MOLERAT 2.0

TERROR BURROWS

Lee Gabel

FRANKEN*SCRIPT*

Frankenscript Press
Box 717, #105 - 1497 Admirals Road
Victoria, BC, Canada V9A 2P8

Molerat 2.0

Cover illustration and design by Lee Gabel

Cover images supplied by DepositPhotos

Body font (ITC Galliard Pro) by International Typeface Corporation
Folios, heads, and caps (Zapf Humanist 601) by Bitstream Inc.

ISBN: 978-1-9991856-1-9 (ebook)
ISBN: 978-1-9991856-2-6 (paperback)

Want to join Lee's Reader Group or find out more about Lee and the books he writes? Please go to:
LeeGabel.com
LeeGabel.com/facebook
LeeGabel.com/twitter
Or follow Lee on BookBub at LeeGabel.com/bookbub

DETEST-A-PEST: CASE #3

DETEST-A-PEST: CASE #3

MOLERAT 2.0

TERROR BURROWS

Titles by Lee Gabel

Detest-A-Pest Series
Molerat 2.0
Arachnid 2.0
Vermin 2.0

Standalone
Snipped
David's Summer
Tied

For Stephen.
Thanks for keeping me flying straight.

Incommunicado

It all happened so fast. In a matter of seconds Sam found himself hanging upside down, three-quarters of the way into the chasm, a rope tangled around his right foot. His eyes struggled to adjust between the bright blue of the sky and the dark cavern floor. Right now he needed to see the floor but his eyes favored the sky.

Blood rushed to Sam's head and pounded at his temples, clouding his thoughts with every heartbeat. His right leg ached as it bore the weight of his muscled frame. He had no doubt that the rope would hold his weight. He had come to trust Harry implicitly. But the haphazard snarl around his ankle was nothing like Harry's infallible bowline knot.

Sam heard what roamed below and as his eyes adjusted to the darkness he could sense motion in the periphery. That alone should have scared the bejesus out of him but right at that moment he felt no fear. Instead he thought about his friends up top, people he cared about and who cared about him. He thought of his son Bradley back in Los Angeles. And Claire. Gooseflesh rose on his legs and arms. The cool air of the subterranean cavern washed over him, carrying with it the smell of damp earth and something else. Something foul.

This was not the way he wanted to remember the Bahamas.

SIX DAYS EARLIER, while Harry Harcourt and other staff and guests of the Mar-A-Verde resort slept, horror chose this predawn May morning to test the air outside its subterranean dwelling. But it was the sun cracking the horizon, slicing the creature's skin with shards of light, that forced it back into its secluded burrow.

Harry's day began at five-fifteen in the morning. The smell of fresh auto-brewed coffee that drifted out from the vintage Mr. Coffee machine never failed to pull him out of sleep. Alarm clocks were overrated.

He rolled out of bed, ran his fingers through his closely cropped natural hair, and tossed on his clothes for the day. The top half of his work "uniform" belonged to Mar-A-Verde. All staff were required to buy and wear purple shirts with the gold embroidered resort logo in the upper left corner. The shirt was adequate but Harry had far more comfortable shirts in his closet. Occasionally on cooler days he'd wear one under this purple abomination. God help you if stepped off the corporate branding train. At least he didn't have to exert any mental energy on choosing the day's attire.

The bottom half was up to him. He slid his legs into well worn jeans, the denim permanently stained with dirt and worn thin in the right spots. The warm feeling of the fabric against his skin maintained the illusion of choice.

The staff apartments were located far from guests in a separate building at the north end of the Mar-A-Verde property, where Harry had been head groundskeeper for 19 years. Living here, on an exclusive island in the Bahamas, would be a dream come true for most. But as with all of Strunk's properties, the staff were undervalued and loyalty was in short supply. Staff were allowed off the island only under special circumstances or upon termination.

Initially Harry had set his sights on a bachelor's degree in aviation but switched to horticulture halfway through his second year of study. He loved to fly, but he loved the earth more, working the soil through his hands, watching seedlings take root and flourish. For him, keeping plants alive was simple. Give them sun, water, fertilizer, and proper care; simple things he could easily master. But his aviation knowledge rounded out his experience and made him an asset to Mar-A-Verde.

He managed a small crew of groundskeepers who got along for the most part. Being paid to work outside all year round in a Bahamian paradise, plus piloting the occasional flight to Palm Beach, was enough to keep him happy. Complaints would only get him a one-way trip to the Biminis.

Harry's small but adequate one-room suite was located on the top floor, reserved for staff with the most seniority. The building resembled the many budget motels that dotted the beaches of Fort Lauderdale and the east coast of Florida. But looks were deceiving, like how the embroidered logo on his shirt made his skin underneath itch something fierce. The exterior of the building appeared nice enough from a distance but upon closer inspection, chips in the paint and cracks in the walls snaked out from corners like a spider trapped under a cinder block. Fine lines that signaled instability. The state of the resort was much the same but less severe.

The room had minimal amenities (a bed, an old television, bathroom, dresser) and its only set of sliding glass doors opened onto a meager east-facing balcony. Weather permitting, and most mornings it did, Harry took in the sunrise as he nursed a steaming cup of coffee, always black. This month the resort's featured blend was a Brazilian dark roast with hints of chocolate and citrus. It had become his favorite.

Technically, the Mr. Coffee machine was contraband. Mar-A-

Verde liked to control its employees in all aspects of their lives, including when and where they drank their coffee. The ground floor staff cafeteria was self-serve pay-as-you-go, as was the small connected staff convenience store that carried a few snacks, drinks, and toiletries. There were better supplies at the golf course's pro shop and the resort dining room offered marginally better food, but price and discrimination kept most employees away from both.

Harry had worked out a deal with Greta, the cafeteria's head cook and his only neighbor to the north. She supplied him with the coffee maker and free freshly ground beans each week, and in return he turned a blind eye to her amorous adventures, often with guests of the resort, a fireable offense.

"You're going to win a one-way trip off this rock," Harry often joked.

Greta would kiss his cheek and whisper in his ear, "I'm not worried." She lived her life moment to moment, secure knowing that things would always work out somehow. Being a planner himself, it was a quality that Harry admired.

Mar-A-Verde, an exclusive members-only resort with its own marina and golf course, was located on Marjerio Cay. The island, east of Palm Beach and forty-four miles south of Freeport, Grand Bahamas, had been owned since 1992 by Kyngston Strunk, a wealthy real estate developer.

The staff had no shortage of nicknames for Strunk, but Harry remained content to keep his head down and do the work required of him. After all, living all year in the Bahamas rent-free *and* earning a living at the same time was a sweet deal, even if it was barely over minimum wage. With the exception of his coffee maker, Harry made sure to follow the rules.

The resort had been built in 1929 and despite being in the middle of the Atlantic's hurricane row, the island and its structures had escaped most hurricane damage of the past ninety years, including 2019's Dorian. In 1984, Mar-A-Verde added its own private air strip, making it accessible by air and boat. No vehicles were permitted except for those used by resort maintenance, with exception of the resort's fleet of golf carts.

Poinciana trees with their vibrant red blossoms contrasted the greens of the palms lining the fairways and main resort buildings. Dahlia shrubs dotted the paths around the resort and through the course. Even the staff apartments had vegetation surrounding them, due in part to his crew's work. Foliage was cheaper than repair and hid the cracks.

The main entrance to the resort encircled a lone guayacan tree, known to locals as lignum vitae or "wood of life." The trees had been long celebrated throughout the Bahamas for their bright yellow foliage, durability, and strength. Strunk had had the remaining guayacan trees removed from the small island to make way for a golf course expansion. Harry thought the course would have been better off with the trees than without, but getting in the way of so-called progress was above his pay grade. Most things were. The only way he'd get his hands dirty would be in the rich soil the resort stood on.

With cup in hand he chose to watch the sun rise over Northwest Providence Channel. It was turning out to be another perfect morning. Harry finished his coffee, pulled on socks, laced up his workboots, and headed out the door to the staff cafeteria for breakfast to go. But he was about to discover just how quickly a perfect morning could turn to disaster.

HARRY PAID FOR his breakfast wrap, an overstuffed offering that almost looked like the breakfast burritos advertised on television.

He handed the cashier his resort charge card. "Not bad, huh? Greta outdid herself this morning."

The cashier swiped his card and returned it to him with a

shrug. She either didn't care or couldn't speak English. Harry hoped it was a language issue but knew indifference was common among the staff.

"Chief!" a young voice called out. "Wait up!"

Harry glanced back and spotted Logan Murphy stowing his dirty dishes in a rolling cart. Logan wiped his mouth with a napkin, tossed it in the trash, and trotted up next to him, walking and talking.

"What's on the docket today, Chief?"

Harry smiled. Logan was the only member of the grounds crew that called him "Chief" and he never tired of it. "The usual. In a week or two we begin hurricane season." He noticed Logan raise his eyebrows. "You've never worked through hurricane season, have you?"

"No. I started in November last year. Remember?"

Harry nodded between bites of his breakfast. "Dorian missed us last year by a couple dozen miles. If our luck holds, it'll be business as usual."

"Business as usual is good." Logan jammed his hands into his purple Mar-A-Verde-branded coveralls.

Harry looked the young man over. The coveralls were a step too far in corporate branding but most new hires followed every suggestion given to them. Logan had to be half his age, and what he lacked in experience he more than made up for with enthusiasm. He'd come around eventually. "You okay?"

Logan took a deep breath. "So, I'm going to pop the question."

Harry was caught with his mouth full. "Rebecca, right?"

Logan nodded.

"That's fantastic news." Harry wiped his right hand on his jeans and extended it towards Logan, sharing a firm shake. "Congratulations. When's the big day?"

"I'm not there yet," Logan said. "I got to make sure I can

afford a ring first. I just decided this morning I'm going to go for it. You're the only one I've told."

"Secret's safe with me." The two men continued walking.

"Also, I was wondering—"

"You need some time off, right?" Harry chuckled. "Smooth, Logan. Real smooth."

"Well, yeah, eventually," Logan said. "But what I was going to ask is... if you'd be my best man."

Harry stopped again and stared at Logan. His expression must have looked concerned instead of surprised because Logan began to backpedal.

"It's okay if you don't want to. I don't really have any family, so I thought... I consider you a good friend and—"

"Logan. I'd be honored." Harry took Logan's hand and shook it again. "Just name the time and place and I'll be there, under one condition."

Logan swallowed hard. "What?"

Harry looked left and right for potential eavesdroppers, then leaned closer. "Don't do it here. Anywhere but here."

"Why? It's so convenient and—"

"Between you and me, Strunk will bleed you dry," Harry said. "Rebecca's in Alice Town?"

"Good memory."

"There's lots of resorts in the Bimini Islands that would be far better. Just saying."

"Okay," Logan said. "I'll think about it."

"Good man." They resumed their walk to the maintenance building. "One more thing."

"What's that?"

"You got to tell the rest of the guys soon." Harry sported a broad grin. "A secret like this might escape all on its own."

"Will do, Chief."

"Now let's get this beautiful day started."

The two men continued onward to the maintenance

building, the warmth of the rising sun on their backs and a lightness in their steps.

Harry and Logan arrived at the maintenance building just before six. Boisterous laughter greeted them. Tzipora, Brynna, and Jomar huddled around Alejandro's phone, watching a video on the screen.

"Morning folks," Harry said. "What'd I miss? Nothing embarrassing I hope."

"How'd you know?" Brynna doubled over laughing.

Tzipora stifled her laughter just enough to respond. "The usual, Harry."

"What did our fearless leader do now?"

Logan peeked over Alejandro's shoulder to get a look at his phone. It didn't take long for him to join in the camaraderie. "Oh shit!"

"Alright. Let's see." Harry joined the rest of the crew.

"Wait, let me restart it." Alejandro slid the playback control to the beginning. The video began innocently enough with a golfer on a putting green lining up his shot in front of dozens of spectators.

"Wait. Is that...?" Harry looked at Jomar and Brynna, both trying to control their laughter, both failing.

Brynna nodded.

"Wait for it." Alejandro's hefty body shook in a silent body laugh as he moved his phone closer to Harry. In another life, Alejandro could have been a professional wrestler. The man in the video eyed the lay of the green, lined up his golf ball with the hole using his putter, and sank to a squat to get a low view. The man's pants split right up the back seam with an audible *rrriiippp*, exposing his backside.

"Oh, Jesus," said Harry. "Can't unsee that."

"What an *asshole*, huh?" Jomar broke into a fresh fit of hysterics.

"The clip's gone viral," Alejandro said.

"Karma's a bitch." Tzipora bumped her fist with Brynna.

Harry shook his head. "Larsen's going to be in a shit mood because of this. So, let's get started. The clock's ticking." He pointed to the job board he had prepared the night before. "You got your assigned tasks. The resort isn't at capacity, but I'd like to get as much of the bunker maintenance completed before seven."

"Forward the vid to me, okay?" Logan said to Alejandro as he looked to the task board. He had been assigned the thirteenth through fifteenth holes, raking bunkers and strimming as needed.

Alejandro nodded. "No prob."

"Logan, switch with me," Harry said. "Take the first, second, and third."

Every hole on the golf course offered stunning views, but the fairways and putting greens of the first, second, and third holes sat on the highest point of Marjerio Cay and offered a picturesque three-hundred sixty degree view of Mar-A-Verde and the surrounding ocean. It was a choice work assignment.

"You sure, Chief?"

Harry nodded. "I'm in a good mood."

"Lucky son-of-a-bitch," Alejandro said. "You get laid last night or what?"

"I wish." Harry looked at Logan and raised his eyebrows. "You going to tell them?"

Tzipora alternated her gaze back and forth. "Tell us what?"

Logan grinned. "I'm going to ask Rebecca to marry me."

Hoots and hollers followed by congratulations erupted from the maintenance building's open doors.

"And I'm going to be best man." Harry puffed his chest out.

"What am I? Chopped liver?" Jomar elbowed Logan in jest.

"Yeah, what about us?" Alejandro said.

"Chill out. You're all my best men... uh, women. People." Logan faced his smiling work mates. "You're all my best people."

"I'll let it go this time," Jomar said. "As long as you got strippers and booze at your stag."

"Congrats." Brynna wrapped her arms around Logan, hugged him, and gave him a kiss on the cheek. "Becca's a lucky woman. And about freaking time."

"Drinks on me after work," Harry said. "Sound good?"

"Now you're talking like a best man." Alejandro pocketed his phone.

"Let's get to it then." Harry hopped into one of several maintenance carts and peeled out of the building toward the path that connected all the holes. The rest of the grounds crew followed and dispersed with their assigned tasks, all anticipating the celebration at the end of the day.

THE FIRST, SECOND *and third holes. Sweet.* Logan reveled in his plum morning work assignment. *I should get almost-engaged more often.* He chuckled at his own joke as he navigated the modified golf cart to the third hole.

Logan started his assigned tasks at the furthest point from the maintenance building and worked his way back. If his cart ever malfunctioned (it had happened before) he'd have less distance to walk.

Hole three was just shy of four-hundred yards and had a cluster of three bunkers surrounding the green. Logan was in luck. The edges surrounding the bunkers looked in good order already, leaving weeding and raking the bunkers as his main task.

He grabbed a grooming rake, shoved a trowel into the back pocket of his coveralls, and stepped into the largest bunker.

The air was still crisp from a night of ocean breeze. He crouched, grabbed a handful of sand, and let the cool, dry grains flow between his fingers. The top inch of dew-dampened sand remained. He tossed the handful aside and began to level out the sand around the edges of the bunker with the flat edge of the rake.

Once he completed the perimeter, Logan flipped the rake and used the tines to create a consistent playing surface for the bunker. He had barely begun when the rake jumped, like something had poked it from underneath.

Logan groaned. Had the bunker's layer of sand become too shallow? Was it a root, a rock, or a combination of all three?

He set the grooming rake aside and pulled the trowel from the back pocket of his coveralls. He started with a small hole. He didn't have any time to waste and this inconsistency had already put him behind.

Logan dug progressively deeper looking for clues until he had a hole the size of a cantaloupe. Usually the culprit would be exposed with a few shallow digs. When the blade of his trowel hit the clay and dirt that formed the base of the entire course, he rocked back and sat on the heels of his work boots, a perplexed expression on his face.

He unclipped his walkie-talkie and was about to call it in when a tremor ripped through the sand, around the fresh hole, and behind where he sat. He fell backward but regained his balance and returned his radio to his belt.

Logan stood and spun around, trying to pinpoint the source of the tremor. Eyes like a hawk seeking its prey, he stood motionless scanning the sand as it rose to the grassy berm on the edge of the green.

Then movement resumed but this time sand was

disappearing, pulled under, as if falling into an obscured funnel beneath the ground.

"Shit." Logan ran to his maintenance cart and grabbed a long-handled spade, mumbling to himself. "This better not be a sink hole."

In the time he had been out of the bunker retrieving the spade, a gaping hole the size of a basketball had formed in the bunker.

"Damn it!" In an instant Logan's morning had been shot to hell. His hand instinctively went for his walkie-talkie. "Chief? It's Logan."

After a moment Harry's voice crackled back. "Go ahead, Logan."

"I'm on the green of the third hole and I think we got a sink hole developing in one of the bunkers."

"You *think?*" Alejandro's voice buzzed back. It was clear that he was laughing when he said it and Logan's face flushed with heat despite being alone.

"Off the radio, Al," Harry's voice said. "Logan, are you sure?"

"I'm not a hundred percent, but the hole just appeared out of nowhere." Logan crouched and stared into the black opening in the bunker. "Chief?"

"Larsen's going to shit, but better safe than not," Harry said. "Rope it off. We'll investigate later today. Keep me posted."

"Right, Chief. Logan out." He returned his walkie-talkie to his belt with a renewed sense of urgency. He may not get all his bunkers groomed by the time seven o'clock rolled around, but at least he had a new, more interesting task to complete.

Logan pulled a handful of metal stakes and a roll of caution tape from his cart and began staking the perimeter of the bunker. Halfway around, he caught movement in the corner of his eye. Logan turned to look, and *something moved*, shuffling back into the shadows of the hole.

"What the hell?" He knelt and crawled on all fours toward the hole, his eyes wide with curiosity. As he drew closer, his eyes adjusted to the shadow. An animal of some kind sat a few feet into the opening in the side of the bunker, rapid breaths and a rib cage rising and falling.

Logan dug out his phone from his shorts pocket underneath his coveralls but as he crawled forward the creature retreated.

"What are you?"

He tapped the light on his phone and directed its cold brilliance into the hole. A pale and hairless mass retreated even further.

"You're definitely no gopher." Logan turned off the flashlight, opened his camera app, and framed the hole on the phone's display. The phone's flash burst, and a picture of the hole appeared on the screen, the sand overexposed and the hole an inky black.

He moved the camera a foot into the hole and took a second picture. *Flash!* A shriek funneled out of the darkness, amplified by the curved walls of the hole. Startled, Logan lost his grip on the phone and it slid down into the darkness.

"Shit!" He peered into the hole, craning his neck for a better view, but even with his eyes accustomed to the shadow, Logan couldn't see his phone. "Shit shit shit."

He rolled his right sleeve to his bicep and wiggled his fingers to limber them up. He picked up the trowel and after a few short breaths to boost his courage Logan reached into the opening, scraping the base and walls of the hole with the trowel's blade.

The deeper into the darkened maw he went the more he felt its cold, musty breath on his arm, shoulder, and face. The hole felt like it opened into a larger space, but he couldn't be sure without confirming that with his own eyes.

Logan heard the metallic sound of the trowel hitting the phone's case. He extracted his arm, dropped the tool in the sand, and jammed his arm back into the hole again like he was moments away from finding long-lost treasure. His fingertips scrabbled along the base of the hole until they brushed the corner of his phone. It had fallen display-side down.

"There you are, you son-of-a-bitch." He jostled it onto its side and the interior lit up with the dim glow of the phone's display. His fingers caressed the smooth glass face just as he felt a searing jolt of pain in his hand.

Logan screamed and tried to extract himself, but whatever had latched into him was working its way up his forearm, the pain following. He pulled back, bracing his body with his other arm, adrenaline boosting his attempt at extraction. And his resistance almost worked.

Logan managed to pull his biceps out past the entrance of the hole. It was then that he realized his entire forearm below the elbow was *within* the creature's glistening body, like a snake trying to swallow him whole. And it had no eyes. *No eyes.*

Its skin was mottled with a network of dark veins and its pale waxy skin exuded a viscous fluid that turned Logan's skin and any exposed roots black.

The creature's fangs encircled the muscle of his biceps, each tooth hinged independently and inching its way farther up his arm.

With sudden rippling constrictions that moved along the creature's sinewy body, Logan was pulled back into the hole an inch at a time. He had lost his leverage and pain overwhelmed his senses. His attempts to fight back proved fruitless. His only line of defense now was the passive resistance of his shoulder socket jammed against the hole.

He scanned the berm of the bunker in a desperate attempt to find a handhold for his left hand but came up empty. No one could say the grounds crew for Mar-A-Verde didn't do their jobs to perfection.

Despite the warmth of the sunrise, Logan shivered uncontrollably. A sheen of cold sweat and blood soaked his clothes under his coveralls. He managed to rotate himself around the hole in the bunker until his feet touched the underside of the green. He used all the power left in his legs to push away from the hole until all at once he was free of it.

Logan looked back at the hole and his right arm, expecting to see nothing but a bloody trail. But his flesh, the muscles, tendons, and tissue that made his arm work were gone, stripped clean away, leaving a blackened skeleton behind.

He was still bleeding badly. Logan thought of Rebecca, her image compelling him to fight for his life one more time. He pulled himself onto the green, leaving a trail of blood in his wake, and crawled to his maintenance cart. His right arm flopped lifelessly beside his body like a puppet without strings.

With his left arm and legs, he maneuvered himself onto the cart's bench seat and righted himself. He jammed his foot on the accelerator, unprepared for the sudden burst of speed. Without the use of his right arm and seconds away from passing out, Logan lost control of the cart and collided with a palm tree. The collision propelled him forward where he struck his head on the tree trunk and fell to the footwell, his body balanced half over the dashboard.

"Logan?" Harry's staticky voice rose from the walkie-talkie still clipped to his belt. "What's your status?"

Logan couldn't have answered even if he'd tried.

HARRY HAD JUST finished up with the bunkers on the thirteenth hole and was on his way to fourteen. But his mind kept wandering back to Logan at the third hole. Something didn't seem right, whether it was Logan's tone of voice when they last spoke or the fact that no sink hole had ever developed on land in the Bahamas during the nineteen years he'd worked at Mar-A-

Verde. Most had formed during past ice ages through a slow process of chemical weathering and erosion of the limestone that made up the Bahama Banks. But no sink hole had ever appeared this quickly.

Harry jammed his foot on the brake and threw his cart into a short skid as he unclipped his walkie-talkie. "Logan? What's your status?" The handheld radio returned a buzzing silence. "Logan? You there?"

No response.

He hopped off the cart and looked back toward the club house and maintenance building. His feeling of dread ramped up with every second of silence.

"Jomar. What hole are you on?" Harry paced on the paved path next to his cart.

"Two in the pink and one in the stink, boss." Sounds of Jomar laughing crackled over the speaker.

"Knock it off. I'm serious."

"Uh, sorry." Jomar cleared his throat as he stifled his laughter. "Just rolled into five."

"Do me a favor and check Logan on three? I can't raise him on the radio."

"I'm sure he's fine," Jomar buzzed back.

"Humor me."

"Harry? Brynna here. I'm just finishing up on the eighth. I can check, too. I'm closer anyway."

"Do it," Harry said. "And keep me posted, both of you."

"What's this about?" Brynna buzzed back. Harry could hear concern in her voice, even through the tinny walkie-talkie speaker.

"I don't know, but I got a bad feeling. Harry out." He hopped behind the wheel and continued down the path to the fourteenth hole.

Burrow

THE THIRD HOLE ran opposite the eighth and their greens were situated close together, separated only by small copses of poinciana trees, dahlia bushes, and the occasional palm tree.

Brynna was first to reach the third hole. At first nothing appeared out of the ordinary. But as she crested the bank of the green, she spotted Logan's cart, tilted to one side and resting against a palm tree. She threw the cart into park and hopped out.

"Logan?"

She walked out onto the green and spotted a darkened path across the groomed patch of grass. Brynna squatted and was about to touch the substance darkening the green before she hesitated. An overwhelming metallic smell flooded her nostrils and meant only one thing.

Blood.

"Logan?" She traced the path back to a bunker where a pool of fresh blood had soaked into the sand. Worried, she reversed direction toward the maintenance cart. "Logan!"

What she saw stopped her dead in her tracks. The bench seat of Logan's cart was smeared with blood and his body lay perched half over the dash and half into the footwell. Tendrils of smoke rose from the underside of the cart.

"Logan? It's Brynna. You okay?" With hesitant steps she approached the cart. The smell overwhelmed her, a mixture of wet metal, shit, and ozone. From that moment on, she would forever associate the odor with fear.

Brynna stepped around to the right side of the cart. Logan's half-open eyes had no life spark to them. She followed the bloody trails that snaked down Logan's forehead to the shoulder of his coveralls, fighting hot tears behind her eyes.

She reached out and shook his shoulder. Logan's fleshless right arm swung out from underneath his body and settled next to his thigh. Light wisps of steam still rose from the exposed bones and blood continued to drip downward in rivulets and rapid drops from his boney fingertips.

Brynna screamed and stumbled backward. It took her three tries to get her walkie-talkie unclipped.

Trembling, she held the mic to her mouth, fighting waves of nausea. "Harry. I f-found him."

The handheld's speaker clicked. "Good. Put him on," Harry's voice said. "I need to hear his—"

"*Harry*. I... I can't."

The radio buzzed. "What do you mean you *can't?*"

"I... He's..." The walkie-talkie slid out of Brynna's hand. She rolled to one side and threw up onto the grass.

"Brynna?" Harry's panicked voice floated from the walkie-talkie. "Brynna! Talk to me."

Brynna wiped her mouth on her sleeve and picked up the walkie-talkie. "He's dead, Harry." She tossed the radio aside, unable to hold back her tears any longer.

"What? Don't touch anything," Harry's filtered voice said. "I'm on my way."

The familiar electrical *whirr* of a maintenance cart's motor rose over the green from the path leading to the fourth hole. Jomar parked and got out.

"Brynna?" Jomar surveyed his surroundings, his eyes darting back and forth between the blood trail and where Brynna sat. "Bryn? You okay?"

She kept her face buried in her arms and remained silent.

Jomar approached the left side of Logan's cart. He took out his phone and began to record video. "What the hell happened?" He moved around the front of the cart, slowing upon the first sight of blood on Logan's face.

Logan's fleshless arm appeared on Jomar's phone display. With everything in shadow, at first he didn't know what he was looking at. He gazed past his phone and his eyes bugged out as they took in the extra detail. His hand holding the phone dropped as he felt for Logan's carotid artery in his neck. For a moment it looked like he was going to stop recording. "Holy shit."

Brynna looked up from her spot on the green and wiped her eyes with her wrists. "What the *hell* are you doing?"

As if her tone of voice was a reminder, Jomar reframed Logan's corpse in his phone's display and moved closer to the carnage. "What? I'm documenting the scene."

Brynna stormed to her feet and rushed at Jomar, shoving him backward. "Logan was one of us! Show some fucking respect, asshole."

"Hey. This kind of shit happens once in a lifetime," Jomar said. "A video like this? I could retire."

Brynna stood and stared at him, incredulous. "You're going to upload that?"

Jomar shrugged, a guilty grin spreading across his face.

"What if Rebecca sees it? Be a decent human being for once."

"They don't pay me enough—"

"To be decent?" Brynna glared at him. "Ugh. You make me sick." She walked back to her cart.

Jomar spotted Brynna's regurgitated breakfast on the grass. "Looks like Logan made you sick too."

The sound of Harry's maintenance cart grew louder as he burst forth from behind the palms and poincianas that separated the tenth and third holes. He raced across the fairway instead of using the winding path. If Larsen had seen him, it would have meant immediate suspension or worse.

Jomar stopped recording, pocketed his phone, and trotted over to Brynna. "If you say anything about the video—"

"Is that a threat?" Brynna clutched her stomach. It still ached from nausea and grief.

"Maybe. You don't want to find out." Jomar followed the blood trail across the third green to the bunker where Logan was attacked.

"You'll get yours," Brynna grumbled under her breath.

Harry killed the motor on his cart and ran across the putting green to Logan's crashed cart. He stepped around the back to the cart's right side.

"Jesus, Mary, and Joseph." Harry diverted his eyes and placed his hands on his hips. His chest rose and fell in heavy breaths.

Brynna could see he was fighting nausea too. *A normal reaction for anyone with a soul,* she thought.

"Brynna, you were first on the scene," Harry said. "Did you notice anything out of the ordinary, other than..." He managed a quick look back and pointed at the crash site. "Other than all that?"

"The blood trail leads to the bunker over here." Jomar pointed to the hole carved in the sand of the bunker, just under the ridge of the berm.

"Right. I'll talk with you next." Harry crossed the green to Brynna's cart. She was shivering even with the warmth of the rising sun on her back. "Brynna?"

"I only touched his shoulder," she said. "When his arm swung out, that was it. I lost it."

Harry placed a hand lightly on hers.

"Why Logan?" Brynna fought back her tears, her fists leaving white crescent nail marks in her palms. "So many others are *far* more deserving." She shifted her gaze from Harry to Jomar.

"I know you liked him."

"Everyone liked him."

"It should have been me," Harry said. "I'm the one who swapped work detail with him."

"Don't go there, Harry."

"Hard not to." Harry looked up at the sky, the rising sun burning away the blue of night. "God damn it." He sighed and placed his hand firmly on Brynna's shoulder. "If you need some time, let me know," he said, locking eyes with her. "Don't worry about Larsen."

"Thanks," Brynna said.

Harry walked over to the bunker where Jomar stood. "That's it huh? Doesn't look like a sink hole to me."

"No." Jomar crossed his arms. "Looks more like a burrow."

Harry looked back at Logan's cart. "This is bad." He dug his phone out of his pocket. "Can you and Brynna finish roping off this bunker? Then try and finish as much as you can before seven rolls around."

"Sure thing, boss."

"Don't touch anything. And no photos."

Jomar nodded.

Harry had no choice but to bury his shock and sorrow for another, quieter, time. He selected a contact on his phone and dialed. The call trilled in his ear. "Come on." He began to walk back to his maintenance cart when the call connected. "Hey Doc. It's Harry. Sorry to call so early. We have an... incident on the third hole. You better get down here, pronto."

Harry paused, listening. "It's best if I don't say anything over the phone. But we'll need the stretcher... and a body bag. I'll fill you in when you get here." He ended the call and a shiver ran up his back.

"HOLY SHIT, HARRY. WHAT HAPPENED?" Daniela Trejo, the resident resort doctor, had parked the first responder golf cart just off the putting green. The modified cart was equipped with a collapsible stretcher and lockable compartments underneath stocked with supplies.

Like Harry, Daniela wore a similar purple Mar-A-Verde-branded golf shirt but with one important distinction: small red crosses encircled with white embroidered on each of the shortened sleeves. Her khaki slacks featured a crisp pleat down the center of each leg and ended in a pair of black leather ankle-high lace-up boots. She walked with intention.

"I don't know," Harry said. "Brynna found him like this."

Daniela pulled her long dark hair up with both hands and a quick, messy French braid appeared as if by magic. She crouched to get a closer view of Logan and his right arm. "The crash itself shouldn't have killed him." She looked down at the flowing puddle of blood on the deck of Logan's cart, which then dripped into the grass. "If I had to guess, I'd say he bled out. The strange thing is his blood hasn't coagulated yet."

"What would strip off skin and muscle like that?"

Daniela shook her head, a look of morbid fascination on her face. "No idea. I'd have to run tests. But we're not set up for this. I can't officially move him. I don't even have a body bag."

"Obviously we can't leave him here."

Daniela stood. "Freeport is still dealing with the fallout from Hurricane Dorian. Police and emergency responders there are severely limited in scope."

"What about the Biminis? Alice Town?"

"Yeah. I'll make some calls," Daniela said. "It'll probably take a day or two for police and the coroner to come for the body. Don't you love being on an island?"

"Normally, yes." Harry glanced at his watch. "But the course is open now. We have to move him. Police and coroner be damned."

"Yeah." Daniela walked toward the first responder cart. "Help me with the stretcher. Like I said before, I don't have a body bag. Blankets will have to do."

"That's probably best anyway," Harry said. "Can you imagine Larsen seeing a body bag being transported off the course?"

"The guy'd have a coronary. We don't need another dead body to deal with."

They both managed a small laugh, despite the tense and mysterious situation surrounding Logan's death.

Harry helped Daniela guide the stretcher into position next to Logan's cart. After donning rubber gloves, they lifted Logan's body onto the stretcher and secured his body with tightly tucked blankets and belts crossing his chest. They wheeled the stretcher back to the first responder cart and locked it into place.

"Head to the maintenance building." Harry hooked his thumb at Logan's upturned cart. "I'll follow you."

Daniela nodded and headed back down the golf path next to the third hole.

Harry stepped to the driver's side of Logan's cart, righting it. He looked at the bench seat, still slicked with blood, and was overwhelmed with sadness.

"Damn shame." He grit his teeth and sat behind the steering wheel. He could feel the cool stickiness of blood soak into his jeans, its coppery smell flooding his nose.

Harry punched the start button and was surprised when the cart powered up. He backed up and drove back along the same path Daniela had taken moments earlier.

Just over an hour ago he had been asked to be Logan's best man. Now, a life filled with possibility had been snuffed out for no good reason. Harry vowed to find the reason why.

But a makeshift morgue was his immediate priority.

THE FRONT AXLE on Logan's maintenance cart had been bent in the accident. As a result, Harry had to pay attention to his speed on the way back to the maintenance building. Increased speed shook the front end of the cart and reduced his steering control. Slow and easy did the trick.

Daniela paced outside the front entrance to the maintenance building. The double doors opened into a large hangar-style area that could house up to a dozen maintenance carts. In an adjoining space, the ground crew prepared their tools and supplies for tending to the resort's many florae.

It was clear that Tzipora and Alejandro had been briefed about Logan's fate by Brynna and Jomar. Their eyes roamed over Logan's shrouded body on the stretcher, past Daniela as if she wasn't there.

The tension between them was palpable. With the exception of Harry, the crew and Daniela had never seen eye to eye. They regarded her as an extraneous expense; paid too much for no real value. It was true that Daniela didn't know the right fertilizer to use on dahlias or the correct method to prepare a bunker. But the crew had never experienced a severe injury during her time at the resort. Maybe that would change their minds.

Harry crested the path next to the first hole's tee-off area and rolled the cart toward the maintenance building. The front end of the cart shimmied badly.

He hopped out and trotted toward her. "Sorry. Bent axle slowed me down."

Daniela heaved a sigh of relief. "Thank God. I was beginning to think you had an accident too."

"Luckily no," Harry said. "Hang tight. Got to clear some space."

Harry entered the building, eyeing various storage rooms. Alejandro pulled him aside. "Can we... pay our respects?"

Harry gave him a sideways look. "What do you mean?"

"Can we see him... Logan?"

Harry looked past Alejandro to see the rest of the grounds crew staring at him, awaiting a response.

Daniela overheard the exchange and stepped forward. "If I could jump in, Harry. I've already breached protocol by moving the body. So, I think—"

Alejandro scowled at Daniela. "Fuck protocol. Logan was family."

Harry glanced at Daniela then back to Alejandro. A war could erupt if he wasn't careful. "Leave it with me. I'll figure something out." He walked back to Daniela. "Let's get Logan inside."

They slid the stretcher off the back of the first responder cart, lowered the wheels, and rolled it inside. Harry led the way to the machine storage room, typically the coolest area of the building. They lifted Logan's body off the stretcher and placed him gently next to one wall. The right side of the blanket showed a dark red stain where blood from his arm had soaked through.

Harry stood and sighed. "Could we let them, you know, pay their respects? I mean, what's one more protocol violation? We had no choice."

Daniela crossed her arms. "Yeah. Okay." She knelt and unwrapped the blanket from around Logan's head. She wiped the tracks of blood off his forehead and cheeks and closed his eyelids. Standing, she looked at Harry. "If I'm going to breach protocol, may as well go all out."

"Yup." Harry motioned toward the exit. "You tell the crew."

Daniela raised her brows and regarded him with doubtful eyes.

"Go ahead," Harry said. "It'll go a long way toward smoothing things out between you guys."

"I guess it's worth a shot."

Daniela exited the machine room followed by Harry.

He trudged past her, stopped, and turned his back to the grounds crew. "Are you sure? The coroner isn't going to like it."

Daniela furrowed her brow. "What—"

"Never mind. I'll meet you outside." Harry winked, grumbled, and stormed out of the building.

Daniela faced the grounds crew. "Look. I was wrong. Pay your respects but please don't touch anything. Logan's in the machine room."

"What happened to *protocol?*" Alejandro jeered as he walked by.

"I guess sometimes following the law isn't the only option," Daniela said. "Thanks for reminding me."

"Well..." Alejandro choked on his reply. "Good."

As the grounds crew disappeared into the machine room, Daniela joined Harry outside. "I saw what you did back there. Thanks."

Harry managed a smile, but it faded quickly. He stared toward the first hole, focusing on nothing. "I need to know what killed Logan." He turned to Daniela, his face serious, his eyes dark with determination. "Want to be my *plus one?*"

"Harry, this isn't the time to ask me on a date." Daniela gave him a sly grin.

"Call it joining my very small investigation team," Harry said. "You've got the brains. I've got the brawn. A perfect combination."

Daniela didn't need any time to think about it. "Yeah. I'm in."

DANIELA DROVE THE first responder cart back to the putting green of the third hole, Harry perched on the passenger side of the bench seat. He gripped the right front roof support to keep himself from sliding off.

"You really motor when you need to."

Daniela made a tight turn next to where Harry had left his

cart earlier. "Don't tell anyone this but I come out here during the evenings, maybe an hour before sunset, and race around the course like it was my own personal racetrack."

Harry narrowed his eyes at her. "You're putting me on."

"Maybe." Daniela's dark braided ponytail flapped in the breeze. "Maybe not."

"I'd know."

"You don't know *everything*."

"Huh." Harry hopped off the cart. "To be continued." He looked down at the grass. Most of Logan's blood trail had soaked into the ground but there was still enough remaining on the turf to draw attention to Logan's desperate crawl for survival. "It's moments like this when I wish for rain. We can't have guests seeing this. I'm going to have to spray the grass down."

"Maybe take some photos first? Just in case the police ask."

Harry nodded and pulled out his phone. "Good call."

Daniela traced the line of blood from the crash site back to the bunker with her eyes. "Do you think he was trying to get away from something?"

"I think he was just trying to get back to the maintenance building." Harry walked and took photos.

Daniela quickened her pace until she reached the leading edge of the bunker's berm. Logan's blood had long since soaked into the sand, but a maroon patina had been left behind encircling a crumbling hole in the bank.

"Harry, did you see the hole over here? There's a considerable amount of blood around it."

Harry worked his way across the green documenting the carnage. "Yeah, I saw it earlier. That was what Logan had called a sink hole."

Daniela looked up at Harry from the bunker, concern evident on her face. "That's no sink hole."

"No." Harry stepped down into the bunker and crouched,

leveling his eyes with the blackened maw in the sand. "It's not." He ran his hand across the top of the sand, already dry and crusty from the rising sun. "In all my years at Mar-A-Verde, I've never seen a sink hole, or even whatever *this* is."

"It looks too perfect to be natural," Daniela said. "Reminds me of a burrow."

Harry cast her a wary glance. "That's what Jomar said too."

"Has there ever been a rat problem at Mar-A-Verde?"

"Never. Well, let me back up. We've had rats here and there, but never a *problem* with them." Harry looked back at the hole. "Besides, it's too big to have been made by a rat." He reached forward with his hand.

"What are you doing?"

Harry looked back. "I know you're the brains of our duo, but you can relax. Whatever you *think* I'm going to do, I'm not." He moved his hand forward to the entrance of the hole and spread his thumb and fingers as wide as he could make them. The tip of his pinky finger and thumb just barely reached the crumbling edges. He held his phone up to her. "Take a picture for me? I'm no good with one hand."

Daniela squatted next to him and framed up his hand in the phone's display. She tapped the screen and the flash went off, capturing Harry's over-exposed hand and parts of the visible burrow behind.

A shriek rose from the burrow's depths. Both Harry and Daniela jumped back in unison, landing on their butts.

"What the hell was *that*?"

Daniela shrugged and handed back his phone. "Did you see anything?"

"No." Harry pinch-zoomed the photo but saw nothing to suggest the origin of that blood-curdling cry. He stood and brushed off his jeans. "So, what do you think killed Logan?" He offered his hand to Daniela and helped her up. "The coroner will want to know."

"Exsanguination, blood loss, is my guess for the cause of death."

"But what could pull skin and muscle off the bone like that... like meat from a skewer?" Harry asked. "Could an animal do that?"

Daniela shook her dead slowly. "To be honest, I don't know. My expertise is people, not animals."

"I thought you were the brains."

"That's not fair, Harry," Daniela said. "Besides, *you* said I was the brains, not me."

"What's the cause of death? Blood loss due to..."

Daniela stared at the burrow's opening. "Unknown cause." She walked out of the bunker toward the first responder cart, Harry following. "Look, I got to make some calls. The sooner I get on that the better."

"Right. And I get to tell Larsen about all of this. He's going to go ape-shit."

Daniela slid behind the wheel and turned on the cart's electric motor. "Good luck. You're going to need it."

Harry couldn't help but chuckle. "I know."

"I'll keep you posted." Daniela swung the cart around and zoomed back toward the clubhouse.

"Hey! Slow down!" Harry pictured Daniela with the accelerator pressed to the floor, her ponytail flipping wildly in the wind. "This ain't the Autobahn, you lead-foot."

Harry thought he heard Daniela's laugh as she disappeared behind the trees and hills of the course. He pulled out his phone and found Vaughn Larsen's number in his contacts. He picked up on the second ring.

"Larsen. It's Harry."

Larsen launched into tirade about calling so early. He was so predictable that he was becoming a caricature of himself.

Harry waited for Larsen to finish. "Look, we got a big problem. I'll meet you in your office in ten minutes." He hung up, cutting Larsen off mid-sentence, and hopped behind the wheel of his maintenance cart. The drive back to the maintenance shed would end up being the easiest part of his day.

Trilling

Vaughn Larsen had held the position of general manager of Mar-A-Verde longer than any other employee. No one knew his actual age. Bald, stocky, and a dedicated classist, he made a perfect puppet for Kyngston Strunk. He ensured that shit bypassed him and continued to roll downhill.

Harry took the back entrance to the resort's administrative offices. Strunk had a strict policy of keeping staff visibility at his resorts to a minimum, especially the "grubby" grounds crew. Once inside, Harry followed a warren of hallways to Larsen's office.

The door was locked. Larsen was going to make him wait. *What a prick.*

Harry opened the Internet browser on his phone and tapped into the search bar, "burrowing animals Bahamas."

Instead of finding information on subterranean creatures that ate human flesh, the browser spat out hundreds of articles reporting animal deaths due to hurricanes.

"Of course, it's not going to be easy," Harry muttered to himself.

Down the hallway and out of sight, Larsen's voice boomed, "Just do it or you're *fired!*" He rounded the corner and trudged toward his office.

"Strunk hired you because of your people skills, right?"

"Don't test me, Harry. I'm not in the mood." Larsen grumbled and pulled out his keys.

"Just busting your balls."

Larsen glared at him. "Too early to be busting balls." He unlocked his office door and stepped inside. "This better be important."

Harry's nose was flooded with the pervasive smell of body odor and whiskey. He stifled a gag. He knew Larsen well enough to understand that his livelihood depended on getting to the point. "One of our grounds crew died this morning."

That got Larsen's attention. "What hole?"

"Third."

"Tell me you moved the body." Larsen peeled off his tweed sports coat, one size too small based on how he wiggled out of it. "We don't need any bad press. Occupancy is down this season. Dorian really fucked us last year."

"The Bahamas are immune to bad press," Harry said. "Didn't you tell me that once?"

Larsen snorted. "Doesn't mean I want to invite trouble."

"Anyway, we've got the body in the maintenance building until authorities arrive."

"What? Who called the authorities without clearing it with me first?" Larsen hung his coat on a hook in the corner.

"Daniela."

Larsen returned a blank stare.

How can this ass-hat manage anything, much less a resort? Harry thought. "Daniela Trejo. The resort physician. We had to act fast. It's protocol."

"Daniela... Oh, yeah. The hot Latina one." Larsen squeezed himself into his leather chair. "You tapped that ass yet?" He grinned.

Harry ignored the question and instead looked at the two chairs in front of Larsen's desk. "Mind if I sit?"

"Actually, I do. You're probably covered with dirt and God knows what else."

Harry placed his hands behind his back and balled them into tight fists, imagining them around Larsen's neck. "We've got another problem. There's a hole in one of the bunkers. A large one."

"What? A hole?"

"At first we thought it was a sink hole, but it's more likely a burrow. Whatever's living inside might be responsible for the death of my groundskeeper."

Larsen leaned back in his chair, the spring groaning under his considerable bulk. "How big we talking?"

Harry held up his hand. "Maybe nine or ten inches across."

Larsen laughed. "Sounds like nothing. Fill it with sand. Problem solved."

"Aren't you the least bit curious?"

"I got a lot on my mind. Fill it and move on." Larsen lifted the handset of his desk telephone and pressed the intercom button. "Get me a coffee, two sugars." He glanced up at Harry. "Is there anything else?"

"His name was Logan."

"Who?"

"My groundskeeper."

"The dead one."

Harry's anger rose from a simmer to a boil. "Yeah."

"What do you want me to say? I'm sorry for your loss?"

"How about a little recognition?" It took all of Harry's will to keep from exploding. "He asked me to be his best man at his wedding, for Christ's sake. An hour before he died. Logan was one of the good ones."

Larsen pushed himself out of his chair and leaned forward. "I manage a resort with a hundred-fifty rooms. I can't be expected to know the names of all my staff."

"Yet you know all the names of your guests."

Larsen's face flushed red. "Excuse me?"

Harry matched Larsen's stare with his own.

"I think you better leave before I do something rash." Larsen pointed out to the hallway. "Close the door on your way out."

Harry turned and left without another word. He thought about slamming the door but that would have dug an even deeper hole for himself. But he decided he would not be leaving through the back entrance.

Screw that.

Harry followed the hallway out into the main foyer of the resort. Dressed in dirty jeans, Logan's blood on some parts, he stuck out like a sore thumb. And Harry reveled in it as he sauntered out toward the main entryway.

He passed resort regular Shane McCoy on his way out. McCoy had made his fortune by winning a Powerball lottery jackpot in 1998, then invested his winnings in technology. Now an angel investor, he traveled the world looking for promising start-ups and often brought colleagues to Mar-A-Verde for week-long golfing retreats. Beside him walked a man Harry had not met before.

"Back for another working vacation, McCoy?"

"Who said anything about work!" McCoy smiled broadly as he shook Harry's hand. "Damn good to see you, Harry."

Harry glanced at his hands. "Sorry about the dirt."

McCoy waved him off. "I don't think I'd trust you if you *weren't* dirty."

Both men laughed.

"Couldn't have picked a better time to visit. The weather's still cooperating." Harry turned to the man beside McCoy. "I don't believe we've met. I never forget a face."

"The name's Brekken Sinclair."

"Good to meet you, Mr. Sinclair." Harry and Sinclair shared a handshake. "I'm the head groundskeeper." He hooked a thumb toward the foliage outside. "I keep everything out there... alive." He winced at his poor choice of words.

"Sinclair's the inventor of Antagreen, an environmentally safe pesticide." McCoy pointed back and forth between the two men. "You guys should talk. We should get together for drinks later."

"Absolutely," Harry said. "Go on and get settled. Call me tomorrow and we'll set something up. You got my number?"

McCoy patted his jacket pocket.

"Until then..." Harry raised his arms and performed a flourish. "Enjoy all that Mar-A-Verde has to offer." He continued his way outside.

"What's good in the dining room this week?" McCoy called back.

Harry laughed. "Steak. It's always steak. You've been here enough times to know that."

"It's called *filet mignon*." McCoy brought his fingertips to his lips and kissed them. "Strunk's best."

Harry waved him off. "Beef is beef. Go hit the links, will yah." The thought of raw beef brought the morning's events back in vivid detail and a wave of sadness and nausea hit him like a brick.

One thing was certain. Larsen was wrong. The hole that Logan discovered was a sign of bad things to come. Harry knew it in his gut.

HARRY WAITED UNTIL six o'clock to venture back onto the course. He loaded his maintenance cart with a shovel, a spade, and a rake. As he drove the winding path to the third hole, he passed McCoy and Sinclair returning to the clubhouse after an afternoon of golf. The front and back nine at Mar-A-Verde had been designed to converge near the center of the course and funnel golfers back toward the clubhouse. He slowed his cart to a stop.

"How was the game?" The two paths were separated by a few trees and shrubs. Harry raised his voice to bridge the distance.

"An embarrassment." McCoy motioned with his thumb. "Sinclair kicked my ass, but the week's young." McCoy looked back in the direction Harry was traveling. "You heading to the third hole? What's with the caution tape?"

"We think there might be some burrowing critters out there. Maybe gophers."

"Gophers, huh? I don't know about that," McCoy said. "That hole seemed too big. But what do I know?"

"I'll get to the bottom of it. That's a guarantee."

"I know you will. Hey, how about those drinks?"

"Like I said before, buzz me tomorrow," Harry called out. "I'm a little tied up."

"Working on the third hole."

Harry nodded, gave the two men a thumbs up, and continued on his way. What he didn't see was McCoy watching him leave until his sightlines were obscured by foliage.

Harry rolled the cart next to the green and parked. The third hole was getting under his skin. How long would it take before he could drive by it without reminding himself of the morning's horrific scene?

Grabbing his tools, he crossed the green to the bunker with the caution tape surrounding it, fluttering in the wind. The sun was already dipping toward the horizon and he figured he had about an hour of good light left.

He stepped into the bunker and faced the hole. It seemed larger than he remembered, but dismissed the thought as his mind playing tricks on him. However, the hole in the side of the bunker was just as dark and uninviting as before.

A phone trilled.

Harry dropped his tools and instinctively went for his own

phone, but the screen was black. A second trill allowed him to refocus on the sound. The direction of the ringing chilled his blood cold.

Inside the hole.

He got on all fours and crawled closer to the side of the bunker, but not too close. The cool, dank breath of the shadowy opening blew past his face in what felt like a sustained exhalation.

The phone rang again.

There's no way in hell I'm going to stick my hand in there.

Harry grabbed a shovel and began to dig at the hole and surrounding bunker, but the root systems of the grass proved difficult to dig through. It was rare for him to try and undo the work of his grounds crew, but in this case it was necessary.

And there was one piece of equipment back at the maintenance building that could do the job.

Condolences

THE NEXT MORNING, Harry drove one of the two pickup trucks at the resort to the third hole. In the back he had secured a compact backhoe. His goal was to minimize damage to the green and fairway as much as possible while excavating the burrow in the bunker. Brynna and Jomar sat next to him in the cab, chosen because of their firsthand knowledge of the scene.

"Larsen is going to eat your ass for breakfast." Jomar sipped from a travel mug.

"Well, something got Logan. We're going to find out what." Harry cast a wary glance at Brynna and Jomar. "What's the worst that he could do?"

"Uh, fire you?" Brynna said. "Larsen loves to fire people."

Harry shrugged. "He'd never fire me."

Brynna and Jomar exchanged glances.

Harry's eyes flitted between the path ahead and his co-workers. "You really think he'd fire me?"

"Larsen shoots first and *maybe* asks questions later," Jomar said. "He's a lot like Strunk that way."

"He wants to *be* Strunk," Brynna added.

Harry approached the green at the third hole. "If he fires me, so be it. I'm doing this for Logan." He killed the engine and threw the truck into park. "Help me get the backhoe unloaded."

Jomar hopped out of the truck and hoisted himself into the

truck bed. "I call dibs on driving Digby," he said as he climbed into the excavator's cab.

"Be my guest." Brynna lifted some shovels out of the back. "I don't want any of the blame if this goes horribly wrong."

"Don't worry. I take full responsibility." Harry extracted a ramp from the back of the truck.

Jomar started the backhoe's engine and backed down onto the green. He navigated around the edge and into the bunker. Torn caution tape settled to the ground. "How you want to do this, boss?"

"Widen the hole but try and leave the berm above intact if you can." Harry took a shovel and carved some simple guidelines in the sand. "Slow and careful."

"That's what she said." Jomar grinned at Brynna.

She rolled her eyes. "What are you waiting for? I want to be long gone before Larsen finds out about this."

Jomar rolled the small excavator forward and manipulated the shovel, digging through the sand and roots like a hot knife through butter. Brynna and Harry used their shovels to chop up the chunks of dirt from the excavator's scoop and clear away loose rocks and dirt.

The first scoop revealed a secondary branch moving from the main burrow. The second and third scoop uncovered even more branches heading deeper underground. Some of the tunnels were big enough for a man to fit through.

A flash of metal caught Harry's eye. "Jomar, hold up a second." He used his shovel to move a mound of dirt, then fell to his knees, working the earth with his hands. On any other occasion feeling the sandy soil in his hands would be a pleasurable experience, but it was imperative to find Logan's phone. Harry dug in a panic, ignoring his proximity to the other open tunnels, until his fingers found what they were searching for.

He brushed dirt and sand from the phone's smooth metal and

glass exterior. A heart sticker on the back, somewhat moistened and scuffed, bore the handwritten message, "Luv U! XO Bec." Harry held it up for Brynna and Jomar to see.

"Holy shit!" Brynna set her shovel down. "That's Logan's phone."

"That's why we're digging, isn't it?" Jomar retracted the scoop of the excavator.

Harry nodded. "Partly, but yeah. I heard it ring last night."

"Oh shit." Brynna pointed to the path leading to the green. "We got company."

LARSEN TORE DOWN the path toward the third hole in his own custom golf cart. It was black with gold-plated accents and wheel rims. The cart was his preferred method of transportation except when Strunk visited the resort. Then he took either the passenger seat beside Strunk or followed behind in a standard resort cart.

Harry shoved Logan's phone into his pocket and braced for the inevitable fallout. He shared a look with Brynna and Jomar. "Remember. I take full responsibility."

Larsen slammed on the brakes and laid a skid a few feet into the green. Unaware of the damage he had just created, he jumped from the cart and stormed past the flag for the third hole.

"Harry!" Angry veins stood out on Larsen's neck. "What the *fucking hell* are you doing?"

"I'm following your orders," Harry said. "I'm filling in the hole."

Larsen trudged down into the bunker to look at the work that had already been completed. He slapped his hands to his bald head and formed fists like he was looking for hair to pull.

"For Christ's sake you don't need heavy equipment to fill in a fucking hole."

"You do if you want it done right." Harry held Larsen's glare. "That's what you pay me for."

Brynna and Jomar exchanged a covert smile with each other.

"Think of the guests, Harry. Think!" He tapped his head with his index finger. "We want the guests' experience to anchor everything we do here. And we must end this lackluster season on a high note. The third hole *must* stay open."

"What if this was a sink hole? I would've covered up a death trap." Harry pointed at the excavated side of the bunker, tired of arguing. "What if a sink hole swallowed up a guest?"

"Is it a sink hole?"

"No, but—"

"Then it's nothing, just like I told you yesterday." Larsen stepped forward, now nose to nose with Harry. "Fill it."

"I'll cut corners for you, but I won't take the blame if something happens." Harry motioned at Brynna and Jomar. "And I have witnesses."

Larsen tried to raise himself on the balls of his feet to get a height advantage but stumbled in the sand. "The third hole stays open. Fucking *fill it*... or you're fired."

Harry's blood boiled but he was determined not to let Larsen get the better of him. "Sure hope you're right."

Larsen stepped back. "When have I ever been wrong?"

Harry shot a look at Jomar and Brynna.

Larsen waved his hands about like he was casting a spell on the bunker. "I want all this... back to normal before the course opens." He stepped out of the bunker and walked toward his cart.

"But that's—" Jomar began.

Harry held up his finger at Jomar. "We'll do our best."

"Better than your best," Larsen called back without looking.

Harry, Brynna, and Jomar watched Larsen board his cart and drive back toward the resort.

Harry grabbed his shovel. "Let's get to work."

Jomar exited the cab of the excavator and joined Brynna and Harry shoveling sand back into the branching burrows of the bunker.

Jomar compared the size of the burrows and the remaining sand. "Uh, boss?"

"I know. We're going to need more sand. I'll deal with it. Keep working with what you have." Harry headed back to the truck. He pulled out his phone and dialed Daniela. He set the phone on speaker and dropped it into a tray in the center console.

"Shit, Harry." Daniela's filtered voice sounded like she had just woken up. "What's with the early morning calls?"

"I found Logan's phone," Harry said. "Interested?"

"Hell, yeah." Daniela was instantly a hundred percent awake.

"Meet me in an hour."

"You got it."

Digging was a brainless task, whether it was filling the back of a pickup with sand or the burrows of some strange animal. And over the next hour, Harry's mind drifted back to Logan's phone and the answers it might hold.

DANIELA STOOD OUTSIDE the maintenance building, a satchel hanging over her shoulder, when Harry returned with Brynna and Jomar. The compact backhoe was securely tied down in the truck bed. He backed the truck into the garage and stepped out of the cab.

"Thanks for the help, guys. Carry on with your appointed tasks as best you can."

"Will do, boss," Jomar said.

Brynna offered a nod of agreement.

Daniela offered a tentative wave and a smile at Brynna and Jomar. "Morning, guys."

Jomar ignored her but Brynna acknowledged Daniela's greeting with a smile and a wave back.

"One out of two. Not bad," Daniela said to herself. "Achievement unlocked."

Harry beckoned Daniela inside the building. "You didn't have to wait outside. This isn't some forbidden place, you know."

"This is your domain, Harry." Daniela tied her hair back with an elastic. "I'm not quite comfortable barging in without an invitation yet."

They both walked back to the machine room. "Anyone who gives you a hard time, let me know and I'll talk with them. Bottom line is we got to work together on this."

"Then I come off looking like a tattle-tale," Daniela said. "Don't bother. I can take care of myself."

"Fair enough." Harry pulled open the door to the machine room. A cool smell of iron and oil plus undertones of something sickly sweet and foreign flowed around them.

Daniela sniffed the air. "Decomposition is starting. It's not cold enough in here."

"What can we do?" Harry shrugged. "I don't think they'd like a dead body in the cafeteria's walk-in freezer." He held Logan's phone in his hand. "So, ready to break protocol again?"

"Why the hell not." Daniela shrugged. "I'm not going to tell. Are you?"

Harry gave her a sideways look and shook his head. "Any bets which will unlock his phone: his fingerprints or face?"

"Electrical capacitance in the fingers stopped when Logan died, so I'd guess fingerprints are out," Daniela said. "And we're twenty-four hours in, so self-digestion is well under way. If it works at all, it's going to be the face."

"Self-digestion?" Harry swallowed hard.

"It's called autolysis," Daniela said. "Excess carbon dioxide builds up and creates an acidic—"

"A little goes a long way, Doc."

"Noted. Just hope the coroner gets here soon. This is about as pretty as it gets."

Harry shook his head, knelt, and pulled back the sheet covering Logan's head and shoulders. The skin of his face, now locked in a slack neutral expression, held a grey and waxy sheen. Seeing him like this was enough to cause Harry's stomach to do a back-flip. He swallowed dryly. "God, I don't know if I can do this."

Daniela crouched next to him. "Try fingerprints first."

Harry positioned Logan's thumb on the phone's home button. The coolness of Logan's skin and the way it seemed to slide over the flesh underneath sent a shiver down his back. Just as Daniela predicted, nothing happened. The phone vibrated and a lock icon appeared on the display.

"Shit. No go."

"Okay, try his face," Daniela said. "You have to use the front-facing camera."

"Ugh. I hate these things. Remember when a phone was actually a phone?"

Harry held the phone over Logan's face for a few seconds until the phone vibrated. The display showed the lock icon again. He tried a second time with the same result. "Dammit. Why isn't this working?"

"I think I remember that the eyes have to be open."

Harry stood. "You've got to be kidding. His fingertips felt strange enough. I'm not touching his eyelids." He shook his head for emphasis. "Nope. Got to draw the line here."

Daniela's face lit up. "I have an idea." She knelt beside Logan and pulled out a pad of paper and a pen from her satchel. She positioned one edge of the pad next to the tear duct of Logan's right eye and made a mark where his eye lid ended.

Harry watched her; his brows scrunched. "What the hell...?"

Using the measurement, Daniela drew two eyes, complete with irises and upper eyelashes. "Even if we did open his eyelids, his corneas would probably be all clouded. That happens a few hours after death."

"So, you're drawing him some eyes." Harry spoke though his nausea.

"Yeah. That's the idea." Daniela looked around the machine room. "You got a pair of scissors somewhere in this joint?"

"I can do you one better." Harry dug into his pocket and removed a Swiss Army knife. He folded out the scissors. "Will these do?"

"Better than a kick in the head with a frozen boot."

Harry gave her a confused look.

Daniela smiled. "Something my dad used to say." She took the Swiss Army scissors and carefully cut around each hand-drawn eye, then used her fingers to give each almond-shaped paper eye a gentle curve.

"You think this will work?"

Daniela shook her head. "Probably not, but it's worth a try, right?" She knelt and placed each hand-drawn eye on top of Logan's closed eyelids.

"Jesus Christ, he looks like a zombie now." Harry held the phone over Logan's face. A second later it vibrated. Still locked. "Shit."

"Just a second." Daniela gave more curve to the paper eyes and adjusted their position. "Try it one more time."

Harry held the phone over Logan's face.

"Well?" Daniela raised her brows at Harry. "What happened? I didn't hear it vibrate."

Harry flipped Logan's phone over. The display showed icons

of different apps, neatly lined up in rows. "Holy shit. It worked. You're a genius, Doc!"

"You're just finding this out now?" She grinned at him.

"So, this is technically evidence." Harry's face drew serious. "You still want to proceed?"

"After all that?" Daniela cleared her throat. "I mean I do take issue with breaking protocol, but we also need answers. Once it's in police hands, we'll never see it again. So... hell, yeah."

"Okay." Harry opened the photos app. "Let's see what got Logan."

He navigated to the camera roll. Most of the photos were of Logan and Rebecca, with a few of various members of the grounds crew. At the end two photos stood out from the rest.

Harry tapped on the first one. The photo showed the sand of the bunker, overexposed, with the hole extending into a circular black void. "That's it, but the exposure is all wrong." He opened the image adjustments and tried to pull detail out of the shadows but ended up boosting the noise of the image.

"The camera exposed for the sand, not the hole," Daniela said. "Go to the next one."

Harry swiped to the next image and his eyes bugged out.

"Holy shit." Daniela craned her neck forward. "What the *hell* is that?"

The creature in the image was unclear due to motion blur and was partially cast in shadow, as if a portion of the flash had been blocked. A partial ring of teeth could be seen, splayed outward and around a reddened glistening gullet within the center of the creature's head... if it could be called a head. The rest of the creature's body was unseen, contained within the further walls of the burrow.

"I have no idea." Harry felt a chill rip through his body. He pinch-zoomed to the partial view of the creature's head and teeth. "But that's what stripped Logan's arm clean of muscle. It's the only explanation."

Daniela held up her phone. "Send me the photos by Bluetooth. I don't want the police coming after me later. Make sure you send them to yourself as well."

Harry transferred the two photos to both of their phones, then opened the call history. "Last call to the phone was from his girlfriend." He sighed.

"Want me to call? I *am* the resident doctor."

Harry shook his head. "I was his manager… and his friend. I'll do it." He keyed Rebecca's number into his phone. "You take Logan's phone for safe keeping. And get rid of those eyes. They creep me right out."

"Right." Daniela removed the paper eyes and pulled the blanket back over Logan's head. "I'll also give the coroner a poke. Things are going to get nasty in here soon."

Harry nodded and handed over Logan's phone. They exited the machine room, Daniela closing the door after her, and headed outside.

"Let me know when the cavalry's coming," Harry said.

Daniela nodded and continued toward the resort complex.

Harry tapped "dial" on his phone and waited for the call to connect. "Rebecca? Hi. Harry Harcourt from Mar-A-Verde." Rebecca's animated voice at the other end of the line chirped happily, despite the hour of the call. He died a bit inside knowing what was coming. "It's almost like I know you, too." Harry took a deep breath in hopes that it might make his task easier. It didn't. "Look, Rebecca. I've got some bad news…"

Harry began the day by doing two things he had never done before: unlock a phone with a dead man's face, and deliver news of death to a significant other. Neither were pleasant.

He didn't think the day could get any worse. But when it rains, it pours.

CARNAGE

It was mid morning and Harry tended to the gardens next to the clubhouse. The dahlias had been prolific this season. He guessed it was the combination of warm weather, new fertilizer, and an increase in bumblebee cross-pollination.

Remaining true to character, Larsen's presence preceded him. Stealthy he was not. A stream of profanity rose above the whine of his golf cart's electric motor until he skidded to a stop in front of Harry's maintenance cart.

"Have you seen this? Fuck! Have you..." Larsen's face resembled an angry boil ready to pop. "Heads are going to fucking roll, Harry. Mark my words!"

"Larsen, tone it down." Harry glanced side to side. "Your swearing doesn't help improve the *guest experience.*"

Larsen knew when he was being made fun of. He pursed his lips and spoke through gritted teeth. "It's all over the Internet. Breaking fucking news."

Harry's mind raced. "What is?"

Larsen presented his phone. The display showed photos and a video of Logan immediately after the accident that killed him, plus images of him dead in the machine room.

"Aw, Jesus." Harry rubbed his temple, leaving smudges of dirt to mix with the sweat on his brow. The news was bad, but it was made even worse because he had a good idea who had done it.

"I want this dealt with, right fucking now." Larsen's stifled anger caused his voice to squeak. "Or I'll fire everyone, starting with you." He pointed an angry finger. "Get your grounds crew to my office. Now."

Harry stared back. Words escaped him.

"What the *fuck* are you waiting for? Or do you *want* to be fired?"

Harry stood and brushed himself off. "I'm on it." His eyes locked on Larsen as he drove away. He detached his walkie-talkie. "Brynna. Jomar. Drop everything and meet me at the clubhouse. Pronto."

Brynna's voice chirped back. "What's up?"

"Not over the radio. Harry out."

"Someone's in *trou-ble*," Alejandro's voice floated sing-song from the walkie-talkie's speaker.

"Shut your trap, Al. This doesn't concern you. And keep this channel clear. Harry *out*."

Twenty minutes later Brynna and Jomar jogged up to where Harry had parked his cart. Harry had used the time to browse the Internet on his phone.

"What the hell took you so long?"

"We were knee-deep in fertilizer on the fourteenth hole," Brynna said. "You know it's the farthest hole from the—"

"Here's what else I know. You're knee-deep in shit for real." He held up his phone at arm's length. "What do you know about this?" A video of Logan slumped over the dash of his maintenance cart played on the display.

Brynna and Jomar exchanged panicked looks.

"What the *hell* were you thinking?" Harry alternated his glare between the two.

"Harry, I—"

Harry raised his hand and cut off Brynna. "Save it for Larsen. Let's go." He led the group around the clubhouse and into the resort through the back entrance, his anger simmering. Brynna and Jomar remained silent.

Once in the building, Harry turned and backed his two coworkers into a corner. "Look. I don't like Strunk either. Or Larsen for that matter. And I'd never intentionally damage this resort's reputation. But more than that, you took advantage of Logan, one of *us* damn it! For what? Views? Likes? He could've been alive right now, but you were shooting video instead."

"He had no pulse," Jomar said.

Harry stepped closer, nose to nose with Jomar. "And that makes it okay?"

Jomar said nothing.

"Move."

The three arrived at Larsen's office. Livid conversation penetrated through the wood door.

"I hope you got your stories straight." Harry rapped the door with his knuckles. The angry dialog continued uninterrupted. He opened the door.

Larsen locked an angry gaze on Harry, then at Brynna and Jomar. "They just walked in. I'll call you back." He slammed the phone into its cradle. "Where's the rest of them? I wanted to see the whole grounds crew."

"These two are responsible," Harry said. "I'd stake my job on it."

Larsen offered an angered laugh. "Who says you still have a job?"

"I'd stake my life on it."

Jomar looked at the two chairs.

Larsen shook his head. "Don't sit. You're not going to be here long." He took a long look at Brynna and Jomar. "Do you have any idea how much fucking damage you've caused? Strunk is furious."

Brynna panicked. "It's not my fault. I tried to stop him, but he wouldn't listen."

"You didn't try hard enough, did you?" Larsen focused on Jomar. "What do you have to say for yourself?"

Jomar shrugged, a scowl on his face.

Harry looked at Jomar. "Is Brynna telling the truth?"

Jomar remained silent.

The tendons in Larsen's neck stood out like angry ribbons. He pointed at Jomar. "You're fired. And you…" He turned to Brynna.

"Please don't fire me, Mr. Larsen. Please!" Brynna stepped forward and leaned on Larsen's desk. "I need this job."

"Step back." Larsen grimaced and waved his hands at her dismissively. "Hands off the desk."

Brynna complied, tears spilling down her cheeks. "But Mr. Larsen. I didn't do anything!"

"That's right," Larsen said. "You didn't do anything to stop it. You're fired too."

"What? No!" Brynna's face fell into shock. She turned to Jomar and pounded on his chest. "You fucking selfish asshole! God damn you."

"Get off me, you *bitch*." Jomar pushed Brynna backward.

Harry stepped in between the two. "Stop it. Now."

"It was her idea in the first place," Jomar said.

"Liar!" Brynna screamed and tried to claw Jomar from around Harry.

"Quiet!" Larsen stood up behind his desk. "I want you *both* off this island before sundown."

Harry corralled Jomar toward the door.

"Don't be touchin' me." Jomar pushed Harry aside and glared at Larsen. "This isn't over. Just you wait."

"Take it up with our lawyers, fucko."

Jomar disappeared down the hallway.

"Please, Harry." Brynna's eyes pleaded. "Do something."

Harry sighed. "I'm sorry. It's up to Larsen." He watched her run down the hallway, her sobs echoing back.

Larsen squeezed back into his chair, a grin of contentment on his face.

Harry stared at him, incredulous. "You actually enjoyed that, didn't you?"

"Made my morning." Larsen stretched and clasped his hands behind his head, shiny from rage sweat. "Now I get to deliver Strunk some good news for a change."

Harry shook his head. "You—"

"Watch it, Harry."

"You didn't have to fire Brynna."

"Bye, Harry. I'd watch your back if I were you."

Harry gave Larsen his hardest glare before leaving his office. "You fat sadistic slob," he said in a low whisper only he could hear. "You'll have your day."

AFTER THE SHIT show in Larsen's office, Harry's nerves were shot. He returned to his office within the maintenance building and did something he normally reserved for quitting time: he grabbed a bottle of Jack Daniels from his desk and took a healthy pull from the bottle.

Drinking on the job was a fireable offense but at that moment, after the past thirty hours, Harry didn't care. The smooth whiskey hit his stomach and exploded warmth throughout his body, relaxing him in an instant.

Whiskey before noon. Harry closed his eyes and took a cleansing breath. "God, grant me the serenity to—"

"Harry?" Brynna knocked on the door frame to the office.

He shoved the Jack Daniels bottle back into his desk drawer and sat on the corner of his desk. "Brynna. I'm—"

"Don't worry. I'm not here to ask for my job back." She glanced at her feet before continuing. "Just wanted to say thanks. It was great working with you."

"Likewise." Harry clasped his hands on his lap. "And I want

you to know this isn't personal. It's Larsen. He's a mean son-of-a-bitch."

"It was also Jomar," Brynna said. "He didn't have to throw me under the bus."

Harry offered a subdued nod.

"Do you believe me? That I wouldn't record—"

"Absolutely. Your work ethic and integrity are top notch," Harry said. "Text me if you need a letter of reference."

Brynna smiled, her eyes still red from crying. "Thanks." She stepped forward and stuck out her hand.

Harry took it and they shared a firm handshake. "Best of luck to you, Brynna." He looked at his watch. "You better get packing. The last supply boat leaves in about an hour."

"Right." Brynna paused at the door and waved. "Maybe I'll see you around."

"You just might." He stepped behind his desk, sat down, and powered up his computer. As the electronics initialized, he slumped to one side and looked at his desk drawer. Hooking his finger into the pull, he slid the drawer out far enough to see the Jack Daniels bottle and the whiskey it contained within.

"One more won't hurt." As Harry grabbed for the bottle, the computer's desktop announced itself with an auditory flourish. He left the bottle where it was and kicked the drawer closed.

He plugged his phone in and transferred the two images from Logan's phone to his computer. "Let's see if anyone can ID this thing."

Harry spent the next hour posting the image to various social media sites. Within minutes he began to receive responses, but most were questions he had no answers to. The closest he came to an identification was some kind of rodent or caterpillar. None of it made much sense and it left him back where he started. He tried to use an image search but that resulted in poor matches as well. There wasn't enough detail.

Harry stared at the motion-blurred image on the screen, at its ring of teeth and jaundiced skin. "What the hell are you?" he whispered.

His walkie talkie crackled on its charging station. "Boss? Al here. We got an... issue on the first hole."

Harry snatched the radio and brought it to his mouth. "What kind of issue?"

"You just better get down here." A staticky pause broadcast though the office. Harry thought he heard panicked voices in the background. "Make it fast."

Shit, Harry thought. *What now?*

IN THE SHORT time it took for Harry to drive his cart to the first hole, his mind kept returning to one scenario: Larsen, stuck headfirst in a sink hole, dead. The thought brought a morbid smile to his lips. But as he navigated the cart down the path next to the fairway a very different turn of events developed.

A group of three people had gathered most of the way down the fairway, close to the green. One person had raised their hands in the air and was waving them back and forth in a frantic fashion. As Harry drove closer, he recognized Tzipora and Alejandro in their purple coveralls. But the other person...

"McCoy?" Harry cranked the steering wheel a hard right and veered off the path, onto the fairway.

"Stop! Don't get too close," McCoy said.

Harry slammed the brakes and left a short patch of dirt behind each wheel. He hopped out and ran towards the group. "What's going on?"

"Jesus, Harry. It's Sinclair." McCoy placed one hand on his hip, the other raking his hair. He paced back and forth, his golf clubs forgotten.

It was clear that McCoy wasn't going to be any help. "What's going on, Al?"

"It looks like a sink hole."

Harry furrowed his brow in confusion. "Another one?" He tried to walk around Alejandro, but he held him back.

"It's what's *in* the sink hole." Alejandro locked gazes with Harry and motioned at McCoy.

"Oh shit." He pushed past Alejandro.

"Harry, wait!" Alejandro called after him.

"Get on the ground," Tzipora yelled. "Spread your weight out."

Harry looked at her, trying to make sense of her words.

"We don't know how big it is. Underneath."

Harry spotted a hole in the ground directly ahead of him, no bigger than two feet across. Beside it lay an upturned golf bag. A hose had been tied to Alejandro's maintenance cart and the other end disappeared into the hole. Things clicked in his head. He looked back at Tzipora and dropped his body to the ground.

Like a soldier in an army crawl, Harry moved toward the hole. As he drew closer, he could hear screams echoing from beneath the ground.

"Slow down!" Tzipora dropped to all fours. "Be careful."

Harry reached the crumbling edge of the hole, ragged with roots and grass, and looked down. It was almost noon and the sun sat directly overhead, casting a shadow of his head onto the wet dirt floor of the cavern. The hot smell of blood rose from within the cavern and tied his stomach in knots.

Sinclair's face and arms were streaked with blood and his clothes were in tatters. Bloody sockets remained where his eyes used to be.

"Help! Get me—" His voice gurgled into unintelligible mumbling as blood rose in his throat and spilled down his cheeks.

Harry's eyes adjusted to the darkness of the subterranean

space just enough to discern two (maybe three?) masses ravaging Sinclair's body. But there still wasn't enough light. He'd have to get down inside the cavern with Sinclair to see better and that was off the table.

"Is he okay?" McCoy took tentative steps toward where Harry lay.

"Stay back." Harry rolled to one side and held up his open palm. "It's not safe."

"What do you see?" Tzipora stood her ground but Harry could see she was itching to join him at the hole's opening.

Harry shook his head. "Nothing good." He slipped his phone out and opened the camera app. He held it with both hands to direct the camera into the shadows. "Now don't drop the damn thing," he chided himself.

In the time that it took Harry to grab his phone Sinclair had lost the ability to move his limbs and whatever was attacking him was pulling his body more into the shadows.

Harry aimed at Sinclair's legs and took a picture. The phone lit the darkened cavern to focus, then tripped a burst of light.

Screeching funneled out of the opening in the ground, concentrated from being in an enclosed space. Harry rolled to one side, crumbling part of the hole's edge and almost dropping his phone.

"Holy fuck," Alejandro said. "What was that?"

Harry rolled to the other side of the hole and held the camera over the opening. "Damned if I know." He triggered a blast of photos and a blood-curdling chorus of shrieks rose from the hole once again.

He inched his way to the edge and peered in. Sinclair's body was motionless but beyond the sun's reach the darkness still moved. Harry flipped on flashlight mode on his phone and aimed its beam into the hole. What he saw turned his guts to water.

At least four hairless creatures the size of house cats dined on

Sinclair's legs, but it was difficult to see where one creature ended and the next began. The closest two reared their bodies up and shrieked again, a ring of bloodied teeth opening like a hell flower to the sun, before they all retreated from the light. It was then that Harry saw the creatures all had tails, long and slick like parsnips gone bad.

"They don't like light, that's for damn sure." Harry inched backward until he was a few feet back from the hole. "And that's the only way we're going to be able to get Sinclair out of there." He turned to Tzipora. "What do we got in the way of floodlights?"

"Not sure, but I'm on it." Tzipora hopped into her cart and sped back to the maintenance building.

"Al, can you stake this hole with warning tape?" Harry surveyed the fairway. "Give it a fifteen foot radius just to be safe."

"Got it." Alejandro dug through the supplies in his cart. "What are you going to do?"

"Got a call to make." Harry grimaced and shook his head. He grabbed Sinclair's golf bag and dragged it to a safe distance.

Alejandro raised his brows. "Larsen?"

"Who else?"

"What about Sinclair?" McCoy had stopped pacing.

"As far as I can tell, he's dead," Harry said. "I'm sorry. I'll bring in our doctor to make the official call."

"What's going to happen to him?"

"We'll get him out if we got enough lights to make it work." Harry found Larsen in his phone contacts. "And that's only if the lights keep those things away. I'm not going to risk anyone else's life."

"Let me see those photos." McCoy's voice carried an angry tone.

"You don't want to remember your colleague that way, McCoy. But—"

"Show me. Now."

"I knew you'd insist." Harry pulled up the photos, which were far more graphic than he remembered them being, even though he had taken them moments earlier. He looked at McCoy. "You sure about this?"

McCoy nodded and extended his hand.

"Okay. Don't say I didn't warn you." Harry handed his phone to McCoy.

The color drained from McCoy's face with the first photo. "Jesus." He moved through two more before weakly handing the phone back to Harry.

Harry placed his hand on McCoy's shoulder and gave it a light squeeze. "Looks like you need a drink. Al, can you drive McCoy to the clubhouse?"

"Sure thing."

"Get him set up and put it on my account." Harry dialed his phone. "If you run into problems, get Gilles to call me."

Alejandro helped McCoy collect both his and Sinclair's golf clubs and drove him to the clubhouse.

Harry's phone trilled twice before Larsen picked up, already in mid-tirade. "Larsen, you need to shut up and listen." His words must have made an impact because Larsen shut his mouth. "We just had our second death. *Two* deaths in *two* days. The resort has a serious problem that we can't cover up with a layer of sand."

He listened to Larsen's measured response, a departure from his usual belligerent demeanor. "You want *me* to solve it? How?"

Larsen offered no answers.

"Fine," Harry said. "I'm driving this bus and I want full control. Equipment, budget, the works."

Larsen agreed and hung up.

"Holy shit." Harry stared at his phone, taken aback. "What the hell have I gotten myself into?"

It wouldn't take long to find out.

ALEJANDRO HAD THE good sense to bring not one but two extendable ladders with him after dropping McCoy off at the clubhouse bar.

"If you lay one ladder on the ground, anchored by one of our carts," Alejandro had explained to Harry, "you can use the top of that ladder as a rest for the one we drop into the hole."

It was a good plan. Not only did it provide a sturdy entry into the hole, it prevented eroding the sides of the hole any more than they already were.

Tzipora arrived with two LED task lights with stands, extension cords, and a portable gas generator. "You want me and Al to set up the high beams?"

Harry shook his head. "No more deaths, other than my own."

"Seriously?" Tzipora held up one of the LED lights. "If they can't stand the light from a phone, they don't stand a chance against this."

"I'll be the one to confirm your theory."

Daniela rolled up, hopped out of her first responder cart, and strode toward Harry. "Long time, no see."

Harry forced a smile. "No shit."

"You know there are other ways to get my attention." Daniela flashed her brows at him and tucked a lock of hair behind one ear. "Chocolate works."

"Noted." Harry looked at the first responder cart beyond Daniela. "We're going to need your stretcher again." He looked at her with hopeful eyes. "Any body bags yet?"

Daniela shook her head. "Not for at least another week."

"How about garbage bags?"

"Maybe." She nodded toward Tzipora and Alejandro

collecting the lighting equipment just beyond the caution tape. "What happened?"

"Think Logan," Harry said, "but a hundred times worse. The difference is I saw the creatures this time."

Before Daniela could ask to see photos, Harry had them up on his phone's display.

"Oh God. That's so... not right."

"Watching a man die was worse." Harry stared at the ground at his feet. "There wasn't anything anyone could do."

Daniela looked toward the hole in the fairway. "We're all going to need counseling after this."

"You may be right." He took a breath. "We need to extract the body. Feel like helping?"

"I don't think I have a choice."

"Everyone has a choice."

"No. Not with this. Not with a dead body... and those *things*. You're not going down there alone." Daniela walked back to her cart. "Help me grab some supplies."

Harry couldn't help but admire Daniela's pragmatic approach.

"I'M GOING DOWN FIRST." Harry took an LED task light from Tzipora and crawled across the horizontal ladder until he reached the ladder descending into the hole. "Plug me in."

Alejandro pull-started the gas generator and Tzipora plugged in the extension cord. Harry flipped the switch and the LED burned a brilliant white.

Harry directed the light's beam into the hole and screeches rose out of the ground like a tornado. "They're ba-ack."

He aimed the light at the creatures on the floor of the cavern, chasing them along the walls until they scrambled out the one exit tunnel. The light seemed to make their pale skin bubble and smoke.

"Thank God for small miracles," Harry mumbled.

"You say something?" Daniela was already at the top of the ladder, ready to join him.

"One way in. One way out." Harry shrugged. "Could be worse." He aimed the light at the exit tunnel as he descended the ladder. His gut tightened with every step until his work boot treads sank into the red and sodden earth blanketing the floor of the cavern. He couldn't wait to get out of there.

Unfolding the built-in tripod, Harry placed the light at the exit. The tunnel leading out was cast in cold bright light and revealed an area big enough for a person to crawl through.

Daniela dropped some black garbage bags and a blanket into the cavern. "Take the stretcher." She handed down a collapsible stretcher. Harry unfolded it and placed it next to Sinclair's body.

Daniela stepped down the ladder without hesitation. "Jesus this place is creeptastic." She set up her light between Sinclair's body and the cavern wall. "Is this where you take all your first dates?"

If Harry wore glasses, he'd be looking over the rims at Daniela. "Not funny."

"Sorry. My humor takes some getting used to."

"I'm definitely not used to this." Harry looked around the cavern, settling on the exit. "The sooner I'm out of here the better."

"I'm down with that." Daniela tossed Harry a pair of rubber gloves and donned a pair herself. She grabbed a garbage bag and shook it open. "Are you one of those guys that needs to drive the bus all the time?"

Harry shook his head and took a slight bow as he pulled on his gloves. "Not this guy. By all means, lead the way."

"Okay." A hint of a smile crossed Daniela's face. "Here's what we're going to do. You lift the body and I'll slip the bags around it. Then we'll wrap him in a blanket and strap him to the stretcher. Sound good?"

"Sure, doc."

"It's going to be messy."

Harry surveyed the footprints on the cavern floor, ending on his own feet caked with bloody mud. "Yeah, I figured that."

"Throwing up is okay. Lots of rookies do it. Just do it over there." Daniela pointed away from the body.

"Who you calling a rookie? This is my second dead body in two days," Harry said. "That's got to count for something."

"Fair enough." Daniela opened one of the garbage bags. "If you can, grab his pants and lift his legs and hips. Otherwise this is going to get a lot harder."

Even though Sinclair's clothes were shredded, there was still enough fabric attached to allow Harry to grab his pants and belt and lift the lower half of Sinclair's body. Patches of bloodied muscle, veins, and bone showed through the holes in Sinclair's pants and Harry fought to keep his stomach under control.

Daniela slid a garbage bag around the dead man's feet, then worked it up the body, ending at his hips.

Harry exhaled, only then discovering that he had been holding his breath. "Easy peasy, right?"

"Bottom half is the easiest," Daniela said. "But you did great. Just do the same thing to the top half and we're ninety percent there."

The task lights flickered and went out, throwing the cavern into darkness. Then the lights re-lit a second later, followed by a shriek that felt much too close for comfort.

Harry looked up at the ladder and circle of sky above his head, the only escape route. "Tzipora? Al? What the hell is going on?"

"Harry, let's focus." Daniela shook out a second bag. "We don't want to be down here if the lights go out permanently."

"Right." Harry grabbed Sinclair's collar and belt and hoisted him up. The man's gored head lolled backward, his skeletal arms hanging limp from his shoulders.

Daniela worked quickly and guided the garbage bag around Sinclair's head and arms. The two bags met at the man's eviscerated abdomen. "Okay, now the blanket."

Harry unfolded a blanket beside Sinclair's plastic shroud.

"Grab his shoulders and I'll grab his feet," Daniela said. "Lift him onto the blanket and we'll roll the body up."

The light flickered again, and Harry cast a concerned glance at Daniela. She tried to return a look of reassurance, but uncertainty and time pressure was wearing her thin as well.

"Onto the blanket. One... Two... Three!"

It was harder to lift Sinclair's slack and slippery body than it looked. His limbs and torso slid within the slick plastic bags. But after a couple of false starts, they managed to get the man's body onto the blanket.

Harry stepped over Sinclair's body and joined Daniela as they rolled him up in the blanket, the embroidered Mar-A-Verde logo disappearing within the folds of the fabric.

"Okay. On the stretcher and we're done," Daniela said.

"We're not done until we're out of this hell hole."

"Right." She rolled Sinclair's body up onto his shoulder. "Jam the stretcher under him."

Harry did as he was told but kept his eyes half on the exit tunnel. As he rounded the body, he kicked the task light nearest to the cavern wall onto its side. Wet mud struck the LEDs and it fizzled out.

"Shit!"

"Just stay focused," Daniela said. "Scoot it right along the body."

Harry positioned the stretcher as instructed and Daniela rolled and rocked Sinclair's body back onto the center.

"Fasten the straps as tight as they'll go." Daniela began with the straps across Sinclair's chest and Harry started at his feet.

They met at the middle. "Okay, let's get out of here. You want to—"

"You go first." Harry was emphatic. "You pull him from the top and I'll lift from the bottom."

Daniela didn't argue but instead grabbed the stretcher handles nearest to Sinclair's head. "Ready? On three."

"No time," Harry said. "Just lift."

They raised Sinclair's body off the floor of the cavern. Daniela stepped up the ladder backward, hooking the heels of her boots on the rungs for balance.

The remaining light flickered off.

"Daniela, hurry," Harry's fingers and arms strained against the weight of Sinclair's wrapped corpse. "We got no light."

"Tell me something I don't know." Daniela maintained her pace ascending the ladder, which was an impressive feat considering she was facing backwards.

Echoing out of the exit tunnel Harry could hear scuffing and grunting. "Those things are back."

Daniela popped her head out of the hole, the brightness of the day burning her eyes. Tzipora and Alejandro tended to the generator, trying to get it running again. "Forget that! Help us out!"

Tzipora and Alejandro ran toward the hole, then froze at the horizontal ladder.

"Will it hold us?" Tzipora looked to Alejandro.

"What are you waiting for?" Daniela had the first quarter of the stretcher out of the hole. "Harry's going to die!"

Alejandro shrugged at Tzipora. "Fuck it." He ran beside the ladder to Daniela and grabbed the stretcher. Tzipora joined him and pulled it back out of the hole, sliding it on the horizontal ladder.

Harry felt the weight release in his hands as the stretcher disappeared from sight. He had his foot on the first rung of the ladder when he heard several creatures enter the cavern.

"Give me your hand!" Harry grabbed Daniela's extended hand and took a second step.

A creature latched itself onto the back of Harry's boot. "Jesus Christ, one of them's on me!" He tried to kick it off, but its teeth had dug deep into the rubber sole and leather upper. Harry continued to climb the ladder, shaking his foot with each step.

Daniela dug out her phone and flipped it into flashlight mode. She aimed it at Harry's feet. "Show me your heel."

He leaned into the ladder and raised his foot. The sight of this creature for the first time, alive and trying to feed off Harry's foot, caused Daniela to hesitate in horrified fascination.

"Come on, Doc!" Harry reached the top of the ladder. "I don't plan on bringing this bastard out with me."

Daniela slipped back to reality and aimed her phone's flashlight at the creature. She leaned farther into the hole to increase the intensity of light falling on the creature. Its pale, greasy skin began to smoke, and it retracted its teeth in an instant, falling to the floor below where it scrambled about like the others.

Daniela stared for a moment longer. "It doesn't look like they can climb ladders."

Harry pulled himself off the ladder and out of the hole. "I'm not going to give them a chance to prove you wrong." He raised the ladder out of the hole and laid it on top of the one already lying on the fairway. "Get away from the edge."

Harry ran to the gas generator and collapsed from exhaustion next to Sinclair's shrouded body. He rolled onto his back, breathing heavily. He alternated his gaze between Tzipora and Alejandro. "What's the rule regarding gas generators?"

Tzipora and Alejandro shared a sheepish look. "Refill the tank after every use."

"Do you think that was done?" Harry asked between breaths.

"No, boss," Alejandro said.

"Okay. Let's not forget next time, huh?"

They both nodded.

"Can you guys get the lights and generator back to the maintenance building?"

"I'm on it." Alejandro hustled back toward the hole in the fairway, followed closely by Tzipora.

Daniela sat down next to Harry, phone in hand. "Do you think this will get the coroner's attention?"

Harry turned to her and offered a winded laugh. "I think you're going to find out. Thanks, by the way. Best date ever."

"But it's not over," Daniela said. "We got to get rid of the body."

"Give me five minutes."

Ten minutes later, Harry's pulse had settled back to normal, but the day, now half over, had just gotten started.

HARRY AND DANIELA drove to the maintenance building on the first responder cart and transported Sinclair's remains to the machine room, next to Logan's decomposing body. The room carried overtones of human rot.

"Jesus." Harry held his hand over his nose which didn't help a bit with the smell.

"What you're smelling is the first stages of bloat," Daniela said. "It's going to get worse before it gets better if the bodies aren't removed. Speaking of which..." She beckoned him out of the room and closed the door behind them.

"I'm going to call Alice Town Police again. Want to be in on the call?" Daniela raised her eyebrows, expectant. "It might help light a fire under their asses."

"Couldn't hurt."

Daniela dialed and connected on the second ring. "Hi. This is Doctor Daniela Trejo from Mar-A-Verde calling for Chief

Abernathy... Sure, I'll hold." She covered the phone's speaker and turned to Harry. "They're playing 'Mack the Knife.' "

"How appropriate," Harry said.

"I know—Oh, Chief Abernathy? Doctor Daniela Trejo from Mar... Right. I've got Harry Harcourt, head groundskeeper, with me. Mind if I put you on speaker?" Daniela waited, then tapped the icon on her phone.

"What can I do for you, Doctor Trejo and Mister Harcourt?" Chief Abernathy sounded like his lunch had been interrupted.

"I'm following up on a reported death at the resort two days ago."

"I'm well aware of your predicament, Doctor Trejo," Abernathy said.

"Well, we have another death, this time a guest of the resort." Daniela cleared her throat. "That's two in two days."

"This a murder?" Abernathy's voice buzzed through the phone's small speaker. "You got some kind of rich serial killin' mucky-muck on your hands?"

"No, sir. Animal attack."

"What kind of animal?"

Daniela exchanged a worried look with Harry. "We don't know yet."

"Look, Doctor Trejo," said Abernathy. "We got our own fish to fry over here too. A murder. I'll send the coroner and a couple officers as soon as I can spare 'em."

"Chief Abernathy, Harry here. We've got the bodies in our machine room, but it's getting bad. Could you send the coroner ahead of the others to get the bodies into proper storage?"

"When I can, Mr. Harcourt. Will that be all?"

"I sure hope this doesn't get back to Strunk." Daniela winked at Harry. "There's already a viral video out there regarding one of the deaths. Casts the resort in a bad light. Help from the local authorities would sure look good on the eleven o'clock news."

Faint sounds of office chatter filtered through the phone's speaker.

"Chief Abernathy?"

"I'll see what I can do to... expedite things."

"Thank you, Chief." Daniela pumped her fist. "I appreciate your assistance."

"I'm sure you do, Doctor," Abernathy said. "Now, if you'll excuse me, I must get back to my murder investigation."

"I'll keep in touch." Daniela ended the call.

"What do you want to bet that his murder investigation involves ham and swiss on whole wheat?"

"Don't be such a cynic, Harry," Daniela said. "I think the fire under his ass is lit."

"I hope so. I want my machine room back."

Harry's phone rang. The call display read "Mar-A-Verde Clubhouse."

"Ah shit. I got to take this. Thanks for all your work today, Daniela. And especially for saving my life. I owe you one." He quickened his pace toward the maintenance building exit.

"No worries, Harry." Daniela headed to the first responder cart and was off like a shot.

Harry answered the call. "Don't let him leave. I'm on my way."

IT WAS BARELY past one o'clock when Harry entered the clubhouse bar and dining room. The tables were sparsely populated by guests eating lunch. The resort had a policy of serving alcohol with food until three o'clock. After that the alcohol flowed freely. Harry had okayed a free pass for McCoy and in his state of mind he willingly imbibed.

Gilles waved Harry over to the opposite side of the bar. "I've cut him off. Didn't like that one bit."

"I'll bet."

"Could you take him somewhere else?" Gilles pointed casually toward a few vacant tables at the back of the room. "He's loud and annoying when he's drunk, and I got to get ready for this afternoon's rush."

Harry nodded. "Can I get some coffee when you get a chance?"

"Sure thing," Gilles said.

Harry approached McCoy. He was half-perched on a bar stool, leaning over the counter clutching a tumbler half-filled with ice. The man reeked of booze.

"How's the whiskey?"

McCoy shook his tumbler of ice. "Empty... *AGAIN!*" He glared at Gilles at the opposite end of the bar.

"Let's take a walk." Harry guided McCoy off the bar stool toward tables at the back.

"Where we goin'?"

"Just to sit and chat." Harry ignored the stares from other guests as he passed.

"Is Sinclair really dead?" McCoy regarded Harry with watery red-rimmed eyes.

Harry sat McCoy down at a far table and took the chair opposite. "Sadly, yes. We've retrieved his remains and have called the coroner."

A server placed a cream and sugar set on the table, overturned two coffee cups onto their saucers, and poured hot coffee into both cups. The aroma was a refreshing change from dirt and gore.

"Leave the carafe, please," Harry said. The server complied and disappeared back to the kitchen.

"Jesus." McCoy held his head as he prepared his coffee. Lots of cream and sugar. "I still got to break the news to his wife."

"I know how tough that can be." Harry sipped his black coffee.

"God damn it, Harry." McCoy dropped his spoon on his saucer, the clatter drawing attention. "What the *fuck* were those things that killed him?"

"I don't know," Harry said. "We're still trying to figure that out."

"I've never seen anything like it. Ever. But you know what they reminded me of?"

Harry shook his head.

"Uncooked overstuffed sausage. But with rows of teeth, kind of like a sea anemone, but not quite." The word came out like "an enemy".

Harry nodded and thought that was a fair description of those ugly bastards.

"No!" McCoy placed his coffee cup back on its saucer without care, spilling some on the new white linen tablecloth. "A leech. You ever seen one? With all those rings of teeth?"

One can't work the earth without running into the occasional leech. "I have. The only problem is leeches are tiny." But McCoy was right. The creature's mouth did look a lot like a leech's.

"Well your resort has a giant leech problem." The volume of McCoy's voice was still stuck on "annoying."

Harry leaned into the table and lowered his voice in hopes that McCoy would take a hint. "There's something out there, that's for sure. Probably not leeches though."

"Right. It had a tail. And legs." McCoy drank his coffee as his brain worked on a memory. "More than four legs I'm sure of that." His eyes narrowed as he gave Harry a side-eyed glance. "Is this related to what you were doing on the third hole a few days back?"

The coffee was working on McCoy a little too quickly and Harry didn't like where his questions were going.

"I don't know yet," Harry said.

"Yet." McCoy sat back and studied him through his fading stupor. "You know what I think, Harry? I think you're hiding something."

"If I was hiding something, would I have shown you the pictures of Sinclair I took today?"

"Why not show your pictures to everyone here, then?" McCoy pointed at the guests eating lunch. He stood and addressed the rest of the room. "This golf course is dangerous. My business partner was killed on the first hole!"

Gasps from various guests floated across the room.

"Okay. Show's over." Harry stood and jettisoned his chair across the floor. "I think it's time for you to sleep it off."

"Only golf Mar-A-Verde if you've got a death wish!"

Harry grabbed McCoy's arm and led him to the exit. "Look, I'm really sorry about Sinclair. But we're working on it. The last thing we need is mass panic."

McCoy eyed Harry's hand on his arm, then shifted his gaze to Harry. "Get the *fuck* off me."

The two men stared each other down for several tense seconds. Everyone in the dining room fell silent as the drama played out.

"You *knew*, didn't you?" McCoy daggered Harry with his eyes. "It must have been bad, but you kept it to yourself."

Harry released McCoy's arm. "Do you want me to escort you or would you prefer I call security?"

"Fuck you, Harry." McCoy looked Harry up and down, disgusted. "Sinclair would be alive right now if it hadn't been for your... secrets. Strunk's going to hear about this."

"Get some sleep, McCoy," Harry said. "I'll fill you in when you're sober."

"If you still work here by then." McCoy stumbled toward the ornately gilded elevator doors.

Harry rubbed his temples. He could feel a headache coming

on fast, but the pressure of McCoy's ticking clock motivated him more.

HARRY SLUMPED INTO his office chair and dug out a bottle of Tylenol from his desk drawer. The little red pills inside jostled like a children's rattle. He shook out three (one extra for good measure) and washed them down with a swig of cold coffee from his travel mug.

He flipped through his Rolodex looking for the phone number for Big Don from Far 'n' Away Pest Management. Despite the world going almost entirely digital and everyone owning a cell phone, Harry preferred to keep his contacts on paper. It was one less thing of his that was owned by the big corporations.

"There you are, Big Don," Harry said to himself. He pulled out the card, picked up the handset to his office phone, and dialed.

The call trilled in his ear four times, then five. Harry had begun to think he had misdialed the number when the call connected.

"Yo," a burly voice announced from the handset's speaker.

"Big Don? It's Harry... from Mar-A-Verde."

"Harry!" Big Don had a smile a mile wide, one that translated over the phone too. "Haven't heard from you in a dog's age. You're still above the grass instead of under it, so that's good."

A shiver ripped up Harry's back as visions of Sinclair flooded his mind, torn to ribbons by those creatures in the cavern.

"I'm doing okay." Harry began doodling on a pad of paper. "How's the pest control business treating you?"

A deep belly laugh echoed from the handset. "Dorian fucked me and pretty much everything else of value in Freeport."

"Jesus. Sorry to hear that. We missed most of it."

"Yeah, everything seems to miss Verde, don't it? The place has a horseshoe up its ass. But my insurance paid out nicely."

Harry struggled to find an eloquent way to get into his reason for calling. Hiring an exterminator for a pest problem at an exclusive island golf resort sounded like white privilege. The fact that both men were black made it feel even stranger. "Look I'm in a bad spot, but after hearing what Dorian did to you..."

"Better out than in, man," Big Don said. "So spit it out."

"I need your expertise." The doodles on Harry's note pad took frightening shape as he scratched rings of jagged teeth. "We've got two deaths from some kind of creature I've never seen before."

"*Two* deaths, huh. You really know how to sell it, Harry." Big Don sighed, no smile this time. "After Dorian, me and the missus moved to West Palm Beach and bought a place. I'm out of the pest control business for good. Might open a pizza joint instead."

"Sounds better than pest control to me," Harry said.

"That's what the missus said. You should try Nassau or even Palm Beach for that matter. You might get lucky."

"Yeah, I have a feeling my luck is running out."

"Oh hey, you still have that live trap? The one I left with you when you had that feral cat problem? It was..." Big Don clicked his tongue in thought. "Five years ago, maybe?"

Harry cast his mind back as he began sketching a rectangular cage. "I do remember the cats, but I'll be damned if I can remember the trap."

"Well, if you can't find someone, those traps are pretty damn effective."

"I hope the trap is big enough..." Harry's thought trailed off.

"What we talking? Bigger than a cat?"

"Never mind." Harry scrawled the words "FUCK THIS SHIT" onto the page. "I'll make some calls. Just wanted you to be the first."

"Appreciate the consideration, Harry. Let me know how things go. I'll always have a soft spot for killing vermin."

"Will do, Big Don." Harry hung up and thrummed his fingers on the desk. His best chance at winning this battle had just evaporated.

He pulled a tattered 2014 yellow page directory from a nearby shelf, flipped to "pest control," and began cold calling. As it turned out, most businesses were still in operation. But that's where Harry's luck ran out.

No one was interested, despite promises of a huge payday. As a result of hurricane Dorian the previous year, most saw the Bahamian islands encircling Northwest Providence Channel as a war zone. It was inaccurate then and especially so now, nine months later. Grand Bahama and Great Abaco islands were hardest hit and disaster recovery and reconstruction were still ongoing. Most other islands escaped major damage.

"Name your price." That was how Harry was ending his calls now. The desperation must have come across the phone because there was still no interest. The two deaths already didn't help either. Excuses ranged from "too much trouble" to "no offshore jobs" to "not enough employees." His favorite was a company that quoted a million dollars, but they'd first need to purchase boats and supplies which would take a month. Then there was the five-hundred thousand dollar deposit.

After exhausting the phone book, Harry's only option left was the infamous live trap. It was an option he had wanted to avoid. And he had a gut feeling he knew where it was. He collected himself and made his way to the door of the machine room, currently doubling as Mar-A-Verde's morgue.

Harry opened the door. The odor of rot filled his nose and the humid air stuck to his skin like honey. He tried to block the smell by breathing into his t-shirt sleeve, but the fabric did nothing to help. He made his way to the back of the room, past the drill press and metal lathe, where assorted hand tools were stored on reinforced shelves.

He and the grounds crew stored a lot of equipment in the maintenance building, and most of it was well organized. On a bottom shelf sat a cage about half the size of an inkjet printer. On the top, near the handle were hand-painted letters that read "PUSSY CATCHER."

Must have been Jomar's handiwork.

Harry hooked a finger around the handle of the trap and made a hasty retreat to the exit, closing the door behind him.

He looked at the trap in his hand. Harry needed one more thing before proceeding: bait. He had a good idea where to find some. But more than bait, Harry needed to wash off the stench of human decomposition. And it was quitting time.

FRESH OUT OF the shower, Harry threw on some clean clothes (another purple Mar-A-Verde golf shirt) and took the stairs down to the staff cafeteria. He bypassed the lineup and headed to the kitchen. The swinging double doors squeaked when they opened.

Greta stood at the back, a soiled apron wrapped around her body and her long blond hair braided and pinned up in a bun under a hairnet. She held a clipboard with a meal plan clipped to it. She had told Harry years ago that she found it easier to come up with meal ideas when she surrounded herself with food preparation.

"No." Greta flipped her hand as she walked toward him. The way her hips moved, graceful and confident, it was easy to see why guests at the resort found her attractive. "You need an apron and hairnet to be back here. Scoot."

"I need a favor," Harry said.

Greta looked him over with a grin and raised an eyebrow. "What *kind* of favor?"

"Can you spare some raw meat?"

"Oh, Harry. I thought you'd never ask!"

Harry looked at her and furrowed his brows in confusion. "I, uh—"

Greta slapped his chest. "I'm making a joke. What do you need raw meat for?"

"Between you and me, I'm going to use it as bait," Harry said. "There's a critter on the course that needs catching. And it doesn't need to be a good cut either. Even trimmings would do."

"Give me five minutes. And wait outside, okay? Scoot!"

Harry stepped back through the swinging doors into the cafeteria. The talk of meat and the sight and smells of the various hot entrées made his stomach growl, despite what he had seen that day. Context was everything.

He slid his phone out of his pocket and dialed Daniela. She answered on the second ring. "I got a trap to bait. Want to come with?" Harry grinned as he listened to Daniela's response. "Meet me at the first hole in fifteen minutes?" He paused and reconsidered. "Okay, make it thirty."

"Harry?"

"I'll talk to you later." Harry ended the call and turned to Greta. "That was quick."

She handed him a package wrapped in brown paper. "So, when am I going to see *your* raw meat?"

"Greta..." Harry gave her a sideways look.

She wagged her finger at him as she turned back to the kitchen. "One of these days, Harry."

"In another life, Greta. And thanks for this."

"Uh-huh. Vamoose!"

Harry walked back to the maintenance building. Alejandro was locking up as he arrived. "Leave it, Al. I got some last minute work to take care of."

"Sure thing, boss."

"Thanks for your help today," Harry said.

Alejandro nodded then turned to him. "Sorry about the generator. I filled the tank personally."

"I'm still alive, so no worries."

Alejandro waved then disappeared down the path to the staff apartments.

Harry hopped into a maintenance cart he had preloaded with the live trap, a shovel, and some rope. He tossed the package of meat next to the trap and drove out to the tee-off area of the first hole.

Daniela was already there waiting for him. "Nothing lights a fire under me like an invitation to trap strange creatures." She hopped onto the bench seat next to him. "Can I drive?"

"Sure," Harry said, "but on the way back. I'm hauling sensitive cargo." He pulled away, following the path beside the fairway.

Daniela looked into the back of the cart and grabbed the package of meat. "You got a not-so-secret admirer."

"What?" Harry cast a perplexed look at her.

She held up the package of meat. On the top written in broad black strokes was a heart with a "G" in the center. "I think Greta likes you."

"Greta likes *everyone*. Besides, she's not my type." Harry kept his eyes on the path ahead.

"What *is* your type?"

Harry gave her a quick glance and grinned. "Not Greta."

When the caution tape came into view, he turned the cart out onto the fairway. The ladders still lay on the grass as they had been left hours ago. They'd leave a mark on the turf, another thing that Larsen would scream about, but Harry found himself not caring. He parked the cart behind them.

Daniela hopped out with the package of meat in her hand. "Feeling a little déjà vu?"

"Yeah, just a bit." Harry reached into the back of the cart and lifted out the live trap and the rope. "Let's get this done as quick as possible." He set the trap down on the grass, squatted, and tied one end of the rope to the handle.

Daniela sat on her heels and peeled back the paper wrap revealing two pieces of tenderloin, lightly marbled and dripping with blood. "These are nice cuts, Harry." She looked up at him. "Greta definitely likes you."

"And those things down there are going to like them too." Harry unlocked the spring-loaded front door and placed both pieces of beef at the back of the trap, past the trip plate.

"Have you eaten?"

Harry shook his head. "Wanted to get this done first."

Daniela crumpled the bloody paper into a ball, threw it into the hole, then relaxed her hands in her lap. "Let me rephrase. Are you hungry?"

"I could eat."

"Want to go for dinner?" Daniela offered a raised eyebrow with a subtle smile. "After this, I mean."

Harry didn't take too long to think about it. "Are we talking cafeteria or..."

"Let's go to the dining room. Don't want to make Greta jealous. Besides, I've never eaten there before."

"You're joking."

Daniela shook her head. "Cross my heart. Hope to die. Stick a needle in my eye."

Harry winced. "After what we've seen today, that's an image I'd rather not think about." He looked at his clothes, fresh an hour ago but with grass stains already on the knees. "I'd need to change."

Daniela appraised herself. "Me too. I could meet you there."

"Okay. Fair warning, the food is only marginally better than the cafeteria, but the ambiance is nicer, that's if you like everything gilded to the max."

Harry crawled to the edge of the hole.

"Here. Use mine." Daniela had her phone in flashlight mode already. "Just don't drop it or I may have to stand you up."

Harry chuckled and took the phone. He first listened for any creature sounds below. When he detected nothing but the odd cricket, he peeked over the edge, using the phone's light to scan the interior of the cavern.

"We're all clear." He handed the phone back to Daniela and lifted the trap carefully by the handle. The weight of the meat in the back made the trap hang at an angle, but he had to tip the trap up even more to fit it through the hole. "Grab the rope, would you? Just in case I screw up."

"Got it." Daniela tied the end of the rope to one of the ladder rungs.

Harry transferred one hand to the rope as he let go of the handle. The trap began to spin as he lowered it into the cavern. Juices from the bait dribbled from the corner of the cage, drawing a bloody circle on the cavern floor. "I can't see how close it is to the—"

The back end of the trap spun into the floor, stopping it abruptly and tripping the spring-loaded door.

"Shit. I got to reset it," Harry said. "Can you get your light in there until I can land this thing?"

Daniela crawled to the edge of the hole on the opposite side of the ladder from Harry. She peeked over and held her phone out, lighting the trap's extraction. Black criss-crossing shadow lines danced on the floor and walls of the cavern.

Harry didn't have to extract the cage entirely. He disengaged the spring-loaded lock on the door and reset the trap.

A shriek rose from the hole.

"Oh shit." Daniela looked down into the cavern and spotted one creature roaming the muddy floor. It clawed the crumpled paper ball around the cavern with one of its many feet. "One of those devils is back."

"Can you chase it away? Shine it into the exit tunnel."

"I think so," Daniela said, "but you need to lower the cage a bit more first."

Harry released the rope a few inches at a time until the cage hung midway between the opening and the floor. Predictably the cage began to spin again.

Daniela chased the creature with her phone's light until it fled down the exit tunnel, then held the light steady. "Hurry. The tunnel is farther than I thought."

"I'm working on it." Harry used the cage's shadow to gauge how much further he had to lower it. He fed rope into the hole even slower. The corner of the cage scraped the dirt and stopped spinning, but Harry ran out of rope before the trap settled to the floor of the cavern. "What the...?"

"Shit. My bad." Daniela had tied the rope on a ladder rung too far away from the hole. "Raise it up again and I'll hold the rope."

"No, stay with the light. I got it." Harry held the rope with one hand and worked out Daniela's knot with the other. Once the end of the rope was free Harry lowered the cage to the cavern floor. He retied the rope on the ladder rung positioned over the hole, then rolled onto his back and glanced at Daniela.

"How was I supposed to know how long the rope was?"

Harry shook his head and smiled. "You weren't. Let's eat."

Daniela shut off her light and the two of them scooted away from the edge of the hole until they were past the warning tape.

Harry hopped onto the passenger side of the cart's bench seat. "All I ask is you not go *too* fast."

Daniela climbed behind the steering wheel and winked at

him. She jammed her foot on the accelerator, soon zooming down the path toward the maintenance building.

HARRY FOUND A respectable black sports jacket, white dress shirt, tie, and dress pants buried in his closet. The waistline and collar were a bit snug but tolerable and everything coordinated except for his shoes. On his feet were the same work boots that he had worn all day. He had used wet a towel to rub the leather, darkening it.

No one will notice, he convinced himself.

Harry was standing just outside the entrance to the dining room when Daniela entered the resort's foyer. He caught his breath and smiled at her approach.

She wore a white lace camisole top with a gray wrap-around skirt, revealing flashes of her left leg as she walked. Daniela held a small black leather clutch in one hand and her shoes, black also, looked more comfortable than dressy. A bracelet watch with a narrow silver band decorated her left wrist.

"Wow." Harry flashed his eyes and held his arms out like he was trying to collect her beauty all for himself. "You look incredible."

"You clean up pretty good yourself." Daniela offered her free arm. "I'm starving. Let's eat."

Harry hooked his arm around hers and escorted her into the dining room. He nodded at the maître d', who waved them through.

Daniela noticed the exchange. "You eat here a lot?"

"Hardly ever." Harry navigated around a warren of tables to one at the back of the room next to a window. "Bart lives a few doors down from me. He's a party animal and legendary for his ability to kill a bottle of Jack Daniels."

Daniela looked back at Bart the maître d', trying to reconcile his professional appearance with Harry's description. Bart had followed her with his eyes and dipped his head, as if tipping an imaginary hat.

Harry pulled out Daniela's chair and seated her, then took the chair opposite. He leaned in and lowered his voice. "Would you mind if we skipped all things beef on the menu?"

Daniela shrugged. "How's the seafood in this joint?"

"Honestly, I don't know. It's been a long time," Harry said. "But my stomach doesn't care."

Daniela picked up the small menu at her place setting and scanned it. "How about we start with crab cakes and finish with lobster?"

"Nice choice, but that is a lot of food."

"Okay, crab cakes only then," Daniela said. "I don't really want to wear a bib tonight anyway. But dessert is non-negotiable."

Harry nodded and casually flipped through the wine list. "Pair that with a bottle of chardonnay and I think we have a plan."

The waitress appeared, took their orders, disappeared, then returned with a chilled bottle of chardonnay in an ornate gold-plated wine bucket with a matching stand. She uncorked the bottle and poured a sample in Harry's wine glass.

Harry looked up at her. "I don't know wine from Welch's. Just pour the damn thing."

Daniela and the waitress exchanged a look.

"What?" Harry alternated his eyes between the two women. "Do you want to taste it?"

Daniela shook her head. "I'm sure it's fine." She directed her gaze at the waitress and smiled. "Just pour the damn thing." She returned her eyes to Harry. "Your lack of pretense is refreshing."

"Well, I can thank plants for that. Plants don't lie to you."

"Neither do dead bodies."

The waitress raised a brow as she poured their wine and settled the bottle back into its ice-water bath. "Your crab cakes will be out shortly," she said and disappeared.

Harry held up his glass of wine. "Here's to finding strange flesh-eating creatures of the night."

"I'll drink to that." Daniela clinked her glass with Harry's and sipped her wine. "Excellent choice."

"To be honest, I think I like Welch's better." They both laughed. "So, what are we going to do with one of those things if we catch one?"

Daniela set her glass of wine down. "I don't know. Take more photos and video? Maybe someone out there can identify it."

"I was talking to the other golfer, the one who survived, and he mentioned how those things reminded him of leeches." Harry sipped his wine. "Ever seen a leech up close?"

The waitress appeared with their meals on a rolling serving cart. Each plate had a stack of three crab cakes with rémoulade between each layer. On the side were grilled asparagus spears, sautéed mushrooms, and a lemon wedge. Each meal was accompanied by a side salad.

"Hold that thought." Daniela watched the waitress present each plate and the salads.

The waitress pulled a pepper mill from under the cart. "Fresh ground pepper?" Both Harry and Daniela declined. "Enjoy." She wheeled the serving cart back toward the kitchen.

"To answer your question, yes, I've seen leeches up close." Daniela knocked over her crab cake stack and cut off a bite. "Don't forget, I'm a doctor. Leeches are still used to reattach severed limbs." She popped the bite of crab cake into her mouth. "Delicious."

Harry nodded and leaned forward. "They're just as good in the cafeteria. Just saying." He chewed and swallowed. "But back to leeches. It was the ring of teeth that the guy zeroed in on."

"Harry, you're the only one I know who can talk about grisly things and eat at the same time." Daniela took another bite of her crab cake. "Did you know they excrete an anticoagulant to prevent clotting?"

"Maybe that's why Logan and Sinclair seemed to keep bleeding." Harry topped up their wine glasses.

"But those things we saw had legs." Daniela cut up more of her meal. "As you know, leeches don't have legs."

Conversation flowed easily as Harry and Daniela tried to identify what kind of creature they had seen earlier in the day. Bite by bite, their meals disappeared and by the time dessert arrived, they had killed two bottles of wine and had little in the way of answers.

Harry had ordered crème brûlée for both of them which they devoured with Spanish coffees.

"To be honest, the 'beautiful chocolate cake' that Strunk gushes about all the time is no big whoop." Harry air-quoted the words and had stopped reducing the volume of his voice a bottle of wine ago.

"I'll take your word for it." Daniela checked the time on her watch. "I think it's time to call it a night."

"I'll walk you." Harry flagged down the waitress. "Put it on my account. Harry Harcourt, 423S. And give yourself twenty percent."

The waitress nodded. "Thank you, sir. Enjoy the rest of your evening."

Harry stood, a little wobbly on his feet. He had expected to see Daniela stumble a bit as well, but she appeared to hold her alcohol much better. He gently clutched her arm.

The two of them strolled back to the staff apartments under a clear sky. Orange-red remnants of sunset faded to the west as pinprick stars lit the sky overhead.

"You don't drink often, do you Harry?"

"Not with such beautiful company." Harry's words occasionally slurred. "I usually drink alone."

"I had fun tonight," Daniela said. "It was good to cut loose and relax a bit for once. We should do this again sometime."

"Good idea." Harry gazed at her, his face pulled into a dreamy smile.

They arrived at Daniela's door on the first floor of the staff apartments. "This is me." She dug out her key. "Which floor are you?"

"Top floor." Harry, acting in the moment, his courage fueled by chardonnay, leaned in and planted a kiss squarely on Daniela's lips.

Daniela welcomed the kiss. She had been expecting something to happen and was more surprised that Harry had been able to land the kiss at all. It was a nice kiss to end a fun evening.

But the heat of the kiss increased. Harry ran one hand over Daniela's camisole and up the small of her back, while the other slid under her hair, past her ear, and behind her neck. A shiver popped her eyes open and she knew where things would likely lead if she didn't slow them down. She raised a hand and placed it on his chest, sensing firm muscles underneath.

"Whoa." Daniela broke the kiss and took a step back. "Is it hot out here or what?"

Harry stepped back, his hand tracing a line on her neck for a moment longer before it returned to his side. "Yeah, it's hot."

Daniela's face flushed but she managed a smile. "We don't have to rush this."

Harry grinned, then nodded. "No. We don't." He smoothed out his jacket. "Shall I meet you here tomorrow morning? To check the trap?"

"Yes. I'd like that."

He took a wobbly bow. "Until then, my lady." Harry turned and stumbled to the elevators.

Daniela watched him go. She inserted her key into the deadbolt of her apartment. It took her two attempts to align her key with the keyhole but that would remain her secret. She closed the door and locked it.

On the fourth floor, Harry pushed open his door, kicked off his work boots, and tore off his tie. He managed to prep the coffee maker for the morning before flopping on his bed. He was asleep within minutes.

Five-thirty in the morning came fast. The smell of coffee roused Harry from his slumber and chipped away at his pounding headache.

He groaned and rolled over on his bed. Each throb of his temple he reminded him why he kept his alcohol consumption limited to a couple of good sips of whiskey at quitting time.

Harry stripped off his evening clothes and left them in a heap on his bed. He pulled his well-worn denim pants over clean underwear, a fresh purple t-shirt, and dry socks. The relaxing feeling of cotton on his skin knocked his headache back a couple of notches.

He pulled on his work boots, which had remained dark despite being dry to the touch. He headed to the bathroom and took down a bottle of Tylenol from a shelf next to the sink. He shook out a couple red pills, tossed them in his mouth and washed them down with a gulp of water straight from the faucet. Instead of placing the Tylenol bottle back on the shelf, he pocketed it.

The coffee had ended up more like espresso from his heavy-handed preparation the night before. He poured himself a cup and began his morning ritual on the balcony. The sun had begun to rise into another cloudless Bahamian sky. He rolled last evening's events through his mind and smiled.

Harry leaned over the railing of his balcony and looked down to the first floor apartments to see if maybe Daniela was up too. She wasn't. No one was ever up at this hour, except perhaps Greta, but her balcony window was dark this morning as well.

He finished his coffee, shuffled back to the kitchen, and rinsed his cup in the sink. He found a clean paper cup in his cupboard and filled it with coffee.

The red digital numbers on the Mr. Coffee machine read 5:55 a.m.

He locked his door, took the elevator to the ground floor, and found his way back to Daniela's door. With the cup of coffee in one hand, Harry dug out the bottle of Tylenol with the other and knocked on her door.

Silence greeted him.

He waited a minute before knocking again. This time he heard movement inside.

The dead bolt clicked and Daniela cracked open the door. She had wrapped herself in a bathrobe and had her hair tied up in a loose messy knot.

"Does the lady require a special morning elixir?" Harry gave the bottle of Tylenol a quick shake and held up the steaming cup of coffee.

Daniela looked up at him and grinned. She stepped out of the doorway and up onto her tiptoes, grabbed his t-shirt with both hands, and pulled him into a kiss. The coffee went flying.

Harry stood in a daze as Daniela stepped back into her apartment, her robe falling open to reveal a thin glimpse of bare skin. She reached out, pulled him into her room, and closed the door.

HARRY AND DANIELA strolled into the maintenance building a few minutes before seven o'clock. Tzipora and Alejandro had already completed their appointed course tasks and were prepping for non-course-related gardening.

"Daniela and I set up a trap last night on the first fairway." Harry hooked a thumb toward the tee-off area of the first hole and hopped into a maintenance cart. Daniela took the seat beside him.

Alejandro raised an eyebrow. "Need any help?"

"No, we're good." Harry started the cart's motor. "Hopefully we'll be back with something cool to look at."

All four waved their goodbyes as Harry pulled out of the garage.

"It's good to be the boss." Alejandro glanced at Tzipora. "Do you think they're—"

"Smashing? Totally."

"About goddamn time," Alejandro said. "You can only pull your own weeds for so long."

The both shared a laugh as they collected their gardening tools.

Harry pulled up behind the ladders on the fairway like he had the previous evening, lining up the cart with the tire tracks Daniela had made in the grass when she had peeled out.

"Oh shit." She put her hand over her mouth, stifling a nervous laugh. "Sorry."

"I'll let it go this time." Harry winked at her. "Let's go."

The two of them approached the ladder and dropped to all fours to redistribute their weight.

"Hold on." Harry held up his hand. "Do you hear that?"

Unfamiliar sounds rose from the hole in the ground, a high-pitched growling mixed with metallic scraping.

Daniela smiled. "I think we got lucky."

"I'll say." Harry smirked and crawled forward. "Let's go see *how* lucky."

Harry brought out his phone, switched it into flashlight mode, and aimed it into the hole. The cage, which had been knocked on its side and dragged, had been just big enough to contain one creature. It screeched and writhed inside, twisting and flexing its body and tail against the cage's woven metal sides. The rope ran taut from the upturned cage to the ladder rung it was tied to on the grass.

"If it had been any bigger..."

Harry pocketed his phone and looked at Daniela. "I know. Lucky. Let's pull it up." Hand over hand, he raised the cage out of the cavern. Daniela untied the end of the rope from the ladder and collected it in a neat pile.

The creature inside used what little extra room it had to spin and turn itself around. Its tail caught on the mesh of the cage more than its slicked, vein-mottled body, snagging the creature and preventing it from moving forward. A shriek would escalate, the creature would reverse, and the whole process repeated. As the cage drew closer to the edge of the hole, the growling snarls and screeching increased in volume.

"It's the daylight that's making it freak out," Daniela said.

Harry nodded. "I hope the cage holds."

The same problem presented itself at the opening of the hole: the cage was too large to fit through horizontally, even when slightly tilted. The inherited motion from the creature's frenzied escape attempts didn't help.

"I'm going to have to raise one end up." Harry reached for the end where the spring-loaded door had closed and locked.

"Are you trying to be a macho man or just an idiot?" Daniela flashed eyes of concern at him.

"Unless I unlock the cage door..." Harry pointed to an interlocking group of metal bars, painted yellow for easy identification. He continued, "it's not going to open. That thing can't get over here."

"I'm not convinced."

"Only one way to find out." Harry held the rope with one hand and reached toward the spinning cage with the creature jostling inside. He touched the yellow bars with his fingers. Mysterious fluid transferred to his fingertips and a shot of pain ripped through his hand and up his arm. "SHIT!" Harry recoiled in shock, letting go of the rope to the cage.

"Harry!" Daniela divided her attention between Harry's mysterious injury and the pile of slack rope that was disappearing back into the hole at a furious pace. She leaped for the rope and caught the last of it just as it pulled itself free of the ladder rung and disappeared into the hole.

The grassy edge crumbled under Daniela's shifting weight. She lost her balance and careened headfirst into the cavern below.

"HARRY!" Daniela hung upside down, her hand still firmly grasping the rope.

"I've got you." Harry had grabbed her legs. "Hold on. I'll pull you up."

"Make it fast. I can't see anything, but I don't like what I hear." Daniela struggled to control both her fear and her nausea. "I don't like how it smells either." The cavern still held a heavy coppery odor from Sinclair's blood the day earlier.

Harry worked his arms up Daniela's legs, wrapping them around her thighs like they were taking part in an insane wheelbarrow race. He dug his heels into the turf and flexed his leg and back muscles with all his strength.

Daniela slid back out of the hole, her head face-down at Harry's feet and her legs straddling his chest. "I'm feeling a little déjà vu again," she said between harried breaths. "How about you?"

"Yeah." Harry laughed as he caught his breath. "The good kind."

Daniela tied the end of the rope to one of Harry's ankles. "Great idea."

"I thought so." Daniela raised a leg over Harry's head, and knelt beside him. "Let me see your hand."

The tips of Harry's left thumb, index, and middle fingers were red and inflamed.

"How does it feel?"

"Like I'm holding hot coals."

Daniela looked back at the hole. "My gut says this is an acid burn but that doesn't make any sense." She stood and ran back to the maintenance cart, retrieving the shovel from the back. "Let's get that thing out of there and back to where we can examine it properly."

Harry propped himself up on his elbows, crawled back to the hole, and began pulling up the rope and cage. "Last I checked this wasn't part of my job description."

He raised the cage back to the level where he had burned his fingers moments before. Daniela hooked the shovel under the cage near the locked door and raised the cage to an almost vertical incline.

With the sway of the rope and the frenzied motion of the creature inside, it took a couple of tries to get everything aligned just right. Then Harry lifted the cage out of the hole and set it on the grass.

"We make a good team," he said.

Daniela smiled, ran her hand over his short natural hair, and kissed him on an unsoiled spot on his cheek. She looked down at the agitated creature in the cage. "Let's get that thing off the course. Remember to lift it with the rope. I need your hands to remain uninjured." A grin slid across her lips.

"Of course, my lady." Harry hoisted the cage into the back of the maintenance cart and tossed the rest of the rope beside it. Minutes later he parked the cart back in its spot in the maintenance building's garage.

Harry unlocked his phone and tossed it to Daniela. "Want to shoot some video and photos as I unload?"

"Sure thing, Spielberg."

Harry grabbed the rope and lifted the cage out of the back of the cart. The creature was breathing but it appeared to have lost its will to fight. He held it up so Daniela could get a good shot. He glanced at the black plastic runner in the back of the cart. "Holy shit. Get a shot of that."

Harry set the cage on the concrete floor and held up the plastic runner. Holes were burned through where the cage had been sitting, with sections drooping as if heated to melting point.

"Acid, like you were talking about?"

Daniela nodded. "Looks like it, but we'd have to test it to make sure."

"How?"

"Got any cabbage juice?"

Harry looked at her, confused.

"You're a gardener. I thought you'd know about this." Daniela handed the phone back to Harry. "Let's put this ugly bastard somewhere safe and I'll show you."

"Not in the machine room."

"Definitely not in the machine room."

Harry transported the cage to the back corner of his office and left with Daniela on a quest for cabbage.

It took a bit of negotiating, but Harry secured cabbage juice from Greta at the cafeteria. Daniela waited outside, not wanting to rock the boat.

"It's better if Greta doesn't know we're working on this together," Daniela had said.

Harry strolled out of the cafeteria with a clear jar filled with purple liquid. "Greta even strained it for me. Didn't even ask *why* I needed it."

"She must *really* like you." Daniela said.

Harry sighed. "She said I owe her big-time now." He looked into Daniela's hazel eyes. "I don't know why we didn't go out before now. I think we got something good here."

"I think so, too." This time it was Daniela's turn to blush. It looked good on her.

"So, what's the secret with cabbage—"

A scream rose from the maintenance building. Harry and Daniela shared a look of concern mixed with panic and they both ran toward the open garage.

Alejandro lay sprawled on the concrete floor. A creature had latched onto his left leg with most of his shoe within the creature's gullet. He thrust his right foot at it, but it kept slipping, as if he was kicking a long fat balloon covered with oil.

Tzipora stood a few feet away, frozen in a panic. "Do something, Harry!"

"I can't get it off me!" Alejandro tried to crawl away, continuing to kick as he went. "Get it off!" Blood had begun to pool around his feet as the creature worked its way over his foot and toward his ankle.

Harry set the cabbage juice on the ground and scanned the garage for a weapon. He drew a blank.

"Your flashlight!" Daniela pulled out her phone. "Everyone get your flashlights on. Real close."

Harry and Tzipora turned on their flashlights. Alejandro managed to pull his out as well but couldn't turn on the light.

"Al, take mine." Harry exchanged phones with Alejandro and turned on his flashlight.

Harry, Daniela, and Alejandro aimed their lights at the creature dissolving Alejandro's foot. Tzipora held her light up from where she stood frozen.

The light was working. Thin wisps of smoke rose from the creature's skin where the lights focused but it was difficult to keep the beams on target.

Harry shook his head. "Tzipora, you got to get *closer.*"

"I can't. I—"

Harry looked around for another weapon, then directed his gaze outside. "Shit. Of course!"

"What?" Daniela shot Harry a worried look.

"The sun! Get him outside."

Harry pocketed his phone, grabbed Alejandro's free hand, and dragged him out of the garage. "There!" He pointed at a bright area out of the shadows of the maintenance building and surrounding trees.

Daniela took hold of Alejandro's other hand and threw all her strength into dragging him out into the open. Alejandro abandoned his kicking as he watched a trail of diluted blood draw out from his left leg like a gruesome paint stroke.

The farther Harry and Daniela dragged Alejandro out of the garage, the more the creature began to smoke. For the first time since they arrived, the creature appeared to be reversing off Alejandro's foot.

"I think it's working," Daniela said.

"God, I hope so."

Harry and Daniela continued to pull Alejandro's body into the full sunshine, his head first followed by his feet. The creature writhed violently, its skin turning black in patches. In a rhythmic rolling motion, the creature extracted itself off Alejandro's foot.

Its eight stubby legs terminated in a grouping of sharp claws, each working into the cracks and paved aggregate to propel its slick smoking body into the shade of the building.

The creature followed a line of dahlia bushes and stopped like it sensed something in the ground. It raised its body and dived, maw first, burrowing into the ground as easily as a diver breaking the surface of a pool.

Then it was gone.

"My foot!" Alejandro stared at the remnants of his work boot, a bloody skeletal foot showing through the holes.

"We need a tourniquet to stop the bleeding," Daniela said.

Harry was off like a shot, digging through equipment in the backs of the parked maintenance carts. It only took a moment to find a piece of rope long enough to do the job. He passed Tzipora on the way back.

She was sitting, back to one of the carts, shaking. "I'm sorry, Harry. I couldn't move."

"It's okay. Al's going to be alright." Harry gave her a quick once-over, looking for injury. "I'll be back." He ran to Daniela and tossed the rope to her. "What do you think?"

"Blood's not clotting so the leech theory is looking better and better." Daniela wrapped Alejandro's thigh with the rope and tied it tight.

"Am I going to lose my foot, doc?" Fear watered in Alejandro's eyes.

Daniela exchanged a quick glance with Harry, then settled her gaze firmly on Alejandro. "It doesn't look good."

"HARCOURT!" Larsen appeared from around the maintenance building, leading a police officer, two paramedics pulling two stretchers, and another man Harry assumed was the coroner.

"And I'm going to lose my head." Harry stood to face Larsen's charge.

THE PARAMEDICS WRAPPED Alejandro's leg and secured him on one stretcher. The state of Logan and Sinclair's bodies allowed their individual body bags to be stacked on the remaining stretcher and transported to the dock.

"Thanks for saving me, Harry." Alejandro propped himself up on his elbows. "That thing came out of nowhere."

"It wasn't just me who saved you. It was everyone." Harry

gave Alejandro's shoulder a squeeze and looked at Daniela checking his vitals one more time. "How's he doing?"

"As good as he can be under the circumstances," Daniela said. "The medics did a good job."

Harry turned to Tzipora. "Stay with him. You both need to be away from here for a while."

"But what about our jobs?" Tzipora fidgeted with her hands. "We're going to be fired and—"

"Don't worry," Harry said. "Your jobs will be waiting when you get back."

Larsen had been standing several feet away going over details with the coroner and police officer. But he heard Harry's promise. He thanked the emergency responders as they left with Alejandro and Tzipora and charged over to face Harry, his demeanor flipping like a switch.

"You can't guarantee their jobs." Frenzied spittle collected on Larsen's lips. "They need to be fired and replaced. Immediately."

"You need to shut up." Harry pushed Larsen in the chest with his index finger. "Right now."

Larsen's eyes bugged out and his face turned a light crimson. Before he could respond, Harry continued.

"You gave me full control, remember? I've got a recording right here on my phone if you need reminding." Harry tapped his pocket. "There's no way I'm hiring anyone else when those things are killing people."

"But the course requires daily maintenance," Larsen said. "You can't do it all."

"All maintenance is on hold. Those creatures are my first priority."

"That's unacceptable." Larsen vibrated with anger. "Strunk will not be pleased."

"Then I suggest you don't tell him," Harry said. "I'm choosing to save lives. You need to stay out of my way and let me do my job."

Larsen rose on his tiptoes and glared at him. "This isn't over."

"It is for now." Harry looked past Larsen at the first responders leaving with Alejandro. Several guests were watching the proceedings. Some had their phones out, recording photos and video. "Besides, looks like you have some damage control to take care of."

Larsen mumbled some obscenities under his breath and ran towards the guests, trying to distract them with lies and promises of complimentary steak, drinks, and beautiful chocolate cake.

Harry shook his head, then rubbed his temples.

Daniela approached him from the garage entrance, stepping around the streaks of Alejandro's blood still on the pavement. "Nice job with Larsen."

"He's an ass-hat. A Strunk wannabe." Harry's doubt showed. "Do you think he'd fire me?"

"Larsen? No. He a windbag." Daniela brushed dirt off his shoulder.

"Yeah, but he's got a serious mean streak."

"You're too valuable and Larsen knows it."

Harry managed half a smile. "That's what I'm afraid of."

"Know what? You're too good for this place," Daniela said. "What did you tell the police officer?"

Harry shrugged. "What *could* I tell them? Some kind of unidentified wild animal is injuring people at the resort. And that we're dealing with it."

"I said it could have been a ground hog, the way it burrowed into the ground afterward," Daniela said. "Honestly, I don't think she cared. She was more interested in Logan's phone."

"Damn, I *wish* it was a ground hog."

Daniela nodded. "Come on. Let's gather some more facts. I've got a craving for cabbage juice."

The two of them walked back to the garage. Daniela picked

up the jar of cabbage juice and shook it, watching its contents swirl.

Harry stepped into his office and found the live trap just where he had left it except the metal mesh had been eaten away, leaving a hole big enough for escape. "What the hell?" He reached to grab it, but Daniela stopped him.

"Don't pick it up."

"Why?"

"Remember my hunch about acid? When you burned your hand on the cage earlier?"

Harry looked at his left hand. His thumb, index, and middle finger were still red and inflamed. "Right."

"And look. There's a trail leading to the door." Daniela pointed to a smear of clear fluid running across the floor. "I'm going to need a pair of tongs and an old rag or sponge."

Harry searched the maintenance building's inventory in his mind. "How about a pair of pliers and..." He scanned his office, then snapped his fingers. "Would a tissue work?"

"It should."

Harry grabbed a box of tissues off the corner of his desk, pulled out several, and handed them to Daniela. He hustled out of his office and into the machine room, returning with a pair of snub-nose pliers.

"God damn, it's still ripe in there."

"It's going to be like that for a while," Daniela said. "Ventilate and scrub with a disinfectant."

"That's last on my list now." Harry handed her the pliers..

"Excellent." Daniela had already folded the tissues into a compact square. She clamped one side in the teeth of the pliers, entered Harry's office, and squatted next to the cage.

"Cabbage has an interesting characteristic, besides being great in coleslaw." Daniela moved the tissue through the fluid on the floor, soaking the fibers. "It has something called anthocyanin in it that can tell us whether something is acidic or basic."

Daniela raised the tissue bundle, now soaked with the mystery fluid and darkening in parts. "Open the jar of cabbage juice."

Harry popped the lid off and set it aside.

"The cabbage juice is purple when it's neutral. If you mix it with something basic, the color will change to blue, green, or even yellow depending on strength." Daniela held up the wad of soaked tissue. "My guess is this is some kind of acid. And acid turns cabbage juice red. The redder it is, the—"

"The stronger the acid. I get it." Harry raised his eyebrows in anticipation. "What are you waiting for? I'm dying here."

Daniela grinned. "I love an enthusiastic audience." She dunked the sopping tissue into the cabbage juice and swirled it around. The juice's color changed from purple to a vibrant red, reminiscent of Alejandro's blood still staining the concrete floor just outside Harry's office.

"Confirmed." Daniela looked past the jar of cabbage juice and locked gaze at Harry.

"So that thing sweats... *acid?*"

"Strong acid. Strong enough to eat through the mesh of that cage. And Al's foot."

"And Logan's arm." Harry rubbed his temples. "Jesus. This just keeps getting weirder. I think we're in over our heads."

"Yeah, just a bit." Daniela dumped the juice down a drain in the floor and threw the jar in the trash. She stood and offered her hand. "I'll help you clean up."

Harry took her hand and stood. "First some Tylenol."

"I've got some back at my place."

They both smiled.

Road Trip

Sam's parole in the State of New York had ended five months ago, almost a year to the day of his release from prison. His calendar had supported that milestone, filled with days crossed out with red "X"s. But receiving the official paperwork proved to be difficult.

The first time he applied, the Department of Corrections and Community Supervision claimed that they never received his application, even after a month and a half of follow-ups.

Sam tried again and instead of mailing his application, he hit the open road and made the two and a half hour drive north to Albany to hand-deliver it. Despite the additional effort, he never heard back.

March rolled into April and more red "X"s marked the days without response. It was like being in prison again, except the bars existed in Sam's mind. He refused to celebrate until the official paperwork arrived. In desperation, he enlisted help from his parole officer, Sara Armstrong. "I'll rattle some cages," she had said. That had been six weeks ago.

Sam checked his mailbox daily just before dinner, after fixing whatever needed fixing in the building. Between five tenants and a steady but manageable influx of rats and other vermin, he was kept busy most days. His mailbox was usually empty, with the exceptions of his monthly phone bill and direct mail fliers for things he either couldn't afford or didn't want.

Today, a different letter sat waiting in his mailbox. The envelope was correctly addressed to #102, 616 Casanova Street, The Bronx, NY 10474. His name, Sam Shaw, was emphasized in bold-face. He had been picking up his mail in this run-down foyer for nearly eighteen months. Now a letter from the New York State Department of Corrections and Community Supervision lay in his trembling hands.

Part of him still believed the letter would never come, that this was a mistake or a product of his imagination. Unable to shake the feeling of being watched, Sam peered over his shoulder.

"Fuck it." He tore into the envelope and pulled out the single sheet of folded paper within. There it was in front of him in black and white. The title read, "CERTIFICATE OF RELIEF FROM DISABILITIES." At the bottom he spotted Sara Armstrong's signature among a sea of others.

Sara had managed to tack a sticky note onto the certificate before it had been mailed. "Finally! Congratulations, Sam. Proud of you," her note read.

Relief washed over him and his knees weakened. Sam returned to his apartment and sat at the old Formica table that had served him well during his parole. He stared at the certificate on the table, not quite knowing what to do next. Then reality dawned on him.

"I'm officially a free man. I can do anything I want," Sam said to himself. His low voice echoed through his sparsely furnished kitchen. "Anything." The concept would take some getting used to.

Then a wide grin spread across his face. He knew of only one way to celebrate this moment. Sam collected his keys and wallet and headed out the door.

Eight minutes and a few blocks later Sam found himself pulling open the doors of Kingsley's Fried Chicken and Pizza. A heated breeze of flash-cooked food flowed around him.

Kingsley's was the kind of place where one left with a fine patina of grease coating the skin.

The three booths were occupied and Sam found his memory replaying the last time he had eaten here with Bradley eight months ago. But things were different now. Better. They called each other at least once a month. Sam had even talked to Claire a couple of times and it hadn't been terrible either.

Marcus stood behind the counter, a permanent fixture at Kingsley's. "Sam! My homie."

"Hey Marcus." Sam waved.

Marcus shuffled his stout frame over to the register. "What can I do you for?"

"I'd like a large deluxe pizza, a Coke, and a slice of apple pie."

Marcus raised his brows. "Apple pie, huh?" He wagged his finger at Sam. "I never seen you order apple pie before. You celebrating something?"

Sam glanced down at the tattoos on his arms peeking out from under his work shirt, then back at Marcus. "Freedom," he said, smiling.

Marcus nodded as he punched Sam's order into the cash register. "I hear you, brother. Say, how's your son... Brad?"

"Good memory. He's doing well. Graduates high school this June."

"That's fine." Marcus placed his hands on the counter and smirked. "Tell me, does he got any franchise leads for me in L.A.?"

"Not sure, but he wears your shirt all the time."

Marcus laughed, his belly rolling. "Couldn't ask for more."

Sam paid for his food and waited outside. Now that he was officially free, the world looked different. Colors seemed more vibrant, more alive.

Ten minutes later, Marcus brought his order out to him. "Thanks, Sam. Appreciate the business." The two men shook hands and Sam headed home.

Hope stood in the foyer sorting through her mail when Sam passed her with his dinner.

"Damn that smells good. What's the occasion?"

"No occasion." Sam dug his keys out of his pocket as he walked to his apartment door.

"Not buying it, Sam." Hope crossed her arms. "You only eat Kingsley's on special occasions."

Sam paused at his door, then turned to face her. "I'm officially a free man and you're the only one that knows, besides my parole officer and a few other folks in high places." He paused. "So keep it under your hat, okay?"

Hope's jaw dropped and it looked like she was about to cry. She ran over and hugged him, even though both of his hands were occupied. "What wonderful news. I'd be shouting from the rooftops."

When she stepped back, Sam spotted a tear on her cheek. "Why are you crying?"

Hope quickly wiped the evidence away. "Oh, I'm not crying. I'm just happy for you." Her stomach growled. "Want some company?"

"Normally I'd say yes but tonight it's going to be just me."

"Come on, you can't celebrate alone."

Sam shrugged and smiled. "Tonight I do."

Hope nodded. "Okay." She leaned in and kissed him quickly on the cheek. "Congratulations."

"Thanks."

Sam unlocked his door, stepped inside, and set the food on the table. Second thoughts about Hope's offer of company ran through his mind, but celebrating alone had its place.

He peeked in the pizza box to find his pizza loaded with toppings, more than usual. He took the Coke and pie out of the paper bag. On the top of the pie lid Marcus had scrawled out "Here's to freedom!" Inside sat two slices of apple pie.

Sam grinned. "Marcus, you're a class act."

Three quick knocks sounded on his door. He opened it to find Hope standing there with a bottle of champagne and two wine glasses.

She smiled and said, "I'll go if you want me to, but freedom should be celebrated. Just wanted you to know that."

"You're right." Sam pulled the door open and swept his arm toward his kitchen table with a flourish. "Come on in. But I don't drink, remember?"

"You mean this?" Hope held up the bottle as she walked in. "Sparkling apple juice. You're all good."

"You just happened have sparkling apple juice chilling in your fridge?"

"I assumed you were on parole when you spilled your guts last summer. I knew it would end eventually, so..." Hope shrugged and smiled.

"That apple juice might be cider by now."

"Let's find out. Got an opener?"

Sam dug out a bottle opener and handed it to Hope. She popped the cap and took a swig right from the bottle.

"Nope. Regular apple juice all the way." She poured juice into both wine glasses, handed one to Sam, and raised her own. "To freedom!"

Sam smiled and clinked his glass with Hope's. "To freedom." They both drank.

Hope sat and took ownership of the plate, knife, and fork already on the table. "Let's eat. I'm starved." She lifted a slice of pizza out of the box, took a bite, and placed the rest on her plate.

Sam grabbed another plate and cutlery for himself and sat opposite from Hope. "I'm glad you insisted." He filled his plate with pizza. "You ever watched *Welcome Back, Kotter?*"

Hope furrowed her brow. "What's that?"

Sam took a bite of pizza and grinned. "You'll see. Let the celebrations begin." He raised his wine glass again. "Cheers!" Hope reciprocated.

Freedom felt great and Sam couldn't help but wonder what lay ahead for him.

O'CONNOR BALANCED THE computer on her lap, her left prosthetic leg resting bent in a sitting position but her right leg raised and stretched out onto the desk as if she was reclining on a chaise lounge. Her stump had been acting up during the last few months. Cysts and phantom pain had slowed her down, and by association Detest-A-Pest business was down too.

The laptop's screen, track pad, and keyboard were caked with dirt and cigar ash. If it hadn't been for the computer's essential role, it would have been long since buried under her usual mountain of paperwork.

O'Connor gnawed at her cigar and stared at the screen of the laptop. VerminWorx.com, the website that had kept Detest-A-Pest afloat for the past eight months, had stalled. A small spinning tombstone that usually preceded a screen full of search results maintained its virtual spin. After a few minutes the screen blanked to white and spit out a "500 Internal Server Error."

"What the fuck? Not again." O'Connor brought her paper cup of coffee to her lips, temporarily removing her cigar, and downed it in one gulp. She crushed the cup and flung it in the general direction of the garbage basket. A growl floated from her mouth as she placed the cigar back firmly between her teeth. "Bring back the goddamned phone book," she muttered.

VerminWorx.com connected exterminators with possible jobs across the United States either via a bidding system or through direct selection, and O'Connor paid a yearly subscription fee for access. As more exterminator and pest control businesses sprouted up around The Bronx and beyond, O'Connor found herself taking larger, more remote jobs to pay the bills and avoid competition. She was fast becoming the queen of the unwanted job.

O'Connor reloaded the page and the spinning tombstone returned. "Come on, you fucker." She blew a smoke ring at the screen and thrummed her fingers on a pile of invoices, expecting to get an error page again. But the website spat forth a list of search results covering most of New York State. She had filtered her results to include only jobs relating to rats but most had small budgets that made the potential jobs impractical.

"Maybe I should retire," O'Connor said to herself. "Go beach myself on some tropical island." She began to laugh. Her girth shook and made the springs in her chair squeak and strain beneath her.

Then she noticed a little red "message" icon in the top right corner of the screen.

"What have we here?" In all the time O'Connor had used VerminWorx, she had always initiated messages through job bids. This was different.

She clicked the icon and her list of past job messages displayed in date order. At the top of the list was an unread message titled "URGENT" from a user named "MarjerioCay", sent less than an hour ago.

O'Connor clicked on the title. The message that expanded underneath read, "We have an urgent situation that requires your expertise. More details will be provided after initial contact. Please submit your bid at your earliest convenience."

"MarjerioCay." O'Connor scrunched her brow in thought. Since buying her laptop and learning to secure work through the Internet, she vetted all potential jobs. She clicked the username and VerminWorx displayed all past requests for bids. There was only one and the account had been registered the day before. "This is smelling more and more like a *dead* rat."

O'Connor typed "MarjerioCay" into her browser's search bar. When the browser returned zero results, it altered the search terms to "Marjerio Cay" instead, revealing the top result, an island in the Bahamas and home to the well-known Mar-A-Verde golf club and resort.

"Well I'll be dipped in shit." O'Connor sent a plume of cigar smoke toward the ceiling to join the low-hanging grey haze already above her head. She clicked on images of the resort and surrounding island. The place looked beautiful, idyllic. "Bahamas in late spring sounds great." But her bullshit meter was on full alert. "Why me?"

She sat up and swung her right foot off the desk, knocking a pile of paper to the floor. "Wait. Why not me? Damn straight."

She clicked on "Reply" and began typing: "$10,000. Detest-A-Pest's bid covers all incidentals and retains the right of refusal pending further details. Respond ASAP."

O'Connor hovered her mouse pointer over the "Send" button. A wide grin spread across her face. "Fuck it." She added another zero to her bid, changing it from $10,000 to $100,000. "They can afford it. And I'm worth it, goddamn it."

She clicked "Send."

SAM AWOKE TO loud knocking on his apartment door. He rubbed sleep from his eyes, pulled on a t-shirt, and padded barefoot down the hallway to his door.

Between knocks a familiar voice rose up. "Sam? You awake?" More rapid knocks morphed into loud pounding. "Sam?"

"Hope?" Sam's anxiety ramped up as he retracted the deadbolt and opened the door. "Quit the racket. You're going to wake everyone in the building." His mood shifted when he saw the concern on Hope's face. "What is it?"

"Did you know anything about this?" Hope held up a pink eviction notice.

Sam took the notice and gave it a cursory read. "Where did you get this?"

"It was in my mailbox."

Sam handed the notice back to Hope, grabbed his keys, and walked out to the foyer. He unlocked his mailbox to find the same notice. He picked it up and unfolded it, half expecting it to say something different. "I had no idea, I swear."

The notice stated that the building had been sold to make way for "community improvements."

"They drop this shit in the middle of the night? Money-grubbing cowards. And they're giving us thirty fucking days to get our stuff out." Hope was furious. "I can't afford to go anywhere else."

"I'll be out of a job *and* a place to live."

"Can't you do something?"

"I'll make some calls," Sam said, "but this doesn't look good. In the past year and a half I've spoken with the landlord... maybe three times? Don't hold your breath."

"Shit." Hope ran her fingers through black hair which had grown considerably over the past eight months. "What am I going to do?"

"Leave it with me," Sam said. "Everything will work out."

"I thought you said, 'don't hold my breath?' "

"Relax." Sam raised his hands and spoke in calm tones. "Trust me on this one."

Hope looked at him with a cautious eye. "What are you going to do?"

"Just trust me. I'll make things right."

Hope let out an anxious sigh. "Thanks, Sam."

He nodded and watched Hope as she headed down the hallway toward the elevator. She stopped and offered a wave back before she pulled open the stairwell door beside the elevator and headed up. Ever since the Gambian whitetail invasion last summer, both Sam and Hope avoided the elevator like the plague.

Sam propped himself against the door frame to his apartment and watched the stairwell door close itself in a slow arc. "I'll make things right," he said to himself. "How the hell am I going to do that?" He had no clue.

Sam's second day of official freedom took on a new look and it terrified him.

SPEAKING TO THE landlord proved to be a bust. The man wasn't interested in anything Sam had to say. Despite having just booted the occupants of six apartments onto the streets, the landlord cared more about the price of the real estate. The call ended and Sam's one and only plan evaporated with it.

Apart from his parole officer, the tenants of his building, and O'Connor, plus a few business owners like Marcus, Sam's connections in The Bronx and New York City were limited. And even though he loved the food at Kingsley's, Sam couldn't see himself working behind the counter, or worse, in the kitchen. Eating was a skill he excelled at. Cooking, not so much.

That left O'Connor, who had been solely responsible for some of the most exciting and equally dangerous times of his life. And even though they sniped at each other now and again, Sam and O'Connor got along well most of the time. She became his new grand plan. With a job, he could find a new place to live.

Sam hopped into Rusty and to his surprise started the engine with the first turn of the ignition. That never happened. The old Ford F-250 usually required two or more tries at the ignition switch before the engine turned over. He took it as a sign of good things to come.

Fifteen minutes later Sam found himself in familiar territory.

It had been eight months since he had rolled the truck down Colgate Avenue, but it felt like yesterday. Would O'Connor feel the same way?

Sam parked half a block away from Detest-A-Pest, choosing to use surprise as an advantage. O'Connor's rusted company van occupied its usual spot and the building's vermin-themed mural looked just as he remembered it, with one important difference. The caricature of Washington held a propane torch that blasted orange and yellow flames across the front of the building. Some of the cartoon-style vermin depicted were singed and looking concerned, with wisps of smoke rising from their heads.

Sam pulled open the door, ringing a bell attached to the top of the door frame. The inside of Detest-A-Pest looked messier than usual with newspapers, magazines, and coffee cups strewn across the counter and floor. Sam couldn't help but wonder how O'Connor was managing.

Sam could smell the pungent aroma of her cigar. He stood and listened for a moment. Apparently, the entry bell wasn't enough of an attention grabber. "Bertha?" Sam grinned.

Rustling of paper sounded from the back office, then a creak of metal springs. Sam heard footsteps and saw a shadow move behind the blinded window of the back office.

"Is that who I *think* it is?" O'Connor's voice preceded her as she reached the office door. She looked at Sam, took her cigar out from between her teeth, and rolled it between her thumb and index finger. A grin a mile wide spread across her face. "Well, fuck me sideways. Sam *motherfucking* Shaw is in the house."

O'Connor flipped the hinged countertop over, sending paper flying. "Give me some sugar." She raised her arms and walked toward Sam with a more pronounced limp than he remembered.

"Hey, O'Connor," Sam said. "Long time."

"Too long."

They embraced, patting each other firmly on the back.

O'Connor's hands moved down Sam's back and gave his butt a two-handed squeeze.

"Yup," O'Connor said. "Your package still delivers."

Sam took a step back, heat rising on his neck. "Same old O'Connor."

"Watch who you're calling old, bucko. Got yourself a woman yet?"

Sam shook his head. "Not yet."

"Better find one soon." O'Connor gave Sam's chest a playful tap. "People are going to think you're gay."

"What people?"

O'Connor gave him a sideways look. "*I'm* going to think you're gay... and if you are, that's okay, but damn, you'd make some good looking babies with the right woman." She laughed, causing her whole body to shake.

"Thanks."

O'Connor stepped backward, put her hands on her hips, and looked Sam up and down. "Sam *motherfucking* Shaw. What brings you to this side of town? More rats?"

"My building's been sold," Sam said. "They're going to demolish it and rebuild."

"Finally!" O'Connor raised her hands above her head. "The answer is yes."

Sam looked at her, confused. "What?"

"You're finally asking me for a job and the answer is yes," O'Connor said. "Abso-*fucking*-lutely."

Sam smiled and chuckled.

"Took you long enough." O'Connor walked back behind the counter and dug through the piles of paper. "For the record, I never doubted your ability." She pulled out a smart phone and tossed it to Sam. "That's the one I used in L.A. with those goddamn spiders. Works great but I've upgraded already."

Sam turned the phone over in his hand, marveling at its size and smooth edges. "Thanks."

"I hate those damn things. All this 'tech.' " O'Connor air-quoted the word. "It's all designed to become obsolete. But you should see my phone case. It's da bomb."

Sam shrugged. "I wouldn't know. All I have is a pushbutton phone back at my apartment."

"Well, say hello to your new little friend. We'll sort out the details later," O'Connor said. "How is Brad, by the way?"

"Doing well. We talk often."

"You Shook Me All Night Long" by AC/DC played from the back office.

O'Connor laughed. "New ringtone. Hold on." She walked into the office and answered her phone. "Yeah?"

Sam propped himself against the front counter and listened.

"Yeah. The name's O'Connor... Who?" She stepped to the doorway of the back office and raised her eyebrows at Sam. "Why are you calling me? Wait. Can I put you on speaker?" She tapped the display of her phone and placed it on the front counter. "Sam, my second in command, is here too."

Sam cleared his throat. "Hello."

"Like I said before, this is Harry Harcourt. I manage the grounds at Mar-A-Verde."

Sam scrunched his brow and mouthed "Mar-A-Verde" without realizing it.

"You submitted a quote on VerminWorx," Harry's voice said. "I'm calling to formally accept."

O'Connor's jaw dropped and her eyes went wide. She grabbed a pen and began scribbling on a piece of paper. "No one else wants the job? Why?"

She turned the paper to Sam. O'Connor's scrawl read: "I quoted $100K."

"Look, I'm not going to sugar coat this." Harry took what sounded like a fortifying breath. "After seeing what we've been dealing with, no one wants the job."

"Bunch of pussies." O'Connor winked at Sam. "What could be that bad?"

"I'll send you some pictures," Harry said. "Just a second."

Sam didn't like where this call was headed.

O'Connor leaned toward him and whispered, "Probably some rogue groundhogs, or some shit like that."

"You should receive the images in a bit," Harry said. "And they're not rogue groundhogs."

A chime sounded the arrival of the images.

"One moment, Harcourt." O'Connor switched to her photo app. "Taking a look at the pictures now." She swiped back and forth between the photos, pinch-zooming for clarity.

One picture showed a group of creatures in the bottom of the cavern on the first hole. Their pale veined bodies were streaked with blood and mud. The second picture showed one of the creatures trapped in a cage, its ring of razor-sharp teeth hooking into the metal mesh.

"Harcourt? Going to put you on hold for a second." O'Connor didn't wait for Harry's response. She looked at Sam, her eyes serious for a change. "That's definitely not a groundhog."

"I don't know what the hell that is except something new to haunt my dreams at night."

"You know what I see?" O'Connor examined one of the photos up close then looked up at Sam. "I see retirement."

"I don't know. That's a lot of blood. Maybe you'll get lucky and be eaten alive."

"I'm serious," O'Connor said. "This kind of payday comes once in a lifetime." She took the phone off hold. "That's pretty bad-ass, Harcourt. What is that thing?"

"We don't know." Harry's voice buzzed through O'Connor's cell phone speaker.

"We'll take the job, but it'll be a hundred K all upfront, no refund."

Harry paused like he was conferring with someone else nearby. "We can do twenty-five percent upon acceptance, twenty-five percent when you arrive, and the rest when the job's complete."

O'Connor countered. "Fifty percent upfront."

"Going to have to remain firm on my original offer," Harry said.

O'Connor looked at Sam. Beads of sweat had begun to pepper his brow. "Okay, Harcourt. You got a deal," she said. "Send me the paperwork."

"One other thing," Harcourt's voice buzzed. "Work needs to start as soon as possible. Like Monday morning."

O'Connor took a set of keys off a row of hooks on the wall. A great white shark fob hung from the keyring. "You got it, Harcourt. Send me the deets and let's get this ball rolling."

"I'm on it," Harry said.

O'Connor tapped her phone and hung up the call. She looked at Sam, an amazed look on her face. "I give you Exhibit A, the 'Fuck Off' quote."

"You never expected to get the job?"

"Not really. I mean a hundred K? Who goes for that?" O'Connor scratched her head. "Jesus."

"Someone who's desperate," Sam said.

"Nervous, Sam? You know who owns Mar-A-Verde, right?"

Sam gave O'Connor a sideways glance. "I may have been in prison for fifteen years, but I wasn't living under a rock."

"That's why I wanted payment upfront," O'Connor said. "The fucker has a tendency to stiff his contractors." She walked around the counter. "What do you say, Sam? Want the job?"

Sam grinned and held out his hand. "Abso-*fucking*-lutely." They shared a firm handshake.

"Yes!" O'Connor pumped her fists. "Finally. Sam Shaw on payroll."

"Do you think that thing looked like a rat?" Sam wiped the sweat from his brow. "You saw the tail, right?"

"Definitely not a rat." O'Connor scrutinized Sam's face. "You haven't relapsed, have you?"

"Uh, no, but we should have an academic on the team."

"Uh-uh. No way." O'Connor shook her head. "I know where you're going with this and the answer is no."

"But you like Hope." Sam smiled, knowing full well that Hope and O'Connor were like oil and water most of the time. "Send her the photos."

"No fucking way." O'Connor crossed her arms.

"We need as much information as possible, because...?"

O'Connor stared at Sam and shrugged. "What?"

"Because knowledge is power."

"Oh God." O'Connor rolled her eyes. "This ain't an episode of Schoolhouse Rock, for fuck's sake."

"Send Hope the photos."

O'Connor sighed. "I may have to fire you."

"You won't." Sam pointed at her phone. "Send the photos."

"Fine, if it'll shut you up." O'Connor gritted her teeth as she selected the two photos Harry had sent. "What's her number?"

Sam blanked for a second. "Sorry. Had to picture it on my trusty pushbutton phone. It's 646-480-6649."

O'Connor sent the images.

"How long do you think it'll take before she responds?"

"Fuck if I know. Maybe five—"

A text chimed on O'Connor's phone.

Sam laughed. "You were going to say five seconds, right?"

O'Connor grumbled and read the text message. "I give up." She tossed her phone on the counter and entered the stockroom.

"Correction. Adapt or die." Sam picked up O'Connor's phone and flipped it around in his hand. The case was made of brushed stainless steel surrounded by a black rubber seal to keep dirt and moisture out. On the back a multicolored rotatable disk covered the light or camera or both. Sam didn't know for sure. "The case on your phone is something else."

"Top of the line," O'Connor called back. "Cost me a fuck-ton so I hope it's worth it."

Sam turned the phone over and looked at Hope's text message.

It read: "WTF IS THAT?!?"

Sam tapped back: "No idea. Thought you might know."

After a few seconds Hope responded: "Nope. Can do some digging tho."

Sam: "Ok. Let me know if you find anything. Gotta go."

Hope: "L8R."

"We got to stock up the trailer," O'Connor yelled from the stockroom. "We roll out tomorrow morning." She entered the front office and spotted Sam with her phone. "What are you doing?" She grabbed it out of his hand and read the text conversation. "Ugh. You made me sound *polite*. I'll let it slide this time but don't do that again."

"You're getting soft in your old age."

O'Connor glared at Sam across the front office. "Don't try me. I can still kick your ass into next week. And that's with one leg. Now let's get to work."

Sam followed O'Connor into the stockroom to gather supplies for the trip. All the while he wondered if the images O'Connor had sent to Hope had set loose a bee in her bonnet.

SAM RETURNED FROM Detest-A-Pest to find Hope waiting outside his apartment door. He smiled to himself knowing the images had worked their magic.

"Hey, Hope." He pulled out his keys and unlocked the door.

"I've got a few slices of cold pizza if you're interested." He stepped inside.

"You know why I'm here, Sam." Hope followed him inside.

"I do?"

"Don't play dumb. O'Connor, who I haven't seen or talked to in months, sends me two very strange but interesting images? Out of the blue?" Hope placed one hand on her hip and held her phone out. On the display was one of O'Connor's images. "I call bullshit."

Sam raised his eyebrows. "You thought these images were *interesting?*"

"So you *do* know about them."

Sam nodded.

"How do..."

Sam pulled out his new smart phone. A Detest-A-Pest logo sticker was clearly visible on the back. "You're looking at O'Connor's newest employee."

Hope's eyes went wide, her aggravation temporarily forgotten. "No way."

"Yup." Sam turned the phone's display toward her. The phone's wallpaper displayed the exterior of Detest-A-Pest and its cast of vermin characters.

"Is that Washington?"

A wistful smile floated across Sam's face. "Yeah. O'Connor had it done last summer. After he died. As a tribute."

"That's cool," Hope said. "I still think of him after all this time."

"He made a big impression on all of us."

Hope remembered her phone in her hand. "So, what are these images all about?"

"Did you find out anything?"

"Wait. Did *you* send them?"

"I convinced O'Connor to send them," Sam said. "She was dead set against it."

"Figures." Hope shook her head. "That bitch carries a grudge."

"And you don't?" Sam looked at her with soft eyes. "What did you dig up?"

"Nothing. I even did image searches and came up with nothing."

Sam walked toward his bedroom, then stopped and turned around. Hope had been following so closely that she bumped into him before stepping back. "So I was wondering... can I borrow your suitcase again?"

"Going on a trip?"

"It's work-related." Sam grinned.

Hope narrowed her eyes and gave Sam a sideways look. "This trip... it wouldn't be related to those images would it?" She wagged her phone.

"You're quick," Sam said. "It's almost like I laid out all the clues for you."

Hope crossed her arms. "Very funny. Where are you going?"

"I really shouldn't say."

"Come on, Sam."

"Okay, you twisted my arm." Sam leaned in. "Ever heard of Mar-A-Verde?"

Hope's eyes became big as saucers. "No freaking way! Take me, too. You need an academic."

"I told O'Connor that," Sam said. "You'll have to convince her. So... about that suitcase."

"Absolutely. A hundred percent. I'll go get it now." Hope ran out to the hall.

Sam followed. "Hope! Wait."

She turned. Her hair bounced and her eyes sparkled with excitement. Sam hoped her enthusiasm would not be in vain.

"I can't promise anything," Sam said, "but you better pack tonight. We leave in the morning."

Hope jumped once, ran to Sam, and planted a kiss square on his lips. Then just as quick, she was off down the hallway again.

"What about Harriette?"

"She'll be fine for a few days," Hope called back. "I'll give her extra food."

"And your job?"

"I have some holiday banked." Hope pulled open the stairwell door and disappeared up the stairs.

"No promises! You're going to have to convince O'Connor." Sam's voice echoed through the hallway as the stairwell door closed. He didn't hear a response and doubted Hope had heard him at all.

AFTER HOPE DROPPED off her now infamous hot pink suitcase, Sam didn't hear a peep from her all night. He had expected her to hang around, excited about a potential trip to the Bahamas. He enjoyed Hope's company but tonight it was equally pleasant to take his time packing alone, in silence.

This was as much an adventure for Sam as it was for Hope, maybe more. He hadn't done much traveling and had never visited the Bahamas before. His life had barely started before he was sentenced to fifteen years for drunk driving and manslaughter. So many opportunities had evaporated because of one dumb decision.

Sam was finishing off a slice of cold pizza and a cup of mediocre coffee when a knock sounded on his door. He opened it to find O'Connor standing there wearing work boots, khakis, and a white shirt with the Detest-A-Pest logo on it. Her branded baseball cap sat firmly backwards on her head.

"Ready?" O'Connor looked tired. "We got a long day of driving ahead of us."

Sam poked his head out of the doorway and scanned the empty hallway.

O'Connor furrowed her brow. "Looking for something?"

Sam shook his head. "No. Let me grab my stuff." He returned towing Hope's loaner suitcase.

"Oh right." O'Connor began to laugh. "You're the hot pink pariah. Didn't realize you added Spongebob Squarepants to your entourage."

Sam hadn't noticed while packing but Hope had added Spongebob Squarepants stickers to the exterior of the suitcase. It was a strange choice considering the number of Bratz, Disney, and My Little Pony stickers already permanently in attendance.

"Neither did I."

"To be honest, Spongebob is pretty cool," O'Connor said. "And who wouldn't want to live in Bikini Bottom."

Sam gave her a confused look.

"So much to learn." O'Connor laughed. "Got your one-of-a-kind Detest-A-Pest-branded phone?"

Sam tapped his front pocket. "Yeah."

"Let's roll."

Sam locked his door and followed O'Connor out of the building, stopping in the foyer to pop hand-written notices about his absence into the mailboxes of the other four apartments.

Bruce, O'Connor's pristine white 1956 Buick Century, was parked by the curb towing a beat-up Detest-A-Pest trailer. Resting on her forearms out of the back passenger window was Hope, the grin on her face a mile wide.

"Hey, sleepyhead," Hope said. "Let's get a move-on. Time's a wastin'."

O'Connor pulled open the wrought iron gate in front of building and glanced at Sam, her eyes dark and annoyed. "Don't ask."

Sam smirked. "Oh, you know the *pink pariah* always asks."

O'Connor unlocked the trunk and Sam added his suitcase next to the other two. He opened the passenger door and slid onto the slick vinyl bench seat.

"Hey, Hope." Sam twisted in his seat to address her. "Surprised to see you. I didn't think you were coming."

O'Connor hopped behind the steering wheel and sent Sam another glare.

Sam alternated his gaze between Hope and O'Connor. Already he could sense the heat within the car and the sun had barely risen yet.

"Okay, I bribed her," Hope said. "With cigars. Nat Sherman 1930s."

"They're not Cohibas." O'Connor gripped the steering wheel until her knuckles turned white.

"I couldn't afford Cohibas. Besides, I was told those were pretty close."

O'Connor scoffed. "Don't forget about you laying down in the street in front of the car."

Hope smirked. "Oh yeah. There's that."

Sam tilted his head back and sighed. "Is this how it's going to be? Two alpha females at each other's throats for a week? Because if it is, you can count me out." Sam got out of the car, walked to the trunk, and rapped his knuckles on the trunk.

O'Connor took a deep breath and turned to face Hope. "Nat Shermans are pretty good." She shrugged and held out her hand. "Truce?"

Sam knocked on the trunk again.

Hope tilted her head slightly, trying to gauge O'Connor's sincerity. "A forever truce? Or just for the trip?"

"I don't do forever. Let's start with the trip."

Hope shot her hand forward and shared a firm handshake with O'Connor just as Sam appeared at the passenger side window.

"A change of heart?"

"A truce," O'Connor said to Sam. "Now get your butt in the car so we can go."

Sam sat and closed the car door. "This is good. You'll see."

Hope and O'Connor were locked in a stare, still gripping but no longer shaking each other's hand.

Sam eyed them both. "Life's too short to hold grudges." He alternated his gaze back and forth. "Right?"

The two women's hands began to tremble as they stared at each other, through each other. Sam imagined smoke would rise from their fingers soon.

"You guys said *truce*, right?" When he received no response, Sam leaned in between them and broke their stare, addressing them in turn. "Truce?"

Hope nodded. "Truce."

O'Connor gave one last shake and released Hope's hand. "Truce."

Sam sat back and buckled his seatbelt. "Let's get this show on the road."

Both women rubbed their right hands to get the blood flowing again. O'Connor started the Buick's engine, settling it into a low buttery growl. She threw the car into gear and pulled away from the curb.

She stuck her left arm out the window, giving Casanova Street an early Friday morning thumbs up. "Bahamas or bust, baby!"

Hope leaned out her window. "Woo hoo! Bahamas here we come!"

"God help us." Sam whispered to himself as he rubbed his temples. He had no idea what to expect, except more of those creatures.

O'Connor piloted the Detest-A-Pest caravan out of The Bronx and south on I-95. As road trips went, this was a popular route, passing through fifteen states, the most of any U.S. Interstate highway.

"Did you plan this route?" Sam watched the world fly by at fifty-five miles per hour, although he couldn't be completely sure. Bruce's speedometer needle bounced between fifty and sixty-five like a pinball flipper. Anything above fifty-five miles per hour was illegal on many sections of I-95, but he found he didn't care. He was a free man and it felt good to be on the road again.

"You're kidding right? I'm following the directions from my new fancy phone." O'Connor crossed the George Washington Bridge, cigar smoke trailing out the partially open driver-side window. "So if we get lost, don't blame me."

"Phone navigation is pretty good these days." Hope had sprawled herself out on the back seat reading articles on her phone. "Did you know that Bahama's hurricane season officially begins in a few days?"

"Don't give a flying fart," O'Connor said. "We'll be in and out in a few days. Besides, Mar-A-Verde lucked out. Most hurricanes haven't touched that place in the last hundred years."

"Well, I hope you brought some shorts. It's eighty-five degrees there right now."

"Nope," Sam said. "Nothing but jeans and long sleeves for me."

"Is it the tats?" Hope scanned the neckline of Sam's shirt, spotting the ends of a few tattoos sprouting underneath. "I say flaunt 'em."

"I second that," O'Connor said.

"Not going to happen." Sam crossed his arms over his chest. The cuff of his shirt rode up his forearm slightly and he pulled it back down. "They aren't a point of pride. Just a constant reminder."

"Sorry," Hope said.

"Don't worry about it." Sam closed his eyes.

Hope flicked through more articles on her phone. "Did you know there was a rat infestation in the White House? We go through D.C., right?"

O'Connor nodded. "Far as I know."

"It'd be cool if you got *that* job."

"If you see one, there's ten you can't." Sam chuckled. "Sounds accurate for the White House."

"They'll never be free of rats." O'Connor clamped down on her cigar. "That's why I do what I do."

"Holy shit," Hope said.

O'Connor glanced at Sam and rolled her eyes. "What is it now?"

"Get this. There was a sink hole on the White House lawn." Hope spoke as if the information was a newfound secret.

"Old news," O'Connor said. "At least three years."

Sam shook his head almost imperceptibly. "No, it was 2018."

O'Connor afforded him a brief look before redirecting her gaze back to the road. "What makes you so sure?"

"The last year I was in prison, I remember the jokes going around. Stuff about an escape tunnel."

"Yeah it was May 2018. Almost exactly two years ago. Wouldn't that be hilarious?" Hope smiled. "Inmates escaping from a hole on the White House lawn. The Secret Service would shit."

"Not that this party is dull–it is–but I think we need some music to complement this sweet ride." O'Connor turned on the car radio to static. "Sam, would you do the honors?"

"On it." Sam leaned forward and worked the knob for the analog AM tuner. It didn't take long for him to find a station. "The Sound of Silence" by Simon and Garfunkel was just finishing up.

"AM? Oh God," Hope said. "I thought you didn't want to live in the past?"

Sam shook his head. "Music's different. It's timeless."

"Born to Be Wild" by Steppenwolf began playing. Sam and O'Connor looked at each other and grinned.

"Couldn't have done better if you'd planned it." O'Connor began tapping the steering wheel to Steppenwolf's power chords.

Sam burst into song and O'Connor joined him moments later. Much to her surprise, Hope was powerless to stop the enthusiasm and began bopping her head and tapping her leg to the beat. It didn't take long for her to learn the chorus.

"Born to be wild!" they all yelled as they zoomed through New Jersey and south toward Pennsylvania, Delaware, and Maryland.

O'Connor stopped around noon on the outskirts of Richmond, Virginia for gas and food. The choice for food was McDonald's or Waffle House, with Waffle House winning hands down.

After securing a window booth, all three ordered burgers, with O'Connor choosing a Double Angus Cheeseburger with the works.

Mid-meal Hope pulled out her phone and opened the two creature images O'Connor had sent her. "How big do you think these things are?" she said between bites.

Sam spotted the bloody images across the table. "Ugh. Not while I'm eating."

O'Connor nodded at Hope in approval. "Not a stranger to gore, huh? That's kind of hard core." She pulled Hope's phone across the table and flipped back and forth between the two images. "Hard to tell without knowing the size of the cage. I'd guess a bit larger than a squirrel. Maybe a small dog?"

"Goddamnit, put the phone away." Sam dropped the remainder of his hamburger on his plate. "It's bad enough dreaming about those things. Now I got to eat looking at them?"

"Jesus, Sam. Chill." Hope clicked off her phone. "You sound like my dad."

Sam locked gaze with her. "Is that bad?"

Hope averted her eyes and looked at the half-eaten burger on her plate. Her cheeks warmed to a rosy pink. "Uh, kind of."

"What do you mean *kind of?*" Sam looked at her curiously.

"Never mind." Hope took a bite of burger and looked out the window.

"You dream about those things?" O'Connor adjusted her baseball cap.

Sam shrugged. "It was the tails that brought it all back. I for one hope they're smaller than squirrels."

"Bigger makes an easier target." O'Connor made a gun with her index finger and thumb, shot Hope's phone, and blew the pretend smoke from the tip.

"I knew you'd say that," Sam said.

O'Connor licked her fingers and pushed her plate aside. "Finish up. I want to hit the road." She downed her coffee, dug her cigar stub out of her front pocket, and secured it in place with her molars. She took out a business card, a top-down picture of a baited snap trap with contact information on the opposite side, and laid it on the table. "I'm going to pay up and hit the can. Better be ready when I get back."

Sam and Hope were already in the Buick by the time O'Connor joined them, Sam stretched out in the back and Hope riding shotgun.

O'Connor relit her cigar. "Who said you could sit upfront?"

Hope shrugged. "Sam took the back seat. I had no choice."

"Don't get used to it." O'Connor started the engine, pulled out of the Waffle House parking lot, and navigated back onto I-95 South.

"What took you so long in there? Gut issues?"

"It was like solving a difficult math problem."

Hope scrunched her brow. "Huh?"

"Had to work it out with a pencil." O'Connor laughed and slapped her leg.

Hope recoiled in disgust. "Gross."

"Did you hear that one, Sam?" O'Connor spied Sam in the back seat through the rear view mirror. He was asleep, snoring softly.

Hope looked at him. "Sam has left the building."

"Hopefully not dreaming of those things." O'Connor accelerated to cruising speed. "We're going to need him at a hundred percent."

Hope flipped on the radio. "Ready to be schooled in modern music?" She began tuning the radio, stations fading in and out as she went.

"Hold it," O'Connor said. "Go back."

Hope sighed and reversed the dial.

"Stop. There." O'Connor smiled.

"Godzilla" by Blue Oyster Cult belted from Bruce's single mono speaker.

Hope listened for a moment and slouched back in her seat in exasperation. "This is *old people* music."

"My car, my music." O'Connor grinned.

"What about the truce?"

"This *is* part of the truce." O'Connor turned up the volume. "Listen. You might learn something."

"Doubtful." Hope connected ear buds to her phone and placed them in her ears. "Let me know when you want a change of pace."

O'Connor settled into the drive and let technology keep the peace between her and Hope. She had been driving just over two and a half hours when Sam awoke with a yelp and a jolt that came from nowhere. He pushed himself upright and scratched his head.

O'Connor looked at Sam in the rear view mirror. "I see the Xanax I slipped into your coffee worked its magic."

"What?" Sam rubbed his eyes.

"Just fucking with you." O'Connor grinned and turned the music down. "Glad you caught some zees."

Hope popped her earbuds out. "Welcome to the land of the living."

Sam looked out the windows with confusion. "Where are we?"

"We just passed Smithfield, North Carolina," O'Connor said. Her cigar sat dying at the side of her mouth, a sodden clump. "I figure we'll stop in Florence, South Carolina. There's a Holiday Inn and lots of places to get grub just off the highway. My ass has had enough driving for one day."

"I could relieve you for a while." Sam smiled, knowing what would come next.

"No one drives Bruce except me." O'Connor shifted her gaze from the rear view mirror to Hope and back. "No one. Got it?"

Sam waved her off.

"What were you dreaming of, Sam?" Hope twisted in her seat to look at him. "It sounded intense."

"I'll give you one guess."

"Rats." O'Connor smirked.

"Specifically, those things," Hope added.

"Yeah, trapped with them in that damn basement from hell."

"At least that basement won't be an option soon." Hope faced front, stared at the upholstered ceiling of the car, and sighed. "If I'd known they were going to evict everyone in a year I would have never moved in."

"Then you wouldn't be with us on this trip either." O'Connor rubbed her chin as if she was in deep thought. "Yeah that would have been better."

Hope glowered at O'Connor.

"Just busting your chops, honey." O'Connor raised one hand from the steering wheel, pointed at her, and winked. "Truce, remember?"

"Yeah, truce. Right. Where are you going to move to, Sam?" Hope asked. "I mean after this job."

"No idea."

Hope looked at O'Connor. "Where do you live?"

"I got a place near the shop."

"Whereabouts, exactly?"

"What's with the fucking third degree?" O'Connor gripped the steering wheel with white knuckles. "Where I live is on a need to know basis and you don't need to know."

"Whoa." Hope shot a look at Sam. "Sorry."

A silence filled Bruce's interior like a fog. Hope took the opportunity to pocket her phone and find some O'Connor-appropriate music on the radio. After bypassing static, religious, and contemporary fare, she selected WGBR 1150 AM, Goldboro's greatest hits. "Start Me Up" by The Rolling Stones was playing.

O'Connor and Hope exchanged glances and O'Connor gave her a nod and a smile.

"Music soothes the savage beast," Sam said.

"I'll take that as a compliment." O'Connor focused on the road ahead. Two hours later she stopped in Florence, South Carolina, having divided the trip almost exactly in half. They checked into the Holiday Inn and ordered room service, none of them having the energy to walk to any of the nearby restaurants.

After a dinner of pizza and beer (and Coke for Sam), they each took hot showers. O'Connor took the queen bed all for herself. Sam offered to sleep on the floor, but Hope insisted he take half of the pullout sofa-bed.

"No hanky-panky unless I'm invited." O'Connor grinned and flashed her eyebrows.

Sam sighed. "I want to know where you get your energy. I need some."

"I just live my life like each day could be my last," O'Connor said.

"Good philosophy." Hope rolled to one side, her back to Sam, and pulled the covers over her shoulder.

O'Connor turned the lights out at 9 p.m. Fifteen minutes later the room rattled with three different levels of snores. Sleep may have come easily for O'Connor and Hope, but Sam's nightmares followed him down.

O'CONNOR'S SIX O'CLOCK alarm sounded on her phone. "Rise and shine my lovelies."

Sam awoke to find Hope partly snuggled into his back. The warmth of her body and the light smell of soap brought back faint memories of his marriage, spending lazy Sunday mornings in bed with Claire. But that was then, before he had screwed everything up.

He sat up on the edge of the sofa bed opposite Hope and scratched his head. "You sleep okay?"

"God yes." O'Connor stretched her arms. "Best sleep I've had in months. You?"

Sam shrugged. "Meh."

"More dreams of those weird sons of bitches?"

"Yeah."

"I wouldn't worry about it." O'Connor sat up, grabbed her prosthetic leg, and began the multi-step process of putting it on. "Those things are probably not much bigger than actual rats."

"Hope you're right," Sam said. "They look downright nasty."

"Be careful what you wish for." Hope had propped herself up on her elbows and squinted around the room.

"I wish for bacon, eggs, hash browns, and coffee." O'Connor pulled up her pants and tucked in her Detest-A-Pest-branded shirt.

"Second that." Sam collected his clothes and dressed. "I'm starving."

"Holiday Inn's continental breakfast is awesome. Bottomless scrambled eggs and bacon." Hope threw off the covers and walked to the bathroom.

Sam hadn't seen what Hope was wearing when she had gone to bed the previous night, but this morning as she passed by his eyes caught a glimpse of a familiar t-shirt: black with an icon of a donkey and the words "Stop staring at my ass," just long enough to preserve her modesty.

Sam found his eyes traveling down her bare legs and averted his eyes to discover O'Connor had been watching the entire parade, including Sam's reaction, the whole time.

O'Connor flashed her eyebrows at him.

"No." Sam shook his head. "Don't even go there."

O'Connor laughed and began shoving the rest of her things into her suitcase. "Sam, you're so screwed."

"What do you know about love, Miss Reverse Harem?"

"You'd be surprised."

The bathroom door opened and Hope walked back to the sofa bed to get dressed. "Surprised about what?"

"Surprised at how much I'm going to eat." Sam sent a look of warning at O'Connor. She got the message.

"So let's get cracking." O'Connor snapped her fingers. "I want to be first in line."

The three of them finished packing and headed down to the small kitchen area near the lobby. O'Connor ended up third in line and made a considerable dent in the buffet's unlimited bacon and eggs.

They ate their fill, washing it all down with lots of coffee. O'Connor went back three times, mostly for the bacon. Sam became an expert with the Belgian waffle maker and Hope concluded her meal with a brimming bowl of Froot Loops.

O'Connor grimaced. "How can you eat that garbage?"

"Reminds me of being a kid." Hope crunched on a spoonful of cereal. "Try some." She pushed her bowl forward. "Both of you."

O'Connor and Sam exchanged a look. They each plucked a colored loop from Hope's bowl and popped it into their mouths.

Sam chewed and swallowed. "Okay. I see the appeal." He strolled back to the cereal bar and filled his own bowl with the candied cereal.

"It's like crack, Sam." O'Connor stood behind him holding her own empty bowl.

"Yeah, it's addictive alright." Sam poured milk over the cereal.

"If I don't have diabetes yet, this'll seal the deal," O'Connor said. "But what the fuck, huh? Got to die somehow."

"I think we'll be okay. Somehow I don't think they serve Froot Loops at Mar-A-Verde."

They both returned to the table, Hope pleased as punch that she could spread some joy with sugary cereal.

O'Connor had Bruce traveling highway speed by seven o'clock. She continued to follow I-95 south, crossing two state lines and skipping Georgia (except for bathroom breaks) before stopping for lunch in Daytona Beach, Florida.

O'Connor chose a restaurant off the highway, right on the Atlantic Ocean. Blue sky and blue water stretched as far as the eye could see. She texted Harry and gave him their arrival time.

"About three more hours to Palm Beach International Airport," O'Connor said. "Then it's a private flight to our tropical paradise."

"Private flight?" Hope raised her brows. "Sweet."

"Paradise and ugly-as-fuck creatures don't mix." Sam popped the last bite of a turkey club sandwich into his mouth.

"You worry too much, Sam." O'Connor punched him in the shoulder.

"Someone has to." Sam shoved O'Connor back.

Three and a half hours later O'Connor pulled up to Strunk Industries' private aircraft hangar, located on the western perimeter of Palm Beach International Airport.

Harry stood waiting on the tarmac beside the massive hangar door, a Gulfstream G650 parked nearby. With his purple Mar-A-Verde t-shirt, a baseball cap to match, and jeans, he stood out like a sore thumb. A pair of mirrored aviator sunglasses hid his eyes. He walked over to the Buick's driver side window. "I'm guessing you're O'Connor?"

"You guessed right." O'Connor gave Harry a once over, then shared a firm handshake with the man.

"Harry Harcourt." He ran his eyes over Bruce's flowing lines and smiled. "Sweet ride. You can park it over there." Harry pointed to the right side of the hangar.

O'Connor pulled Bruce into the hangar far enough to cover the trailer and parked next to a small control booth that doubled as an office. She killed the engine and stepped out. Sam and Hope followed.

Harry walked to greet Sam and Hope. "Harry Harcourt." He shook both their hands.

"My name's Sam and this is Hope."

Harry nodded to both, his eyes lingering on Hope a second longer. Sam noticed. "How was the drive?"

"Smooth," O'Connor said. "Not many jackasses on the road this weekend."

"Good to hear." Harry clapped his hands, rubbing his palms together like it was cold. "I know you all must be tired from the drive, but if I could ask that we pack up and get in the air, I can promise a premium suite and a luxury dinner." He motioned to the Gulfstream, the Strunk Industries logo emblazoned on the fuselage.

Hope's eyes went wide as saucers. "We're going on that?"

"You bet." Harry smiled. "Nothing but the best for guests of Mar-A-Verde." He pulled open the plane's cargo doors.

"Holy shit." Hope looked at Sam. "I knew it was a private flight, but…" She scanned the smooth lines of the Gulfstream, her eyes alive with excitement.

"And this is how the one percent live." Sam stretched and pulled suitcases from Bruce's trunk.

"Before we unpack, I want to get business out of the way," O'Connor said. "I believe it was fifty percent upon arrival."

"I think you mean twenty-five." Harry placed a firm hand on O'Connor's shoulder and squeezed. "Let's start things off on the right foot."

"Right. Twenty-five."

Harry tapped something out on his phone. "Done. You should have an etransfer waiting in your inbox."

O'Connor confirmed the email and initiated the etransfer. "What's the password?"

"Mar-A-Verde, all one word and lower case."

O'Connor tapped in the password. A chime sounded from her phone to confirm the deposit. "Fucking-ace! Let's get packed up." She stepped to the back of the trailer and unlocked the doors.

With everyone helping, it took just under twenty minutes to load Detest-A-Pest's equipment into the cargo hold of the Gulfstream.

O'Connor locked the trailer, rolled up Bruce's windows, and locked its doors. "Got a place to store my keys?"

Harry beckoned O'Connor to the small office. In one corner on the floor sat a safe. He punched in the combination code and the door popped open.

"Who else knows the combo?"

"Just me." Harry tapped his temple. "Mind's like a steel trap."

"Just don't die on me." O'Connor dropped the keys into Harry's hand and motioned at the Buick. "Bruce is my pride and joy. And those things look vicious."

Harry paused, as if he was going to say something, then

placed the keys into the safe and closed the door. "SECURED" in digital letters appeared on the front display of the safe.

"Don't worry," he said. "Dying isn't on my agenda. Let's get going. I don't like flying at night."

"You're a pilot, too, huh?" O'Connor followed Harry, joining Sam and Hope at the plane.

"Strunk likes his employees multi-skilled. Cheaper that way." Harry smiled and motioned toward the stairs leading into the plane. "After you."

An interior that rivaled the poshest hotel suite met O'Connor, Sam, and Hope at the top of the airstairs. An extended sofa plus individual seating all in top grain leather, a dining area with place settings for four, a big screen television, a well-stocked wet bar, and a business center with laptop and Internet access rounded out the amenities. All edges were lined with gold trim.

"Fuck me." O'Connor's jaw hung open. "I could live here permanently."

"No kidding." Hope ran her hand across the backs of one of the chairs. "The leather's warm. I swear. Feel it."

All this luxury felt foreign to Sam. None of it seemed real. He had spent almost half his life living with nothing and in this environment he felt like an impostor.

"Crazy, huh Sam?" O'Connor sat down in one of the chairs and spun herself around.

"Yeah. Crazy." Sam took off his shoes and sat down on the sofa. Hope was right. The leather did feel warm. He buckled himself in and closed his eyes.

Harry pulled the airstairs closed and engaged the lock in the door. "Please take a seat and buckle up. Once we're at cruising altitude, feel free to roam around and make yourself comfortable, but not too comfortable. It's door-to-door in less than an hour."

O'Connor peered out at Bruce from one of the large oval

windows. "Who's going to close the hangar door? That's my precious down there."

Harry spoke back from the cockpit. "The hangar doors have a proximity sensor and close automatically when the plane is a safe distance away." He fired up the two jet engines and after obtaining clearance from air traffic control, taxied to the runway and entered the queue for take-off.

O'Connor watched as the hangar doors closed just as Harry had described.

"Fasten your seat belts and prepare for take-off," Harry's voice broadcast through the cabin speakers. The engines throttled up, setting the plane into a subtle vibration and emitting a high-pitched whine from the turbines.

Hope watched the runway zoom past the window, then appear to fall away as the plane took flight.

"Ladies and gentlemen," Harry's intercom voice said, "we have lift-off. Out the windows you can see Palm Beach directly below us and, in a few minutes, we'll be cruising over the Atlantic bound for the Bahamas. Flight time approximately thirty-eight minutes."

O'Connor and Hope had their faces glued to the windows next to their seats as the east coast of Florida made way for the Atlantic. Sam had reclined and was already in a deep sleep, dreams of strange creatures replaced by blue sky, at least for the time being.

TRUE TO HIS word, twenty-three minutes later Harry began his fifteen minute descent. "Seat belts back on everyone. Off the port side you can see the Grand Bahamas. It's still recovering from 2019's hurricane Dorian. From starboard you can see the

Bimini Islands and Alice Town. Our destination is a small island directly between the two."

Harry navigated the Gulfstream in a wide arc as he made his approach. A mile out the runway's landing lights engaged.

Hope placed her hand on the porthole window. The sun dipped toward the horizon, casting the sky in blue and orange. "Can you imagine living here year round?"

"I don't want to imagine," O'Connor said. "I want the real thing."

The plane landed with a gentle bounce. Harry engaged the flaps, decelerated the plane, and taxied toward a hangar similar to the one they had just left in Palm Beach, the doors open and waiting.

Harry buzzed through the intercom. "Ladies and gentlemen. Welcome to Mar-A-Verde. Please keep your seat belts on until we have come to a full and complete stop."

"Fuck that." O'Connor unbuckled her seat belt and popped her unlit cigar into the side of her mouth. "I want a steak and an ice-cold beer." She walked the length of the cabin to the cockpit and peeked inside. "This is one fine piece of machinery."

Harry nodded and gave O'Connor a short glance over his shoulder, paying note to her cigar. "It's good that you didn't light up during the flight. I would have thrown you out."

"I may be getting up there in years, but I do know the rules of air travel."

"You sure don't listen." Harry kept his eyes forward as he taxied the Gulfstream into the hangar, beside a small six seat Cessna Turbo 206.

"Just out of curiosity, would you throw me out with or without a parachute?"

Harry turned the plane in a stationary circle until it faced toward the doors of the hangar and the runway beyond. "Over the open ocean it wouldn't matter. You'd either die upon impact, or drown tangled in your parachute." He glared at O'Connor and began the plane's power-down sequence, pressing buttons and flipping switches on the expansive dashboard. "Let's get your stuff unloaded." He stepped out of the cockpit, unlocked the door, and engaged the airstairs.

O'Connor met Sam and Hope at the plane's door. "Harry Harcourt is a bit of an asshole."

"Kind of like you when people don't follow *your* rules." Sam nudged O'Connor's shoulder as he exited the plane.

Hope grinned and exchanged a look with O'Connor as she passed by.

"Not a word, Missy," O'Connor said.

"Who me?" Hope laughed and followed Sam down to the concrete floor of the hangar.

O'Connor grit her teeth and stepped to the door of the plane. She dug out her Zippo and lit her cigar. Plumes of grey smoke floated partially in and out of the plane.

Harry parked a windowless panel van next to the open cargo hold of the Gulfstream and got out.

O'Connor stepped to the pavement. "Okay people. Let's get her loaded up." She lined up supplies at the edge of the hold's door.

Hope and Harry carried the Kill-O-Matic out first due to its size and Sam intercepted it at the back of the van.

"Watch it with that." O'Connor scrutinized the Kill-O-Matic's delivery. "That's why you're paying us the big bucks."

"Do I want to ask?" Harry said.

"Best you don't." Sam snugged the Kill-O-Matic along one wall of the van. "Let just say I've seen it fry more rats all at once than a New York City pizza joint."

Harry raised his brow in curiosity. "I look forward to seeing it in action."

"Maybe you don't," Hope said. "It's not pretty."

O'Connor pointed at the Cessna parked to the right of the

Gulfstream. "I see why you chose the jet. Our stuff would have never fit in that piece of junk."

"Lucky for you Strunk likes to impress people with his fancy toys," Harry said. "And it's not a piece of junk. If I had my choice, I'd take the 206 over the Gulfstream any day."

They finished transferring supplies and closed the van's rear doors.

"Grab your luggage and I'll walk you to the lobby." Harry started down the path leading from the hangar to the main resort building.

"Why not drive?" O'Connor extended the handle on her luggage in anticipation of Harry's response.

"Not enough seats for everyone," Harry called back. "Plus your equipment takes up all of the cargo space."

"Why not drive me?"

Harry said nothing and continued along the paved path.

Sam laughed and followed Harry. "You're a charmer, O'Connor."

"At least I don't have My Little Pony stickers all over my luggage."

"I thought you wanted a steak and a cold beer?" Hope rolled her suitcase forward. "Let's go."

O'Connor hobbled along behind Hope, playing caboose on this train of fools.

THE EXTERIOR OF Mar-A-Verde showed signs of disrepair, with sections of the exterior stucco cracked and crumbling. The brochure and website photos had either been retouched or weren't taken close enough to expose the damage in detail. Being there in person exposed some of the secrets of the ninety-year-old building. Upkeep obviously hadn't been a high priority.

Harry led the Detest-A-Pest crew toward the front entrance. "Normally, I'd take contractors through the back. Strunk, and by extension our G.M. Vaughn Larsen, frowns upon anyone who doesn't look like they belong here."

"But…?" Sam appraised his clothing and his pink suitcase, then shared a glance over his shoulder at Hope and O'Connor.

"Some rules are meant to to be broken," Harry said. "Larsen's been a huge pain in my backside the past few days."

"We don't want to cause trouble," Hope said.

O'Connor gnawed on her cigar. "The hell we don't."

Harry grinned. "Trust me. It's no trouble."

Larsen spotted the motley crew enter the lobby. He grimaced and scanned the area for guests before raising his arms and sporting a wider-than-normal smile. Harry knew it was fake, all for show, and wondered if his guests would see through it too.

"Friends! Welcome to Mar-A-Verde. Glad to see Harry delivered you safely. Vaughn Larsen, general manager, at your service." He took a bow.

O'Connor, Sam, and Hope exchanged looks.

"This is the crew from Detest-A-Pest." Harry initiated introductions with O'Connor. "Owner and operator... I'm sorry, what's your first name?"

"It's just O'Connor." She shook Larsen's hand.

"Or Bertha to her friends." Sam winked at O'Connor. "I'm Sam." Evidence of his extensive tattoos escaped from under his sleeve cuff as he reached to greet Larsen. He noticed the bald man's brows rise.

"And I'm Hope, the resident animal behaviorist." She took Larsen's hand and gave it a quick shake.

The elevator chimed its arrival and two guests emerged. They shot disapproving looks at the Detest-A-Pest crew as they walked past on their way to the dining room.

Larsen intercepted the guests and tried to block their view. "Ah, Mr. and Mrs. Desjardin. We have your usual table ready for you." He escorted the the Desjardins to the dining room entrance.

Larsen turned back to the group, but his eyes betrayed his motive: scanning the lobby for any other guests. "Well, Detest-A-Pest is it? You're quite the unique team. You all must be tired from your journey." Larsen ushered O'Connor, Sam, and Hope towards the elevator, their beat-up luggage in tow. "Let's get you to your room so you can relax."

Larsen pressed the elevator call button. The elevator doors slid open, he stepped in, and directed everyone to follow.

"O'Connor." Harry motioned behind him with his thumb. "I'll move your equipment to our maintenance building. Can I join you all for a late dinner? Say eight-thirty?"

O'Connor clamped her cigar and nodded from within the elevator as the door glided closed. "Steak and a cold beer... or five."

Larsen pressed the second floor call button and the elevator jerked into motion.

Black marble with gold trim lined the walls of the elevator. Sam ran his finger along the trim and gold flecks peeled off and stuck to his finger.

"It's beautiful here, Mr. Larsen," Hope said.

"Thank you." Larsen stared at the closed elevator doors.

"Will we be meeting Mr. Strunk?"

"He doesn't visit during summer."

"I thought Mar-A-Verde was his permanent residence now."

O'Connor elbowed Hope and glared at her.

The elevator chimed for the second floor and the doors slid open. "This way, please." Larsen stepped into the corridor. "Follow me."

O'Connor, Sam, and Hope passed a dozen doors, each suite featuring an ornate carved design surrounding the room number, all black and gold.

At the end of the corridor, Larsen opened a heavy fire door

that led to a shorter, narrower hallway. The air smelled heavy and musty. He swiped the electronic lock and opened the door to their suite.

"I hope you find your stay enjoyable while dealing with our... problem." Larsen handed the card key to O'Connor and turned to leave.

"Hey, hold up, Jack," O'Connor stepped aside as Sam and Hope entered the suite. "I thought we'd be getting separate rooms."

"This is the best we can do on such short notice." Larsen gave O'Connor a dismissive once over. "Our members take priority. I'm sure you understand. Will there be anything else?"

O'Connor grit her teeth and spoke around her cigar. "No."

"Oh. One more thing, *Bertha*." Larsen leaned in. "There will be no smoking anywhere inside or within fifty feet of the premises. That abomination in your mouth should be thrown away. Good day."

O'Connor watched Larsen leave until the heavy fire door blocked her view. She followed Hope into the suite and closed the door. "What an asshole."

"At least the asshole is easy to read," Sam said.

Hope sat on the edge of the king bed, sniffing the air. "Does anyone smell anything strange?"

"Yeah." O'Connor dropped her suitcase on the bed. "That's piss. This whole place stinks."

"It's falling apart." Sam pulled open the curtains to the balcony. The sun kissed the horizon to the west, a view even the worst resort couldn't spoil. He opened the sliding glass door to let in some fresh air. "Did you see the cracks on the exterior?"

"It's like there was an earthquake and no one bothered to fix the damage," Hope said.

"Hope. Only going to tell you once." O'Connor leaned in close. "Earthquake talk is forbidden. Got it?"

Hope eyed Sam and he nodded his head in response, drawing a line with his finger across his throat. "Okay. Whatever."

"O'Connor, did you bring a black light?" Sam grinned.

"Please say no." Hope swallowed hard with a grimace. "Gross."

"And what was with Larsen's handshake?"

"Limp as a fucking dead fish," O'Connor said. "I don't trust limp handshakes. And as much as I'd love to talk about that douche all day, I'm starving. Let's go eat."

"Should we change?" Hope unzipped her suitcase. "These places always want you to dress a certain way."

"Fuck 'em," O'Connor said.

"Just give me five minutes." Hope pulled out a few articles of clothing and headed to the bathroom.

O'Connor and Sam shared a knowing glance. "Five minutes. Clock's ticking."

Four minutes later, Hope emerged wearing a long flowing skirt with a tunic top, both black. She had elevated herself from academic to socialite with ease.

"Don't let Strunk see you in that," O'Connor said.

"He's not here during summer, remember?" Hope twirled in front of the mirror, pleased with how she looked. "Let's go."

"You look amazing."

"Why thank you, Sam." Hope headed for the door.

"Oh please." O'Connor rolled her eyes.

Sam looked at his usual ensemble: jeans with white t-shirt and flannel button-up work shirt. "I feel underdressed now."

"Like I said before, fuck 'em." O'Connor said. "We're being paid to be here. Let 'em gawk."

They left the room and walked back down the hallway, through the fire doors and to the elevators. O'Connor pressed the down call button. She pointed at a giant golden-framed picture of Strunk on the opposite wall: bleached teeth, fake tan, and holding two thumbs up. "Jesus. As if anyone needs a reminder."

Sam observed Hope's reflection in the black marble of the elevator doors. "Anyone get the impression that we're being hidden? Like from other guests?"

"Fuck 'em," O'Connor said. "How many times do I have to say it."

The elevator dinged and the three of them stepped inside. A minute later, Bart the maître d' stopped them at the dining room entrance on the main floor of the resort.

Bart smiled and nodded at Hope, then turned to Sam and O'Connor, his smile dissolving away in an instant. "A jacket and skirt are required for dinner. And there is *no* smoking."

O'Connor leaned in so much that Bart was forced to step back. "I ain't wearing no skirt, numbnuts."

"Take it easy, O'Connor," Sam said in a whisper.

Harry appeared beside Hope and caught Bart's eye. "It's okay. They're with me."

"Rules are rules, Harry." Bart spoke softly through gritted teeth.

"We're going to have to let go of the skirt rule, but grab a couple of spare jackets and bring them to my table," Harry said. "This way, folks. And O'Connor, the cigar has to go. Can't do anything about that rule."

O'Connor stowed her cigar in her front shirt pocket. The fabric had been stained ash grey at the bottom seam from storing past unfinished cigars there.

McCoy sat at the bar nursing a scotch neat and watched Harry lead the crew to their table at the back of the dining room.

Just as O'Connor had predicted, people stared and whispered as the Detest-A-Pest crew filed by. She leaned toward one elderly couple. "Take a damn picture. It'll last longer." They gasped and recoiled from O'Connor's intrusion.

Harry took O'Connor's arm. "You're in a different world now. I'd recommend trying to fit in."

O'Connor pulled her arm away and glared at him. Sam prepared for an onslaught of profanity and was pleasantly surprised when she refrained.

Bart appeared with two black jackets. Sam's fit perfectly and completed the illusion that he belonged there. O'Connor's jacket was at least one size too small and she was barely able to pull it on over her work clothes.

Harry nodded at Bart. "Thanks."

"If you require anything else..." Bart tipped his imaginary hat, a sly grin on his face as he left.

"The fucker gave me a small jacket on purpose," O'Connor grumbled.

Hope examined the menu. "What's good here?"

"Define good." Harry laughed. "I actually ate here a few nights ago and the crab cakes were tasty. Can't speak for the lobster."

"I want one of Strunk's famous steaks and a cold beer," O'Connor said.

"She's been jonesing for steak the whole trip out," Sam said. "It would be wise not to disappoint her."

"Damn straight." O'Connor squirmed in her jacket. "Fuck this." She wriggled out of the jacket and draped it over her shoulders instead.

"How about steaks for everyone?" Harry glanced around the table.

"I'm having the lobster." Hope smiled and flicked her eyes at Sam. "Two pounds is a lot. Helpers will not be turned away."

"Steak is fine by me," Sam said.

"I'm not a wine guy, so what goes well with steak...?" Harry glanced at O'Connor. "Besides beer?"

"Malbec is nice." Hope propped her chin up with her hand. "So is Cabernet Sauvignon."

Harry snapped his finger and pointed at Hope. "Our wine expert has been revealed. Malbec it is."

"Club soda for me," Sam said.

Hope scanned the room, taking in the expansive and elaborately decorated ceiling surrounded by golden moulded edges. "This place is crazy."

"You ain't seen nothing yet," Harry said.

The waitress appeared and took everyone's order, returning afterward with a bottle of Malbec for the table, a Dos Equis for O'Connor, and a club soda with lemon for Sam.

"Mexican beer." O'Connor emptied the bottle into a frosted glass. "How ironic."

"I've heard only the most interesting people in the world drink it. So you got that going for you." Harry poured wine for Hope, then himself. He raised his glass. "To Detest-A-Pest. May your work go smoothly."

Everyone clinked glasses and sipped from their drinks.

"What work would that be?" McCoy, well on his way to blitzville, settled his hands and his tumbler of scotch on the table. "Eh, Harry? Finally killing those things out there?"

"McCoy, keep your voice down." Harry looked around at other diners taking notice of the disruption and pulled an empty chair to the table. "Sit down." He didn't wait for McCoy to comply. Instead he pulled him into the chair by his belt. "O'Connor, Sam, Hope. This is Shane McCoy."

McCoy took a sloppy gulp of scotch. "What if they kill again? What if they get me, Harry?"

O'Connor held up her hands. "Whoa whoa whoa. What do you mean *kill again?*" She exchanged an uneasy glance with Sam and Hope, then focused on Harry. "You didn't say anything about killings."

"He didn't tell you?" McCoy slumped back into his chair. "Surprise, surprise."

Harry leaned forward and kept his voice low. "Look, it's not that simple."

"But it is. You knew something was out there, Harry. But you did nothing. You said nothing." McCoy gulped at his scotch. "Sinclair's dead because of you, so that makes you complicit."

"I had no idea there'd be a sink hole on the first hole," Harry said. "That's the God's honest truth."

"I've been coming here longer than you've been employed. How many other lies have you told me over the years?" McCoy crumpled in on himself and held his head with both hands.

A hush fell over the table, but O'Connor was first to break it. "I want all the deets, Harry. Now. Or we walk."

Harry sighed. "McCoy's right. There's been deaths. Two, plus one serious injury."

McCoy laid his head on the table and closed his eyes.

Sam's face went ashen. "Jesus." He grabbed Hope's hand and gave it a squeeze before he realized what he was doing. "Sorry," he said before pulling it away again. Hope didn't seem to mind.

"I want specifics. Everything," O'Connor said.

"And you'll get it, but not here." Harry motioned to the rest of the guests dining. "The less people know about this, the better."

"That's not working too well for me," O'Connor said. "I've dealt with bullshit like this before, but my crew didn't sign up for this."

"I swear. You'll know everything by tomorrow morning," Harry continued. "It's just that no one would take the job if I mentioned the deaths."

"So you pull a bait and switch? This is going to cost you... what do you think, Sam? Hope?"

Hope shrugged.

"Creatures that kill people wasn't part of the deal to begin with," Sam said. "Not sure I'm down for that."

O'Connor grinned. "Come on, Sam. You've dealt with death before, and these aren't rats, so... what? An extra fifty K?"

Harry scoffed. "No deal."

"Then we're out of here." O'Connor crossed her arms.

"What are you going to do? Swim home?" Harry crossed his arms too, unknowingly mimicking O'Connor's pose. "And Strunk will sue you for breach of contract."

"A fraudulent contract that misrepresented our agreed upon tasks," O'Connor said. "It'll cost Strunk a hell of a lot more to sue us."

Harry stared at O'Connor. "Okay. An extra fifty K, paid when the job is completed to my satisfaction."

O'Connor pulled out a small and weathered black leather-bound booklet and a pen from her front pocket. She scribbled some notes on it and presented it to Harry. "Sign it. I want this contract addendum in writing."

Harry took the booklet, read it over, signed it, and slid it back across the table. "I'll send you official paperwork."

O'Connor gave the booklet to Sam. "You and Hope sign it too, as witnesses."

Which they did. The signed contract worked wonders to calm the tension at the table. They all took sips from their respective drinks while a soft snore rose from McCoy.

"He's going to have one hell of a hangover," Hope said.

Harry shrugged and swished his wine around in his glass. "Won't be the first time."

"So I got to ask." O'Connor narrowed her eyes at Harry. "Why Detest-A-Pest? I mean thanks for the gig and all. We'll pound those things out there into mush. But why us?"

"To be honest, you were the first serious quote we received," Harry said.

"You've got to be shitting me."

Harry shook his head. "Nope. There was no one in the Bahamas who wanted to take the job... or could do it right away.

When we posted the job on VerminWorx, we got a few bogus quotes. Then yours rolled across my screen. Damn expensive, though."

O'Connor leaned back in her chair and grinned. "And tomorrow you'll find out why we're worth every penny."

"But I'm no dummy. I checked you out," Harry said. "Your case study on the Gambian rat invasion in New York was morbidly fascinating. But it was how you dealt with the spiders out west in L.A. last year that cinched it for me." He drank more wine. "Your company has quite a colorful history."

O'Connor shot a glance at Sam and Hope. "Wait. Where did you read this?"

Harry scrunched his brow, confused. "Detestapest.com of course. That *is* your website, am I right?"

O'Connor nodded. "Right, right. It gets confusing with all those social media pages and crap. Simplicity is underrated."

Sam pulled out his cell phone and tapped at the display apathetically. He handed it to Hope and whispered, "Can you call up websites on this thing?"

Hope took the phone, opened the Internet browser, and soon had Detestapest.com loaded up. She raised a brow and handed the phone back to Sam. "Looks good."

McCoy grunted, almost waking himself up. He pulled his cheek away from the table where it was partially stuck with dried saliva, and settled his head on the opposite cheek.

"Look, I'm going to run McCoy back to his room," Harry said. "He's overstayed his welcome." He bent down and wrapped McCoy's arm around his neck and shoulders, lifting him to his feet. "Back in five."

The movement woke McCoy. "Hey. What's going—"

"Room service awaits, big guy." Harry guided a stumbling McCoy out of the dining room.

"Brad made your website." Sam slid the phone across the table. "See at the bottom? Designed by Bradshaw Creative."

"Boy's got a knack for it, I'll give him that." O'Connor flipped through the pages. "I'll send him payment when we're done here."

"I'm sure he did it without expecting to be paid," Sam said.

"Professional work should be paid for." O'Connor raised her glass. "To Bradshaw Creative."

All three drank.

"So..." O'Connor now spoke in a serious tone. "Sam, Hope, you two okay with me steamrolling you for another fifty K?"

Sam and Hope looked at each other for a moment.

"Yeah, sure," Hope said. "I mean it's fifty *freaking* K."

"Sam?" O'Connor focused on him.

"Still don't like the death part, but sure."

"I wasn't about to let the deal go sour," O'Connor said.

Hope looked around the dining room. "Harry caved pretty easily, don't you think?"

"He's either desperate or the real deets, besides the deaths, are more fucked up than he let on."

"Or both," Sam said.

A team of servers followed the waitress with their meals. They presented Hope with a lobster the size of a football. The crustacean's spindly legs were tucked under its body and the massive claws sat facing each other like it was about to go into battle with itself.

"Holy shit." Hope stared at the brick red creature on her plate with wide eyes.

"I thought you didn't like spiders," Sam said.

"I don't."

"Well, lobsters are part of the arachnid family—"

Hope turned to Sam. "You need to shut up and eat your steak."

"Oh yeah." O'Connor started to laugh. "Brings back memories, eh Sam?"

Hope glared at her. "Don't start, *Bertha.*"

"Maybe we should've used lobster shell crackers against those spiders." O'Connor slapped her knee and rolled her head back laughing.

Hope returned her attention to her own plate. "How the hell do I eat this?"

"I'll show you the ropes." Harry had returned and took his seat at the table. "First put on your bib."

"A bib?" O'Connor slipped into hysterics.

Harry raised his brow. "Is she going to be okay?"

"She'll be just *fine*." Hope kicked O'Connor under the table.

"Wrong leg, honey!" O'Connor laughed as tears streamed from her eyes.

Harry gave Hope a quick crash course on eating lobster as Sam and O'Connor dug into their steaks. Considering how the evening began, the meal ended up a success. The crew enjoyed camaraderie and a satisfying feast, necessary requirements before waging war.

HARRY KNOCKED ON Detest-A-Pest's door just past six on Monday morning. He held a bag of pastries and coffee from the cafeteria.

Sam opened the door looking reasonably alert and already dressed in his standard everyday attire: blue jeans, white t-shirt with a flannel work shirt over top.

"Good, you're up." Harry presented the cup holder with four coffees. One of the coffees was in a thermal mug.

"I'm up, but Hope and O'Connor are still out." Sam took the coffees.

"The day's wasting. May I come in?"

Sam stepped aside. Harry entered the suite, set the bag of pastry on the dining table, and folded down the sides. Sam set the coffees down next to the pastries and took a coffee for himself.

"You get some rest last night?" Harry took a bite of an apple turnover.

"Not really." Sam sipped his coffee. "Holding back the death part was a dick move."

"Yeah, sorry about that," Harry said between bites. "Once everyone's up, I'll take you to the maintenance building and introduce you to our resident doctor. She's been working with me on this."

The odor of hot brewed coffee pulled O'Connor and Hope out of sleep. O'Connor sat up and began to attach her prosthetic leg.

Harry noticed and raised his brows. "You're an amputee."

"Good deduction, Captain Obvious."

"How did you lose it, if you don't mind me asking?"

O'Connor worked the neoprene suspension sleeve over her knee and stood. "Of course I mind, but everyone asks. What's one more time? I lost it in Operation Desert Storm, IED took out my convoy. And that's where this conversation ends."

Hope pulled on pants and a t-shirt, then helped herself to a pastry and a coffee. Sam shot a glance at her and smiled. They both knew O'Connor's real story.

"Oh." Harry cleared his throat. "Thank you for your service."

O'Connor paused, caught off guard, then nodded. "Yeah." She walked to the dining table and reached for a danish and the thermal mug of coffee.

"Not that one, if you don't mind," Harry said.

"Why not?" O'Connor's words came out almost like a growl.

"That one's for Doctor Trejo. The others are plenty hot. Right, Sam?"

Sam nodded. "It's good, too."

O'Connor narrowed her eyes at Sam. "Who the hell is this *Doctor Trejo?*"

Sam shrugged and took careful sips of his coffee.

"Let me introduce you." Harry collected the remaining pastries and the thermal mug. "Follow me."

He led O'Connor, Sam, and Hope out through the lobby and down to the maintenance building. "We won't run into Larsen at this hour. He doesn't clock in until at least eight."

Sam rolled the name through his head but came up blank. "Larsen?"

O'Connor tapped Sam's shoulder. "The douche."

"Limp fish," Hope added.

Harry laughed. "That's the one. The only people you see up at this hour are the ones that actually keep this place running."

Daniela sat on a bench outside the maintenance building. When she saw Harry strolling toward her, she stood and smiled, smoothing out her shirt and pants with her hands.

Harry smiled back and raised the thermal mug and bag of pastry. "I got goodies."

"*That's* who gets the thermal mug." O'Connor leaned toward Sam and Hope. "They're fucking."

Daniela took the thermal mug and pulled Harry's face to hers, planting a quick but full kiss on his lips. She let her finger drag a line down his jaw before taking the bag of pastry.

"What'd I tell ya?" O'Connor chortled.

"So what if they are?" Sam said.

"Workplace romances never work."

Sam shook his head. "I prefer to do my own research."

Hope smiled to herself for a moment, noting a few prison tattoos escaping the cuffs of Sam's long sleeve work shirt.

Harry placed his hand on the small of Daniela's back. "Sam, Hope, O'Connor, this is Doctor Trejo."

"The crew from Detest-A-Pest." Daniela presented her hand. "Good to finally meet the legend."

Sam and Hope looked at each other, then at O'Connor.

"Legend? I'll take it." O'Connor shook Daniela's hand.

"Thank God. A firm handshake. What are you a doctor of, exactly?" She worked her cigar stub out of her pocket and back into her mouth. She relit it with a quick flip of her Zippo.

"General practice. I'm charged with maintaining the good health of the staff and guests. You can call me Daniela, by the way."

"We need to fill them in on everything," Harry said. "Let's go to my office."

Daniela stepped next to O'Connor. "A cigar smoker, huh?"

O'Connor eyed her and laughed. "What gave it away? And I know the dangers, but you can tell me again if you want your lifespan shortened too."

Daniela took the hint. "Don't let Larsen see you."

"The douche? Too late for that." O'Connor laughed. "I'd like to see him try and stop me."

They followed the others past the marks etched in the concrete where the creature had attacked Alejandro's foot. The marks led right back into Harry's office.

Harry held up the old cage with a hole dissolved into the side of the metal mesh. "Okay. Full disclosure. You remember the images I sent you? This is the cage I caught it in."

"That's a big cage." Sam scanned the cage with a nervous eye. "And an even bigger hole."

"You could catch a medium sized dog in that," Hope said.

Sam leaned toward O'Connor. "You said these things were no bigger than rats. I remember that photo. The cage was barely big enough to hold one."

"Looks like I was wrong." O'Connor stepped to get a close look at the hole in the side of the cage.

"To be fair, you never asked how big the things were," Harry said. "But yeah, they're big. They stripped the flesh off the entire arm of one of my groundskeepers."

"Are they okay?" Hope asked.

Harry shook his head. "Dead. Bled out."

"Oh." Hope averted her eyes. "I'm sorry."

O'Connor looked over the top of the cage at Harry. "What's with the hole?"

"Getting to that." Harry looked at Daniela. "Want to talk about this part?"

"Sure." Daniela sat on the corner of Harry's desk. "The creatures exude strong acid, like how we sweat when we're nervous. We believe it's a defense mechanism."

Hope glanced at Sam in time to watch his face drain of color. She placed her hand on his shoulder, but he remained rigid and still.

"Not only that," Daniela continued, "their saliva has anticoagulant properties, like a leech. And if you've seen a leech, their mouths are remarkably similar to these things. Rows of concentric teeth."

Hope shook her head in disbelief. "I've never heard of an animal sweating acid before."

"Brings new meaning to 'get off my back,' " said O'Connor. "But I've got the perfect thing for these acidbacks."

"What's that?" Harry asked.

"All in due time." O'Connor nudged Sam. "Ain't that right, Sam?"

Sam didn't respond. Instead he stared at the empty cage, through it.

O'Connor raised a brow at Hope and she answered with a shrug. "Like I said before, this is why you're paying us the big bucks." She puffed on her cigar, jettisoning smoke toward the office ceiling.

"Acidbacks." Daniela smiled. "I like that. The Bahamian acidback."

"I have many talents." O'Connor chuffed. "Let's get to work. You going to give us a tour?"

"Yeah. We'll take two carts." Harry set the cage on the floor next to his desk. "Daniela is quite a speed demon, so if you like it fast, go with her."

Daniela waved Harry off, but her eyes were on Sam. Hope noticed her attention and was surprised to feel a twinge of jealousy.

"Sam?" Daniela stepped into his line of sight to get his attention. "You feeling okay?"

Sam shook his head. Hope sidled up to him looking for an opportunity to assist.

Daniela positioned a chair behind him. "Sit down. Slow and easy."

Hope placed one hand on Sam's arm and one on his back and guided him into the chair. She could feel the scar that her screwdriver had made in his back when she had moved in last summer. It felt like such a long time ago.

Daniela looked at Hope. "Keep doing what you're doing." She took Sam's wrist and measured his pulse. "Are you feeling weak or dizzy, Sam?"

Sam closed his eyes and took in shaky breaths. "Yeah. And my heart feels like it's going to explode."

"Okay. You and Hope are going to stick with me," Daniela said. "You're just having a mild anxiety attack."

"Doesn't feel mild."

"Stay right here. Relax and breath." Daniela motioned at Hope and walked to the doorway of the office. She spoke in hushed tones. "Has Sam ever had an anxiety attack before?"

"He's had an ongoing fear of rats." Hope looked back at Sam with concern. "Last summer he helped rid his apartment building of rats, because it's New York, you know? He had a few attacks back then. But he's been handling it well, desensitizing himself and all that. We thought he had it beat."

"Relapses are common. It would be better if he remained above ground for now."

Hope blinked. "What do you mean above ground?"

"Where did you think the tour was going to be?" Daniela studied Hope's reaction. "These creatures live underground."

O'Connor stepped to the office doorway. "What's the holdup? You ladies comparing academic papers? Let's go."

Hope helped Sam to his feet and walked him out to the cart. Daniela was already behind the wheel. Hope helped Sam into the back bench seat and sat next to him, her arm around his shoulder.

"Don't worry," Daniela said. "I'm not going to speed today."

"Wagons ho!" O'Connor yelled.

The two carts drove down the path to the first fairway, back to the sink hole where acidbacks had consumed Brekken Sinclair in a feeding frenzy.

HARRY AND DANIELA parked their carts just beyond the caution tape surrounding the sink hole and everyone gathered around. Sam's complexion still resembled that of a bloodless corpse as he propped himself up on the open tailgate of the cart.

"I think Sam should sit this one out." Daniela took his wrist and measured his pulse again.

O'Connor crossed her arms. "He's out only if I say he's out."

"He's still exhibiting signs of anxiety-induced panic." Daniela stood her ground. "If you want him to be any use to you in the future, cut him some slack."

"It's okay," Sam said between breaths. "I can do it." Sam stood up on wobbly legs.

"Bullshit. Sit down." Daniela ensured Sam was seated back on the tailgate. "As the official doctor of everyone at this resort, including contractors, I refuse to allow it."

O'Connor leaned toward Hope like she was going to

whisper, but spoke loud enough for Daniela to hear. "Someone's got a massive ego."

"Excuse me?" Daniela had a good six inches on O'Connor, but she seemed taller when they were toe to toe. Squaring off, she said, "If Sam goes down there right now, he's going to come up in a body bag. If you can't see that, then you're an idiot."

A hush fell upon the group as Daniela and O'Connor held their ground for a few tense seconds.

"You might have a point, Doc." O'Connor looked at Hope. "You're up. Let's go."

Hope glanced at the dark opening to the sink hole, then back at O'Connor, hiding her trepidation as best she could.

"This is what I call a live substitution," O'Connor said grinning. "You like my big words?"

"Took you long enough." Hope walked between Daniela and O'Connor, pushing them apart. "Let's do this."

O'Connor raised her brow. "Someone grew a pair."

Harry got onto all fours and pulled one ladder forward. "I'll lower the ladder into the hole, but don't go far."

O'Connor gave him a sideways glance. "What, you're not coming with? I thought you were going to give us a grand tour?"

"Hell no. I've already been down there twice." Harry tilted the ladder up, pivoting it on the bottom rung of the ladder resting on the ground. He lowered it into the hole, with the top supports just long enough to rest on the topside ladder. "Recon only, just to see what you'll be dealing with. You got me?"

"This ain't my first rodeo, chief."

"There's one tunnel leading out," Harry said. "No idea where it goes. It's big but you'd have to crawl if you want to go farther in." A shiver ripped up his back. Both O'Connor and Hope noticed. "I wouldn't recommend it."

O'Connor squatted next to the topside ladder. "Anything else?"

"Light enrages those things—"

"Acidbacks."

"Right. If you have a filter for your light, use it."

O'Connor pulled her phone from her pocket. "What color would you suggest?"

"Use red," Hope said. "Wasps can't see the red spectrum."

"These aren't wasps, honey."

"We don't know *what* they are." Hope locked her eyes on O'Connor. "They might sense body heat too... and if they do, we're fucked."

"Also assume that they can sense ground vibration and sound," Harry said.

Hope nodded. "Good point."

"Turns out the expensive high-tech phone case was a smart choice." O'Connor rotated a plastic filter attached to her phone case over the exterior light. "Red filter engaged. No vibration or sound. Anything else?"

"White light enrages the things because it burns their skin," Harry said. "But with a phone you need to be close to do maximum damage. It's risky."

O'Connor nodded, looked at Hope, and puffed a cloud of smoke into the blue sky. "Ready to dance?"

"Yeah." Hope swallowed hard. "Quick before I lose my nerve."

O'Connor lowered herself down the ladder first, followed by Hope. The cavern was cast in a bluish tinge from the skylit hole above them. O'Connor turned on the light on her phone, the filter converting the light to a deep red and plunging their surroundings into purples.

"Just like back at the apartment last year," O'Connor said. "Remember?"

"Lower your voice. Sound will amplify in the tunnel" Hope whispered. "And I remember. But this is worse." She looked at her feet as they sank into the soft muddy floor. "We're the bait."

O'Connor released a silent cloud of smoke. "Shall we?" she whispered.

They crouched at the opening of the tunnel. O'Connor held up her index finger, then cupped her ear. A gentle rumbling emanated from deep within the tunnel, almost like a heartbeat. And there was something else. Soft squeaks?

O'Connor motioned toward the tunnel and Hope nodded. They dropped to their hands and knees. O'Connor held her phone up with one hand, lighting the tunnel with blood-red light three feet ahead of them, and they crawled in.

HARRY SQUATTED NEXT to the ladder descending into the sink hole. He glanced back to see Daniela standing next to Sam still sitting on the tailgate of the cart. He knew she was just doing her job, making sure Sam was okay, but part of him resented it. He pushed the thought away as best he could and refocused on the sink hole and the cavern below. He prided himself on being a better man than that.

Daniela made a point of giving Sam space. "Is the fresh air doing anything for you?"

"Maybe a bit." Sam took in a couple of deep breaths as if to confirm his words. "I feel like a failure. I thought I had beaten this."

"Phobias are tough to kick." Daniela made a point of not lingering too long on Sam's muscular features under his well-fitting button-up work shirt. "And relapse is common. I know, it's easy for me to say that, but what you're experiencing is completely normal."

Sam shook his head. "Not normal for me. Not anymore. If I can't get a grip on this, right now, I'm useless. I may as well go back to New York."

Daniela stepped to the tailgate and sat next to Sam. She caught a glimpse of Harry watching her and mouthed "He'll be okay."

Harry nodded and returned to monitoring the sink hole.

"How long were you in for?"

Sam looked at her, surprised. "How did you know? Was it the tattoos?"

"I've been monitoring your pulse pretty regularly over the past hour," Daniela said. "The watch with no hands inked around your wrist was hard to miss."

Sam grabbed the wrist in question and rubbed it like he was trying to remove the offending tattoo from his skin. He sighed. "Fifteen years. Drunk driving causing death. Now I'm a free man, but not exactly free." He tapped his temple.

Daniela hopped off the tailgate. "I'd be worried about anyone who's *not* scared of those things."

A yell rose out of the sink hole. Harry fell backward but regained his balance and leaned out over the opening.

Daniela ran to join him, falling to her hands and knees halfway there to lower her center of gravity. She looked back expecting to find Sam back on the cart's tailgate, but he was right behind her.

"You don't have to do this," she said.

"I'll never get over it if I don't face it." Sam smiled. "A little bit at a time."

Daniela nodded and took a position next to Harry. "What's going on?"

"Look."

O'Connor's light, no longer red, flashed around wildly within the cavern. And Hope was on her way up the ladder.

THE TUNNEL DESCENDED and about twenty feet in the walls opened up to another larger cavern. The sounds O'Connor and Hope had heard before, the thumping and squeaks, increased in volume.

The red filtered light on O'Connor's phone gave them no clues except for a general sense of motion beyond the light's reach. Hope and O'Connor may as well have been blindfolded.

Hope leaned to O'Connor's ear and whispered, "What now? I can't see anything."

"Photo op?" O'Connor whispered back.

Hope could barely make out O'Connor's grin. "That's crazy. They'd be after us in seconds."

"Maybe they move slowly."

"They've got eight legs," Hope said. "I'm not taking that bet."

"You head back. I'll give you a sixty second head start."

"You're crazy."

O'Connor smiled as tendrils of red smoke floated from her mouth. "I love you too, honey."

"Why am I even here?" As Hope turned around O'Connor grabbed her arm.

"You got guts, you're smart, and you're faster than me. That's why. But don't tell anyone I said that, or I'll have to kill you." O'Connor eyed her. "Make sure that ladder's ready."

Hope paused and sniffed the air. "You smell that?"

"Forget smell. Can you *feel* that?" O'Connor swung the phone's red light in front of her. "It's like—"

Hope looked over her shoulder at O'Connor. "Something's breathing on us."

O'Connor began to turn when an acidback appeared from the darkness, its circular maw expanding and contracting, the teeth moving independently like sharp fingers. She looked at Hope. "Move your ass. *Now.*"

Hope crawled forward, faster now that she could see the dim

light in the exit cavern ahead. She looked back once and could see nothing, not even the treads of O'Connor's boots.

As Hope reached the cavern, a flash lit up the tunnel from behind, bright and white, casting her shadow on the wall ahead. A second burst of light flooded the tunnel for a less than a second and went dark again.

"O'Connor!" Hope squatted at the entrance to the tunnel, facing a void of black.

The light illuminated the tunnel a third time, but instead maintained its brilliance. What Hope saw turned her guts to water. She screamed.

O'Connor's silhouette shuffled backward on her backside several inches at time. She held her phone in front of her, broadcasting a bright white light that kept an acidback at a safe distance but close enough to see its gaping undulating gullet lined with teeth.

"Move. Your. Ass!" O'Connor's voice hissed from within the tunnel.

Hope turned to the ladder and saw Harry and Daniela peering in from the sink hole opening.

"What's going on? We heard a scream," Harry said.

"That was me. I'm coming up." She grabbed a rung and took a first step, then stopped.

"What's wrong?" Harry looked down at Hope, concerned.

Sam's face appeared at the sink hole's opening. He locked gazes with Hope and nodded. "Go."

Hope stepped off the ladder and dug her phone out of her pocket. She turned on the flashlight and positioned herself at the tunnel.

O'Connor was halfway through, making good progress, but the acidback was following just as quickly. "That better not be you, Hope, my dear."

"Sorry," Hope called back. "Hate to disappoint."

"You don't listen too well."

"I've got a good teacher."

O'Connor continued moving, now five feet from the cavern. "Promise me you'll be on that ladder before I get out."

Hope didn't answer.

O'Connor backed out of the tunnel to find Hope standing by the tunnel's entrance. "God damn it, you stubborn bitch."

Hope shrugged. "Take my phone. Twice the light, twice the fun."

O'Connor eyed her and smiled. "Thanks. Now MOVE YOUR ASS."

Hope stepped onto the first rung and pulled herself up the ladder with rapid steps. Sam helped her over the top.

"What about O'Connor?" Harry alternated a panicked glance between Sam and the floor of the cavern.

"She'll be fine," Hope said between breaths. "Watch."

O'Connor reversed out of the tunnel holding both phones in one hand at arm's length. She stood and backed up toward the ladder, the acidback a safe distance away. But every step back for O'Connor meant fewer options for escape.

She caught her heel on a root and fell backward between the ladder and the cavern wall. She braced her fall with her hands, momentarily taking the light off the acidback.

The creature charged forward. O'Connor raised the phones, but the lights were caked with mud, obscuring their beams of light.

"Fuck you." She blew a dense cloud of cigar smoke at the acidback, stopping it long enough for her to clear the mud from one phone's light. The creature reversed and tried to climb over the bottom rung of the ladder, its body scraping the ladder supports and the next rung above as well.

A tight fit, the acidback made it through, flopping onto the muddy cavern floor, its eight stubby legs and razor sharp claws working the dirt. The ladder began to fizzle where it had come in contact with the creature's skin.

O'Connor pocketed one phone and stepped onto the first rung of the ladder. Weakened from the acid, the rung buckled under her weight. She brought her foot up again and the second rung gave way as well.

She took an extended drag from her cigar and blew the smoke at the acidback. It recoiled and gave O'Connor the time she needed. Pocketing the second phone, she launched herself up, grabbing an upper rung.

The ladder's side supports collapsed at the base where acid had eaten them away, and the whole structure fell vertically. With nothing to anchor the ladder at the top, it began to fall to one side.

"FUCK! Sam!" O'Connor looked up to find Sam was already there. He held the top rung in his hands.

"Climb, you silly bitch." Sam grit his teeth, his arms straining under her weight. The earth where he lay crumbled under his armpits. "CLIMB!"

O'Connor pulled herself up and positioned her good foot onto an undamaged rung. The acidback snapped at her feet from below. Soon after, a second and third acidback entered the cavern, all attempting to bite O'Connor's feet. Their circular mouths flexed open and closed, casting globs of saliva like a demonic fish out of water.

Harry and Daniela helped O'Connor out of the sink hole and onto the fairway. She rolled onto her back, breathing hard.

Sam hoisted the remains of the ladder out of the hole and rolled next to O'Connor. "You got a death wish, you know that?"

"A death wish for acidbacks." O'Connor took a long drag from her perpetual cigar and released a cloud into the morning breeze. She pulled Hope's phone out of her pocket, caked with mud, and tossed it to her. "Sorry about the dirt."

Hope rubbed the phone on the grass, cleaning most of the clumps of mud off the display. "Still works. So what's next?"

O'Connor propped herself up on her elbows. Her clothing

was covered in mud, caked to her back, the seat of her pants, and the heels of her work boots. "First on the list is a kick-ass breakfast. None of that pastry shit. I want heavy fuel."

"You got it," Harry said. "All you can eat. What about a change of clothes?"

"I have nothing to change *into*, bucko... unless you don't mind me going starkers." O'Connor threw her head back and laughed.

Harry grinned at Daniela. "I'll arrange for your clothes to be cleaned. And for... *heavy fuel* sent to your room."

Daniela stood and helped the others to their feet. "What was it like to be face to face with those things?"

"I can show you," O'Connor said. "A picture's worth a thousand words." She held up her phone and grinned. "Acidbacks are going to go viral. Come on."

Harry and Daniela drove the Detest-A-Pest crew back to their suite to regroup and recharge.

INNARDS

With everyone back at the Detest-A-Pest suite, O'Connor insisted on being the first to shower. "I'm the dirtiest bitch here," she laughed before disappearing into the bathroom.

"Hold on, O'Connor." Harry rapped the bathroom door, three plush terrycloth bathrobes tucked under his arm. "Let Sam and Hope change out of their clothes first."

Sam watched O'Connor crack open the bathroom door. He couldn't hold back his smile. "You still get to shower first. Promise."

One at a time, Sam and Hope changed into their bathrobes. O'Connor returned to the bathroom, grabbing the remaining robe from Harry on her way by. Moments later she kicked out all their soiled clothes in a big wet ball. "Watch out for the skid marks." Raucous laughter rose from behind the bathroom door.

Harry chuckled to himself. O'Connor's laugh was infectious. He collected all the soiled clothes, dumped them into a wheeled linen hamper, and rolled it to the door.

Daniela stopped him. "You're a good man, Harry." She took his face in her hands and kissed him.

"Thanks." Harry smiled. "Your clothes have seen better days. Can I take them too?" He flashed his eyebrows.

"Later." Daniela grinned at him.

"Be back soon with your grub, folks," Harry called back before disappearing down the hallway.

Hope caught their interaction. She glanced at Sam and smiled to herself. "I don't like the room, but I'm not taking *this* off." Hope sat on the bed with her back against the headboard and stretched out her bare legs. The robe was a little too big for her and she looked like she was floating in it.

"You should take one home with you," Daniela said.

"Maybe I will." Hope wrapped her arms around her body like she was hugging herself. "What do you think, Sam?"

Sam stood in a corner of the room looking out the sliding glass door, a towel wrapped around his waist underneath the bathrobe. He had stuck his hands and arms into the opposite openings of his sleeves, successfully concealing almost all his tattoos. "Feels good."

Hope turned to Daniela. "What kind of acid do those things excrete? It practically melted that ladder."

"I can't be a hundred percent sure, but I'd guess hydrochloric or even sulphuric," Daniela said. "Don't even ask me about the physiology."

"I've been thinking. From my studies of rats, I know that naked molerats have a buildup of acid in their body tissues." Hope sat up and crossed her legs under her robe. "Living in high levels of carbon dioxide increases acidosis in their bodies. But it's not a strong acid. Nowhere close to hydrochloric or sulphuric. And it stays in their system."

"It certainly is stranger than fiction," Daniela said.

"Molerats have tails, right?" Sam's voice echoed from the corner of the suite like a ghost.

Hope nodded. "Yes."

Sam looked back at her. "Do they have eight legs?"

"Of course not," Hope said.

"If I hadn't seen it myself, I'd say it was made up." Sam returned his stare to the sliding glass door.

The bathroom door cracked open and released a cloud of steam into the room.

"Everything about this place is bad," Sam said.

"Not everything." O'Connor stepped out wearing a bathrobe, the bottom hem collecting on the floor. "Jesus Christ, I feel like a million bucks." She looked out into the room and sniffed. "Where's my breakfast?"

"Soon," Daniela said.

"Better be." O'Connor hobbled to the bed. "Hope, your turn. Go get hot and wet. The fucktards here don't know how to decorate but boy, they can do a shower."

Hope swung her legs off the bed and padded to the bathroom. Sam watched her legs go. She slipped her robe off her shoulders and looked back to find Sam watching her. She batted her eyelashes.

Sam smiled and averted his eyes for a second, then looked back. Heat rose on his cheeks as he watched Hope turn in the doorway, clutching her robe together in front of her chest. She pushed the door closed with her bare foot.

Both Daniela and O'Connor looked at Sam, his cheeks now beet red.

"Someone's crushing on you, Sam." Daniela walked to the couch near the sliding doors.

O'Connor tapped Sam on the shoulder. "If you like her, you should go after her."

Sam shook his head. "She's too young."

"Bah." O'Connor waved him off. "She's just what you need." She looked around the suite. "And I need food."

Fifteen minutes later Harry returned with a feast on a multi-tiered rolling food cart: scrambled eggs, bacon and sausage, toast and waffles, fruit salad, plus juice and coffee. "Good news and bad news, folks. The good news…" He presented the food with a flourish. "Food has arrived."

O'Connor made a beeline for the bacon and eggs and began filling a plate. "What's the bad news?"

"It's going to take a bit longer to get your clothes back," Harry said. "I figure by the time everyone's finished eating. So dig in."

Everyone filled their plates and found a comfortable place to sit and eat.

"My compliments to the chef," Sam said between bites.

Harry sipped his coffee. "I'll pass that on to Greta. She runs the cafeteria and loves meeting new people. She'd like you, Sam."

Daniela raised her eyebrows, almost choking on a bite of food. "*Meeting*? Perhaps in the abstract sense."

"So how about I start our featured presentation?" O'Connor had set her plate down and now stood beside the wide screen television. She held up her phone and wiggled it in her hand. "Anyone want to see what we're up against?"

Hope looked at her plate. Partially eaten bacon, two sausage links, and eggs with ketchup stared back at her. She swallowed hard. "Do we have to watch it now?"

"No time like the present," O'Connor said. "Who's with me?"

Everyone exchanged glances, said nothing, and continued eating.

"It's unanimous." O'Connor cackled. "I'll set it up." She went to her suitcase and dug out a specialized connector cable. She returned to the television, examining the back.

Hope looked at Sam, shrugged, and mouthed the word "sorry."

Sam sat down next to her on the edge of the bed. "No worries. She was going to play it no matter what we said. O'Connor's a force of nature." He speared a piece of sausage with his fork, juices spraying out of the side, and took a bite. "Desensitization, right?"

"You're damn right, Sam." O'Connor winked at him from across the room. "About the force of nature bit." She made the last connection and turned on the television. The big screen mirrored her phone's display.

Harry and Daniela moved closer and sat on the couch. "Did you get photos? Or video?"

"Both." O'Connor flashed her abundant grey eyebrows. "I started recording when an acidback got a little too close for comfort. I got the sense that they could either pick up our body heat, or smell us, or both. We could sure smell them, right Hope?"

Hope grimaced and pushed her plate of food aside. "Thanks for reminding me."

O'Connor started the video. The shot showed O'Connor pushing herself backward with her feet, swearing as she went. The light on her camera kept the acidback at a safe distance while providing enough visual detail.

"Holy shit," Harry said. "Look at that thing."

Everyone was looking except Daniela, who looked at Sam instead. "How you holding up?"

Sam nodded. "Actually, not too bad. That thing is goddamned ugly but I'm surviving."

"If you begin to feel overwhelmed, look away. I think it's safe to say that your team needs you at a hundred percent."

Sam grinned. "I'll never be a hundred percent."

On the screen O'Connor had just scolded Hope for not leaving the cavern. She paid O'Connor back by handing her a second phone, flashlight blazing.

"Such an ungrateful bitch," Hope said smiling.

"You're lucky I said thanks."

Daniela stood and walked closer to the television. "Back it up. I want a good look at the teeth."

O'Connor scrubbed back and settled on a frame with clear detail. The outer ring of teeth were stained red and pointed in random directions. In the center lay what could only be the acidback's throat. The opening looked like a festering sore. Sam shivered.

Daniela tapped each tooth with her finger. "There's twenty-two teeth on the outside and they appear to be independently articulated." She traced the gumline on the screen. "The next ring of teeth don't, or can't, move as much."

"If you think that's interesting, just wait." O'Connor closed the video and pulled up an image. "This was taken a second or two earlier. See anything strange?"

The image showed the same acidback a little further away, its stubby legs and claws propelling itself across the dirt floor.

Sam pointed. "Is there something in the top left corner?"

"Bonus points for Sam. This is an HDR image so let me boost the levels."

Harry furrowed his brow in confusion. "HDR?"

"High dynamic range images. Gotta keep up with the tech, Harry." O'Connor winked as she fiddled with the image controls, raising the exposure. The acidback in the foreground brightened until its detail faded out. But the dark background revealed more detail, more acidbacks.

O'Connor pointed to one part of the image. A long distended and stretched acidback lay on a shelf of dirt with multiple nubs protruding from its side.

"Oh my god. Are those…" Hope's eyes widened as she locked gaze with O'Connor. "Baby acidbacks?"

"Yeah."

Daniela tilted her head and took a few steps back. "It looks like they're nursing, a dozen of them."

Harry closed his eyes and rubbed his temples. "Jesus. There could be hundreds in there."

"Maybe thousands," Hope said.

"With a tunnel system to match." O'Connor's eyes gleamed with excitement. "Have you spotted any other openings on the course?"

"Actually, yeah," Harry said. "The third hole. That's where one of my groundskeepers died. But it's not underground."

"As much as I love crawling in the dirt in pitch black, I love being above ground more."

Daniela looked at Harry, then at O'Connor. "We need to catch another one of those things. And this time it can't get away."

"So we can figure out the best way to kill them." O'Connor raised a sausage link to her mouth like an edible cigar and bit into it. She flashed her eyebrows as fat and juices dribbled down her chin. "Detest-A-Pest has just the answer."

HARRY DELIVERED CLEAN clothes to O'Connor, Sam, and Hope shortly after breakfast. "We'll regroup down at the maintenance shed in ten minutes."

O'Connor had pulled a new cigar from her suitcase and held it under her nose, inhaling its unlit aroma. "Don't think I can wait ten minutes to light this baby up."

Harry held up an open hand. "Just not inside, okay. Otherwise it's my ass."

O'Connor nodded as Harry left the suite. "Move it, Missy. We got acidbacks to catch and a cigar with my name on it."

"Be right out," Hope said from inside the bathroom.

Sam pulled on jeans over his boxers, his chiseled muscles working the fabric up to his hips.

"Jesus, Sam. I always forget about your wicked tats." O'Connor grinned and let her eyes roam over his body, taking in the mixture of profanity and artistry. "You should just skip the shirt."

Sam grabbed his white t-shirt and pulled it over his head. "Very funny." He layered his flannel button-up work shirt over top.

"No, seriously. You'd get fucked faster than a rat in heat."

"Give it a rest, O'Connor."

"Give what a rest?" Hope stood in the doorway of the bathroom dressed and ready for action.

"Never mind." Sam walked past O'Connor, glaring at her. "Let's go."

The three met up with Harry and Daniela at the maintenance building's garage door. All Detest-A-Pest's equipment had been unloaded and lined up against the wall.

"What the hell is a... Kill-O-Matic?" Harry hooked a thumb back at the metal box.

O'Connor chuckled, her whole body shaking. "All in due time. But now, let me present you with the cage to end all portable cages." From a nearby storage container she pulled out a cage that looked like the one Harry had used.

He shrugged. "So what makes this one better?"

"It's one of Washington's creations, God rest his soul." O'Connor swallowed hard. "All the metal bars have been coated with porcelain making them resistant to heat, acid... everything."

Harry raised a brow. "I can see how that would be helpful."

"Who's Washington?" Daniela asked.

Sam leaned closer to Daniela and lowered his voice. "He was a genius inventor and O'Connor's right-hand man. He died last summer."

"I'm sorry."

"O'Connor pretends that she's over his death, but it's pretty clear that she's not." Sam straightened up. "I'd recommend not asking about it again."

Daniela nodded in understanding.

"About the two people that died..." O'Connor bit both ends of her cigar and lit one end, rotating it under her Zippo until a decent cherry ember glowed at the tip. "Did they bite it in that pit of hell I was just in?"

"I? Don't you mean *we*?" Hope crossed her arms against her chest. "I *saved* your ass."

"What? Yeah, yeah." O'Connor waved her off. "To be honest, I wouldn't be disappointed if I didn't have to go in that death trap again."

"The first person to *bite it* as you put it was on the third hole, just off the side of a sand trap," Harry said. "Logan was his name. A good guy, about to propose to his girlfriend."

"He was our version of your Washington." Daniela and Sam shared a brief glance.

"Right." O'Connor offered a nod. She drew in a puff of cigar smoke and released it in a thick cloud around her head. "Take me to the third hole." She placed the porcelain cage into the back of one of the carts. "But first we're going to need bait."

"We should use what we used last time," Daniela said.

O'Connor raised an eyebrow. "And that would be what exactly?"

"Raw steak," Harry said. "The bloodier the better."

"Strunk steaks are always bloody..." Daniela added. "Bloody expensive."

Everyone laughed.

"I've had better steak at an Outback Restaurant." O'Connor's stomach growled. "Hear that? Let's move."

"I'll get the bait." Harry hopped into one of the carts. "I'll meet you at the third hole."

Daniela stepped into another cart. "Everyone else, hop in."

"I call shotgun." O'Connor chortled as she pulled herself into the passenger seat beside Daniela. "You lovebirds can sit in back."

Sam rolled his eyes as he pulled himself onto the cart. His

neck flushed in a gentle red, almost too subtle to notice except for Hope. She smiled to herself and sat next to Sam.

The two carts diverged from the maintenance building's garage, each on their separate path.

Harry floored the accelerator of his cart back toward the cafeteria. His job securing the bait from Greta would be easy, but no one could have predicted the horror that would come next.

THERE WAS A trio of golfers finishing up on the third hole when Daniela and the Detest-A-Pest crew arrived.

O'Connor jumped out, smoke following her like a steam engine. "Okay, chuckleheads. Move your asses." She waved her arms at them. "Professional exterminators at work."

"Carry on, gentlemen." Daniela grabbed O'Connor by the arm and spun her around. "Don't forget where you are. Anyone here could destroy your life with one phone call. The amount you're being paid for your *work* here is how much they pay each year just to set foot at this place."

O'Connor pulled her arm out of Daniela's hand and blew smoke in her face. "They're getting ripped off, then."

Sam stepped between the two women. "Rein it back a bit, O'Connor." He looked to make sure the golfers had moved on to the next hole. "Not everyone is used to your larger than life personality."

"O'Connor!" Hope stood next to the bunker marked with caution tape. "You got to see this."

O'Connor trudged off toward Hope.

Sam watched O'Connor go. "Operation 'Diffused and Distracted' successfully accomplished."

Daniela raised a brow and looked at Sam. "You and Hope set that up?"

Sam grinned. "Too obvious?"

"It seemed to have worked didn't it?" Daniela offered a small wave at Hope and she waved back. "You and Hope make a good team."

Sam narrowed his eyes at her. "Let's go see what's so important."

"Wait. Harry's back." Daniela pointed at his approach. Harry pulled up his cart beside the putting green and hustled toward Daniela and Sam. He clutched a brown paper-wrapped package in one hand and waved at them with the other. "I got the goods."

"Did Greta finally get *your* goods?"

"Ha. You're funny. Although Greta says I have to put out next time." Harry tossed the package to her.

Daniela caught it with ease. "Why are you giving it to me?"

"Thought you might want to unwrap my package and examine my meat."

"Jesus." Sam shook his head. "You guys are worse than O'Connor. Come on."

The three of them approached the bunker where Hope and O'Connor stood. The caution tape rippled in the warm breeze coming off the ocean. Black plastic had been staked down in front of the hole in the side of the bank and the sand at the base was stained reddish brown. Sections of the plastic appeared melted.

"Is that blood?" Sam asked.

"Looks like it." O'Connor crouched to pull the plastic away.

"Careful." Hope exchanged glances with O'Connor.

"Or what?" Smoke leaked out of O'Connor's sly grin.

"You know they like blood already," Harry said. "Thought that'd be a big clue."

Daniela looked at the package of meat in her hands. Bloody juice dripped from a corner into the sand at her feet. "Harry?"

She tossed the package back at him. "No offense but I don't want it anymore."

Harry caught the package. "I'm crushed."

"You two need to get a room," Sam said.

"And I need to unwrap *this* mysterious gift." O'Connor pinched the side of the black plastic and pulled it up.

A circle of teeth centered around her fingers, punctured the plastic, and yanked the black covering back into the hole. O'Connor pulled her hand back just in time, lost her balance, and fell backward into the slope of the bunker.

Hope tried to break her fall but wasn't quick enough. She offered her hand instead.

O'Connor took Hope's hand and pulled herself up. "Thanks. That was close huh?" She brushed herself off in time to see the color drain from Sam's face.

"Holy shit," Harry said.

"What?" O'Connor returned her gaze to the now uncovered hole in the bank of the bunker. Pieces of torn flesh and bloodied bones lay scattered around the entrance.

Half covered by the black plastic sat an acidback, its ring of articulated maroon-tinged teeth flexing inward and outward. Clear fluid dripped from its pulsating gape.

"Jesus Christ." O'Connor took in the carnage. "Looks like a cannibal's back yard."

"I'd move very slowly if I were you. They're getting bolder." Daniela noted the sun's position in the sky. "This side of the bunker is in shade most of the day."

Harry scanned the ground surrounding them. "Where's that cage of yours?"

"Shit," O'Connor said. "It's back at the—"

Hope appeared at the berm of the bunker with the porcelain cage in one hand and a putter in the other. "Need this?"

O'Connor broke into a wide smile, cigar smoke drifting from the corners of her mouth. "You read my mind, Hope, darlin'."

"It's not that difficult," Hope said.

Harry backed away from the hole in the bunker in slow steps and met Hope at the side of the bunker. He unwrapped the meat and placed it within the porcelain cage. "Bloody enough for you?"

A shiver ran up Hope's back. "I think I'm going to become a vegetarian after this."

Harry took the cage with its sodden bait and the putter and presented them to O'Connor. "I figured you'd want to do the honors."

"And you'd be right." O'Connor armed the cage's locking mechanism, hooked the putter's end into the cage's handle, and lowered the cage toward the hole.

O'Connor struggled with the weight of the cage at the end of the putter. She couldn't hold the cage steady enough to place the cage at the hole's entrance.

"Here," Sam said. "Let me try."

O'Connor backed up, her eyes flickering toward argument mode, but relented. "Are you sure? I know your arms are like pythons but it's the lack of muscles between your ears that I'm worried about."

Everyone shared concerned glances. The acidback sat just inside the hole's entrance as if it was taunting everyone.

"Those muscles between my ears need some exercise." Sam stood firm and beckoned. "Let me try."

"Okay." O'Connor handed the cage and the putter to Sam.

"You got this." Hope gave Sam a thumb's up.

He nodded in acknowledgment and re-hooked the putter into the cage's handle. Sam raised the cage up, his arm muscles tensing in hard lines under his shirt.

Sam held the putter with the cage hanging from it directly in front of his body. He had about four feet between safety and a fate he cared not to imagine.

As he drew near to the hole Sam bent his knees and lowered

the cage, but even with Sam's strength it was difficult to keep the cage steady. He tried to gauge the timing of the cage's swing... one, two, three.

Now!

He lowered the cage almost exactly at the hole's entrance, but it landed too hard and tripped the spring-loaded door, closing the cage.

Before anyone could react, the acidback shot forth and latched its ring of teeth around the porcelain mesh of the cage. Its body pulsed as if it was trying to absorb the bait through the mesh.

"Shit!" Sam dropped the putter and stepped back to regroup. "I screwed that up. Now what?"

"Only one thing to do," O'Connor said. "Get the cage and try again."

Sam scanned the rest of the group. Even without words he was met with the same answer.

"Get the cage." Sam took a deep breath and steadied himself. "Wait. I got to get that thing off the cage first. Any ideas?"

Hope piped up immediately. "Flashlight mode. Everyone activate their phone's light. We'll slowly advance, two to a side, and force that thing back inside. Sam can reset the trap and set it back down again."

"Look at the big brain on Hope," O'Connor said.

Hope shrugged. "I just remembered the tunnel on the first hole. We should have done this from the beginning."

"Have to say you're growing on me, kid."

"Like a fungus." Hope and O'Connor spoke in unison.

"You owe me a beer." O'Connor flashed a toothy grin still clamped to a cigar.

Hope stared back at O'Connor, dead serious. "Ready?"

O'Connor nodded and turned on her phone light. The others had their lights on already.

"Everyone move forward together at the same speed so that

fucker has nowhere to go except back into the hole." Hope glanced at Sam. "You ready?"

Sam gave her a thumbs up.

"Let's do this," Hope said.

Harry, Daniela, Hope and O'Connor moved toward the acidback, adjusting the aim of their lights as they went.

"Watch for acid, Sam," Harry said. "I burned my fingers a few days ago and they still hurt."

"Thanks." Sam nodded in appreciation.

As the four lights closed in, the acidback began to writhe in violent spasms, its teeth still clutching the cage mesh.

"It must really like Strunk steak," Daniela said.

Harry chuckled. "There's no accounting for taste."

The acidback flipped wildly back and forth until it dislodged itself. It scurried backward into the hole just as fast as it had moved forward earlier.

Sam looked at the cage, then the putter. "Fuck it." He clutched the back end of the cage where the bait sat and scrambled up the berm of the bunker to the grass.

O'Connor craned her neck. "I can't see. What the hell is he doing? Sam?"

Harry looked over his shoulder where he saw Sam rubbing the front of the cage on the grass. "He's wiping off the acid. Good plan."

Sam tilted the cage upright and sent the bait back to the rear of the cage, past the trip plate. He engaged the spring loaded door and jumped back into the bunker.

"Locked and loaded." Sam set the cage at the entrance of the hole. "Cage set."

Harry, Daniela, Hope, and O'Connor took several steps back and turned off their lights.

Like a switch, the acidback reversed direction again and propelled itself into the cage, striking the trip plate and causing the door to close. But the acidback hadn't gone far enough into the cage and most of its hairless white tail hung out of the cage's opening.

"Goddamn it!" Hope said. "It's reversing again."

Harry picked up the putter and used the end to push down on the door, locking the cage and trapping the creature inside. To his horror, the force severed the rest of the acidback's tail from its body. A small rivulet of dark, almost black blood trickled from the wound.

Everyone stared as the fleshy veined creature devoured the meat, then began a fruitless attempt at escape. The sudden loss of most of its tail had no effect.

"Did it even feel that?" Daniela watched the acidback bite the back of the cage repeatedly. There was no room for the creature to turn itself around and instead used its many claws to rotate its body lengthwise inside the cage like a demented corkscrew.

Harry shrugged. "Looks like it just wants out."

"We got you now, motherfucker." O'Connor laughed. "I'm going to call it Stubby McSausage."

"Ugh," said Hope. "Going vegetarian is definitely in my future now."

"Let's get it back to the maintenance building." Harry hooked the putter around the cage's handle and carried it back to his maintenance cart. "We need to cover it. I don't want any guests seeing this thing."

"We also don't want it to burn to death from sunlight on the way," Daniela said.

Everyone looked at each other for ideas.

"You got your wish, O'Connor." Sam unbuttoned his flannel shirt and revealed his muscular arms decorated with prison tattoos. "All I ask is you keep your questions to yourself." He tossed the shirt to Harry and hopped into the back of Daniela's maintenance cart. Hope and O'Connor followed, whispering to each other and giggling.

"Let's see what makes these things tick." Daniela turned on

the cart's power and floored the accelerator. The cart's small rubber tires gripped the pavement and shot them back down the path toward the maintenance building.

Harry followed at a cautious speed considering the volatile cargo squirming and screeching in the back.

Soon they'd have more questions than answers.

EVERYONE REGROUPED AT the maintenance building. The porcelain cage had stood up well against the caustic excretions from the acidback's skin during the short trip back. The back of Harry's cart told a different story.

The cage had left a melted imprint in the plastic lining the back of Harry's cart and Sam's flannel shirt showed ragged holes and blackened patches.

"Sorry Sam." Harry put on a pair of industrial rubber gloves and lifted Sam's shirt off the cage. "Your shirt's toast. I'll replace it."

"I'll be fine." Sam rubbed his arms. "The flannel made me sweat. I feel cooler already."

"Got the time?" O'Connor jettisoned a plume of cigar smoke and motioned at the tattoo of a watch encircling his left wrist.

"I said no questions, remember?"

"I wasn't asking about your tattoo," O'Connor said. "Just wanted to know the time."

Sam pushed O'Connor against the wall with his index finger. "We all got phones so don't try and bullshit me."

"No. You got it all wrong. I—"

Hope offered a consoling glance at Sam, pulled O'Connor aside, and lowered her voice to a whisper. "You need to shut your mouth."

"Excuse me?" O'Connor straightened up into a defensive posture. "Just as I was taking a shine on you, you do this—"

"Look." Hope peered over her shoulder to make sure she was out of earshot. She grabbed O'Connor's shirt and pulled her close. "Did you happen to notice the lack of hands on that watch tattoo?"

"Now that you mention it, yeah. That's—"

"God you're so stupid sometimes. It means a long prison sentence. Same with the spider webs on his elbows." Hope held O'Connor's gaze. "Leave it alone. He doesn't need any reminders." She released O'Connor's shirt and pushed her back.

O'Connor stood expressionless, glanced at Sam, then back at Hope. She blew a thin stream of cigar smoke from the corner of her expanding grin. "You really like him, don't you?"

"Oh, for pete's sake." Hope let out an exasperated sigh and rejoined the rest of the group on the opposite side of the garage.

"Who made *you* an expert on prison tattoos?" O'Connor said to herself. Sam looked back at her and rubbed his wrist with his right hand. It was clear they both regretted their words.

"O'Connor." Sam beckoned her over. "You're missing deets."

O'Connor straightened her shirt and rejoined the group. "What deets?"

Harry had hooked the cage's handle to a chain and a snatch block suspended from the ceiling. He raised the cage to a comfortable viewing level.

"Something we missed from your video." Daniela stepped closer to the rear of the cage but far enough away to avoid acid splatter from the struggling acidback inside. She picked up the putter and oriented the cage, pointing at the acidback's razor sharp teeth. "It's got two pairs of incisors, top and bottom, similar to a—"

"A rat." Hope looked at Sam and O'Connor.

"Ugliest fucking rat I've ever seen," O'Connor said. "I want to poke it with a stick until it pops."

Everyone stared at O'Connor in silence, with the acidback's sounds of distress in the background. It was as if the creature understood what she had said.

"What?" O'Connor alternated her eyes between the rest of the group and blew a cloud of smoke out the side of her mouth. "I'm an exterminator. I exterminate."

"Let's try and figure out a bit more about this thing before we kill it," Daniela said. "It might help us later."

O'Connor shrugged. "Yeah, maybe."

"Its claws look as sharp as its teeth." Sam stood the farthest away from the acidback in the cage.

"Yeah, and with eight legs, four claws on each..." Hope trailed off.

"That's a lot of claws," Sam said.

"It appears to have amazing healing properties." Daniela spun the cage slowly and pointed to the stub of where the acidback's tail had been cut off minutes earlier. It had already healed itself.

"No eyes," Harry said. "That's what freaks the crap out of me. How does it know where it is or where it needs to go?"

"Probably smell." Daniela nudged the cage in the opposite direction. "The tunnels are probably laced with pheromones."

"That's why they avoid cigar smoke," O'Connor said.

Daniela nodded. "Makes sense."

"If you ignore the freaky-ass mouth and the eight legs, the thing reminds me of a naked molerat. Listen to this." Hope read off her phone. "Molerats are the only mammals to be eusocial. In other words, one queen produces offspring by mating with up to three breeding males, and the rest become workers, finding food, caring for pups, and guarding the nest from attack. It's a lot like how ants and some bees live."

"It's good to be the queen." O'Connor placed her hands on her knees and crouched closer to the acidback. "This sorry son of a bitch must be a worker."

"Most can live over thirty years," Hope said. "And they can survive without oxygen for up to eighteen minutes."

"I'll assume they produce offspring like crazy." Harry tightened his grip on the chain. "That means there could be thousands of those things underneath us. Maybe millions."

"Not millions." Hope consulted her phone again. "Queens live for eighteen years max and produce an average litter of eleven pups every seventy days. Since only the queen produces pups..." She cast her eyes to the sky and her tongue stuck out a bit as she calculated in her head. "Definitely thousands."

Harry swallowed hard. "Great."

"But this is a mutation of some kind," Hope said. "There's no telling how many there are or how many miles of tunnels run underneath our feet, maybe even under the resort too."

O'Connor looked at Harry. "Any other *accidents* you're not telling us about? And you better not lie."

Harry shook his head. "No. Not since the last three. I swear."

O'Connor straightened up. "I know what our first test is going to be." She disappeared into the garage and returned with a plastic trash bin, emptying the contents on the floor. "Let's drown the sucker."

"Drown?" Daniela looked at O'Connor with concern.

Harry looked at the mess from the trash bin and glanced at Sam and Hope. "She always such a slob?"

"Yeah." Sam chuckled. "You should see her office."

O'Connor nudged Harry. "Where's the water?"

Harry led O'Connor to the water hose connected to the side of the building. She uncoiled a section of hose and dragged it and the trash bin next to the hanging cage.

"You're seriously going to do this?"

O'Connor crossed her arms and faced Daniela. "I was hired to do a job and I'm going to do it. Consider this research."

Daniela looked at Harry for support, but he offered nothing but a shrug instead.

"You've seen what these things can do," he said. "Larsen is going to fire my ass if they're not gone soon. So I'm on board with extermination by whatever means possible."

O'Connor placed the hose in the trash bin and turned on the water.

"Drowning seems so inhumane."

O'Connor snickered. "Trust me, Doc. Detest-A-Pest has far more effective ways to kill these things than water."

"Then why do it?"

O'Connor paused for a moment to think. "Call it professional curiosity. I need to know all the options."

"Sure it isn't because you're a psychopath?"

"Thanks for the compliment." O'Connor winked at Daniela, turned off the water, and pulled the hose out. "Harry? Lower the sucker in."

"I'm going to sit this one out, if that's okay," Sam said.

"Sam..." O'Connor tilted her head, poised to rebuke, but caught sight of Hope's annoyed reaction instead. "That's... a good idea. We're going to need you at the top of your game later."

Hope nodded subtly. "How about we take the thing out a few times along the way and check to see if it's still alive?" She raised a brow. "For the sake of science."

"How about you time how long it takes for the thing to stop moving?" O'Connor blew a smoke ring towards her. "For the sake of science."

Hope nodded. "That works too."

Daniela sat next to Sam.

"You're going to miss the festivities."

Daniela looked back at O'Connor, Hope, and Harry prepping to lower the cage into the trash bin. "I think they got it under control. How you feeling about... all this."

"Pretty good, I think." Sam stared through the maintenance

building's garage, at some distant imaginary object. "Just trying to ease into the horror, you know?"

"Good plan. And we got front row seats." Daniela smiled. "Lucky us."

"Okay, you guys ready?" O'Connor alternated her gaze between Hope and Harry.

Hope had her phone out, ready to start the timer. Harry had unlatched the lock pin from the chain holding the caged acidback. Both nodded affirmative.

O'Connor stood at the side of the water-filled bin like a kid about to tear into a present on Christmas day. "Let her rip!"

Harry let chain links slip through his hands a few inches at a time, letting the chain work its way though the snatch block and lowering the cage into the water.

Because the acidback had been unable to turn itself around in the cage, its ring of teeth entered the water first, gnashing at the mesh. Its struggle intensified as the cage sunk deeper into the water until the cage submerged completely. The acidback's struggle turned the surface of the water into a froth of bubbles.

Hope started the timer on her phone.

"Give it another six inches, Harry." O'Connor watched the submerged cage and chain attached send shock waves through the water.

"One minute," Hope said as she watched her phone's display.

O'Connor took a puff of her cigar and held it between her thumb and index finger. "Still going strong."

Harry latched the lock pin on the chain, preventing the cage from descending any farther. He walked up next to Hope and O'Connor and directed his eyes at the strange creature beneath the water's surface.

"How can you watch this?" Harry eyed O'Connor. "Do you get pleasure from it?"

"It's like finding a long lost puzzle piece," O'Connor said.

"You get a clearer overall picture and that's gratifying. So yeah, that's pleasurable."

"I never liked puzzles much." Harry hooked a thumb at Daniela and Sam. "I'm going to join the live studio audience."

"Suit yourself."

"Two minutes." The surface of the water still churned with struggle and the reality of what was happening chipped away at the mental blinders Hope had set up for herself.

After the third minute passed, Hope bowed out. "Just let me know when it stops moving." She sat next to Sam and placed her head on his shoulder.

"You're all a bunch of pussies," O'Connor said.

Sam shook his head slowly. "Unless you want a mutiny on your hands, I'd recommend shutting your big mouth."

"Aw, you guys are no fun." O'Connor laughed and returned her attention to the submerged acidback.

"It sure is different when you don't have a horde of the bloody things after you," Harry said.

Daniela took Harry's hand in hers and turned toward Sam and Hope. "I know you said no questions, Sam. But Hope. What's your story?"

Hope ran her fingers through her jet-black hair. "Not much to tell really. I studied zoology at the University of California in Santa Barbara. Moved to New York to observe rodents in their natural urban habitat and fell in with these yahoos. The rest is history."

"Your focus of study was rodents?"

"Yup. In fact, I left my beloved Harriette back in New York to come here. So this job better not last much longer."

Harry raised a brow. "You live with a pet rat?"

"Lots of people do." Hope smiled. "She's an albino Wistar and she's beautiful, isn't she, Sam?"

Sam growled.

Daniela nodded. "Smart women outnumber the men in this group. I like those odds."

"Now I just got to pay off my student loans," Hope said.

"Studies not paying off job-wise?"

"I'm employed by a cigar-smoking exterminator with anger management issues. What do you think?"

"If this year's election pans out the way I hope it will, student loans may be a thing of the past."

Hope glanced at the seconds ticking by on her phone's stopwatch. "I'm not going to hold my breath."

After minute fifteen O'Connor pulled the cage part way out of the water, but the acidback's stub of a tail twitched back and forth and its clawed feet worked at the cage's mesh.

"Won't be long now," O'Connor said. "I can feel it."

Except it was. It took another thirteen minutes for the submerged acidback to die. Even O'Connor's glee had evaporated by then.

Harry raised the cage out of the bin. The light pink tinge of the acidback's skin was gone, leaving a dull yellowish-white pallor. The vast network of once purple veins just under the skin had turned black.

"Just over twenty-eight minutes." Hope pocketed her phone and sniffed the air around the trash bin. "What's that smell?"

"Like anything fighting for its life," Daniela said, "the thing lost control of its bladder and bowels. You're probably smelling a mixture of urine and feces."

O'Connor leaned forward to get a closer look at the acidback in the cage, tracing the black veins with her eyes. "At least we know we can scare the shit out of it."

Hope stepped back, holding her nose. "Can we dump the water?"

"Remember, the water likely has acid in it as well. Who knows how much." Daniela glanced at Harry. "It would probably kill any plant it touched."

Harry nodded. "Leave it. I'll dump it in the ocean after Detest-A-Pest works its magic."

O'Connor spun the cage to face the acidback's fanged maw. "Sam. Get your butt over here. School's in sesh."

Sam took his place reluctantly beside O'Connor. Hope sidled up next to Sam, brushing her arms against his.

"Look at that face." O'Connor pointed at the ring of teeth locked in a death grip on the cage's mesh, each one razor-sharp. "Only a mother could love that face. And we're going to kill it."

"Let's perform an autopsy," Daniela said.

Everyone stared at her and for once O'Connor didn't have a snappy comeback.

"It'll be just like gross anatomy at Stanford." Daniela winked at O'Connor. "That's academic for 'poke it with a stick until it pops.' "

"It'll be gross, alright." Hope grimaced.

"Think of it as an extension to your university education." Daniela raised an eyebrow at Hope. "You dissected a rat, right?"

"Unfortunately."

"Stop whining. This isn't Harriette, honey." Smoke drifted in lazy wisps from O'Connor's cigar.

"We're going to need some tools." Daniela began to search when Harry appeared with a knife and a rubber mat. "You read my mind."

"The knife isn't a scalpel, but it's sharp. And the mat…" Harry shrugged. "I thought it'd be better than exposing the floor to acid. We already know it eats right through it."

"I'll need gloves. Rubber if possible."

Harry disappeared into the back recesses of the maintenance garage and returned with industrial rubber gloves with long cuffs that ended mid-forearm. "We use these for mixing pesticide."

"They're perfect." Daniela rolled down her sleeves and slipped her hands and shirt cuffs inside.

Sam looked at the creature in the cage. "I hope they're acid resistant."

Daniela grinned at him. She was in her element. "I guess we'll find out."

Harry maneuvered the cage to an open area of the floor and lowered it onto the rubber mat.

O'Connor rubbed her hands together. "Want to see something cool?"

Everyone exchanged looks with one another, not knowing what to expect.

"I'll need your knife for a second."

Daniela handed over the knife to O'Connor, handle first.

"Watch." O'Connor knelt and used the tip of the knife to pry out a corner pin that ran the length of the cage. She slid it out, pushing with the blade's dull edge, and the sides of the cage flipped open and laid flat on the mat. The acidback lay completely unrestrained, except for its teeth still firmly clamped on the far end of the cage's mesh.

"Jesus Christ." Sam took a panicked step backward. "I'm glad that thing is dead... It *is* dead, right?"

"Deader than a doornail." O'Connor handed the knife back to Daniela.

"You know what this reminds me of?" Daniela turned to the rest of the group. "A tardigrade."

Blank faces stared back at her.

"Water bear? Moss piglet?"

O'Connor shrugged. "Sorry Doc, you're speaking nonsense."

"Hope? I'm surprised you don't know what I'm talking about." Daniela set the knife down beside the bloated acidback. "A tardigrade is a little creature about a millimeter long, with eight legs and claws. It doesn't have eyes or teeth."

"Doesn't sound like much of a threat," Harry said.

"The surprising aspect of tardigrades is their indestructible nature."

O'Connor balked. "Indestructible? Bullshit. Nothing's indestructible."

"Tardigrades can survive hundreds of degrees of heat and cold, radiation, massive pressure, like bottom of Marianas Trench kind of pressure, and even the vacuum of space."

"That *is* pretty amazing." Hope pulled out her phone and tapped the display.

"But what about my fucking boot heel?" O'Connor flashed her brows and took a puff from her cigar.

Sam pointed at the lifeless acidback. "That thing's dead so it's obviously not a tardigrade."

"But it could have some tardigrade DNA in it," Daniela said.

"Luckily not the DNA that makes it indestructible." Harry shifted uneasily on his feet. "Time's ticking, people."

"Just thought I'd mention that. Let's see if this thing has any guts." Daniela picked up the knife and positioned it near the mouth, the tip of the blade hovering over the acidback's pallid skin.

"Dani, wait." Harry ran into the depths of the maintenance building and returned holding a clear plastic face shield with a head mount.

"You think of everything."

"It's my garage. Safety first."

Daniela placed the shield on her head and positioned it in front of her face. "Anything else I'm missing?"

"How about an acid resistant suit?" Hope smiled with a shrug.

"Appreciate the thought." Daniela looked to the rest of the group as if giving a last farewell. "Here goes nothing."

She pressed the knife blade's tip into the acidback's skin until it broke the surface.

Daniela ran the knife blade down the length of the acidback's body, its skin splitting open like an overcooked sausage. Clear fluid mixed with dark blood filled the incision and the surface of the knife blade began to sizzle. With each pass she cut the incision deeper until the acidback fell apart, split in two pieces.

Hope covered her mouth and turned away, trying to suppress her gag reflex.

"What the hell?" O'Connor pointed at the knife. "It's like the blade's hot."

"That's the acid at work." Daniela held the knife up, its blade pocked by acid bubbles. "And yes, there's going to be heat as well. Acid metal reactions produce heat. Harry? Can you grab some tissue?"

"One second." Harry disappeared into his office and returned with a box of tissues. He pulled out a couple and handed them to her.

Daniela balled the tissue up and ran it along the incision, blotting blood and acid. In seconds the tissue began to blacken.

Sam stepped beside Hope. "That was pretty gross. You doing okay?"

Hope swallowed. "I'll be fine. Blood and surgery's never been my thing." She looked at him. "You seem to be okay though."

"Yeah, it's weird. Cutting the thing open has demystified it a bit for me." Sam smirked. "A bit."

"Then you should go back and watch. I just needed a little air."

"Sure?"

Hope nodded and Sam rejoined the group.

"The physiology looks a lot like a snake." Daniela pointed out body parts as she spoke, beginning with a small dark red orb connecting the veins that covered its body. "That must be the heart, although I can't see any lungs."

"Maybe it doesn't have any," Harry said.

"It's got to get oxygen somehow." Daniela poked around the innards with the tip of the knife blade.

"Maybe it's like an earthworm." Hope had rejoined the group. "They breath through their skin."

"That's possible and would explain the network of circulatory veins throughout the body and on the surface." Daniela scanned the length of the acidback. "I can't seem to find a stomach or that steak it ate."

"It probably liquefied it," Harry said. "Looks like acid plays a major part of this thing's existence."

"Just show me where its asshole is so I can jam a taser rod up there." O'Connor grinned. "Give 'em a taste of my disco stick."

Screams rose from the clubhouse.

"Shit!" Harry shot a panicked look at the others and took off like a shot. "Come on!"

The others followed not knowing what they would find, but Harry fought a sinking feeling that had become all too familiar over the past week.

Little Bitch

Harry rounded the corner of the clubhouse at top speed and his momentum carried him toward the edge of a vast sink hole, many times the size of the cavern on the third hole. He dug his heels into the turf and dropped to the ground like he was sliding into home base.

If only it was home, he thought as his feet and legs sailed over the edge.

A muscular tattooed hand grabbed Harry's forearm and pulled him back. He looked up and saw Sam's familiar grin. Relief washed over him.

"We almost lost you there, partner," Sam said.

"Thanks."

The rest of the group arrived moments after. Daniela knelt next to Harry. "Are you hurt?"

"Forget about me. Worry about him!" Harry pointed at the golfer stranded at the bottom of the sink hole. "I'm going back for rope and my shotgun."

Harry bolted back the way he came.

"Follow him, Sam," O'Connor said. "Bring back taser rods and anything else you can carry."

Sam nodded and tapped Hope's shoulder. "I could use an extra hand. Got it in you?"

"Absolutely."

Sam and Hope ran after Harry.

Beside his upturned golf cart fifteen feet down, the golfer made futile attempts to scramble up the crumbling dirt sides but nothing supported his weight. Potential handholds disintegrated in his grasp.

"Someone get me out of here!" the golfer yelled.

Daniela peered over the edge and cupped her hands around her mouth. "Help's on the way."

O'Connor pulled her back. "You're too close to the edge. You're no good to us down there with him." She addressed the crowd collecting around the edge of the sink hole. "Everyone stay back. The edge could give way at any second."

Daniela shot a concerned look at O'Connor. "You see the smaller tunnels leading into the sides?"

"Yeah," O'Connor said. "Lunch is served." She called down to the golfer. "Grab a club."

"What?" The golfer cupped his ear to help him hear better.

"You need a weapon," O'Connor repeated. "Grab a golf club!"

"I need a what?"

"Jesus Christ. Deaf as a post." O'Connor lowered her voice so only Daniela could hear. "The fucker's going to die right in front of us." She plucked her cigar out and raised her voice again. "A CLUB. PICK UP A CLUB GOD DAMN IT."

This time the golfer got the message. He scaled his toppled cart, found his golf bag, and grabbed a driver. He needed no explanation why. As if on cue, acidbacks began poking their fanged maws out of the shaded tunnels.

Several spectators took out their phones to take photos and record video.

O'Connor laid down on her belly. "What's your name?"

The golfer looked up at her, his blond comb-over a rat's nest on his balding pate. "Ronald."

"Okay, Ronald. Can I call you Ron?" O'Connor didn't give Ronald a chance to answer. "We're getting a rope to get you out.

Until then, you got to use that club against those bastards crawling out of those tunnels around you."

Ron turned around, scanning the walls of the sink hole. "What? I don't see anything."

A spectator followed O'Connor's example, laid on their stomach, and lowered their golf club in hopes it would be long enough to connect with Ron's. "Hook your club on mine and I'll pull you up!"

Daniela waved her arms to gain the spectator's attention. "Sir, help's on the way. Back away from the edge."

"No, I got it." The spectator yelled into the sink hole. "Ron, buddy, hook your club on mine." He inched forward until his hips rested on the edge.

"Sir, as the resort physician, I insist you back up."

"This ain't going to be pretty." O'Connor surveyed the mayhem as she drew in a mouthful of cigar smoke and let it escape in a lazy drift.

Ron climbed to the highest point of the sink hole's bottom and held up his club. Just another few inches would do it.

"Fuck this. Outta my way!" O'Connor circumnavigated the edge of the sink hole, pushing other spectators aside as she went. "Hey jackass. This is no time for heroics."

O'Connor had ten feet to go when the edge crumbled beneath the prone man, sending his body toppling forward and his legs into the air. She managed to grab one leg and dig her feet into the turf, stopping the spectator's fall.

O'Connor looked around at other spectators swooping in with their phones. "Quit your fucking gawking and give me a hand."

The extra distance allowed Ron to hook his golf driver onto the spectator's club. He jumped and begin climbing but the added weight was too much. The spectator's club slid out of its rubber grip and fell to the bottom of the sink hole, burying itself mid-shaft in the soft soil. Ron fell backward onto his back.

"Shit!" The reality of his situation sunk in and the spectator began to squirm. "Pull me up! Pull me—"

An acidback emerged from a tunnel in the sheared edge and latched its fangs on the spectator's head. He didn't have a chance to scream. The creature twisted its body and reversed back into the tunnel, yanking the man's leg from O'Connor's hands and leaving her holding his right golf shoe.

The spectator tipped over the edge. His falling momentum pulled the acidback out of the tunnel and into the bright sunshine. Both plummeted to the bottom of the sink hole, narrowly missing Ron.

The gripless golf club already at the bottom shot through the spectator's chest like a hot arrowhead. The acidback, its skin smoking in the sun, released the man's head, now a ghastly and bloody skull, and backed into the shadows.

Ron stared in horror and scrambled backward, chunks of dirt and turf flying from his heels.

"Oh Jesus." Daniela placed her hands over her mouth and shot a look at O'Connor across the void.

"That can't be good," O'Connor mumbled as she got to her feet and ran back to where Daniela stood. She took out her cigar and cupped her hands around her mouth. "Ron! Stay in the sun!"

Harry arrived in a loaded maintenance cart, with Sam and Hope riding shotgun. He slammed on the brakes and threw his golf cart into a drifting skid. The three of them grabbed armfuls of supplies and joined O'Connor and Daniela.

Harry dropped a twisted coil of rope and a break action shotgun when his eyes fell on the other golfer impaled on the club. "What the hell happened?"

"What's wrong with his face?" Hope asked.

"Someone tried to be a hero." O'Connor spoke without emotion. "Didn't listen to us and paid with his life."

"This is going to get ugly," Daniela said. "I'm going to try some crowd control."

Harry grabbed her arm. "Be careful."

Daniela smiled back.

"Here. Take this." O'Connor handed her a taser rod. "Anyone who doesn't listen, zap 'em."

"Worst case scenario."

"Look around," O'Connor said. "What do you think's happening here?"

"Touché." Daniela smiled and began working her way around the edge of the sink hole, moving spectators farther back.

"Oh shit, look." Sam pointed across the open sink hole to the sidewalk next to the clubhouse as Larsen charged down its length. "The douche is back."

"Harcourt! What is the meaning of—" Larsen stopped short when he saw the carnage before him.

"White noise." Harry knelt and placed two shells from his pocket into the double barrel of the shotgun and snapped it closed. "I got bigger fish to fry."

In the time since the sink hole had opened up, the sun had moved further west, casting one side of the hole in more shadow. Acidbacks emerged from their tunnels with more freedom to roam. Several were already ripping into the dead golfer's feet.

Ron looked up at O'Connor. "Get me the fuck out of here! Right fucking now!"

"Working on it, Ron." O'Connor grabbed the rope and tied it to Harry's maintenance cart.

"Ron?" Sam looked a question at O'Connor.

"Yeah, we're on a first name basis now." O'Connor threw the rope over the edge, its knotted end hanging five feet above the floor of the sink hole.

"Ever think of getting a longer rope?"

"Don't look at me." Sam glared at O'Connor. "But there's other rope. We could tie them together."

"No time," O'Connor said. "Harry? You good?"

"For now." Harry wrapped his hands around the rope.

O'Connor grabbed three taser rods and threw two of them to Sam and Hope. "Work the perimeter with Daniela. It's all we can do."

The three of them spread out along the edge, following Daniela's path.

Acidbacks scuttled back and forth along the terminator line between sun and shadow, as if they knew a possible food source was escaping. A venture into the direct sunshine caused their skin to smoke and char, forcing them back into the shade.

Harry shook the length of rope and yelled down at Ron, "Hurry. You don't have much time."

Larsen stormed up to Harry. "What the hell is going on?"

"Not now, Larsen. Peoples' lives are at stake."

"People are recording this." Larsen scanned the crowd surrounding the edge of the sink hole. Daniela, O'Connor, Sam, and Hope were making good progress keeping people back, but it was far from perfect. "It'll be all over the Internet. This is bad. Very bad. Strunk will *not* be pleased."

"Then shut up and do something about it, Larsen." Harry looked down at Ron scaling the side of the sink hole. "I'm done talking."

"Don't let him die, Harry," a voice called out.

Even though they were on opposite sides of the sink hole, Harry and Daniela recognized the voice immediately. McCoy stood two dozen feet away from her with his phone out, recording the mayhem. She ran toward him.

"Back away from the edge and put your phone away."

"Or what?" McCoy evaded the business end of Daniela's taser rod. "Going to shock me?"

Larsen saw McCoy and Daniela arguing and followed the edge of the sink hole to intercept them.

"Or you have to deal with him." Daniela pointed at Larsen, sweaty and red-faced, charging toward them both.

As McCoy pocketed his phone, Daniela noticed Ron halfway up the side of the sink hole, climbing toward a tunnel in the dirt wall.

"Ron! The tunnels," Daniela called across the chasm. "You're headed straight for one."

Manning the rope with Ron below, Harry couldn't see any tunnels from his vantage point. But he understood Daniela's message loud and clear. "Ron, stay away from the tunnels in the side."

"What tunnels?" Ron spoke between labored breaths.

"The tunnels. The holes in the side."

"Ron, you've got to stop!" Daniela waved her arms. "Stop him, Harry."

O'Connor, Sam, and Hope joined to try and warn Ron.

"I've only got a little bit more to go." Ron continued his ascent, hand over fist, a step at a time.

From the opposite side, the crowd watched as Ron's body passed over a tunnel opening, his body casting the hole in shadow.

An acidback within launched itself at Ron, its ring of pointed teeth sinking into his soft belly. He lost his grip on the rope and fell backward, landing next to the dead golfer and knocking the wind out of himself.

The impact knocked the acidback off Ron's abdomen by several feet, with uneven chunks of skin and fat still caught in the creature's teeth. Its bloodlust overpowered its aversion to the sun and it relaunched itself back at the man.

Blood flowed freely from Ron's torn belly thanks to the creature's anticoagulant saliva. He raised himself on his elbows and tried to drag himself away from the charging animal. Rapid blood loss and the sight and severity of his injuries threw his body into shock.

Harry raised the shotgun and tracked the acidback's charge across the uneven sink hole bottom. He pulled the trigger. Buckshot ripped through creature's side and ejected jets of blood and acid but did nothing to slow the acidback's advance.

"Shoot it in the head!" O'Connor yelled across the sink hole opening.

Harry had only seconds left before the acidback would be on top of Ron again. Everything moved in slow motion in his mind. He aimed a half foot ahead of the creature's direction of travel, exhaled, and pulled the trigger.

The acidback's ring of teeth and head area, if it could be considered a head, exploded in a mist of fatty tissue, blood and acid, coating the back wall of the sink hole and parts of Ron's face. The momentum of the acidback's approach caused it to flip end for end, coming to rest upside down in a smoking charred heap, two feet from Ron's body.

Ron screamed and rolled away from the dead creature, clawing at the acid burning tracks into his face.

Harry dug into his pocket for two more shells, broke open the shotgun and reloaded.

"Stay out of the shadow," Daniela yelled. Soon everyone in the group as well as a few spectators were yelling variations of the same warning.

It was all white noise to Ron. He heard none of it as he clawed his way toward the side of the sink hole, forgetting the rope that had been his savior moments earlier.

"Not into the shadow!" Someone yelled from the crowd.

Spectators clambered for better views, many restarting their video recordings.

"No! Put them away." Larsen began pointing and trying to grab phones out of peoples' hands. "Stop recording!"

Acidbacks not already feeding on the dead spectator wasted no time latching onto Ron's bulky frame. His head and blond comb-over were first to go. A ring of teeth stretched around his head and down to his chin, extracting everything that made Ron recognizable, including his voice. Left with lidless eyeballs and a permanent skeletal grin, Ron looked more like the Cryptkeeper.

Four additional acidbacks joined the attack and tore through Ron's clothes and skin like he was an old trash bag.

The crowd fell silent. The only noise in the immediate vicinity was the creatures' furious appetites awash in blood and acid.

Larsen looked down in horror at the carnage below, then redirected his eyes to the crowd above as if to memorize everyone there. He ran back towards Harry and grabbed his shotgun.

Locking the barrel, Larsen leveled the shotgun at the crowd and swept it back and forth. Many spectators ran. Others ducked.

"Hold on, Larsen." Harry spoke calmly with his hands raised. "You don't want to do this."

Larsen singled out McCoy. "You'll all pay for this. All of you."

McCoy raised his hands, making sure his camera lens faced forward to catch Larsen's act of desperation.

Harry seized the moment and grabbed the barrel of the shotgun, aiming it toward the sky. The sudden movement surprised Larsen and he pulled the trigger. The gunshot rang out across the golf course, sending birds into flight.

Harry pulled the shotgun away from Larsen and cracked open the barrel. "What are you, an idiot?" He dropped the shotgun to the ground. "This kind of shit gets you fired, isn't that right, Larsen? Guess you're going to find out."

Larsen took out his phone and took photos of the crowd. "I'll identify you... all of you. And ban you from Mar-A-Verde for life."

Harry stepped up to Larsen and shoved him backward hard. "Get the hell out of here."

"That's it." Anger flared in Larsen's eyes. "Once all this is done, you're gone. You're fired, Harry."

"Oh, I'm fired *after* the job is done?" Harry managed a laugh through his anger. "You can try."

Larsen trudged toward the clubhouse with furious footsteps. "Your career is over. I'll make sure of it."

"You're a damn fool."

Spectators began to clap.

"Seriously? Two men are dead and you're clapping?" Harry pointed at the crowd as he raised his phone to his ear. "Show's over you depraved assholes. Police are on their way. Go back to whatever the hell you were doing, but don't do it here unless you want to be arrested." He spotted McCoy among the crowd. "You too, McCoy."

McCoy pocketed his phone and approached him. "Got to hand it to you, Harry. You did what a lot of people have wanted to do for years. If you need a job, let me know, I've got connections."

"Thanks, but Larsen is full of hot air and empty threats."

"The offer stands." McCoy offered a half-hearted smile and merged with the dispersing crowd of spectators.

Daniela appeared by Harry's side. "Nice going, but the cops? It'll take days."

Harry shrugged. "Smokescreen. But we do have to take care of *that* ugliness." He motioned at the skeletal remains at the bottom of the sink hole. "And fast."

O'Connor, Sam, and Hope rejoined Harry and Daniela.

"What a clusterfuck." O'Connor plucked her cigar from her lips and rolled it between her finger and thumb. "What's the power situation like here?"

"We got a direct submarine cable connection from the Biminis plus diesel backup generators."

"Good, because we need lights." O'Connor clamped her

teeth on her cigar and spewed out a cloud of smoke. "Lots of them."

"More than lights, we need a plan." Sam looked down into the sink hole. The acidbacks that had attacked Ron and the other golfer had disappeared back into their maze of tunnels, leaving behind a pile of skeletal gore. "Because I'll bet we've stepped in a bigger pile of shit than we think."

"But we're paid to step in shit. Ain't that right?" O'Connor slapped Sam's back.

Sam cast her an uneasy glance, then focused past her toward the blue Bahamian sky.

The sun continued its daily trek above with each passing second. Soon it would be dark and the acidbacks would have the advantage they had thrived on for hundreds of years.

LARSEN CHARGED INTO his office and slammed the door behind him. He paced the small space while he weighed the few options in front of him.

He could close Mar-A-Verde and send everyone home until the infestation of strange creatures had been eradicated. A press release or an on-camera statement downplaying the peril might help but with all the social media coverage and viral videos it would come across as a lie.

"FUCKING HARCOURT." Larsen swept his arm across his desk, knocking pens, paper, the phone, and an empty mug to the floor. The phone's handset bounced off its cradle, a busy signal buzzing from its speaker. He slumped into his chair and ran a furious hand over his bald head. The computer monitor with an open Internet browser window stared back at him.

Larsen typed, "Mar-A-Verde" and hit the enter key. Hundreds of results flowed across the screen, all variations of the same theme: unexplained deaths rock Strunk's exclusive Bahama resort. The Internet moved fast, especially when Strunk was involved.

He scrolled down further and noticed a new story trending. "Mar-A-Verde Meltdown. General Manager Has Tantrum," the headline read.

"I'm fucked." He slammed the keyboard tray into his desk. Even with events unfolding out of his control, the silence of the office calmed him until the phone began its wailing off-hook signal.

Larsen stood, picked the phone off the floor, and returned it to its rightful spot on his desk. He hesitated for a moment before placing the handset back in its cradle.

Immediately the phone began to ring. He knew who it was without looking at the call display. Few people knew his direct office number and even fewer called it. Larsen contemplated not answering and walking away, catching a boat off the island and starting a new life somewhere new.

But he couldn't let Harry win.

Larsen picked up the phone and was met with Strunk's livid voice on the other end of the line. He held the handset a few inches away from his ear until he thought it was safe to speak.

"I know sir, but I had no control," he said.

"No control? What do you mean no control? It's a tidal wave of bad press." Strunk's voice crackled through the handset's speaker. "You're a little bitch, Larsen. Don't make me regret hiring you."

"No, sir... Mr. Strunk, sir. I'll do—"

"Fix it or you're fired, little bitch. I'll fire you then sue you into the stone age. Believe me."

The telephone line clicked and reset to a steady dial tone. Larsen bashed the handset against the cradle several times as if he was murdering someone.

Murdering Harry. This was all his fault.

Larsen moved to the window and looked out at a vast expanse of green.

"I can save Mar-A-Verde," Larsen said to himself. "I'll be a hero." But even though he heard his spoken words, in his head all that echoed back was *little bitch*.

SHOCKING REVELATION

AFTER STAKING OUT the clubhouse sink hole with caution tape, Harry, Daniela, and the Detest-A-Pest team regrouped at the maintenance building. The dissected acidback lay on the rubber mat exactly as they had left it.

"Maybe we shouldn't have killed that thing," Daniela said. "We could have learned more, like its strengths and weaknesses."

Hope nodded. "I agree."

"Bah." O'Connor dismissed the two with a wave. "You academics are all the same."

Hope furrowed her brow and strutted up to O'Connor, close to bumping chests. "What's that supposed to mean?"

O'Connor took a step back. "Forget it."

"Oh shit." Sam rolled his eyes and shared a glance with Harry. "Here we go again."

"I expect nothing less from a group of alpha personalities," Harry said.

"Yeah." Sam stepped between Hope and O'Connor.

"No, tell me, O'Connor." Hope ignored Sam's attempt at mediation. "If you're such hot shit, tell us why *us academics* drag you down."

"Okay. You want to know? You talk too much." O'Connor moved her fingers and thumb like a puppet and blew cigar smoke into Hope's face. "Talk, talk, talk. All talk and no action. If you haven't noticed, we don't have a lot of time."

"I've been pulling my weight." Hope's voice rose in anger. "I even saved your sorry ass once. I'm beginning to regret that."

Daniela stepped in. "O'Connor's right. We're wasting time."

"Look." O'Connor removed her cigar. "I can appreciate that you have knowledge that I don't. So what do we know?" She counted off on her fingers. "Those fuckers are fast. They've got sharp teeth. They're bloodthirsty. They sweat acid. And they don't feel pain. That's a fuckload of badass." She looked at Hope and Daniela. "What else do we know?"

Hope spoke first. "They burn up in bright light."

"What else?" O'Connor alternated her gaze between the two women. "Let's hear some answers from those big brains of yours."

Daniela looked at Hope, momentarily flustered. "They're probably electrically conductive."

"Not proven yet, but I'm itching to find out," O'Connor said. "What else?"

Hope snapped her fingers. "You can drown them, shoot them, cut them open, and probably kill them with fire."

"Yes. Thank Christ we can kill them." O'Connor puffed her cigar. "Anything else?"

Hope shrugged and looked to Daniela.

"This isn't about the creatures, but there's probably tunnels everywhere," Daniela said. "Which means potential sink holes everywhere."

"What about ground-penetrating radar?" Hope asked.

Harry shook his head. "A good idea, but it would take forever to scan the entire course. And getting the equipment here, that's a whole other story."

"Why not do what we always do." Sam looked at the others. "Get them to come to us."

"In other words, be the bait." O'Connor clamped her teeth on the end of her cigar and laughed. "Never thought I'd hear you say that again."

"Occam's razor... slightly modified." Daniela nodded, grinning. "The simplest solution tends to be the correct one."

Sam looked at O'Connor with a sly smile. "Are you thinking what I'm thinking?"

O'Connor returned his smile with one of her own. "Time to break out the Kill-O-Matic?"

"Bingo." They bumped fists.

Harry turned to Daniela. "Kill-O-Whatsit?"

"One problem," Hope said to O'Connor. "The cage is metal. Acidbacks and metal don't mix."

"Good point, my fine young academic." O'Connor narrowed her eyes on Hope. "Two questions. How many acidbacks could fit in the cage, and how long would it take the acid to burn through it?"

Hope shook her head. "No idea."

"Looks like we're going to have to find out." O'Connor flashed her eyebrows at her. "And if they're conductive, that improves our odds."

"What *are* our odds, exactly?" Sam asked.

O'Connor shrugged and puffed out a cloud of cigar smoke.

Harry scrunched his brow at the Detest-A-Pest team. "Wait. Back up. What's a Kill-O—"

"Kill-O-Matic? That's another one of Washington's inventions," O'Connor said. "It's an electrified cage, a Detest-A-Pest exclusive. It can fry a thousand rats at once, ain't that right, Sam?"

"Don't remind me." Sam swallowed, his dry throat clicking. "Having enough issues getting past these things."

O'Connor turned to Harry. "We need a buttload of lights. It's one thing we didn't pack."

Harry nodded. "I've got a bunch of portable LED lamps plus a couple gas generators if we need them."

"Fucking ace." O'Connor rubbed her hands together. "We

also need to be able to raise and lower people and supplies into that sink hole. Any ideas?"

Harry gave the question some thought. "I've got no shortage of ladders. There's two still out on the first hole. But I'm pretty sure there's a small amount of scaffolding in the back. Haven't used it for a few years though."

"Let's get to work, people," O'Connor said. "We're losing daylight and that's our best ally."

Sam, O'Connor, and Daniela began unloading more equipment, including the Kill-O-Matic.

Hope grabbed Harry before he disappeared into the maintenance storage. "Do you decorate for Christmas by any chance?"

"Are you kidding?" Harry laughed. "Strunk loves all things shiny and twinkly. Follow me."

He led Hope into a separate storage room filled with every kind of gilded Christmas decoration imaginable.

"Looking for anything in particular?"

"Lights," Hope said. "LED if you got them."

"I think I know what you're up to." Harry grinned and pointed out at least two dozen plastic bins along the back wall. "They're all LED, pretty much. Saves money and Strunk's a cheap bastard. I'll leave you to it."

Daniela appeared at the door. "Need any help?" Harry gave her a light peck on the cheek as he passed by.

"Sure." Hope pointed along the wall. "Grab a bin. We're looking for LED rope lights."

As the crew gathered and transported supplies to the clubhouse sink hole, shadows grew longer and darker and acidbacks lay in waiting, growing hungrier by the minute.

IT TOOK LONGER to transport materials to the clubhouse sink hole than it did to assemble the scaffolding. Harry directed Sam and O'Connor where and how the pieces fit together. Hope and Daniela were nowhere in sight.

Half-way through assembly, O'Connor stepped aside. "I got to pace myself. The leg is being a bitch today. Going to go see what the *academics* are up to."

Sam glanced at her over his shoulder. "O'Connor. Don't raise shit, okay?"

O'Connor threw her head back and laughed. "You're funny, Sam." She hopped into a maintenance cart and sped back to the maintenance building.

Sam sighed. "She's going to be the death of me."

"She's a force to be reckoned with. I'll give her that."

"More like a runaway train, most days," Sam said.

Twenty minutes later Sam and Harry completed a scaffold six feet tall on both sides of the sink hole. The occasional screech and squeal from an acidback echoed up from below.

Sam wiped his brow with the bottom of his t-shirt, now looking more gray than white. "Sometimes I wonder why I do this. I mean those creatures have as much right to be here as we do."

"But if they're killing people, that's where I draw the line." Harry crossed his arms against his chest. "As for Strunk, it's basic greed. If those things kill his guests, they kill his cash flow."

"Wouldn't it be cool to just blow the entire resort up, acidbacks and all?" Sam chuckled. "Load the property with dynamite, light the fuse, and walk away."

Harry laughed too. "That would be quite a sight. Larsen would love that. But I'd have no job."

"A guy with your skill? You'd have a job in no time. And the way you handled Larsen's tantrum earlier." Sam looked at him. "I'd bet people would be knocking on your door."

"Thanks." Harry looked back at the scaffold and past toward

the sun moving steadily toward the horizon. "We better get back to it. We're losing daylight. Don't want to give the ladies any excuse to call us lazy."

"They wouldn't do that."

"I believe O'Connor would."

Sam gave it some thought, then nodded. "Yeah, she would." The two men laughed. "Let's tie those two ladders together and span the gap."

Sam and Harry extended two ladders to their maximum forty foot length and bound them together with rope for strength. Sam took another rope and tied it to the leading rung of the fortified ladders.

"I was thinking of pulling it across," Sam said.

"Sounds as good an idea as any. But I want to attach a pulley and the snatch block to the middle first." Harry looked down to the bottom of the sink hole, now murky with shadows. "I'd rather not climb out to the middle to tie that hardware on."

Harry tilted the doubled ladder on its side and got to work affixing the pulley and snatch block. The sound of a maintenance cart approached.

Sam stood and shielded his eyes with his hand. "I think the rest of our crew has returned."

Hope hopped out, followed by O'Connor and Daniela. Silver rope wrapped around Hope's legs and waist. "What do you guys think?"

Harry finished tying the pulley and the snatch block assembly to a rung near the middle of the double ladder span and looked up. "What are we looking at?"

"Watch this." O'Connor adjusted something at Hope's belt line. The silver rope lit up Hope's legs like it was a Christmas tree. A spill of intense light five feet in all directions surrounded her.

Hope raised her arms like she was presenting a showcase on The Price Is Right. "Anti-acidback pants."

"Huh." Harry smiled. "That's out of the box thinking right there."

"And the lights plug into those new battery packs I picked up originally for the taser rods." O'Connor stepped around Hope to get a better view.

"Anyone who doesn't know our situation would think you're crazy. But I love it." Sam clapped. "Brilliant! In more ways than one."

"I hope they're bright enough."

"Don't worry, Hope," Harry said. "They're plenty bright. With the LEDs we've got, those acidbacks won't be able to get anywhere near you."

"Academics sure are useful, huh?" Sam slapped O'Connor on the back. "Another idea that'll save your ass."

O'Connor shot him a look and grumbled.

"We have enough lights for two people, maybe three." Hope unplugged the lights and Daniela helped her unwrap the lights from around her legs.

"Looks like you two have been busy." O'Connor stepped around the doubled ladder and surveyed the scaffold.

"And y'all arrived at just the right time." Harry raised the leading end of the ladder supports and rested it on the top of the scaffold.

He flipped the support rope over the top and threw the remaining tow rope across the opening of the sink hole. "O'Connor, Daniela, I'd appreciate some help lifting the back end up."

"Hope, I'm going to need some help on the other side." Sam ran around the edge, picked up the rope's end, and took up the slack across the top of the other scaffold structure.

Hope followed. "What do you need me to do?"

"You can help me support the weight of the ladders once it gets more than half-way past the other scaffold," Sam said. "It'll be a bit like tug of war. Then it'd be great if you could pull the ladders onto the top of this scaffold to form a bridge."

"Got it." Hope grasped the rope and stood behind Sam. She watched his muscles work under his shirt and caught the musky smell of sweat rising in the breeze from his t-shirt.

"Ready?"

Hope snapped to attention. "Ready."

"Go, Harry." Sam pulled on the lead rope as Harry, O'Connor and Daniela lifted the back end of the ladders.

The two ladders slid over the top of the first scaffold like it was on rails. A few feet at a time, the reinforced ladders slid across the chasm.

But every plan hits a snag, and in this case, it was an actual snag. The ropes that bound the ladders together got hung up on the top crossbar of the scaffold.

"Can you lift the ladder a bit more on your end?" Sam called out.

"I'll see what I can do." Harry stretched his arms up as far as they would go and rocked up on his toes. Too high for O'Connor and Daniela to safely reach, they let go of the ladders. "It's not too bad. The scaffold and Sam's rope is taking a lot of the weight."

It was just enough extra height to scoot the binding ropes past the scaffold's crossbar. The ladders shot forth and began to tip towards the sink hole's bottom, pulling Harry up like he was holding onto the end of the world's most insane teeter totter. The leading tips of the ladders dipped and swung wildly from side to side.

"Quick! Grab my legs or I'm going to lose control of the end."

O'Connor and Daniela wrapped their arms around Harry's legs and pulled him down. The ladders rose again, the scaffold acting as an off-center fulcrum.

Across the sink hole opening Sam and Hope pulled up the rope's slack as fast as they could manage.

"Let's pull off his pants." O'Connor flashed her eyebrows and gave Daniela a mischievous grin around her cigar. "What do you say?"

"Be serious."

O'Connor shrugged but maintained her grip on Harry's legs. "Shit. You're no fun."

"I'm right here," Harry said. "I can hear you."

"Take it as a compliment." O'Connor spoke through teeth clamped on a soggy cigar that somehow remained lit. "Just trying to lighten the mood a bit."

"I'd rather you focus."

Sam and Hope pulled the ladders across the chasm until the leading ends reached the scaffold's top crossbar on the other side.

"Hope, it's your time to shine." Sam motioned to the top of the scaffold. "You're going to have to climb up and lift the ends of the ladders so it clears the top crossbar."

Harry, O'Connor, and Daniela watched in intense silence as Hope dropped her section of rope, crawled into the interior of the scaffold on the other side, and used the crossbars like steps.

"Go slow."

Hope's eyes locked with Sam's. On any other day a look like that would have made her weak in the knees, but she could sense that he was gravely serious. She smiled to acknowledge his concern.

She ascended halfway up the scaffold, grabbed the leading rung of the ladders, and raised the end over the crossbar. "Got it!"

Sam pulled the ladders over the scaffold by a few inches. "Okay, back down, just as slow. I'll wait until you're safe."

Hope moved with cautious intent, step by step.

Seconds played out like minutes in Sam's head until Hope

was down and had taken her position behind him again, grasping the remainder of the rope. He sighed with relief as he and Hope pulled the ladders onto the scaffold. He dropped the rope and looked across the chasm at Harry, O'Connor, and Daniela.

"Nice work," he said.

Harry hitched up his pants as he raised his eyebrow at O'Connor. "Seems solid enough, although I'd like to tie down the corners."

O'Connor bowed in front of the scaffold structure. "I dub thee, 'Jungle Gym of Death.' "

"You might want to rethink that one," Harry said.

O'Connor laughed in response.

Daniela's phone rang. She extracted it from her pocket and looked at the display. "Shit."

Harry narrowed his eyes in concern. "What?"

She held up her index finger. "Hey Abernathy. What's up?"

Harry groaned.

Hints of Chief Abernathy's unmistakable voice floated from Daniela's phone speaker as she listened.

"Yeah, another two dead." Daniela gazed down into the sink hole chasm. "Viral videos sure do spread fast these days." She paused and listened. "No. Honestly Chief, there's nothing left except bones. We're in the process of extracting them now."

Sam and Hope rejoined the group. He glanced at Daniela, then the others. "We are?"

Daniela raised her finger to her mouth and shushed him. "We don't have any way of identifying the bodies except going through the entire resort and knocking on doors. And dental records, but that would take weeks." She listened. "That's not my job. Besides, I'm knee-deep in the extraction operation. Larsen's better suited to identify the deceased... yes, I'm sure. He's got a lot of damage control to take care of himself as well. He needs a serious wake-up call."

Daniela paced back and forth, then shook her head. "No, we don't need more police presence, but an evacuation order would help. And stop anyone trying to get here by boat." Chief Abernathy chattered in her ear. "It's bad but we got the situation under control." She glanced at O'Connor. "We got a team of professional exterminators on the scene."

Daniela's body relaxed. "Okay. I'll keep you posted. Thanks, Chief." She pocketed her phone and looked at the rest of the group. "Mar-A-Verde is fucked, reputation-wise that is. The videos that people shot earlier today are blowing up online."

"Yeah," Harry said. "I saw that coming... *bigly*." He chuckled.

Sam spotted Larsen standing in a bay window of the clubhouse, glowering down on them and their scaffold structure spanning the sink hole. "You think *Larsen* saw that coming?" He motioned at the clubhouse window.

Harry looked up and connected his gaze with Larsen. "If he didn't, he does now."

A shiver ran down Hope's back. "How long do you think he's been watching?"

Harry shrugged as he raised his phone to his ear. "Call Larsen." His phone obeyed and almost immediately he heard the call trilling in his ear.

Larsen raised his phone to his ear.

Harry heard the line click as Larsen picked up the call. "Larsen. Don't say anything. Just listen."

For once, Larsen did as he was told.

"I've heard about the videos," Harry said. "There was nothing you or anyone could have done. People have become attention whores. But we've got a workable plan. We can redeem ourselves and Mar-A-Verde. Just do me one favor. Get people out of here, including yourself. The less variables we have to deal with the better."

"You'd like that, wouldn't you." Larsen's voice sounded calm even though Harry knew there was an undercurrent of rage buried beneath.

"Look. I'm trying to help you... and Mar-A-Verde." Harry pleaded with his eyes, although at this distance he doubted Larsen would see it. "Get people off the island."

Larsen tapped his phone and disconnected the call. He reached beside the window and lowered the blind, obscuring himself from view.

"Well that was dramatic," O'Connor said.

Hope redirected her gaze from the clubhouse window to Harry. "You think he'll do it?"

A solemn expression crossed Harry's face. "No. He's too pigheaded. He's got a personal vendetta against me now."

"It doesn't matter what Larsen thinks," Daniela said. "We have to move forward."

"Damn straight." O'Connor released a couple of smoke rings. "Let's get to work."

Harry looked to the sky. "I got a better idea. I'm beat and I'm sure everyone else is too. We all deserve a good meal and a good night's sleep."

O'Connor held up her cigar and grinned ear to ear. "Slumber party at our room! Attendance is mandatory."

Harry laughed. "If that means a good night's sleep, I'm in."

"It means whatever you want it to mean, Harry." O'Connor clicked her tongue and winked at him.

Sam grabbed some rope and metal stakes. "Let's tie down the scaffold first."

Working together, the group secured the makeshift bridge spanning the sink hole and collected the equipment in an organized pile. Most of the Detest-A-Pest supplies were locked in plastic bins and the collapsed Kill-O-Matic was secured with its own padlocks.

BACK AT THE Detest-A-Pest suite, Harry ordered room service for everyone on his own resort charge card. After filling their bellies with the best Mar-A-Verde's cafeteria could offer, O'Connor pulled out her set of Cards Against Humanity. Both Sam and Harry were newcomers to the game, which made it more interesting. Harry laughed more in one hour than he had in years.

"Okay peeps. This is the final round. Normally I'm a party animal. Sam can back me up on that. But I'm fading fast." O'Connor drew a black card and read it aloud. "This is your captain speaking. Fasten your seat belts and prepare for..." She looked at the rest of the group holding their collection of white cards with answers. They selected their best card and threw them in a pile.

O'Connor shuffled the cards looked at the answers. "I'm calling an audible and reading the best answer. Any objections?"

Hope yawned as she shook her head.

"And the winner is: 'Fasten your seat belts and prepare for... sweet, sweet vengeance.' "

"That was mine." Sam bumped fists with Harry.

Hope had crashed on one side of the king bed. As she snored softly, O'Connor took the other side. Sam stretched out on one of the sofas.

Harry looked at Daniela then eyed the other sofa. "Can we crash here tonight?"

"This sounds a bit weird coming from me, but be my guest." Sam said.

"Just keep the fucking to a minimum unless I'm invited." O'Connor chuckled from the opposite side of the room.

"Noted." Harry laid down on the sofa and Daniela snuggled

in between his body and the backrest, using his shoulder as a pillow. She fell asleep in minutes.

Soon the entire room buzzed with the cadence of four different snores. Harry stared at the stars through the balcony window until sleep overtook him as well.

But Harry's sleep was a restless one, floating over images of Larsen's untapped rage.

HARRY WOKE AT four in the morning, his stomach in knots. The room carried a stillness, the cacophony of snores at a surprising minimum. But something felt off and he couldn't let it go.

So much for a good night's sleep.

He extricated himself from Daniela's arms, taking care not to wake her, and grabbed his shoes. He had been on far too many one night stands in his youth to forget how to leave quietly in the middle of the night.

Harry unlatched the door, stepped out, and eased the door closed again. He padded down the hallway until he was out of earshot. He slipped on his shoes and disappeared down the emergency stairwell.

Outside, his autopilot kicked in. He headed towards the clubhouse sink hole before he knew exactly where he was going. His guts were making the decisions.

All his life Harry had trusted his gut instinct. It had never failed to steer him in the right direction. In the wee hours of the morning, it had worked its magic again.

As he approached the scaffold and ladder structure spanning the clubhouse sink hole, he saw a darkened figure bent over the supplies. He slipped his feet out of his shoes and skulked closer.

The mystery man was dressed all in black, but the idiot had forgotten to wear a hat. His bald white head gave him away.

"Hey!" Harry broke into a soundless sprint, his bare feet tearing clumps of turf between his toes.

Larsen looked back, startled, and began pushing equipment into the chasm.

"What the *fuck* are you doing?" Harry ran top speed, but even that wasn't fast enough as he watched Larsen push thousands of dollars of equipment and hours of hard work into the sink hole.

Larsen pushed the large silver Kill-O-Matic case over the edge just as Harry tackled him. The two rolled across the grass. Harry swung his leg out and stopped himself. He grabbed Larsen's collar and slammed him into the ground repeatedly.

"Are you *crazy?*" Harry unloaded his fist against Larsen's face, opening a gash along his cheekbone. "We're trying to help you, you damn fool!" He hit Larsen two more times in the face before a force pulled him off.

Sam stood beside the two spent men. He grabbed Larsen's shirt with one hand and lifted him up to eye level, the tips of Larsen's shoes barely touching the ground. He headed toward the sink hole with brisk steps.

"Wait!" Larsen tried to crane his neck around to see where Sam was heading, but the panic in his eyes made it obvious he already knew. "Where are you going? Let go of me."

Sam showed no signs of slowing down as the edge of the sink hole drew closer with each step.

"No, Sam." Harry ran after the two men. "He's not worth it."

"No, stop," Larsen cried. "Please!"

Sam halted inches from the edge, holding Larsen's life with one muscular tattooed hand. "You want to know something?"

Larsen's dangling feet crumbled the edge with his toes. "What? That you're crazy?"

"I'm not afraid to die. Are you?" Sam shook Larsen and the bald man screamed. More turf and dirt fell away into the blackened chasm. "You fight me and we both go over. I don't give a shit."

Larsen lost his fight and began to whimper. "Please. Don't drop me down there."

"Give me one good reason why not." Sam shook Larsen again for emphasis.

"I'll do anything you want," Larsen said. "Stay out of your way. Anything. Now please let me go."

"True fact. If I dropped you right now, the fall wouldn't kill you, but you'd be dead within minutes anyway. Torn to pieces by the very things you asked Harry to get rid of." An evil grin spread across Sam's face. He was enjoying this. "Sounds like poetic justice to me."

Sam rocked forward on his feet toward the chasm. Larsen waved his arms wildly then began tugging on Sam's arm.

"No no no... no please." Larsen cried. "No." Liquid streamed from his left pant leg. "I'm sorry. I'm sorry."

"If I were you, I'd be more worried about O'Connor." Sam pulled Larsen back from the edge and threw him on the grass. "She shoots first and *sometimes* asks questions later." Sam hooked a thumb at the sink hole. "And you just destroyed her pride and joy."

Larsen jammed his heels into the grass attempting to scramble away from Sam.

"You're going to let us do what we need to do." Sam crouched near Larsen, making the man cower. "If we're lucky, we'll save this resort and maybe your career. But don't fuck with me or anyone on our team. Or our equipment." Sam stood. "If you do, I'll find you and kill you with my bare hands. We clear?"

Larsen nodded rapidly.

"Remember." Sam crossed his arms over his chest, his muscled prison tattoos flexing. "I've got nothing to lose."

Harry stepped next to Sam holding the break-action shotgun in one hand and his phone in the other. He had been recording the entire exchange on video. He shrugged at Larsen. "Insurance."

Larsen stood, brushed himself off, and ran his dirty hands over his face and bald head. A piss stain spread out from his crotch and down his left leg.

"I'll put in a good word with Strunk for you," Harry said. "And I'll keep you informed."

Larsen said nothing. He turned and hustled back to the clubhouse and disappeared inside.

"Holy shit, Sam." Harry grinned. "Where the hell did that come from? I thought for sure you and Larsen were going over the edge."

"After fifteen years in prison you come away with certain... skills." Sam glanced at him sideways. "Our little secret, okay?"

Harry nodded. "Sure, sure."

Sam looked into the black chasm of the sink hole. "O'Connor's going to be pissed."

"Nothing we can do about it now. I don't suppose you want to try catching some shut-eye?"

"No. I'll stay here just in case that fuckwit decides to return. But you should. You've got a damn fine woman waiting for you."

"But Sam, I—"

"Go. I'm not taking no for an answer."

Harry nodded. "Thanks Sam. See you in a couple hours." He walked back to the resort's side doors and stepped inside.

Sam laid back on the grass but the squeals of acidbacks below and knowing he was just feet from certain death eroded his attempt to relax. He moved back towards the clubhouse and found safer ground. But was it really safer? Or was there unknown tunnels below this new position too? He pushed the thought out of his head.

On his back, his hands clasped behind his head, the early morning air felt cool and sweet against Sam's skin. A cloudless and star-filled sky expanded above. It wasn't true. He had a lot to lose and this moment was just one of many.

As the impending glow of sunrise began to simmer on the horizon, Sam set a goal to take in another night like this one. But he'd have to get through the day first.

THE NEXT MORNING Harry arrived with his maintenance cart loaded with two large plastic bins. Sam and O'Connor were engaged in an argument by the remaining pile of equipment. He hopped out of the driver's seat, grabbed one of the bins from the back, and ran toward them.

"Larsen fucked us," Hope said as he passed her.

Harry exchanged a look with Sam as he dropped the bin next to the other supplies. "Why'd you tell her?"

"I didn't. She just knew. What's in the bin?"

Harry tapped the sealed lid. "Bait."

"I'll kill him!" The veins in O'Connor's neck stood out in angry ropes and her face flushed red. "I'll find him and rip his fucking head off. Use *it* for bait."

Harry joined Sam's struggle to keep O'Connor from enacting her rage upon Larsen.

"He's not worth it," Harry said. "Let's just get the job done and we all can go home."

O'Connor grit her teeth around a fresh cigar. "If I see that motherfucker again, all bets are off."

Daniela approached the three of them. "I took a look around. It's not as bad as it looks. The soil at the bottom of the sink hole is soft and most of the equipment that Larsen pushed over is stuck, not smashed."

"Doesn't change what he did." O'Connor paced back and forth in an attempt to calm herself.

"O'Connor." Sam held up a lighter and sparked a flame. "Relax."

She offered a small smile. "You're getting to know me a bit too well, Sam." O'Connor rolled her cigar in the flame, drawing air in and puffing thick smoke out, roasting all sides of the hand-rolled tobacco until she developed a cherry of coals at the tip. She closed her eyes and let go a sigh of relief. "Now that's the stuff."

Sam stood at the edge of the sink hole. "Look on the bright side. We don't have to lower all that stuff into the hole. We just have to set it up."

That flipped O'Connor's mood. "First things first. We need to know how acidbacks react to electricity." She looked at Hope. "Help me suit up."

Hope scanned the collection of supplies still above ground for the plastic bin that held her rope lights. She stepped to the edge of the sink hole and her shoulders deflated. "Fuck me. The asshole pushed them over."

"Then it looks like we're going underground together." O'Connor slapped Hope's shoulder. "Again."

"Great," Hope said. "Can't wait."

Harry pulled the snatch block over to the side of the sink hole. "I tied a loop underneath for your feet, plus there's extra rope on the end that I want to tie around your waists."

"Why?" O'Connor sent a smoke ring that encircled Harry's head.

"Because it's a sink hole. And sink holes are unpredictable."

"So am I." O'Connor clicked her tongue at him.

Hope fastened a battery pack to her waist and handed another to O'Connor. They both plugged in their taser rods and clipped walkie-talkies to their belts.

O'Connor triggered the weapon and a blue arc bridged the gap at the end. The acrid scent of ozone filled the air. "I'll never get tired of these babies."

"Maybe we could incorporate a light into the design next time." Hope found two large hunting knives with leather scabbards, attached one to her belt and flipped the knife, handle first, to O'Connor.

Hope pulled up a pair of binoculars. "What about these?"

O'Connor shook her head. "Like I want to see those things up-close."

"These will help." Daniela held two flashlights with lanyards attached. "Hang them from your necks."

"A couple of brainiacs, you two are." O'Connor guffawed. "Where would we be without you?"

"Dead? Or maimed?" Hope offered a playful grin. "Or both?"

"That's the spirit."

Harry tied the extra rope around Hope's waist in a bowline hitch and repeated the procedure for O'Connor.

Hope eyed the knot with a wary eye. "You sure that's going to stay tied?"

Harry smiled. "Bowlines are failure-proof. Everyone should know how to tie one. In fact, gather round." He grabbed a short length of rope. "Imagine your rope is a tree." Harry made a loop at one end of the rope. "This is the rabbit hole next to the tree."

"Jesus," O'Connor said. "What is this, Sunday School?"

Harry gave O'Connor a cool gaze. "This knot might save your life some day."

"So zip it." Sam elbowed O'Connor and refocused his attention on Harry's demonstration. "Continue."

"The end of the rope is the rabbit," Harry said. "It comes out of the hole, runs around the back of the tree, and goes back down the hole." He pulled the ropes tight. "That's it. One of the best knots you'll ever learn."

"Stupid rabbit. Now step aside." O'Connor placed her right boot into the foothold and hooked her elbow around the two ropes passing through the snatch block. "You sure this rope is going to hold both of us?"

Harry crossed his arms against his chest. "The rope's rated for 500 pounds. You and Hope don't weigh that much combined. Plus, the snatch block cuts the load by half."

O'Connor cocked her head to one side. "Did you say *snatch?*" She threw her head back and roared with laughter. "What a coincidence. Two women hanging from a *snatch* block."

Hope realized she still had the binoculars in her hand and handed them to Harry. She stepped into the foothold and settled her foot next to O'Connor's. The ladder creaked but held. "Could be worse. We could be hanging by our... you know."

"Wait." O'Connor furrowed her brow. "How would that work?"

"Forget it."

Daniela shook her head and chuckled to herself.

Hope glanced back at Harry, then above her head. "How much can the... ladders hold?"

"That I don't know." Harry had run the rope from the scaffold structure to a second pulley attached to a nearby tree. "You ladies ready?"

O'Connor held up her thumb. "Go for it, Harry my man."

Harry tossed the binoculars to the grass and untied the anchor. "Everyone on deck." Sam and Daniela took hold of the rope behind Harry and all three began lowering Hope and O'Connor into the sink hole.

"What's your plan?" Sam asked.

"Zap some acidbacks and see if they conduct."

"Don't be a hero."

O'Connor gave Sam a sideways look as she and Hope descended below the turf. "Hero? When have I ever done that?"

Hope turned on her flashlight and scanned the bottom of the sink hole. The morning sun cast only half of the bottom in direct sunshine, but she wasn't taking any risks.

"Hey." From the foothold O'Connor stood face to face with Hope. "You on the rag?"

"What the fuck, O'Connor." Hope grimaced.

"No, I'm serious." O'Connor surveyed the bottom's steady approach. "Think about it. These things are like leeches on steroids. Leeches love blood, so..."

"Oh shit." Hope's face went ashen. "No, but I see what you mean." She looked up the two ropes suspending them. "I've got a bad feeling about this. Fifteen feet suddenly seems a lot deeper."

O'Connor stepped off the foothold. "Shut your mouth. Let's get to work."

Hope placed one foot into the soft floor of the sink hole. Patches of grassy turf scattered the area. The Kill-O-Matic looked still intact, leaning to one side near the opposite wall. The two LED lights lying next to it were too far to assess damage.

She righted the plastic tub containing the rope lights and placed the spilled contents back inside. "Want to get the light suit on?"

"Quiet." O'Connor cocked her head. "Listen."

Hope froze. Muted sounds of birds from above filtered into the hole but there was another sound beneath it all. A low thumping and squealing. And it was getting louder.

"I think I want to get the fuck out of here." Hope snapped the lid on the tub of rope lights and dragged it by its handle to the snatch block's foothold. "O'Connor. Come on!" Hope hissed as she placed her foot in the foothold loop.

O'Connor ignored her. She turned her head slowly side to side. She took a puff from her cigar. "I can't locate the source," she said in a low whisper.

"Fuck the source. Let's go."

"But we just got here." O'Connor clicked on her flashlight and scanned the smaller tunnel openings exposed on the sink hole wall. "Come out, come out, wherever you are... little acidback fucks."

As if on command, five acidbacks emerged from different tunnel openings near the floor of the sinkhole, their fanged orifices twisting on their bloated bodies, locating O'Connor's position. A sixth acidback wriggled down an exposed root to join the others.

"Uh, O'Connor..."

"Yeah. I can handle one or two at once, but this..." O'Connor backed toward Hope. "No fucking way."

The acidbacks, sensing motion, sound, heat, or a combination of all three, shot forth converging on Hope and O'Connor's position.

"SAM! HARRY!" Hope unclipped her walkie-talkie. "Get us out of here!" She saw Sam poke his head over the edge and thought she heard him swear as she grabbed the handle of the plastic bin. She returned her walkie-talkie to her belt.

The ropes began to snake through the snatch block, but the foothold below it remained slack.

"Get your taser ready." O'Connor set her foot next to Hope's in the foothold.

"Can't. I got to carry the bin."

"What? Drop it."

Hope shook her head. "We need the rope lights."

The acidbacks closed in, gnashing their fangs.

"You better be right." O'Connor went to grab her radio but her taser rod took priority. She yelled instead, "Faster, Sam, goddamn it!"

The snatch block lifted Hope and O'Connor off the soft dirt floor just as the acidbacks reached their launch point.

"That's right, my pretties. Come to mama." O'Connor crouched on her right leg, hooked one arm around the snatch block itself, and extended the end of her taser toward the onslaught of acidbacks.

The electrified prongs touched the veined skin of the fastest acidback and blasted it backward in a smoking heap.

"Stop."

Hope glared at O'Connor, confused, her free arm straining under the weight of the bin of rope lights. "What?"

"STOP." O'Connor called up. "Hold our position."

Command received. The snatch block stopped with a bounce and Sam poked his head over the edge. "You okay?"

"Just hold for second," Hope called up before turning to O'Connor. "You know what you're doing?"

The remaining five acidbacks clambered over the dead one in an attempt to get close to O'Connor. The mass of mottled flesh contorted and twisted together, resembling a meat grinder from hell.

"Trust me." O'Connor chose her moment and jammed the taser rod into the center of the writhing acidbacks. "Eat my disco stick, you fat fucks."

Like a land mine going off, the remaining five creatures exploded backward toward the tunnel openings they had emerged from. But instead of slavering in a feeding frenzy, they lay dead, their bodies in pieces, their skin smoking and charred.

"I love the smell of burning acidbacks in the morning." O'Connor grinned. "Sam! Get us out of—"

The floor of the sinkhole crumbled and fell away. The dead acidbacks, the two LED lights, and the Kill-O-Matic descended into a dank cavern with no discernible bottom, except for the sound of equipment smashing in the darkness below.

"Holy shit." Hope faced O'Connor, wide-eyed. "Those taser rods really work."

"Maybe a little too well." O'Connor yelled up the rope. "Sam! Resume Operation 'Get us the FUCK out of here.'"

"Fast," Hope said. "My arm is about to drop off."

The two women ascended to the top of the sink hole, safe for now. But the expansive cavern below remained poised to swallow everyone whole.

HOLDING ON TO the scaffold, Sam reached out into the chasm and took the plastic bin from Hope's straining hand. As he set the bin next to the remaining equipment, Harry pulled him back.

"Not so close to the edge," he said. "Don't want any more deaths. We're flirting with disaster as it is."

"Got it," Sam nodded. He grabbed a hoe, hooked the rope connected to the snatch block, and pulled Hope and O'Connor closer to the edge.

"You see the bottom drop out?" O'Connor narrowed her eyes below and tried to spot detail with her flashlight.

"We felt it first," Daniela said. "Heard it second."

With one end of a rope wrapped around his arm and the other end tied to a nearby tree, Sam offered his hand to Hope, then O'Connor, pulling them to safety. "What about the Kill-O-Matic?"

Hope shook her head.

"Fuck if I know." O'Connor clicked off the flashlight around her neck and unplugged her taser rod. She motioned at Hope to do the same. "It sounded pretty bad down there, but we won't know for sure until we go back. One thing's for sure. Larsen just sealed his fate. Next time I see him—"

"We did save the rope lights." Hope pointed at the bin Sam had taken moments earlier. "And the taser rods work."

"Like a hot damn." Excitement returned to O'Connor's eyes, her momentary hatred for Larsen placed on the back burner where it needed to be. "Should have seen it, Sam. Zap-kaBOOM!" She mimed an explosion with her hands.

Harry stepped to within a couple feet from the edge. "How far down are we now?"

Daniela picked up a stone and casually tossed it into the chasm. She counted to herself *one... two... three* before the sound of impact echoed back up the hole. "About three seconds drop time equals..." She did the math in her head. "About fifty meters. One-hundred sixty feet. Or half the height of the Statue of Liberty."

"Thank God for academics." Sam smirked at O'Connor. Hope noticed the exchange.

"Holy shit." Harry slapped his hand to his forehead and rubbed it. He looked back at the clubhouse to judge distance. "That might be too far to tap into the resort's power supply."

"Just plug a bunch of power cords together." O'Connor brushed her hands together like she had just finished a project. "Easy peasy lemon squeezy."

Harry shook his head. "It's not that simple. Doing shit like that could start a fire."

"Just get someone to monitor the plug," O'Connor said. "If it bursts into flame, just unplug it."

"We do have generators." Hope shifted her spot to get a better view of the equipment. "Looks like two."

Harry nodded. "They'll work for what's left of the LED lights but I'm not sure about your Kill-O-Matic."

"If it still works," O'Connor said.

"What does that thing draw? How many amps?"

O'Connor shrugged. "No idea. As much as it can? Washington was the genius in that department."

"Probably fifteen amps." Harry thought a moment as he scanned his pile of equipment. "I might have a ten or a twelve gauge extension cord long enough."

O'Connor grabbed the bin with the rope lights. "Hope, set me up with a light suit?"

Given a task that could potentially save the day, Hope sprang into action.

"Can I assist?" Daniela raised her brows at Hope.

"For sure."

The two women anchored the rope lights at the base of O'Connor's feet and began a process of weaving them around her legs, working up toward her hips.

"Watch the crotch, ladies." Cigar smoke blasted from O'Connor's lips. "I'm pretty volatile down there." She threw her head back and laughed.

"Noted." Hope rolled her eyes at Daniela and they exchanged a smile. She plugged both rope lights together and finally into the battery pack on O'Connor's belt.

O'Connor's legs lit up like bright beacons. "Hope, you're a damn genius. That's why I need you down there with me." She switched off the lights.

Hope balked. "I don't know, O'Connor. Twice is enough. What about Daniela?"

"I need someone familiar with the Kill-O-Matic and…" O'Connor peered at Sam. "I'd rather Sam's muscles stay up top."

"I could do it," Daniela said. "I'm a quick study."

O'Connor regarded her, assessing her ability. "I'm sure you are, but—"

"Okay." Hope sighed. She knew she had a choice but the reality of the situation chose for her. "Let's get those lights on me too."

One leg at a time, Daniela wrapped Hope with rope lights. The ends met at Hope's waist where she plugged them into her battery pack. They shone just as brightly as O'Connor's had moments ago. Hope turned the lights off to conserve power.

Daniela crossed her arms, satisfied with her work. "You're good to go."

WHILE O'CONNOR AND HOPE suited up with rope lights, Sam and Harry collected the necessary equipment for the next entry into the sink hole.

Harry examined several coils of extension cord. None were long enough. "With the bottom falling out like that, I don't trust this apparatus." He looked past the scaffold and out onto the golf course. "This entire resort could be sitting on an expressway to hell."

"We can only work with what we can see." Sam had lined up a generator and three LED task lights. "We got any more extra rope long enough to lower these down?"

"No. Just short pieces. We'll have to lower the equipment in a second load."

"Great." Sam said. "You can break the news to our enforcers."

"Speaking of which." Harry pulled out his phone and dialed. The call connected after one ring. "Larsen?"

There was no response. Typical behavior from a coward.

Harry carried on anyway. "Listen. The sink hole by the clubhouse. It's expanded into something much larger. But it's subterranean. The whole resort could be sitting on an underground house of cards that could go at any minute."

He paused for a response from Larsen but was unsurprised when he received none.

"I still recommend you evacuate the resort immediately, staff and guests, just to be safe." Harry listened for a moment. "Larsen? You hearing this?" He ended the call and shook his head. "That fool's inaction is going to cause more deaths."

Hope had just finished testing her newly applied "light pants".

Harry looked at O'Connor and Hope. "Looking pretty blingtastic. Shall we get phase two under way?"

"What's phase two?" O'Connor gnawed at the end of her cigar.

"I thought you could tell me," Harry said. "What I can tell you is we'll have to lower the generator and task lights after you two are down there."

O'Connor crossed her arms and gave Harry a dubious look. "Why?"

"One, we only have one rope long enough to reach the bottom," Harry said. "And two, we need someone down there to untie the generator from its harness."

"So you'd be stranding us down there for a while?" Hope eyed Harry and Sam with concern.

Harry nodded. "Maybe five minutes. But once the generator is down there, you'll have hours of light and potentially enough juice to run your Kill-O-Magic."

"Kill-O-*Matic*," O'Connor corrected. "Although it is almost magic."

Sam laughed. "As magic as a toaster in a bathtub. So what's the plan?"

"After our last shindig, we won't be doing anything except waiting for that generator and those lights." O'Connor crouched as much as the rope lights would allow. "How does the generator work?"

Harry pulled the unit closer on its back wheels. "Pretty simple really. I've already done a pre-check and set the fuel valve open. Make sure there's nothing plugged in and hit this switch." He pointed to a rocker switch. "Just flip the switch to 'on', then yard on the rip cord here." He demonstrated and the generator roared to life. He turned it off and the motor died. "You might have to adjust the choke here, but that's easy."

"Okay, what are we waiting for?" O'Connor itched to get moving. "Let's go."

"What about carbon monoxide?" Hope focused on Harry.

"Smart question," Harry said. "Obviously run it only when you need to. With no ventilation down there, you can imagine what would happen if you kept it running." He alternated his gaze between Hope and O'Connor. "I'd leave it off until you're ready to come up."

"So set up the Kill-O-Matic and bait it, kill the queen, and get the hell out of there," Hope said.

"Gee, is that all?" O'Connor placed her hands on her hips. "Why don't I mine for diamonds while I'm at it?"

"We can't really use the LEDs right away unless we run them off batteries. Or we risk dying from carbon monoxide poisoning. Oh, what fun." Hope picked up a task light to look at its rating. "Thirty-five watts? Holy shit. We *could* run them off batteries. Do we have extras, O'Connor?"

"Who the hell do you think you're talking to?" O'Connor strolled with indignant steps to a plastic storage bin. She held up an armful of belt batteries with plug-in receptacles on the side. They were the same type as Hope and O'Connor were currently wearing around their waists. "Of course we got extra. I'm always well-stocked for any job site."

"Okay, I propose a change to the plan," Hope said.

"Shoot." Sam motioned at her to proceed.

"O'Connor and I get down there with a few LED lights and battery packs and we set up a perimeter big enough to surround the Kill-O-Matic. With me so far?"

O'Connor shifted her eyes with boredom. "A toddler could understand your plan."

"Would you rather do this alone, *Bertha?*" Hope glared at O'Connor.

"Ladies, please." Harry spoke in calm tones. "Everyone has a role to play. Hope, please continue."

"Kiss-ass." O'Connor blew cigar smoke at Harry.

Harry let the gray cloud pass his head. "Look, O'Connor. I

still hold your purse strings. So you might want to shut up, okay?"

O'Connor shrugged indifference, but it was clear Harry had taken some of the wind out of her sails.

"As I was saying, build a perimeter, set up the Kill-O-Matic, hopefully it still works, and bait it. We kill the queen and you guys pull us out."

"A good plan but still ambitious as fuck." Everyone turned to Daniela. "What? I can swear too, you know."

"Clearly." Harry grinned at her before turning to O'Connor. "Let me check your tether." He ran his hand along the piece of rope connecting Hope and O'Connor, checking the integrity of the knots as he went. "Bowlines never fail."

Sam draped two battery packs over Hope and O'Connor's shoulders. The two women resembled militia carrying belts of ammo. He hung three LED task lights off each of the belts.

Sam eyed O'Connor and Hope. "Okay. You two ready? You're not going to rip each other's eyes out, are you?"

"I'm good now," O'Connor leaned her head toward Hope and fluttered her eyelashes. "How about you? Do we need to have make-up sex?"

Hope shook her head in exasperation but shared a small grin with Sam. "Yeah, I'm good."

Sam picked up the hoe and pulled the snatch block with its rope foothold close to the sink hole's edge. He held up an arm for O'Connor steady herself on. "Age before beauty." He winked.

"You're an asshole." O'Connor stepped into the foothold. "Harry, hand me another taser rod, will you?"

Daniela had already grabbed one and relayed it to Harry. He passed it on to O'Connor.

"Thanks. You can never have enough of these babies."

It was Hope's turn. She took Sam's hand and guided her foot next to O'Connor's. "How many times are we going to do this?"

"Third time lucky, eh Missy?" O'Connor laughed. "It's always the women who save the day. Let 'er rip!"

Harry, Daniela, and Sam let the rope out, faster this time.

O'Connor began to sing the opening riff to "Start Me Up" by the Rolling Stones. She switched on the rope lights covering her pants. "Light me up! Once you light me up I'll never die..."

Hope mouthed "Oh my God" as she switched on her rope lights as well. Harry, Sam, and Daniela laughed and waved goodbye as the two women disappeared into the chasm once again.

O'Connor's butchered rendition of The Rolling Stones echoed back out of the sink hole, but it did nothing to settle the overwhelming sense of unease.

HAND OVER FIST, Harry, Daniela, and Sam fed rope through the pulley on the scaffold structure in steady lengths. Sam was first to reach the end.

"Whoa. That's it, folks. We got to tie it off." Sam pulled the rope back and around the trunk of the tree. "I'll hold it and you do your magic with that knot."

Harry took the end and fashioned a double bowline.

O'Connor's voice broke over Sam's walkie-talkie. "What's the holdup, folks?"

Sam pressed the talk button on his walkie-talkie. "What do you mean?"

"I mean you're supposed to lower us to the bottom." O'Connor's voice crackled. "We've got another...five feet to go."

"Shit." Sam looked at Harry. "Can we tie on another half dozen feet?"

"You mean a dozen feet," Daniela said. "The snatch block doubles everything."

Harry nodded. "She's right. And I might have enough." He ran to a plastic bin and began digging through its contents.

Sam raised the walkie-talkie to his mouth. "Hold on, we're working on something."

"We're not going anywhere but hurry it up," O'Connor's filtered voice said. "Our feet are going numb."

Harry found pieces of rope and spanned them across his chest and outstretched arms to get an idea of their length. They kept coming up short. He grabbed the last piece of rope in the bin.

"Come on come on." Harry counted one chest and arm width. Two. Three... and a bit. "That's going to have to do." He ran back to the tree. "I'll tie a new knot around the tree, then untie the old one." He looked at Daniela and Sam as he began the new knot with the shorter rope. "Can you to keep them suspended until I tie the two ropes together?"

Sam and Daniela exchanged doubtful looks. "Looks like we have no choice."

"We'll be okay, right Sam?" Daniela raised her brow waiting for the only possible answer.

"We'll be fine."

Harry nodded as he yanked the new knot tight. Sweat slicked his face and arms. "Okay, pull them up so I have some slack to work with."

Sam and Daniela pulled back on the rope supporting Hope and O'Connor.

"What the fuck's going on up there?" O'Connor's annoyance came through loud and clear over the walkie-talkie's cheap speaker. "We're supposed to go *down* not up."

"Harry, take my walkie." Sam motioned at his belt.

Instead, Harry pressed the talk button without removing the handheld radio from Sam's belt. "Harry here. Going to be some bumps. Hold on."

"Hold on to what?" O'Connor's electronic voice echoed back. "My tits?"

Harry held out his hand. "Give me some slack."

Sam and Daniela pulled up enough rope for Harry to work with but holding the rope stationary took enormous effort.

Harry tied a small bowline loop on the end of the rope tied to the tree. He inserted the end of the support rope through the loop and was about to secure it with a second bowline when a gunshot rang out.

Sam and Daniela flinched and ducked, losing their grasp on the rope. The end shot out of Harry's sweat-greased fingers, headed for the pulley on the scaffold bridge, and plummeted to the bottom of the sink hole.

Larsen stood next to one side of the scaffold structure with the break-action shotgun in his hands, one barrel releasing wisps of smoke.

Harry exchanged worried glances with Daniela and Sam. He stood and raised his hands, palms forward. "What are you doing with the shotgun, Larsen?"

"I've had a change of heart, Harry," Larsen said. "I saw one of those things. So I shot it."

"What the FUCK is going on up there?" O'Connor's voice buzzed from Sam's walkie-talkie. "Nearly broke my goddamn ass. And what was that noi—" Sam reached back and turned the walkie-talkie off.

"As you can see, we got people down there." Harry eyed the shotgun in Larsen's hands. "There are better ways to help. How about you give me the gun?"

"I think I'll hold on to it, thanks."

Harry took a few slow steps forward. "It's dangerous, Larsen. It's going to send the wrong message to the guests."

"It's too late for that." Larsen dead-eyed Harry.

Harry scanned the immediate area for anyone else, but the course looked deserted. Maybe Larsen had listened to him and sent out an evacuation notice to the staff and guests. "You know this is going to get back to Strunk eventually."

Larsen shook his head. "Don't give a shit. I'm his *little bitch* now."

Harry took another step forward, putting him within five feet of Larsen.

Larsen leveled the shotgun at him. "That's far enough."

"Easy, Larsen. Easy." Harry froze but managed a glance back at Daniela. She shook her head slowly, almost imperceptible, pleading him to stop with her eyes. He winked at her and turned back to Larsen. "I want you to give me the gun."

"I want you to step back."

Harry nodded and took a step back. "Okay. I did what you asked. Now give me the gun."

"It doesn't work that way, Harry." Larsen shifted his cool lifeless gaze from Harry to Sam and Daniela and back. "Who's Strunk's *little bitch* now?" He raised the barrel of the shotgun under his chin.

"NO!" Harry leapt forward, his hands reaching for the shotgun's barrel.

Larsen pulled the trigger.

Click.

Bewilderment set in when he realized his head was still in one piece. Harry tackled him and ripped the shotgun away from his hands. He broke the barrel open, dumped the shells to the grass, one used and one live, and tossed the gun aside.

"But I pulled the trigger." Larsen began to sob.

Harry took Larsen by the shoulders and shook him enough to get his attention. "Larsen, you need to get off this island. I suggest you do it as soon as possible."

Larsen nodded, still in a daze. "It was loaded and everything."

"I'd say you just got a second chance at life." Harry stood. "Make the most of it."

Larsen wandered back toward the clubhouse muttering to

himself when he spotted McCoy standing in the bay window. He stood recording the action on his phone.

"You!" he yelled, pointing his finger. "I want you off the premises immediately." He ran toward the nearest entrance as fast as McCoy disappeared from view.

Daniela ran to Harry, kissed his neck, and hugged him tight. "I thought I was going to lose you."

"How did Larsen survive?" Sam asked. "I saw the shells. One was live."

Harry sighed and grinned. "Larsen might know how to run a golf course, but he doesn't know shit about guns." He picked up the shotgun. "This old shotgun has a switch that controls which barrel is live. He didn't change barrels, so in effect he saved his own life by accident."

"Lucky son of a bitch," Sam said.

"Did you know he hadn't flipped that switch?" Daniela gave Harry a serious glare.

He shrugged. "The odds were in my favor."

Daniela slapped him on the chest hard. "Damn you, Harry Harcourt."

"Oh shit." Sam grabbed his walkie-talkie and turned it on. "Sorry O'Connor, Hope. We had a... situation."

"While you guys were having a threesome, we got some serious work done down here," O'Connor's voice crackled back. "The perimeter is set and guess what? The Kill-O-Matic survived. That Washington was a fucking engineering genius. So we need the bait and the generator."

"Seen any acidbacks?" Sam released the talk button to listen to O'Connor's response.

"We've heard them, but they've been keeping their distance." O'Connor paused. "From the looks of things, the tunnels don't run this deep. Bait will change all that."

"May I?" Harry beckoned for the walkie-talkie.

Sam handed it to him.

"O'Connor? Hope? Harry here. Before we can get you those supplies, I need you to do something for me."

"For the last time, Harry, I'm not sending you nudes." O'Connor chortled through the walkie-talkie's speaker.

"Very funny. Look, we lost the end of the rope," Harry said. "I need you to tie a big knot in the end of it so it can't pass through the snatch block."

"Hope's already on it," O'Connor's voice said. "In fact, you could probably start pulling up the rope any time."

"Got it. Harry out." He handed the walkie-talkie back to Sam.

"Excuse me, boys." Daniela stood behind them holding the hoe. "And keep the jokes to yourselves." She stepped forward, hooked the anchored support rope tied to the ladders and pulled it to the side of the sink hole.

Harry helped her raise the rope and Sam made sure the rope fell in neat coils to avoid tangling later. They had the snatch block in their hands less than three minutes later.

Hope had secured the end of the rope to the snatch block with a bowline knot.

Harry smiled. "I see someone's paying attention." He untied the bowline and fed a length of rope from the pile back through it. He held the end up for Daniela and Sam to see. "We've got to pass the end of this rope through that pulley." He pointed out to the middle of the ladders where one end of the rope was tied. "This is the end we pull to get Hope and O'Connor out of there. So... any volunteers?"

Sam didn't look at Daniela or pause with his response. "I'll do it. I was always good on monkey bars."

"You sure?" Harry appraised him seriously. "I could find some other gardening tools to try and do it remotely."

"It's only a matter of time before acidbacks attack Hope and O'Connor," Sam said. "Besides this is what you're paying us for."

"True." Harry shrugged and nodded at him. "So the end of

the rope has got to go through the pulley from the back side, so it comes out pointing toward us. Make sense?"

"Got it." Sam took a deep breath, clapped his hands, and rubbed them together. He raised the walkie-talkie to his mouth. "Hope, O'Connor, watch your heads. About to do something stupid." He tossed the walkie-talkie to Daniela. "Just in case I fall to my death."

She narrowed her eyes in warning. "Don't you dare."

Harry surveyed the scaffold and ladders on top. "How are you going to do it? Crawl out over top?"

Sam shook his head. "Brute force it, hanging from the rungs."

Harry and Daniela shared a look of concern. "I think we should tie a safety line to you, just in case."

Sam waved him off as he stepped to the side of the scaffold. He placed the end of the rope between his teeth, reached up to the ladders, and grabbed a rung. Sam let his weight settle into the structure and stepped into the void. With no time to waste, he swung himself rung by rung out to the center of the ladder. He stopped next to the pulley.

The strength of his arms and hands were all that separated him from a one-hundred sixty foot drop to the bottom. O'Connor and Hope could watch him die.

Sam let go with his right hand and took the rope from his mouth. He could hear Daniela's gasp from the edge. He began to insert the end of rope into the gap at the top of the pulley.

"Sam, the other way." Harry had cupped his hands so he didn't have to speak as loud. "The rope needs to go the other way!"

"Right," Sam mumbled. He pulled the rope end out and clamped it between his teeth. He placed his right hand one rung back which rotated his body to face the pulley.

Sam let go with his left hand this time, took the rope from

between his teeth and pushed it through pulley toward Harry and Daniela.

"You got it," Harry said. "Now get the hell back here pronto."

Sam clamped the rope in his teeth again and swung himself back to the edge of the sinkhole, Harry and Daniela feeding him slack as he went. He grabbed one side of the scaffolding and Harry gave him his hand.

Not quite ready for Sam's heft, both men began sliding back toward the edge.

"Dani!" Harry reached out to Daniela and they locked arms. Her efforts tipped the scale back to safety and solid ground. Sam grabbed the rope from his mouth, wrapped it a couple times around his wrist and collapsed to the grass.

The walkie-talkie on Daniela's belt crackled to life with O'Connor's voice. "You're the king of the apes, Sam. A jungle VIP."

Daniela pressed the talk button. "Sam says thanks."

"I don't want to do that again," Sam said between breaths. "Tie this fucker to the tree for me, Harry."

Without a moment's delay, Harry took the rope end from Sam, damp from his saliva, and fed it through the bowline loop tied to the extension. "And one more bowline will do it." He finished the second knot and tightened both ropes against each other.

Daniela had begun the task of pulling the support rope back through the ladder pulley. She grabbed the walkie-talkie from her belt. "Generator and bait will be down shortly."

"Good," O'Connor said. "I'm getting hungry."

Daniela looked at Harry. "Speaking of bait, did Greta get off all right?"

Harry raised his brows at her.

"Did she get off *the island* all right?"

Smirking, Harry continued. "I knew what you meant. And

yeah, she's long gone. Safe." He dragged the bins of bait next to the generator. "These were her final offerings."

Sam looped rope around the generator's frame. "Let's make it count."

The three set to work securing the generator for its descent into the sink hole. Every second of delay meant increasing danger to Hope and O'Connor. The acidbacks wouldn't stay away for long.

THE KILL-O-MATIC SAT on a mound of dirt and turf, slightly off-balance, in the center of the sink hole's expansive cavern. Higher up on the walls, just within the perimeter lights' reach, darkened tunnel openings looked down on Hope and O'Connor like black, lifeless eyes.

"Generator's on its way down," Sam's voice buzzed through O'Connor's walkie talkie.

She looked up to the small blue expanse of sky overhead, bisected by the ladders and scaffold. The generator's rectangular frame descended at a steady pace until it settled next to the Kill-O-Matic.

Hope and O'Connor untied the support ropes.

"Release the bait, Sam my boy." O'Connor stowed the walkie-talkie back to her belt as she watched the snatch block rise back up the chasm.

Hope handed the power cord for the Kill-O-Matic to O'Connor. "Thought you'd like to do the honors."

"Don't mind if I do." O'Connor plugged in the unit. "It's going to be a real treat to see these fat bags fry."

A rumbling passed under their feet and the floor lowered by a few inches.

"Did you feel that? Was that an earthqu—"

"Ah!" O'Connor held up her index finger. "Don't say it. And yeah, I felt it." She'd been spooked and couldn't hide it.

"I don't like this." Hope scanned the sides of the sink hole for signs of danger.

"Then let's get this done and get the fuck out."

"Bait on its way," Sam's voice squawked.

"Finally." O'Connor watched the plastic bin descend.

Hope traced the length of rope between her waist and O'Connor's. "How long is our tether?"

"I don't know." O'Connor shrugged without taking her eyes off the bait. "Maybe fifty feet?"

"You know... we could just say we couldn't find the queen, set the trap, and get out of here." Hope raised her brow in anticipation of a "yes."

"Where's the fun in that?" O'Connor blew a cloud of cigar smoke out into the cavern and glanced at the rope between them. "Besides 'tied together, die together' has a certain ring to it, don't you think?"

"No."

The bait bin touched down. O'Connor untied its rope harness. "Give me a hand with this."

The two women lugged the bin to the Kill-O-Matic and placed it just inside the mesh door. O'Connor was about to pull off the lid when Hope stopped her.

"If that's what I think it is, it's going to be bloody."

O'Connor paused. "Right. Let's wait until the last minute."

"So which way are we headed?"

O'Connor glanced up at the ladder and scaffold above and oriented herself. "The first hole is that way. Remember the first hole?"

A shiver ran through Hope's back. "How could I forget?"

"I say we try one of those tunnels. It goes in the same direction." She pointed to a large tunnel about three feet in diameter and twelve feet up a slope from the base of the cavern.

"I was afraid you'd say that." Hope swallowed hard. "Can someone develop claustrophobia after the fact?"

"Come on, you're with me." O'Connor flashed her eyebrows. "What could go wrong?"

"You really want me to answer that?"

"Nah. Let's go."

"Just a sec." Hope maneuvered to the front of the Kill-O-Matic and picked up two of the LED task lights and their battery belts. "We could use these." She slung them over her shoulder.

"Good plan." O'Connor stepped up the slope, loose dirt and grass breaking away under her feet. "You remember what the queen looks like, right?"

"Yeah." Hope followed, less enthusiastically, the task lights and batteries rattling against her chest.

"That's right. Long and fat with twelve tits." O'Connor stopped and plucked the cigar from her mouth. "I wish I had twelve tits. It would make my sex dungeon the hottest spot in New York."

Hope stared at her. "I often find myself wondering if the words that flow out of your mouth are for real."

"Don't believe me? I'll invite you over sometime." O'Connor popped her cigar back in its designated spot. "But you got agree to put out."

Hope sighed. "Just go."

O'Connor plucked her walkie-talkie from her belt. "Sam, heading into the belly of the beast. Over and out."

As she clipped her walkie-talkie onto her belt, Sam's response crackled through. "Rog... O... nor."

"The walkie reception is getting spotty down here," O'Connor said.

Hope gathered the rope tether in loose loops so they could walk into the tunnel as close to each other as comfortable.

Armed with taser rods, rope lights on their legs, task lights, and large hunting knives, Hope and O'Connor stooped over and entered the tunnel. They looked like a Christmas parade gone terribly wrong.

Hope scrunched her nose. "Ugh. Smells like shit in here."

"Acidback B. O." O'Connor appeared not to notice. "The fuckers probably shit where they eat."

As the two progressed farther, the tunnel narrowed so much that they had to drop to their knees and crawl. Moist dirt, muddy in patches, oozed between their fingers.

"O'Connor, I'm not sure how much help I'm going to be." Hope realized that she was hyperventilating and made a point of slowing down her breathing. "Plus, the air in here is thin."

O'Connor took her cigar out, held it in front of her, and watched the wisps of smoke rise from the sputtering embers at the end. Tendrils collected in the nooks and crannies of the tunnel next to her head.

"Yeah. There's no air movement."

The tunnel joined with a larger tunnel running perpendicular to it. O'Connor checked both directions with her flashlight and turned right.

Using the renewed freedom to move, Hope stripped off the battery packs and LED task lights. She aimed one light down the path O'Connor hadn't taken, half expecting to see a bounding pack of acidbacks rushing towards her. She was met with nothing but light receding into darkness. Somehow that seemed worse.

She placed the second light facing the opposite direction, illuminating O'Connor's light-bedazzled backside and followed her. After what seemed like an eternity, the large tunnel snaked to the left and joined with another cavern, much like the one they left. The exception being no opening above leading to the sky.

About forty feet in diameter, the cavern resembled an ancient amphitheater that spread out from the tunnel's opening, with concentric stepped ledges leading down to the floor. Shadows breathed on the back wall.

This wasn't like the sink hole on the first hole. It was bigger, excavated with more precision. "I wonder how long it would have taken to dig a chamber like this," Hope whispered.

"Don't care." O'Connor cocked her head to one side. "There are things moving in here. I can hear them."

"And the squeaks. You remember the—"

"The squeaks. Yeah." O'Connor's cigar was completely out. She stowed it in her front pocket. "I got to get closer."

Hope tugged on O'Connor's shoulder. "We need to keep the element of surprise. As much as I hate to say it," she whispered, "we got to turn off our lights. Use your phone with the red filter."

"Good idea." O'Connor engaged the red filter on the back of her phone case and turned it on. "Are we fucking crazy?"

"Probably." Hope and O'Connor cast their fears behind them. "Lights out?"

"Lights out."

Both women turned off the lights around their legs. O'Connor grabbed one of her taser rods and eased herself out of the tunnel, the tether trailing behind her.

"Oh God. It reeks." Hope unhooked her own taser rod. "I'm going to stay right here if that's okay."

"More than okay, Missy." As O'Connor moved further into the cavern the red light on her phone pulled more detail out of the darkness. "Because if my hunch is right, I'm going to need you to stay put."

"Don't get too close," Hope said. "You need surprise on your side."

O'Connor winked at her and followed the ledge around the top of the exterior wall, the tether connecting her to Hope almost used up. Opposite the tunnel, part way up the back wall and within the reach of her phone's red light, lay not one but three acidback queens, all nursing their broods on a shelf of dirt. Their skin pulsed as the suckling pups fed.

She reached for her walkie talkie, then froze when one of the acidback queens shifted its position. O'Connor took careful steps back to the exit tunnel where Hope sat.

"Did you see that?" She spoke in a whisper. "We got babies and I didn't see any workers."

Hope nodded, both their faces awash in red light. "And multiple queens. It goes against the rules of eusociality. But there's something else."

"What's that?"

"This nest isn't connected to the one on the first hole," Hope said. "And that means there's more queens out there."

"Well, shit. We're just going to have to kill 'em all, one by one," O'Connor whispered. "Here's my plan. You wedge yourself into the tunnel and hold the line tight. I'll run along the top edge of this hell hole 'til the tether runs out and zap the fuckers as I go by in one fell swoop. Like a rope swing on its side, you get me? I should be able to fry them all in one go. Then we'll bug the fuck out of here."

"Who do you think you are, Cirque du Soleil?" Hope whispered. "You've got a limp for fuck's sake."

"Got any better ideas?"

Hope had nothing.

"Didn't think so." O'Connor turned her phone off and plunged their enclosed world into total darkness. "Disabled is a state of mind," her disembodied voice whispered. "Ready for Operation Cirque d' O'Connor?"

Hope scooted backward a couple feet and dug her heels into the earthy walls of the tunnel. Her nose had acclimatized to the smell, but she longed for fresh air. "Ready." She wrapped the rope around one hand to strengthen her grip on the tether.

O'Connor's voice floated like a ghost. "Lights on in three... two... one... Go!"

The LED leg lights blazed on both women, casting the cavern in an eerie glow. O'Connor grabbed the tether with one hand and ran around the top edge of the cavern until the rope reached its maximum length, snapping taut and nearly pulling Hope out of the escape tunnel.

O'Connor's momentum boosted her running speed and carried her around the back ledge of the cavern. She leaned out, pulled the trigger on the taser rod, and dragged blue arcing electricity across the veined skin of the first queen.

An easy target, the acidback opened up like a hot knife through gelatin. A gurgling screech echoed through the small dank space as a torrent of liquid guts cascaded down the cavern's stepped ledges to the floor below. The remaining two queens sensed danger and ejected their pups from their teats. Fanged orifices pulsed and squealed, following the heat of O'Connor's approach.

"Hurry!" The muscles in Hope's arms stretched to their limit. "They're pissed!"

"No shit." O'Connor's taser sliced open the second queen, narrowly missing the creature's ring of teeth, but the third had managed to orient its enormous body toward her. Her speed and the arc of the rope gave her no other choice but to run over the third queen. "Ramming speed!"

O'Connor leaped with her right foot, the tread of her boot sinking into the oily skin of the acidback's skin. The tread of her boot began to sizzle. The third queen flipped its mouth and undulating fangs around in an attempt to lock onto O'Connor's position. Instead, the creature's bulk acted like a springboard to propel O'Connor until she landed hard on her backside in the dirt. She jammed the taser's electrified prongs into the third queen's side and split the creature open. The acidback rolled to the cavern floor with a meaty *splat*.

"Suck it, bitch!" O'Connor stood and awkwardly began to run.

Most of the pups ejected from their mother's teats had tumbled into the growing slurry below. The pups that did survive scrambled along the edge of the cavern, in O'Connor's wake.

Hope strained against both O'Connor's weight and momentum combined. The plan was working, but like so many of her plans, the conclusion was open-ended.

O'Connor stumbled on a rock and slipped down to the next ledge toward the pool of bloody acid, bubbling entrails, and certain death. It was now or never.

Adrenaline surged through Hope's body and energized her arms and legs. She pulled back the tether quickly, hand over hand as O'Connor ran, helping to raise her up the stepped ledge of the cavern and back to the tunnel where Hope sat. She extended her hand to O'Connor and pulled her up.

Both breathing hard due to low oxygen levels, O'Connor still managed a hearty laugh. "Did you *see that shit?* God damn I'm good!"

"We're not out of danger yet." Hope flipped over and crouch-walked as fast as she could. "Those little bastards still know how to bite."

"What little—" O'Connor looked behind her to see the surviving acidback pups scrambling over themselves, up the side of the cavern's ledges like they were playing hopscotch. And there were no acidic entrails on this side of the cavern to slow them down. Once they got to the tunnel there would be no stopping them.

"Fuck me." O'Connor had to shuffle on both hands and one knee due to the limited bending range of her left knee within her prosthetic. She could move fast but would it be fast enough?

They rounded the bend in the tunnel toward the two task lights Hope had left behind. O'Connor looked backward, between her legs. The upside-down image of acidback pups gaining on her kicked her shuffle-crawl into overdrive.

Hope disappeared into the small tunnel that lead back to the sink hole. O'Connor navigated around the task light and sent a bright blast back at the pups, sizzling them in their tracks. But O'Connor's prosthetic leg bumped the light as she entered the escape tunnel. Uninjured acidback pups trampled the burned leaders and their pursuit resumed.

"Fuck. Those little bastards made it past the light," O'Connor called out.

Hope never thought she would feel so elated to be back in the bottom of a sink hole, but the glimpse of blue sky, the ladders up top, and the snatch block hanging nearby renewed her trust that everything would turn out okay. And the air. She filled her lungs with glorious fresh air.

Hope grabbed her walkie-talkie and spoke between breaths. "Get ready to pull us up." She gathered the tether in loose loops as O'Connor's rope-lit legs approached the tunnel's exit.

"Those little fuckers are relentless." O'Connor hopped down from the tunnel opening and unhooked her two taser rods.

"You did just slaughter their mothers."

"Okay. Since you put it that way." O'Connor locked the tasers' triggers to their "on" position and jammed their handles in the dirt, pointing back into the tunnel. Blue arcs buzzed at their tips. "The on-board batteries won't last long, but it'll give us a few more seconds."

From high in the walls of the sink hole, rumbling and screeching echoed from the tunnels above. Adult acidbacks stuck their fanged maws into the open space like they were searching for the rest of the tunnel. The first one dropped to the floor, then another dropped from a different tunnel. Like lemmings to a cliff, an increasing torrent of acidbacks flew out of the tunnel openings, all converging on Hope and O'Connor.

Hope looked toward the snatch block, their salvation. They could still make it in time. "Somehow they know what we did." She tugged O'Connor by the tether. "We got to get out of here."

The first of the acidback pups reached the tunnel exit, immediately fried by one of the taser rods.

"Eat my ozone, you bastards."

Hope yanked the tether and pulled O'Connor into action. They both ran toward the snatch block as packs of frenzied acidbacks gained on them in all directions. The stampede of pups in the tunnel's exit pushed past the taser rods and the collected dead, tumbling out of the tunnel and joining the pursuit.

Hope was first to the snatch block and inserted her boot into the foothold.

"Shit, the bait!" O'Connor skidded to a stop and ran back to the Kill-O-Matic.

"O'Connor! No. There's no time."

But O'Connor was like a dog with a bone. She arrived at the mesh door to the Kill-O-Matic and kicked the bait bin over with her right boot, the tread still soft from acid burn. Several pounds of bloody fat-riddled steaks dumped to the cage's floor. She rounded the cage and pulled the starter cord of the electric generator.

"O'Connor! Forget it!" Hope yelled at the top of her lungs. Up top, her screaming must have caused alarm because the snatch block began to rise. "They're pulling us up! O'CONNOR! MOVE YOUR FUCKING ASS!"

O'Connor looked back at Hope, then to the advancing horde of acidbacks. Her odds of survival diminished with every passing second.

She gave one last tug of the starter cord, but the generator remained silent. "Fucking piece of shit." O'Connor bolted back toward Hope and the snatch block, the foothold now three feet off the ground.

The bait distracted half of the acidbacks and lured them into and around the Kill-O-Matic cage. The remaining half closed in on O'Connor, driven by their instinct to defend the colony at all costs.

Hope crouched on the foothold and reached down with her hand. "Your foot! Give me your foot!"

O'Connor raised her muddied right boot. Hope grabbed the warm tread and slid it next to hers. She locked hands with O'Connor and strained to pull her up as O'Connor straightened her right leg.

A flood of acidbacks encircled the spot directly under the rising snatch block. One creature latched onto O'Connor's left boot. She shook her leg but the creature remained, sinking its teeth further into her boot and prosthetic underneath.

"You better not fuck up my beautiful rubber foot." She raised her left foot up and made a fist.

"No. The acid!" The words were barely out of Hope's mouth before O'Connor followed through with a punch.

Her knuckle connected with the acidback's fleshy section just behind its fangs. The creature responded like any living thing receiving a blow to the head. It released its bite and fell back to the floor to rejoin the slavering horde below.

"Goddamn it." O'Connor's hand sizzled and smoked. She rubbed it against her shirt but ended up burning holes into the fabric. "Hurts like a son of a bitch." Despite what it had done to her shirt, she tucked her right hand under her left arm hooked around the snatch block.

"We're not out of this shit yet." Hope focused her gaze past her feet below. In their haste to get out of the sink hole, she had forgotten to reclaim the fifty feet of tether. Now several acidbacks had latched onto the loop of slackened rope tied between them.

"Am I seeing things?" O'Connor looked at Hope, dumbfounded.

"Unless we're suffering from a mass hallucination, you're not." Hope returned O'Connor's gaze. "Somehow they've developed the ability to climb rope. Maybe they always had it."

O'Connor looked up at the remaining distance between their

position and safety. "We got a ways to go and I've become a useless tit, so... you're up." She looked down at the loop of tether and the advancing acidbacks. "And they can climb a rope quickly, too."

Hope instinctively reached for her taser rod.

"A taser's a good idea, but you have to wait until they're within range. You're smarter than that."

"So what am I..." Hope paused to think, then grinned at O'Connor as she pulled out her Bowie knife.

"Atta girl."

Hope placed the carbon steel blade behind the rope tied to O'Connor's waist and worked it back and forth until her tether fell away. Half of the climbing acidbacks plummeted back to the sink hole floor.

"Harry's bowlines are no match against a knife." Hope grinned.

"Less talking, more cutting."

The acidbacks left on the tether seemed to sense their impending fate and increased their climbing speed. Their stubby clawed feet acted as anchors on the rope as their bodies expanded and contracted like demonic inchworms.

Hope ran the blade under the loop around her waist and cut through it on the fifth thrust of the blade. The rest of the tether fell away, taking the attached acidbacks with it.

The drop proved deadly. Hope and O'Connor watched the falling acidbacks explode upon impact.

"Bullseye." O'Connor threw her head back and managed a short laugh before the pain of her hand interrupted the levity.

Hope peered up at the supporting ladders growing closer by the second. She'd had enough exposure to acidbacks for a while. "Terra firma here I come."

No sooner had her words escaped her mouth than a tremor rumbled through the resort, lowering the bottom of the sink hole another ten feet and crumbling one side of it, taking the scaffold on that side along with it.

Convergence

Sam's heart sank when he saw the scaffold on the far side of the sink hole teeter on the edge as the ground underneath crumbled. "Hope! O'Connor!"

The metal structure tumbled into the expanding sink hole, crashing into dirt floor below. The ladders tipped and slid toward the eroded side but came to rest against the sink hole's opposite wall.

After the dirt and dust settled, Hope's voice floated out. "We're okay... but get us the *fuck* out of here!"

Sam doubled his efforts retracting the rope hand over inked hand, coiling it in a pile beside his feet. From his time in Los Angeles back in September, he knew how unpredictable quakes could be. Harry and Daniela had a difficult time keeping up.

The snatch block rose into view first, followed by a hand with its fingers in a "V for victory" sign.

"Hold it steady," Harry said. "I'll tie it off."

Sam dug the heels of his boots into the grass next to Daniela. "With a bowline, no doubt."

"Lucky guess." Harry pulled a loop of rope around the tree and fashioned his preferred knot, pulling it tight. "We're secure."

Sam and Daniela eased their grip on the rope until Hope's and O'Connor's weight pulled it tight. Daniela grabbed the hoe and used it like a hook around the rope looping through the snatch block.

Sam knelt and extended his hand toward Hope.

She shook her head. "Get O'Connor off first. She really did a number on her hand."

"It's nothing." O'Connor tried her best to remain stoic, but it was clear to Daniela that she was in a lot of pain.

"O'Connor, take my hand," Sam said.

O'Connor winced as she pulled her hand out from under her arm. She wouldn't be able to take anyone's hand for a while. The burns on the top of her hand had begun to bleed, leaving behind blood-soaked fabric where she had stowed it under her arm.

"Take over for me." Daniela transferred the makeshift hook to Harry.

Sam avoided O'Connor's hand as best he could and latched onto her forearm. With her good hand, she grabbed the ladders now balanced at a precarious incline and stepped across to the edge of the sink hole where the remaining scaffold stood. Sam pulled her to safety and Daniela took over.

Sam repeated the rescue operation, grabbed Hope, and pulled her safely into his arms. They shared a short but tight embrace before backing away from the sink hole's edge.

Daniela ripped a strip of fabric from the bottom of her shirt and wrapped O'Connor's hand. "You're burned pretty bad." She ran toward the resort's administration offices in the north section of the main building. "I'll bring back more supplies."

"Be careful...," Harry said but Daniela was already out of sight.

"So Harry, that *fucking* generator didn't start." O'Connor watched blood begin to soak through her temporary bandages in expanding red dots. "We got our Kill-O-Matic still down there waiting for some juice."

"Who knows if it still works or not," Hope said. "In case no one noticed, the earthquake..." She glanced at O'Connor and shrugged. "It caused another collapse down there. The quake... sorry... *it* knocked the cage over, ruined the light perimeter, and maybe even buried the generator." Hope's shoulders slumped in defeat. "We're fucked."

"Not necessarily." Harry peered over the edge, trying to discern the state of the Kill-O-Matic. "We could still daisy-chain a couple of power cords. They might destroy your cage electronics, but at this point I don't think it's coming back out."

O'Connor sat on the grass cradling her hand. "Can you see any of our beloved acidbacks down there?"

Harry shook his head then began sorting through power cords. "I couldn't see anything down there anymore. Shadows are too dark."

"That bloody bait you gave us was the cat's ass." O'Connor held the fingers of her uninjured hand to her lips and kissed them.

Harry struck a pose. "Strunk steak. The choice of carnivorous parasites everywhere."

"Maybe it was low-level vibration from being attacked by those acidbacks that caused the scaffold to fail." Hope motioned at the collapsed side of the sink hole where the support ladders sat on an incline.

"I'm no geologist, but I guess anything's possible." Harry surveyed the supplies lined up near the sink hole's edge. "And on that note..." He began to pull the plastic bins, extension cords, Detest-A-Pest equipment, and other supplies to a safe distance.

"Good idea." Sam joined Harry's rescue effort and together they finished the task in half the time. He dropped an armful of extension cords and rope strands just as the ground began to rumble.

Harry cocked his head and squinted at Sam. "What did you do?"

"Nothing. I—"

"Holy shit." Hope pointed at the resort. The north end of the complex started to crumple like a house of cards, the adobe shingles cracking and sliding off the roof in chunks.

"Daniela!" Harry broke into a run

Hope followed and caught up to him. "No, Harry. It's too dangerous."

Harry hesitated. He knew the dangers but couldn't accept leaving Daniela inside.

"You don't even know where she is. It'd be suicide." Hope held Harry's face in her hands and locked gaze with him. "She'll be back. Trust me."

"How do you know?"

"I just do." Hope grinned. "If I was her, I wouldn't want to let a guy like you out of my sight for too long."

Harry looked back at the dark smoke plumes rising from the north end of the resort. Despite Hope's insistence, he bolted toward the resort.

"I'm sorry," Harry yelled back. "I have to."

Hope took three steps after Harry and stopped. The ground supporting the remaining scaffold disintegrated and took the rest of the structure with it. Metal twisted and bolts popped as the reinforcing bars spun off the edge of the sink hole and plunged into the deep darkness. The ladders remained, just barely spanning the sink hole.

The impact of the last scaffold released a loud metallic *clang* that echoed across the golf course. The ground shook more violently for a second then subsided.

"Not again." O'Connor backed away from the sink hole. "Never again, goddamn it."

One end of the reinforced ladders tore free from the dirt and roots it clung to and tipped vertically into the expanding chasm. Still tied to the tree, Harry's famous bowline knot held the ladders in place by its center rungs.

But when the rope between the ladders and the tree pulled taut, it knocked the top of the coiled tow rope into the chasm, causing a chain reaction. Foot by foot, the rope disappeared over the edge at an increasing rate.

"It's okay. You got through Los Angeles fine." Sam spoke with a focused effort to calm O'Connor. "This is no different. It will pass."

"Sam!" Hope saw what was going to happen and was powerless to stop it. "SAM!"

"What—"

A loop of rope had flipped around and tangled around one of Sam's legs. The weight and momentum of the falling rope pulled him off his feet and dragged him over the edge.

"NO!" Hope ran forward and a hand fell on her shoulder, pulling her back away from both the edge of the sink hole and the mass exodus of rope.

Hope spun around expecting to find O'Connor but found Harry holding her back instead. "This is your fault, you asshole!" She pounded on his chest and sobbed. "Sam's dead and it's *your* fault."

Harry had no words.

When the rumbling stopped, everything fell unnaturally quiet.

Then Hope's walkie-talkie chirped a staticky message. "Cleanup on aisle four."

SAM HUNG UPSIDE DOWN by his right ankle, about three-quarters of the way down the sink hole. Due to the crumbling walls, he had experienced more of a controlled slide than a straight fall to his current location. But the sudden stop still stretched his right leg in ways he wasn't prepared for. His eyes were still adjusting to the shadows after standing in the afternoon sunshine only moments ago, but something was moving down there.

Acidbacks.

"Sam?" Hope's voice squawked on the walkie-talkie in his hand. Even through the radio's small speaker, he could sense her happiness and relief. He turned the volume down.

"The one and only," Sam whispered as his eyes came to terms with the darkness. He could see no movement from his beloved acidbacks in his immediate area but could still hear something. "I'm still about thirty feet from the bottom. Let me get down and I'll call you back. Sam out."

Sam cut off the beginnings of someone's response as he turned his walkie-talkie off. He reached up and grabbed the rope tangled around his ankle. Memories of vertical sit-ups in the prison yard floated in the back of his mind. At least he hadn't been tied to the prison wall back then.

With one hand on the rope above his foot, Sam bore the weight of his body and used his free hand to unwind the rest of the slackened rope.

It never ceased to amaze him how a few simple twists in a rope could cause so much trouble. But once he began pulling at the loops, the rope and nature's random slip knot fell away.

Using both of his hands now, he lowered himself to the bottom of the sink hole. He favored his right leg and avoided the tunnel openings in the walls as he descended.

Sam's eyes had completely adjusted to the dark. The glow he had sensed while he was first upside down appeared like a beacon to him now. An uneven layer of dirt and turf had covered the perimeter lights.

With slow and careful movement, Sam excavated the first light and its battery pack, and turned it off. He had a plan for it. There was more residual glow several feet away.

The lack of sound inside the sink hole made the environment around him feel even more oppressive. He crouched and listened for any other noise, fighting off the claustrophobic screams building in the back of his throat.

Nothing. And for that he was glad. He moved on to the

source of the second glow and found the second perimeter task light. He used it to sweep the base and walls of the sink hole. Poking out from the dirt fifteen feet away was the corner of the Kill-O-Matic.

"Bingo," Sam whispered to himself. He strapped the battery pack to his waist, hung the light from his shoulder, and turned it on. The ground surrounding his feet were bathed in bright light. He reached for his walkie-talkie and turned it on, keeping the volume low. "Harry, can you patch together three-hundred feet of extension cord and throw it down? Female end. Don't care how."

After a moment Hope's voice crackled back low. "He's working on it, Sam. You okay?"

"Yeah, but I got some shit to do. Sam out." Sam clicked the walkie-talkie off again and clambered to where he had seen the Kill-O-Matic.

He pulled clumps of dirt off the side of the cage to find it almost completely packed with acidbacks. Their skin fizzled when his light passed over them. But the acid excreted from their skin was also dissolving the mesh of the cage that kept them from attacking.

High above his head, the first length of extension cord slid down the side of the sink hole.

Sam cleaned away enough dirt to reveal the orientation of the Kill-O-Matic. Following the back edge of the cage, he found the extension cord. He gave it a pull, but the cord wouldn't budge. He sunk to his knees and dug through the loam, following the power cord snaking through it.

He expected to find the generator, but instead he found the end of the power cord. Sam picked out the dirt and clay jammed around the plug's prongs. He looked up at the bright sky above and winced. Squinting, he could see the extension cord dropping every thirty seconds or so.

The cage began to break in spots where the acid had eaten

away the metal mesh. Acidback fangs protruded and gnawed at the hole. Soon those things would be out and after him.

"I'll be dead meat soon," Sam said to himself. He repositioned the perimeter task light to shine on the Kill-O-Matic. "That might buy me some time." Back to the pile of rope at the bottom of the sink hole, he grabbed a length near the bottom and held it in front of him.

Sam had watched Harry tie a bowline at least a dozen times but now that it mattered, he couldn't remember the sequence of loops.

"Something about a damn rabbit and a tree," he muttered to himself as he twisted the rope around in his hands. The sound of trapped acidbacks fighting against both the task light and the cage grated at his patience.

"Fuck it." He made a loop, flattened it, and tied the only knot he knew how to make: a simple overhand knot, in this case an overhand loop knot. Opening the loop, he examined the simple handhold he had created. Six feet farther down the rope, he repeated the process but with a larger loop and tightened the knot to form a foothold.

"Harry, eat your heart out," Sam chuffed. He glanced at the Kill-O-Matic. More acidbacks attacked the weakened parts of the cage despite the bright beam from the LED task light.

Sam scanned the walls farthest away but discovered they were beyond his light's reach. Still, he could sense movement from the tunnel openings higher up. Above his head and on walls closer to him he spotted the intermittent fanged maw test the air outside the tunnel exits.

"Shit." He turned on his walkie-talkie. "Hey guys, how much longer for the extension cord? I'm going to be lunch soon."

"Hang in there, Sam," Hope's voice buzzed. "We're almost done." A staticky pause stretched out a little too long for Sam's liking. "A hundred more feet."

Sam estimated the end of the power cord was fifty feet away.

With the delay becoming dire, seconds felt like minutes. Acidbacks were beginning to push through the mesh on the Kill-O-Matic.

At last the power cord's end was within his grasp, but Sam needed more slack to reach the Kill-O-Matic. He pressed talk, "Come on guys. I don't want to die *under* the Bahamas."

"You're good to go," Hope's voice said. "Tie it on and get out of there."

Tie it on?

Confused, Sam looked up at the extension cord and everything clicked into place. Harry had tied the extension cords together so they wouldn't become unplugged.

Sam ran to the Kill-O-Matic's cord and tied the hanging extension cord to it, then plugged it in. He was no longer concerned about attempts to be stealthy. His mission had become "Get the Fuck Out as Fast as Possible."

He returned to the rope and was about to signal for extraction but above him along the rope's path more acidbacks appeared, screeching and snapping their fanged sphincters.

Sam spotted a support rod from the fallen scaffold and picked it up. He returned to the rope, hooked one elbow though the handhold, and placed his injured right foot into the foot loop.

"Pull me up. NOW." He paused, then raised the walkie-talkie back to his mouth. "Please," he said before snapping the handset to his belt.

Immediately, the rope began to ascend, lifting him off the ground. He grit his teeth and pushed down the dull ache in his right foot as it bore the weight of his body.

Sam planned to use his left foot and leg to maneuver himself side to side and around the tunnels with acidbacks poking out of them. The steel bar was for emergencies. But Detest-A-Pest plans often derailed, and this was no exception.

DANIELA BURST INTO her office and threw open her first aid cabinet. She restocked two first aid kits with more supplies and latched them closed.

First, she felt the rumbling. Then she heard it gradually amplify. "Time to go."

She left her office in a state of disarray, as if thieves had ransacked it. On her way to the lobby of the main building, the north section of the resort fell into the ground. With her two first aid kits, one in each hand, she ran without looking back. If she had, she would have seen that her office was no longer there and most of the corridor she had just run down had been swallowed up by the ground.

Staff and guests that had managed to get out in time scrambled in the same direction. Some pushed her aside and scattered once they reached the main lobby. Others stopped with panic in their faces, unsure which way to go.

Ever-familiar screeching rose from the direction her office used to be.

"Get to the dock. The dock! Llegar al muelle!" Daniela pointed toward the main doors of the resort and beyond. She turned to continue her escape when a beefy hand greased with sweat gripped her shoulder and spun her around.

"You've got no idea how much shit your little fuckboy is in." Larsen spit the words out like daggers. "He's going to prison for a long time. Strunk's lawyers will make sure of that."

Daniela twisted her shoulder out of his grip. "This isn't Harry's fault, or anyone else's for that matter." The rumbling subsided slightly as she looked around the lobby. "This is Karma."

Larsen scowled and glanced at the kits in her hands.

"Someone die? Hope it was that ex-con or that fat, cigar-smoking bitch."

Daniela shook her head and stepped backward. "You need to get to the dock and make sure your guests and employees get off this island safely. Or Strunk will throw you under the bus, too."

Larsen crossed his fingers. "We're like this, Strunk and me. Tight."

Daniela continued her backward steps. "You're so naive. Strunk only keeps you close if you can give him what he wants." Daniela scanned the lobby. Gilt decorations and framed pictures of Strunk fell from the walls and smashed on the tiled floor. "He wants you to fix *this*. Good luck."

A lascivious grin spread across Larsen's face. "You know, Trejo, we should have fucked."

Daniela grimaced at the thought. "You're gross, Larsen. Never in a million years." She turned and ran past the entry to the dining room and toward the side doors that led to the pool and clubhouse.

"Get to the dock, Larsen," she called back. "Get off this island while you still have a chance." She pushed through the double doors and disappeared outside.

All Larsen could hear in his head was Strunk's voice repeating, "You're my little *bitch*." He followed a frenzied cleaning staffer out the main entranceway.

Seconds later a loud metal *clang* sounded from outside, accompanied by a round of heavier vibration. Marble floor tiles began to crack.

The only one left in the lobby to hear it was McCoy. From his concealed vantage point behind the lobby counter, his trusty phone had caught everything on video. He took the cracked tile beneath his feet as a sign to move on. He followed the action and headed for the doors to the pool.

Daniela ran around the edge of the pool. Large cracks had formed in the surrounding concrete deck, but the pool appeared to be intact. On any other day she would have stopped to investigate, but she was needed at the sink hole.

After passing the pool she could see the clubhouse looming in the distance. The structure looked like it had survived the quake, unlike the collapsed administration section of the resort she had just come from. Plumes of dark smoke rose from the crumpled building. Despite the acrid smell scorching her throat, Daniela broke into a sprint.

As she rounded the corner of the clubhouse, the devastation stopped her cold. The sink hole she had left less than ten minutes ago had become a mammoth opening in the ground. The scaffold had been consumed and the supporting ladder hung straight up against the dirt cliffs.

But something else was wrong. Harry and Hope strained against a rope that descended into the earthy depths. O'Connor, with her hand out of commission, stood nearby barking something, hopefully words of encouragement.

Sam was gone.

Daniela broke into a sprint. "Where's Sam?"

She saw relief break on Harry's face despite his efforts on the rope. "On the end of this rope."

"Finally some medical attention." O'Connor cradled her hand and approached Daniela. "Thought you had seen your *last patient,* if you know what I mean."

Daniela dropped the first aid kits next to the other supplies and took up the rope behind Hope. She flexed her legs and arms and added some much needed power to the rescue effort.

"Hey, what am I? Chopped liver?" O'Connor said.

"For the moment, yes. It's called triage. Look it up." Daniela spoke between pulls on the rope. "Why not make yourself useful and try to help Sam."

O'Connor held up her blood soaked bandage. "How am I going to do that?"

"I don't know." Daniela heaved the rope in sync with Hope and Harry. "Get creative."

Daniela expected O'Connor to sulk but to her surprise O'Connor ran to the pile of supplies and dug out a taser rod and several sections of rope.

Using her feet and her good hand, O'Connor managed to tie a basic overhand knot around the handle of the taser. She tied the ends of the ropes together until she had amassed a lengthy strand.

She raised her walkie-talkie. "Sam, listen. Sending down a taser." She stepped next to Harry and dropped the loose frankensteined rope.

He shook his head. "Don't go any farther. The ground's unstable."

"Right." O'Connor pressed talk. "Taser coming down. Watch that tattooed noggin of yours." She aligned herself with Harry's rope and tossed the taser rod into the void.

Harry, Hope, and Daniela continued their synchronized lifting.

Hope motioned to O'Connor, then looked at the rapidly disappearing rope. "Don't forget about the loose end."

"What loose—" O'Connor clued in just in time and stamped on the end of the rope just before it sailed over the edge. She looked at Hope with relief. "Thanks, Missy."

O'Connor dug out the end of the taser rod rope from under her boot. She tugged on Harry's pant leg. "Hey sport, lift your heel."

"Why?"

"Just do it."

Harry obliged grudgingly and O'Connor slid the end of the taser rope under his heel.

"What did you do?"

"You're the anchor for Sam's taser."

Harry let out a groan. "You've got to be joking."

"Don't worry, Harry," Hope said. "You're all good."

O'Connor pressed talk. "Can you see it, Sam?"

After a pause that seemed far too long, Sam's voice crackled back. "I can see it. About twenty-five more feet. Wish I had it now though—" The walkie-talkie went dead.

"Sam?" O'Connor waited for a response that never came. She ran to the diminishing pile of supplies and dug through it. "There you are." She picked up the pair of binoculars and ran around the edge of the sink hole to get a better view on Sam's position.

She raised the binoculars to her eyes with her good hand and used her injured hand to hold the walkie-talkie. "Sam, I got eyes on you."

Tunnels above Sam's head contained acidbacks in waiting, as if they knew that succulent human flesh would be passing by at any moment.

O'Connor watched Sam shifting his position on the side of the sinkhole, trying to navigate around the passing tunnels, but he hadn't moved enough. The friction of the rope on the dirt held him back. He was still within acidback striking range and the taser rod remained out of reach. "Sam, bogies at ten and two."

"Shit." O'Connor's stomach bottomed out when she realized there was no sign of his walkie-talkie in his hands or on his belt. "His walkie's gone."

Sam could not respond even if he wanted to.

"BOGIES TEN AND TWO!" O'Connor's voice echoed down the chasm, but Sam couldn't tell where she was. Both his injured leg and his elbow hooked through the upper handhold hampered his mobility on the extraction rope. At best, he could crane his neck side to side but that offered no additional clues.

"Ten and two, Sam!" O'Connor's voice called out. "Ten and two!"

Sam spotted the tunnel openings approaching above his head and instead of avoiding them, maneuvered to the left to take the "ten o'clock" tunnel head on.

Before he could see into the dark passage, Sam stabbed his steel bar into the opening. Shrieking blasted out of the tunnel and the end of the steel bar he couldn't yet see rattled back and forth.

"One bastard down." He extracted the steel bar and dragged a dying acidback out with it. He flung it away from his body, careful not to touch the creature's acid sweat.

"Three o'clock!" O'Connor's trusty loud mouth came in handy, reminding Sam of the other acidback a few feet away.

He thrust the steel bar into the second acidback, the metal at the end already riddled with dissolving holes. Like he had with the creature moments earlier, Sam swung the bar wide and away from his body, sending the writhing acidback screeching into the shadows below.

The steel bar began to disintegrate in chunks.

"SIX O'CLOCK!"

"Six?" Sam said to himself. "What the..." He looked down to see an acidback wiggling up the rope, its eight legs synchronized in a frenzied approach, its articulated fangs flexing like fingers.

He swung at the acidback but hit nothing but air. Having his elbow hooked into the handhold had decreased his reach. And the acidback ascending the rope below his foothold showed no signs of stopping.

Sam straightened his right arm, his elbow aching from

supporting his upper body, and clutched the handhold. He traded one pain for another and bent his right knee to crouch as far as possible. He raised the eroded steel bar over his head and swung it with as much strength as he could muster.

The tip of the bar connected with the acidback's excuse for a head and laid down a deep scratch. Black blood mixed with acid and who knew what else flowed down the creature's back. But the blow didn't slow it down.

The acidback reached Sam's foot in the rope foothold. It attempted to clamp its honed teeth on his tread. He pulled himself up with his right arm and managed to remove his foot just in time. The eight-legged sausage from hell got a mouthful of rope instead.

Sam planted his right foot on the dirt wall, straddling the rescue rope. Part of him was glad to have given his right leg a break, but now his arm bore all his weight. He swung the steel bar at the acidback and glanced the side of its body, opening another small wound across its skin.

Sam looked up at the same moment O'Connor yelled "TASER" across the chasm. Raised sufficiently high to reach the weapon, Sam wasted no time.

He threw the steel bar at the acidback, missing it entirely. The creature tried to back up and extract itself from the foothold, but its teeth had caught on the weave of the rope.

Sam gripped the taser rod in an instant and pulled it free of the knot. He pushed the electrodes into the bleeding wound on the creature's head and triggered the charge.

The acidback's body went rigid, its eight stubby legs stuck straight out like a fainting goat and released its grip on the rope. At the same time the back end of the acidback ripped open in chunks like a shotgun blast triggered from within.

"Fucking ace, Sam!" O'Connor yelled. "Keep going. You're almost home."

Sam placed his foot back in the foothold but the acid from

the creature's skin, blood, and saliva had weakened the rope's fibers. His leg shot through it and his body slammed flat against the dirt wall. Instinctively his right hand gripped the handhold tight, preventing his certain fall.

"Fuck this." Sam clamped the taser rod between his teeth and started to ascend the rope, hand over hand like a mountain climber without a harness.

He approached a tunnel on his right and predictably an acidback lay in waiting. With the taser rod, combat was easy. He jammed the taser into the hole and let forth a short blue arc of electricity. The slimy creature shot back into the small, dank space, clogging the exit with burnt entrails. Sam turned his nose away from the smell of ozone and burnt acidback drifting back.

With Harry, Hope, and Daniela still pulling on the escape rope, Sam's climb took even less time, even as his limbs burned with fatigue. He couldn't see Harry and the others yet, but O'Connor's boisterous yells carried with her as she ran around the side of the sink hole.

"You da man, Sam!" she called out. "Go go go!"

Sam lifted and stepped, lifted and stepped, and saw Harry's head appear from behind the turfed edge of the sink hole.

"Almost there." Harry broke into a broad smile.

O'Connor rejoined the group, her limp more pronounced than before. "Sammy, get your ass on this grass." She picked up the slack from behind Daniela and ran with it toward the tree, giving Sam one more boost of speed.

The rescue rope had carved a gash in the edge of the sink hole and a chunk two feet wide and fifty feet thick broke free and plummeted to the bottom.

Sam swung to the newly exposed side and continued his climb as if the recent cave-in hadn't even happened. His adrenaline surged and provided him with just the boost of energy he needed to breach the edge of the turf. He transferred the taser rod to his left hand and clawed at the grass, pulling himself closer to safety.

Harry and the others dropped the rescue rope, took Sam's arms, and dragged him toward the tree. O'Connor flipped him over and straddled him.

She grabbed his collar with her good hand and shook him back and forth. "That was fucking awesome." She turned to face the others, the binoculars swinging around her neck. "Saw the whole fucking thing."

Sam grinned between breaths. "Glad you approve of me almost dying."

"Don't mention it." O'Connor plucked her cigar out of her front pocket and clamped her teeth around the soggy end.

"Speaking of almost dying—" Sam pushed O'Connor off his lap and lunged forward with his taser rod. Three acidbacks had climbed the rope and were scuttling across the grass toward the group. Their bodies had already begun to smoke in the bright sunshine. "Cut the rope!"

Sam impaled the taser rod into the first acidback and blasted it back, tumbling end over end into the sink hole. He zapped the second creature, blowing it backward like a loose bag of guts.

O'Connor appeared with a taser rod of her own and lit the last acidback up like a candle. Its skin burst into flames and rolled back into the chasm.

But the damn creatures kept coming, scaling the rope like mutant caterpillars with a thirst for blood.

Hope grabbed the rescue rope and sent a wave through it like a battle rope exercise at the gym. She sliced through the rope with her Bowie knife and threw the end over the edge, taking all remaining acidbacks on the rope with it.

"Easy peasy." Hope slid her knife back into its scabbard and brushed her hands.

O'Connor relit her cigar, a process that seemed to defy

physics. "Let's light up the Kill-O-Matic." She turned to Harry. "Please tell me you got more bait."

Harry turned his head sideways and grinned. "Bitch, *please*." He trotted back to his maintenance cart and peeled open the lid of the bin in the back. A swarm of black flies flew out.

"Jesus, those are Strunk steaks?" O'Connor shielded her nose. "They're a little ripe."

"Not ripe. 'Aged to perfection.' " Harry air-quoted the words before he lifted the bin from the back of the cart. "Got to maintain corporate branding. Although to be fair, they have been sitting in the sun all day." He set the bin down closer to the edge of the sink hole.

"This is corporate branding." O'Connor pointed at the Detest-A-Pest logo on her shirt. "That's—"

"An accumulation of putrefaction?" Hope crossed her arms and smiled.

"I was going to go with a bucket of shit," O'Connor said with a shrug. "But that works too."

"The *academics* thank you." Hope gave a nod to Daniela and took a spot on the grass next to Sam. She closed her eyes and rested her head against his shoulder.

O'Connor glared at Sam and Hope. "While some of you are sitting on your asses, I got to work for a living." She alternated her gaze between Daniela and Harry. "Who's going to volunteer to set this bait?"

"No one's going down there again," Harry said.

Sam gave Harry a thumbs up. "Amen to that."

"And why not?" O'Connor revved herself up in preparation for a fight.

"We have no more rope."

"Then use the power cord."

Harry shook his head. "That'd be a suicide mission. There's no way it would hold our weight."

O'Connor stared at the rest of the group, eyes wide in

disbelief. "I'd do it myself but..." She held up her injured right hand, her bandage tattered, torn, and soaked red. "Speaking of which, I need you to patch me up, doc."

"Even if your hand was fine, underground missions are now off the table," Harry said. "Besides, I still hold the purse strings."

"Always using the money against me, you fucking loser." O'Connor began to pace. "I'm... *we're* just trying to do our damn jobs."

Sam leaned toward Hope. "See that?" He spoke quietly as he motioned at O'Connor. "There's still hope for her yet."

Daniela intercepted O'Connor. "Let's get that hand of yours properly wrapped."

O'Connor had opened her mouth to paint Daniela in profanity when a short-lived tremor rumbled through the area like a wave cresting on the ocean. "Uh, yeah. Good idea."

Daniela picked up her first-aid kits and escorted O'Connor to the back of Harry's maintenance cart.

Sam eased Hope's head off his shoulder and stood. "We're not giving up, O'Connor. If that's what you're thinking."

"Could've fooled me."

Hope took her spot next to Sam. "We don't need to go down there. And there's one good reason why."

O'Connor returned a cold stare at Hope as Daniela wrapped O'Connor's hand. "I'm waiting, Missy."

"Remember electrical conductivity?" Hope said. "All we have to do is get them in close contact, with their skin touching. Then, *ZAP.* The fuckers are toast."

"That's all we have to do, huh?" O'Connor gnawed on her cigar, annoyed.

Daniela smirked. "She's right, you kno—"

"I know she's right." O'Connor snapped. She pulled her bandaged hand away from Daniela and examined the precision work. "You damn smarty-pants got me this time." She flexed her right hand. The bandage followed her hand movements. "Thanks, by the way. Feels better."

"Thank my medical degree from smarty-pants university." Daniela winked at O'Connor.

"Yeah, yeah. Knock it off." O'Connor trudged next to Harry. "So... let's dump that shit and light those little bastards up."

Harry nodded. "Sam, do you remember where the cage is located from up here? It's too steep to see the bottom."

"It was to the left of me," Sam said. "I can tell you exactly where, but I need a marker."

Harry scanned the diminished supplies. "Like what exactly?"

Sam singled out a short piece of bright yellow rope and picked it up. "This'll do." Favoring his right leg, he ran around the edge of the sink hole until he was on the opposite side.

He got on all fours to distribute his weight and peered over the edge. Now that the hole was bigger at the top it was easier to see the bottom. The LED task light he had left behind pointing at the Kill-O-Matic twinkled like the evening star.

Sam repositioned himself perpendicularly in line with the edge of the sink hole and backed away, laying out the yellow rope as he went. "Line up the bait with the rope. The Kill-O-Matic is directly below."

He stood and took a wider route back to the group, wary of the unpredictable nature of the eroding edge.

"You!" a voice cried out from the side of the clubhouse. "Stop!"

Sam skidded to a halt and turned to find Larsen charging toward him. He shot Harry a brief look of panic then shifted his attention back to Larsen.

"Whoa whoa whoa." Sam raised his hands up, palms forward in a placating stance. "Calm down, Larsen. Let's talk about this."

Larsen maintained his speed as he charged toward Sam. "You're going to pay for what you've done."

Sam braced for his inevitable confrontation. "Wait, Larsen. Buddy. We can—"

Larsen blew by him at full speed. Confused, Sam looked back and spotted McCoy jumping out from behind a shrub in front of the clubhouse. McCoy was recording video on his phone.

"Shut it off, you motherfucker." Larsen broke into a trot. "Give me your phone."

McCoy took pleasure in recording Larsen's outbursts. "Going to have pry it from my cold dead hands, you cue-balled son-of-a-bitch." At the last possible moment, McCoy pocketed his phone and ran. But he had failed to consider an escape route.

Sam waved his hands back and forth. "Larsen, stop! Stay away from the edge."

Harry, Daniela, Hope, and O'Connor joined Sam with their own warnings but all of it fell on deaf ears.

McCoy tried to veer toward the rest of the course, but Larsen cut him off, forcing the pursuit toward the edge of the sink hole with no regard to the unstable edge.

McCoy had nowhere to go. In front of him was Larsen, his eyes red and clouded with rage. Four feet behind him lay the jagged edge of the sink hole and the terrors below.

"Chill out, Larsen." McCoy glanced left and right as if expecting a route to safety to suddenly appear.

"Give me the phone." Larsen demanded. "Give it to me now."

"I'll delete the videos, I swear." McCoy shifted his weight back and forth.

"The phone. Now." Larsen took a step forward.

McCoy took a step back.

"Stop. Both of you!" Harry yelled from behind them across the chasm. "Be reasonable, Larsen."

"Reasonable?" Larsen shifted his gaze between McCoy and Harry. "This asshole has cost me a job. You, too. All of you." He waved his arms wildly. "He's fucked this entire resort. There's no coming back from this."

"Exactly." Harry calmed his voice. "This standoff is pointless." He exchanged a quick glance with Sam.

McCoy dug his hand into his pocket and slid the phone out. He raised it above his head. "I'll delete the videos but you're not getting my phone." Veins stuck out like thick ropes on his neck. "My livelihood is on it. You're the last person I'd give it to."

Harry sent a subtle nod at Sam. He broke into a sprint, intent on pulling Larsen away from the situation. But the nod wasn't subtle enough.

Larsen spotted Sam's approach and advanced toward McCoy with quick steps punctuating his words. "Give. Me. The. PHONE."

McCoy took one more step backward.

Sam saw the cracks forming in the turf before anyone else. "Stop! Get out of there!" But he was too late.

The grass under McCoy's feet fell away in a large chunk, taking both him and his phone into the darkened maw of the sink hole.

Sam grabbed Larsen by the back of his collar and dragged the man backward to safety. He threw Larsen to the ground, lifted his chest by his shirt, and slammed it back down once. "You killed him. KILLED HIM."

Larsen stared at Sam, then broke into uncontrollable laughter.

Taken aback, Sam shook his head in disbelief. He felt a hand on his shoulder, pulling him back with a gentle tug. It was Harry, with the rest of the group corralled behind. He stood and walked away.

Hope went to Sam's side without a word and placed her arm around his shoulder. "Let's get the bait bin prepped."

Larsen continued his fit of hysterics on the ground.

Harry crouched next to him. "You need to leave this island, Larsen." His voice was clear and calm. "If I see you again, I'll kill you myself."

Larsen paused, then restarted his laughter. He stumbled to his feet and beat a hasty retreat, laughing all the way to the clubhouse.

O'Connor watched him go. "The guy's bat-shit crazy."

"Yeah." Harry turned to Daniela, concerned. "You think McCoy survived?"

"Depends on how... and where he landed. If he missed the wrecked scaffold, then there's a good chance."

"You're right, doc." O'Connor scanned the bottom of the sink hole with the binoculars. "From what I can see, we've got signs of life." She handed the binoculars to Daniela.

Magnified ten times she saw McCoy moving his head slowly side to side. "He could have a concussion, broken bones, internal injuries." Daniela handed the binoculars back to O'Connor. "No way to know unless I get down there."

Harry waved her off. "Out of the question." He walked back around the sink hole to join Hope and Sam. Daniela followed.

"But he'll die, Harry."

"What can we do?" Harry raised his hands in exasperation. "All we got is that generator and that electrified cage down there. We have no rescue equipment left."

"I can't let him die." Daniela grabbed the frankensteined power cord connecting the Kill-O-Matic to the generator. "I'll lower myself down."

"And how will you get up?" Harry didn't wait for a response. "Sorry. No. The answer's—"

"Help!" McCoy's pained voice echoed out of the chasm. "Someone help."

"Dammit." Harry ran to where O'Connor stood with the binoculars. "If he doesn't die of his injuries, those things will make sure of it."

"Hold on, McCoy," Daniela called down. "Help's on the—"

Harry placed his hand over Daniela's mouth, cutting off the rest of her words. "Sound will draw them out. Any sound. Even us telling him to shut up."

"I think my legs are broken," McCoy yelled up. "Somebody help me."

"Harry's right." O'Connor lowered the binoculars and handed them to Harry.

He saw movement in the shadows. "Shit. The only chance he has is the bait and that generator." He handed the binoculars to Daniela and ran back to where Sam and Hope were lining up the bin with the yellow guide rope on the other side. "And that chance isn't good."

Daniela raised the binoculars to her eyes. Acidbacks crested the mound of dirt at the bottom of the sink hole by the Kill-O-Matic. No more than twenty feet away lay McCoy. Harry was right. There was no easy outcome to this tragic turn of events.

"Let's get that bait down there now," Daniela said.

Sam and Hope had tied short pieces of rope to the handles of the bin to help guide and aim the dumping of its contents from a safe distance.

"Is anyone out there?" McCoy's voice shifted from desperation to panic. "Those things are back. I can hear them but can't see—"

A blood-curdling scream echoed from below.

"Oh Jesus!" Daniela left the binoculars hanging from her neck. "Dump the bait. DUMP IT."

Sam pushed the bait bin with a taser rod as Harry let out more rope. The bin slid over the edge and down the side of the sink hole. The rope tied to the leading edge of the bin reached its limit and flipped the rancid meat over the side.

A little over three seconds later the squelching sound of raw flesh hitting the cage floated up.

Harry locked gaze with Daniela. "Is it working?"

The binoculars trembled in her hand as she raised them to her eyes. The bait had drawn hundreds of acidbacks and had covered the LED task light. The scene playing out in the optics of the binoculars resembled a writhing sea of over-sized earthworms battling for morsels of the rotting meat. Their greasy veined skin stretched and twisted around the Kill-O-Matic.

Daniela scanned down to the last location she remembered seeing McCoy. She didn't need to see much to know that the man was dead. Visions of Sinclair's bloody body back in the cavern on the first hole flashed in the back of her mind. The only part of McCoy's body that held any human resemblance was his left hand. Somehow it had escaped the wrath of the acidback horde and lay limp to one side, a blood-soaked mitten attached to a spindly skeletal arm.

Daniela lowered the binoculars and shot a look at Harry. "It's working... but it's not working, too." Her shoulders slumped as she rejoined the others.

Harry yanked the starter cord on the generator and the engine rumbled to life with one pull. He threw a switch and shared a somber look with Daniela before turning toward O'Connor. "Your cage-thing's got power. Fire it up so we can all go home."

"It's called the Kill-O-Matic. And Mar-A-Verde will be its swan song." O'Connor held the remote in her hand, the "ON" switch under her thumb. "This one's for Washington." She turned the cage live.

The generator lurched for a moment as if it was unprepared for the amount of power it would need to deliver. Then its motor evened out.

The squeals and screeching hit their ears first. O'Connor

beckoned the binoculars from Daniela and ran to the side of the sink hole like it was Christmas morning.

Daniela shook her head in sorrow. "Does she even realize that a man died a horrible death... literally minutes ago?"

Sam stepped next to her. "O'Connor's funny that way. Never been big on grief."

"How does she do it?" Daniela shivered. "I mean look at me. I'm a mess."

Sam shrugged. "She files it away. Compartmentalizes it somehow. I've known her less than a year and I've seen some seriously scary shit. I guess you get desensitized after a while."

"I've seen my fair share of injury and death." Daniela rubbed her arms like she was cold, even though the afternoon sun rode high in the sky. "It never gets easier."

"It takes a special breed of human."

O'Connor lifted the binoculars to her eyes. Blue bursts of electricity arced out of the Kill-O-Matic like bony fingers, laying waste to every acidback in proximity.

"Holy shit, you should see the fireworks down there." O'Connor vibrated with excitement. "This is why you pay us the big bucks."

Some acidbacks split open like overcooked sausages. Others popped, the creatures' partially cooked entrails scattering across the walls of the sinkhole.

Smoke from the electrocution drifted up the chasm. The odor of burnt flesh and ozone stung Sam's nose and eyes, forcing him to take several steps farther away from the edge.

Hope choked on a cough and took refuge next to the nearby tree. "That's nasty."

"That's victory, baby!" O'Connor continued to scan the bottom of the sink hole. "Just one problem. Those little bastards don't seem to be affected on the edges of the group. It's only when they get closer that they pop."

"That's electrical resistance." Harry walked next to

O'Connor. She handed him the binoculars. "The longer the distance an electrical charge must travel, the less power it holds. That's why I wanted to use better power cords. As for those things down there, they are conductive but they're also resistant. Which means—"

"We're not going to kill them all." O'Connor exchanged looks with Harry.

"Yeah." Harry covered his nose with his hand. "Pretty much. And I'm smelling melting plastic, so that's not a good sign either." An electronic chime sounded from his pocket.

"Fine time to get a text, bucko." O'Connor took back the binoculars and resumed her surveillance of the sink hole floor. The blue electrical arcs had lessened both in frequency and brightness, and there was less movement.

Harry pulled out his phone. What he saw on the display turned his face white.

Daniela took several steps toward him. "Harry? What is it?"

He locked gazes with her, a look of confusion mixed with concern filling his face. "It's McCoy."

O'Connor dropped the binoculars to hang from her neck. "What do you mean McCoy? He's—"

"He's dead," Daniela said. "There's no way McCoy's alive."

"Well, his phone's alive." Harry's phone chimed a second time, then a third. He alternated his gaze between the others in the group. "And it looks like he sent me all his videos."

"Holy shit." Sam glanced at Hope.

"Give it here. Let me see." O'Connor attempted to grab Harry's phone. "This could be good for us."

Harry pulled his phone away.

Sam stepped between the two. "O'Connor, this isn't the time."

"No, it's the perfect time." O'Connor stepped forward and blew smoke into Sam's face. "And last I checked, you're *my* employee."

Sam closed his eyes and let the cigar smoke float away. "You don't want to die on this hill."

O'Connor glared into Sam's eyes for a tense moment. "No, I guess I don't."

Harry's phone continued to sound intermittent chimes as he pocketed it.

Hope cocked her head to one side. "Wait. You hear that?"

"What, the fucking text alerts?" O'Connor shrugged indifference. "Of course we hear them."

"No. Underneath all that," Hope said. "Listen."

A low rumble rose from the sink hole.

Sam nodded his head. "I trust Hope's hearing. And I hear it too."

Daniela exchanged a look with Sam, then Harry. "So do I."

"Oh, shit." Harry's face went slack with dread.

"Better not be another goddamn earthquake," O'Connor said.

"Worse."

O'Connor narrowed her eyes at him. "Worse? How?"

Daniela glanced at Harry. "The pool." She stepped closer to the edge of the sinkhole just as gushers of water jetted from the acidback tunnels on the opposite side. "We need to get the hell off this island."

Tsunami

AS ACIDBACKS FEASTED on McCoy, more cracks snaked across the pool deck toward the edges of Mar-A-Verde's ocean water pool.

Water seeped into the gaps and saturated the earth surrounding the below-ground feature. The instabilities and tremors introduced by the clubhouse sink hole could no longer support the weight of sixty-seven thousand gallons of ocean water.

The pool itself sank in sections below the level of the deck surrounding it. White and gold chaise lounges, patio tables, and umbrellas cascaded into the water like dominoes. At the deep end, one corner of the pool dissolved into the ground. The draining vortex belched out its remaining air bubbles as if the structure had given up its last breath.

Then in one fluid motion, the entire bottom of the pool fell away, taking the remaining sea water with it and funneling it through the vast network of acidback tunnels. The pool deck and walls collapsed into the muddy slurry and followed the water's rampage, two-hundred eighty tons of unstoppable momentum.

The turf in front of the clubhouse began to collapse into itself in a winding fissure as an unending hunger of rushing water consumed the earth below. The fissure expanded into a trench, soon reaching the side of the clubhouse itself. Bricks, wood, glass, and stucco broke away and cascaded into the trench like a birthday cake in the rain.

There was no reversing the inevitable collapse now.

"LET'S GET THE HELL OUT OF HERE." Harry ran toward the south end of the resort. "Leave everything. Our escape route's been cut off."

"What about our equipment?" O'Connor grabbed a Detest-A-Pest bin and dragged it by the handle. "We're not done here."

"Whatever you lose, you can buy again."

Daniela, Sam, and Hope followed Harry.

O'Connor dropped the bin and plucked her cigar from her mouth. "Sam! Hope! Get back here."

Sam stopped and looked back. "Stubborn bitch," he said under his breath. He ran back and grabbed O'Connor's arm. "I may be your employee, but I'm calling the shots this time." He managed to drag her a few feet before she yanked her hand from his grasp.

O'Connor turned back to the supply bin. Reality slapped her in the face as the golf course and clubhouse crumbled before her eyes.

"O'Connor! Move your ASS." Sam ran back and grabbed her by the wrist.

"Wait." O'Connor dug into the bin and pulled out a taser rod. "Okay. Now we can go." As if to punctuate her consent, the power generator exploded in a shower of sparks and smoke. The remaining fuel in the tank burst into flame.

Harry, Daniela, and Hope stood at the doors to the resort.

"It's right behind you!" Hope called out. "Run!"

Just as Sam and O'Connor began their charge toward the rest of the group, the turf they had been standing on seconds earlier fell away, taking all their remaining supplies. The rope light suits, propane torches, pellet guns, all of it gone. Except for the logo on O'Connor's shirt, a dirty brown torrent had washed away all evidence of Detest-A-Pest's existence at Mar-A-Verde.

The only pieces of equipment to survive were the fortified ladders tied to the adjacent tree. But the expanding sink hole would soon take that as well, roots and all. Beyond the tee-off area for the first hole, poinciana and palm trees shook as the ground supporting them crumbled inward. The course began to disintegrate like a castle made of dominoes.

O'Connor limped behind Sam. "Have we moved to the *holding hands* stage?" She chomped her cigar firmly in place.

"What?" Sam turned back to see O'Connor batting her eyelashes at him. "Jesus Christ, this island is falling apart and all you can do is joke?" He dropped her wrist and ran towards the rest of the group.

"It's how I deal with stress."

"Find another way." Sam focused on the doors to the resort.

"You know what you need, Sam?" O'Connor called back. "A good fuck, that's what." She mustered the strength to run even though the pain in her stump fought her at every step.

Sam threw his hands up in frustration and turned back again, absolutely aware that he was heading toward a sink hole out of control. He pulled O'Connor's arm around his broad muscular shoulder and carried most of her weight.

"You're right." Sam spoke between strides. "I do need to relax but not here. Not now."

"Can I be your first?"

"Boy, you never let up, do you?" Sam's annoyance melted away, replaced with a grin. "Sounds like you need a good fuck more than I do."

The two of them rejoined the group. Harry held the door open for them.

"Hold on." O'Connor surveyed the resort with a wary eye. "You think it's a good idea to go through the building, with *that* happening?" She pointed at a section of the clubhouse collapsing into the ground.

"Normally I'd say no, but it's the only way to the marina now." Harry watched the golf course crumble in sections. "Come on. This island isn't going to wait for us."

Harry slipped his arm under O'Connor's other shoulder and together with Sam they propelled her down the main corridor. Hope and Daniela led the way.

"A Harry and Sam sandwich." O'Connor grinned. "Me likey."

As the group rounded the corner at the end of the corridor, the resort lost power, plunging them into darkness.

"The marina's this way." Daniela switched her phone into flashlight mode without breaking stride. Hope followed suit.

"To be buried alive in a Strunk resort would be a fate worse than death," Hope said.

"Don't worry. That's not going to happen." Just as Daniela's words left her mouth, the floor of the resort shifted under their feet. Harry and O'Connor were the only ones able to maintain their balance.

The section of corridor they had just traveled fell away in a plume of smoke, concrete ash, and fire.

"You were saying?" Hope scrambled to her feet and pulled Daniela up.

"Just keep moving."

Sam, O'Connor, and Harry followed Daniela and Hope into the main lobby. The marble tile lay unevenly in fractured pieces. Dirt and mud oozed around the edges with each step.

The weakened floor next to the end of the reception counter burst open and two acidbacks emerged. At first it seemed the creatures were looking for escape, but it didn't take long for them to lock onto the sweaty heat of the group.

"Go!" O'Connor unhooked her taser rod and turned it on. "I got this."

Harry exchanged a glance with Sam and he nodded. "You don't got shit. Let's keep moving."

Hope and Daniela had already made it outside the crumbling resort.

The uneven tiles and dirt made it difficult for Harry, O'Connor, and Sam to navigate. The two acidbacks with sixteen stubby legs between them had the advantage. The creatures scrambled toward them with one intent: to feed.

"We're almost there." Daniela pointed to the marina a short distance away.

Sam and Harry dragged O'Connor into the roundabout. "What about that sweet-ass jet?"

"The dock is closer," Daniela said. "Plus planes don't float."

Black smoke rose from destroyed sections of Mar-A-Verde and blocked the sunshine in random intervals. Harry looked back at the encroaching acidbacks gaining ground with an ease that he and Sam lacked. "Uh, we need backup."

"Ready to use that taser?" Sam glanced at O'Connor.

"Thought you'd never ask." O'Connor smiled, a gleam in her eyes.

The three of them spun about-face and O'Connor jammed the taser rod into the lead acidback. A blue arc of electricity blew the creature's body apart. She retracted the weapon and sunk its sharp prongs into the soft side of the second marauding acidback. Its skin and flesh split apart, as if cleaved with a red-hot blade, instantly cauterized.

"I stand corrected." Harry raised a brow and nodded. "You still got it."

"What we don't got is time. Come on." Sam guided Harry and O'Connor toward Hope and Daniela.

"Once we're on a boat, we're home free. Thanks to Dorian and our new disaster protocol, there's enough rescue capacity for everyone at the—" Daniela led the charge only to be stopped cold as the path to the dock disintegrated into the ocean. She lost her balance and fell forward.

"Dani!" Harry let go of O'Connor and ran after her, but Hope got there first. She grabbed the back of Daniela's shirt and pulled her backward.

Daniela landed on her backside with her calves hanging off the edge of the eroded bank. She scrambled backward and Hope helped her to her feet.

Harry scooped Daniela up in his arms and embraced her. "I thought I'd lost you."

Daniela hugged Harry back as she exchanged looks with Hope. "Thanks. I owe you one."

Hope shrugged and smiled. "Who's counting?"

"What the fuck is that?" O'Connor pointed at churning mud and sea water below.

Acidbacks swirled around in the water like helpless grubs. It was clear they weren't meant to swim. A fin sailed past and shredded one creature, turning the water crimson.

"Sharks?" Sam stepped away from the edge. "Fuck *me*." He glared at O'Connor. "Don't say it."

O'Connor drew in a mouthful of cigar smoke as seductively as she could manage, blew a smoke ring at Sam, and laughed. "You're so easy, Sam."

"The sharks might actually help us," Harry said. "But we got one option left."

Daniela raised a brow. "The plane?"

"Bingo."

"Sweet-ass jet, here we come." O'Connor had regained her strength and the five of them reversed their steps to follow the access path to the airstrip. But they hadn't gone far when they heard a cry for help.

"Did you hear that?" Hope looked at the others. "It's coming from over there." She pointed at the section of the resort that ran east to west and faced the expansive front lawn. A walkway pieced together with intricate river rock divided the lawn into two halves.

O'Connor shook her head. "There you go with that super hearing of yours."

"You need a hearing aid," Sam said. "I hear it too."

"Help!" A voice called out. "Anyone."

Harry's face hardened. "Larsen."

"What?" Daniela stopped and sent Harry a sideways look. "I thought he left the island."

Harry grit his teeth. "In case you haven't noticed, Larsen is as smart as a bag of hammers. I guess we have to save him now, huh?"

"I do," Daniela said. "I can't intentionally leave someone to die, no matter who it is."

An explosion rang out from the south end of the resort followed by a burst of flame and smoke.

"We have no time." O'Connor pointed up the path that led to the airstrip. "I vote we leave the fucker behind. Call it Karma."

"There's not going to be a vote." Harry looked back at the destruction behind him, then noted the sun's position in the sky. "We'll all regret it if we don't save him."

O'Connor grunted and crossed her arms.

"Correction," Harry said. "Everyone except O'Connor will regret it. Let's make this fast."

The group veered off the path back toward the resort. They passed a row of palm trees lining the farthest edge of the grass and a tall flagpole. The flag bore the Mar-A-Verde and Strunk logo and hung listlessly from the top, higher than the resort itself.

Harry burst through the doors in front that led to the resort's east courtyard. Most of the corridor was intact. "Larsen!" He stopped and listened.

"Harry?"

"Keep talking." Harry led the group down the corridor as they followed Larsen's voice. As seconds ticked into minutes, dread filled Harry's thoughts. The resort could collapse on top of them at any time.

"Down here."

The end of the corridor had folded into the ground like a broken drawbridge falling into a moat. The tiled floor had become a steep precipice surrounded by fast flowing sea water. The occasional acidback bubbled past, its legs working madly to navigate the current.

Larsen had managed to find a foothold where the water met the floor, but the tiles were chipping away as the earth underneath eroded. His chubby hands slid against the slickened floor and wall and his waterlogged suit provided enough friction to keep him from sliding into the water.

"Harry! Thank God," Larsen called up. "Get me the fuck out of here."

"He's about fifteen feet down." Harry looked to the others.

O'Connor peered over the edge. "A slippery slide directly to hell. Now that's poetic justice, am I right?"

"Fuck you, *bitch*." Angry spittle flew from Larsen's pudgy lips. "Get me out of here, Harry. I'll make it worth your while."

"We shouldn't even be in here." O'Connor blew smoke at Larsen. "That asshole is going to get us all killed."

Harry clenched his fists. "O'Connor, you need to shut up. Right now."

"Or what?"

Harry faced O'Connor but bit his tongue. Nothing good would come of this war of words. He had already moved on when Daniela and Hope stepped in to break up the argument.

"One thing's for sure, time isn't on our side," Harry said.

Sam bolted back down the corridor and stopped at a mirrored box affixed to the wall.

Hope glanced at Daniela. "What is he doing?"

Daniela shook her head and shrugged.

Sam pulled on one side of the mirror and it swung open on hinges. Hidden within sat a fire hose spool.

Harry rubbed his stubbled chin. "I'll be damned. Vanity knows no bounds."

Sam ran back towards the group, holding the nozzle of the hose. "When we passed by earlier, I thought 'a box with a mirror on it?' It was too strange not to check out."

The hose reached its limit three feet away from the break in the floor and yanked Sam backward onto his backside.

"Hurry it up, you dumb fucks." Larsen's voice yelled out of the hole in the corridor floor. "Those things are down here too. You guys did fuck all to contain them."

"Leaving the jackass behind is looking better all the time," Hope said.

"See?" O'Connor winked at Hope. "That's what I'm talking about."

Harry ignored O'Connor and helped Sam to his feet. "Human chain?"

O'Connor pointed to her bandaged hand speckled with dried blood. "Gonna sit this one out due to skeleton hand."

The building shook over their heads and the intact floor of the corridor shifted under their feet. Sections of the ceiling broke away and landed in heaps on the cracking tile.

Sam wrapped the end of the hose around one arm and gripped it with his hand. He held his free hand out toward Hope. "Come on. There isn't much time." He grinned broadly and shrugged. "It's 'Save an Asshole' day."

Sam's smile convinced her. Hope grabbed his forearm as he did the same with hers. Daniela tightened her grip on Hope's other arm and completed the chain with Harry leading the rescue.

"It's about fucking time." Larsen stretched as far as his short and bulky frame would allow.

Harry took a fortifying breath and stepped over the edge. He leaned out with his free arm but there was a two-foot gap between his hand and Larsen's. Harry dropped to his knees to try to close the distance, but he still came up short.

"Nice going, Einstein," Larsen growled. "You always come up short."

"Try this."

Harry looked over his shoulder to see O'Connor holding her taser rod. He furrowed his brow in confusion.

"To bridge the gap." O'Connor raised the weapon vertical. "Ready? You got one chance."

"Your throw better be good, then."

O'Connor laughed. "You son-of-a..." She tossed the taser rod, trying as best she could to maintain its vertical orientation. The weapon sailed through the air in slow motion, all eyes locked on its metal shaft glinting in the ambient sunlight.

The taser rod landed in Harry's open hand. Part of him expected to miss but there it was, the aluminum cooling his palm.

"Hey, dirty Harry," O'Connor grinned. "The safety's off."

Larsen focused on the two sharp prongs at the end of the taser, darkened from past electrocutions. "Wait. What are you going to do with that?"

Harry loosened his grip and the taser rod's handle and trigger slid into his hand. He aimed the business end of the taser at Larsen. "Grab it. I'll pull you out."

An acidback surfaced in the watery current near Larsen's feet and screeched.

"Bullshit." Larsen alternated his gaze between the prongs of the taser and Harry's satisfied smile. "You're going to shock me."

"I guess you're going to have to trust me," Harry said. "Grab it and we'll pull you out. Or..." He motioned at the water.

Larsen glanced backward as if he expected to see something different, another option perhaps. Broken tile, drowning acidbacks, and blue churning ocean water remained. He shook his head. "I don't trust you."

Harry shrugged. "Suit yourself. Guys pull me up."

Sam initiated reversal of the human chain.

"Wait. Wait." Larsen cried.

"Hold up, S..." Harry lost his words before he had a chance to say them. The surface of the water behind Larsen bubbled up in a crimson plume.

Daniela saw the danger. "Grab it, Larsen. Grab it now."

Larsen sneered at her before noticing his rescuers' faces had gone white as ghosts. "What's wr—"

An acidback breached the surface of the water and latched its fangs onto one of Larsen's meaty calves. He screamed and scrambled forward, reaching madly for the end of the taser rod. Survival instinct had replaced his trust issues.

Larsen's blood ran in torrents down his leg and into the water below, creating a bath of purple terror.

"Grab the taser, Larsen!" Harry extended his reach as far as he could and Larsen took the hint. He grabbed the pronged end and punctured his meaty palm. With all the adrenaline pumping through his veins, Larsen didn't register the pain.

"Go!" Harry and the others began to inch backward up the inclined edge of the tiled precipice, Larsen in tow, when a tiger shark emerged from the blood-charged water below.

The shark's maw swallowed the acidback whole and clamped its rows of razor-sharp teeth across Larsen's midsection, severing his body in half. Larsen lost his grip on the end of the taser rod. His eyes glazed over as his body convulsed and slid back down the tile, painting it with the remains of his shredded entrails. As quick as the attack had begun, Larsen sank below the water and out of sight.

"Get me the hell out of here!" Harry dropped the taser and scrambled with his feet, but the tiles were too slick.

Sam used his arms and legs to begin Harry's extraction. With everyone straining, Harry made slow progress up the cracked tile precipice.

O'Connor stepped in ahead of Sam and grabbed the fire hose with her good hand. With a fresh burst of strength, the group pulled Harry to safety in seconds.

Harry panted on the floor. "That was insane."

Hope took in the carnage Larsen had left behind on the tiled precipice. "You can't escape Karma, it seems."

"I almost feel sorry for the guy," Daniela said between breaths.

"You threw away a perfectly good taser rod, bucko." O'Connor blew a cloud of cigar smoke at the crumbling ceiling.

Harry looked up at her, incredulous. He had no words.

"Just fucking with you." O'Connor laughed and offered her hand. "Come on. We got to get out of this shit-hole."

The group ran down the corridor as another section of the floor caved in several feet behind. The doors to the east courtyard, the path they had taken in, was their salvation. But their escape route was about to disappear right in front of their eyes.

Reclamation

THE GROUP BURST out of the double doors and onto the east courtyard. The main lobby of the resort had sunk in a cracked and crumbled heap as the ocean reclaimed its dominance.

The path leading up toward the airstrip began to cave in, the asphalt heavier than the rest of the grounds. The soil underneath could not support its added weight.

Sam scanned the area for escape routes.

"Mother*fucker!*" O'Connor made fists with both her hands. "I knew we shouldn't have tried to save that sorry son-of-a-bitch."

"Easy." Harry cast O'Connor a disapproving look. "We're better than that."

"We're going to end up dead." O'Connor hooked her thumb back at the collapsing east wing of the resort. "And dead ain't better than *that.*"

Harry had had enough. "So what are you going to do besides complain?"

"Me?"

"Yeah, what are our options, genius?"

"Fuck this. There's no time." Sam bolted out onto the grass in front of the courtyard and pushed on the flagpole. His efforts rippled all the way to the top and back. "This is the only way. Come on."

Harry sneered at O'Connor. "Sam just saved our asses."

"We're not saved yet."

Hope and Daniela joined Sam followed by Harry and O'Connor moments later. The group's synchronized efforts bent the flagpole toward the other side of the moat created where the asphalt path used to be. But an endless supply of ocean water continued to eat away at the banks on both sides. The group had to work fast.

Hope looked up at the large Mar-A-Verde flag tossed back and forth with the group's pushes. "What the hell is with Strunk's obsession with insanely tall flagpoles?"

"Inferiority complex?" Daniela said between pushes on the pole. "Maybe he's compensating for something." She winked at Hope and they both laughed.

"The length of this pole is going to save us," Sam said. "So be thankful for that."

The flagpole's anchor in the ground weakened and it became easier to push the pole over. Sam stepped to the opposite side and pulled the pole down farther. Harry joined him.

"Who's first? It's about eighty feet to the other side." Before Harry had finished getting his words out, Hope grabbed the flagpole and hooked her heels and calves over the top. Hanging underneath the pole by her legs and arms, she pulled herself across.

"I've done a few obstacle courses," Hope called back, already having traveled ten feet. "This is the monkey crawl. Move opposite arm and leg at the same time. Position the pole between your heel and calf. Keep moving and you're good to go."

"Easy for you to say." Daniela watched Hope move up the flagpole to the other side.

Sam stared in wonder. "Learn something new every day." He turned to O'Connor. "You going to be able to do that with your fake leg and your fucked-up hand?"

"No problem."

Sam watched O'Connor scan the flagpole's length. He didn't see confidence in her face. "You better go next, then."

Not one to back down from a challenge, O'Connor tapped her hands together gingerly and stepped up to the flagpole. Her bandaged hand limited her grip and kept sliding off the smooth surface of the pole. Hope's technique required modification.

Instead O'Connor hooked her right elbow over, grasped the pole with her left hand, and swung her legs up. She alternated her left and right leg, sliding her right elbow and pulling with her left hand. "See, Sam? Piece of fucking cake." But she was moving at half the speed as Hope had.

Harry eyed chunks of embankment chipping away and falling into the expanding ocean channel below. "Remember, faster is better."

"Yeah, yeah." O'Connor spoke around her clamped cigar. "You can kiss my ass... if you can catch me."

Harry crossed his arms against his chest. "I'll *kick* your ass instead."

"Eat my dust, bitch," O'Connor cackled.

"Keep it going, O'Connor," Hope called from the opposite bank. "You're past the halfway mark."

O'Connor paused and stared at Hope from her upside-down vantage point. "Who are you, my dad?"

"I'm—"

A large chunk of earth fell away from the bank where Hope stood and caused the flagpole to drop half a foot. The unexpected downward movement pulled O'Connor's stump painfully free from its prosthetic.

"No!" O'Connor reached for the mechanical leg with her free arm.

"Shit." Sam stepped forward like he was going to run after her. Harry was ready to hold him back, but Sam stopped on his own. "Let it go, O'Connor!"

O'Connor waved her left arm madly at the prosthetic. She

tried to grab the suspension sleeve but missed it by inches as it rolled off the flagpole. The leg plummeted to the ocean water below and splashed between many groups of dead and thrashing acidbacks.

A tiger shark surfaced from the dark blue water below and swallowed her prosthetic in one bite.

"Fucking shark! God*damn* it!" O'Connor heaved a frustrated cloud of cigar smoke.

"Forget it," Sam said. "Just keep moving."

O'Connor had to modify her technique again. Left with one hand and one leg, she resumed her traversal of the pole, moving like an inchworm.

Ignoring the blood-frenzy of sizzling acidbacks in the ocean moat below her, she gripped the pole with her left hand and slid her right leg forward. Then she clamped her right leg and knee around the pole and slid her left knee and stump forward, all the while with her right arm and elbow sliding over the top of the pole. It was slow going but O'Connor made steady progress.

Once within reach Hope helped pull O'Connor off the flagpole and onto the grass. "Nice going."

"But I lost my fucking leg," O'Connor grumbled. "That thing was damn expensive. Fucking shark better choke on it."

By the time Hope returned to the flagpole, Daniela was already a quarter of the way across. "Have you done this before?"

Daniela let out a breathy chuckle as she moved, hand over hand, leg over leg. "No. Just a quick study."

But she was over-confident. Three-quarters of the way across, exhausted and her coordination impaired, Daniela missed the pole when moving her legs and slipped off. Hanging by her hands, the carnage roiled below her, and she froze.

"Dani! Keep going." Harry ran to the flagpole, his desire to rescue clear.

"It won't support both of you," Sam said.

"I know." Harry paced a nervous track into the grass. "It's fucking bullshit."

"Come on, Daniela," Hope said from the opposite bank. "Don't let the bastards win. We academics need to stick together."

Harry cupped his mouth to amplify his voice. "I'll buy you dinner once we're off this shit-heap. Now move!"

Something clicked in Daniela's head and her will to survive returned with a jolt of adrenaline. She raised her legs to the pole one at a time and finished the last leg of the traversal, slow but steady. She collapsed onto the grass beside O'Connor.

"Can I borrow your cigar for a second?"

O'Connor eyed Daniela curiously. "You're not going to toss it, are you?"

"Just give it to me."

O'Connor gave her a sideways look and complied.

Daniela took the wet chunk of tobacco, somehow still smoldering at one end, and drew in a mouthful of smoke. She handed the stub back to O'Connor. "Hit the spot."

"So you're a closet cigar smoker?" O'Connor jammed the cigar back between her molars.

Daniela jettisoned tendrils of smoke from her mouth. "Even less frequent than that. But right now, it seemed like the right thing to do."

"I hear you, Doc." O'Connor made a fist and the two women bumped knuckles. "Nothing like a near death experience as cause for celebration." She sucked a mouthful of smoke and released several consecutive smoke rings.

Harry hopped off the flagpole and ran to Daniela's side. "You had me worried there."

Daniela propped herself up on her elbows. "I'd be a fool to pass up dinner with Harry Harcourt."

O'Connor rolled her eyes. "Get a room, will yah?"

Hope watched the banks erode in slow chunks. "Hurry, Sam. You don't have much time."

Sam grabbed the flagpole with both hands, lifted his midsection, and hooked ankles in place. He began the final traversal, opposite hands and legs in sync. Being the most muscular of the group proved to be a blessing and a curse. He had strong arms and legs, but he also had increased body mass to carry.

The flagpole curved more under his weight as he moved closer to the center of the span.

Loud snapping and crashing sounded from the resort as the east wing collapsed into itself. The thunderous vibrations of destruction forced cracks to finger through the lawn in front of the east courtyard. Ground cleaved away along the newly formed faults taking the flagpole anchor with it.

"Shit, we got a problem." Hope grabbed the flagpole near its top and tried to pull it toward her. "The pole's falling and it's going to take Sam with it." She leaned as close to the edge as she felt comfortable with. "Hold on, Sam!"

Harry and Daniela joined Hope but the three of them failed to budge the flagpole in a positive direction.

"I'll just sit here and admire the view." O'Connor watched more of the bank peel away as Harry, Daniela, and Hope struggled to keep the top of the flagpole under control. "On second thought..." She butt-scooted backward to safer ground but nowhere was completely safe.

Harry's eyes ran the length of the pole, from the top to halfway where Sam struggled to advance his position. The incline increased as the pole's anchor slid further into the expanding moat.

"Bend it," he said.

"What?" Hope furrowed her brow in confusion.

"Make a hook out of it." Harry pulled down on the top end

of the flagpole and a kink appeared in the tapered surface. "Bend it. Like a hockey stick."

With all three of their efforts combined, the top of the flagpole bent until it resembled an upside-down "L". The Mar-A-Verde flag collected in a heap on the remaining grass.

The anchor at the bottom swung the rest of the flagpole like a massive pendulum. It struck the bank vertically below the turf and the rest of the crew. Because of the newly bent top, the pole stayed put.

"That was genius, Harry." Hope peered down over the edge. "He's okay." She locked gazes with Sam. "Climb, you big beautiful man!"

O'Connor did a double-take. "What the hell did she just say?"

Hope raised her middle finger at O'Connor without looking at her.

Harry joined Hope at the edge. "Looks like you've got company."

Sam glanced down past his legs, down the flagpole to where the concrete anchor had submerged below the water's surface. Despite their burned and bubbling skin, acidbacks wrapped their stubby legs around the pole and began to inch their way up the pole. The acidbacks were built for speed and advanced more efficiently than Sam.

"If he doesn't move faster, those things are going to chew up his feet," Harry said. "Then it's game over."

Bearing his weight horizontally was one thing but climbing vertically was quite another. Already sapped of strength, Sam could barely move.

"I'm not going to make it!" Increased sweat on Sam's hands greased his grip on the flagpole.

Daniela dropped to her knees and rooted underneath the crumpled Mar-A-Verde flag.

Hope watched her frenzied search. "What are you looking for?"

"I should have thought about this before." Daniela found what she was looking for and raised up the rope used to raise the flag. "We'll *pull* Sam up."

O'Connor pointed. "Now *that's* genius."

"Sam, grab the rope." Hope wiggled the braided cord beside the pole. "We can pull—"

"It's tied at the bottom." Sam looked down to see an onslaught of acidbacks closing in on him from below.

"Shit." Hope's eyes flitted between Harry, Daniela, and O'Connor, looking for an answer until her hands settled on her own belt. In a light-bulb moment, she pulled out her Bowie knife. "Sam, you got one chance." She held the knife out over the bank. "Ready?"

Sam, approaching delirium, looked up and understood what he had to do. He nodded and wrapped one arm around the pole. "Ready."

Hope dropped the knife, handle down. The weapon was in freefall for just over a second but seemed to fall in slow motion.

Sam matched the speed of the knife's fall and caught the hilt in his right hand. "Holy shit." He stared at his salvation with wonder.

"Cut the rope, goddamn it!"

Snapping back into reality, Sam lowered the knife to waist-level and sawed at the rope, using the pole as a cutting block. The cord wiggled and rolled under the blade, fraying a thread at a time.

"Hurry, hurry, hurry Sam." Hope whispered to herself as she chewed at her lower lip.

The acidbacks were less than three feet away.

Sam sawed at the rope like it was a piece of uncooperative gristle. Back and forth, cutting deeper through more threads.

The wet sound of the acidbacks' pulsing sphincter of fangs droned in Sam's ear. The creatures were less than two feet away.

The blade cut through the rope, the lower end disappearing

between his legs. He took aim and dropped the knife blade straight into the red and raw gullet of the first acidback. It fell backward and knocked the second creature in line off the pole. Sam had a bit more time before those things ate him alive.

He grabbed the rope and twisted it around his forearm. "I'm good to go!"

Hope, Harry, and Daniela heaved with all their strength. For the first time since the flagpole fell vertical, Sam moved faster than the pursuing acidbacks. During each pull, he raised his legs and anchored the tread of his work boots around the pole. The trio at the top collected the slack and the process repeated until he was within arm's reach of the bank's top.

Harry extended his hand. Sam took it, grasping his forearm. "Damn glad to see you, buddy."

Sam nodded. "Likewise."

Aided by Hope and Daniela, they dragged Sam's depleted body past the edge to safety.

"Welcome to Club Invalid." O'Connor's body shook with laughter.

Sam glanced at her. "Ever think it might be time to retire?"

O'Connor looked at herself, with a bandaged right hand and one functional leg. She shook her head, her stogie smoldering in her jaws. "No rest for the wicked."

Hope and Daniela pushed the flagpole into the moat, which was more like an inlet now. The tiger sharks below circled in a feeding frenzy. The acidbacks that had survived had met their match.

A pile of twisted wood, metal, and cracked stucco replaced the east courtyard and the resort around it where O'Connor and the gang had just emerged. To one side of the rubble lay a framed photo of Strunk's smiling face. A sharp splintered two-by-four had pierced the photo right through his nose, making him look like Pinocchio's narcissistic brother.

The sink holes and cave-ins induced a ripple effect

throughout the golf course. Sections of the course disappeared into the ocean as if Mother Nature had reset the island to its defaults. Poinciana and palm trees with their red and green foliage toppled into newly cracked fissures in the ground and most of the man-made structures still above ground lay in ruin. The marina had been reclaimed and the dock had been reduced to just its support posts. Several boats floated off shore, crammed with Mar-A-Verde staff and guests watching in awe.

Harry maintained a safe distance from the bank's edge and surveyed the destruction. "Never thought I'd see the day..."

"Crazy isn't it?" Daniela tucked her arm around Harry's waist and rested her head on his shoulder. "I guess we need to find new jobs."

Sam and Hope helped O'Connor up on her one leg.

"Well that was a total fuck-up," Sam said. "We didn't do anything."

O'Connor hooked her arm around Sam's neck. "We destroyed Mar-A-Verde. I'd say we succeeded beyond our wildest dreams."

Hope shook her head. "Correction. *Acidbacks* destroyed Mar-A-Verde. The videos on Harry's phone prove it. And with all the tunnels running under the property, it was just a matter of time."

Sam looked her with a half-hearted grin and raised his brows. "I guess that's a plus?"

"Whatever it is, I'll take it." O'Connor's stomach let loose a loud growl.

Hope stared at her and laughed.

"What? Those sizzling bastards smelled like pork soup." She inhaled through her nose. "Anyone up for Chinese after this?"

No one had a chance to answer as the edge of grass the five of them stood on chipped away and slid into the ocean.

Harry raised his arms like he was making an invisible barrier and stepped back from the crumbling edge. The rest of the group followed his lead and backed up with him. O'Connor had to hop.

"We got to move or we're not going to have a runway or a plane." Harry turned, set to run toward the hangar, when Sam caught his eye.

"A little help?" Sam motioned at O'Connor hanging from his neck by the crook of her arm as the two of them hobbled away from the edge.

Harry ran back and slid O'Connor's other arm around his neck. The two men stood and lifted O'Connor off the ground.

"I'm in heaven, boys. Feel light as a feather." O'Connor grinned ear to ear. "Now, ándele! Ándele!"

Daniela and Hope sprinted toward the hangar. Fissures in the turf formed alongside them and followed their path like dark snakes.

Hope turned and ran backward. "Watch the cracks! They're—" Her heel caught on an upturned root that had burst from the ground and she fell on her backside.

With O'Connor in tow, Harry and Sam maintained their speed across the grass.

"Hope! Behind you," Sam yelled between breaths.

Hope flipped herself over and scrambled forward when the ground opened underneath her.

Daniela descended to one knee, grabbed Hope's hand, and pulled her safely to her feet. Hope turned to look back but Daniela's grasp on her hand tightened.

"Just run! There's no time."

"But what about the others?"

Daniela had no answer except to maintain her stride and pull Hope along with her.

Sam, Harry, and O'Connor watched the fissure expand in front of them as they approached.

Harry focused on Daniela and Hope. "I'm getting tired of this shit. What do you want to do, Sam?"

Sam scanned the crack in the ground looking for options. With his brain addled and body fatigued, he came up empty.

"Jump," O'Connor said.

Both Harry and Sam turned to her at the same time. "What the *fuck?*"

"You heard me. Try and get ahead of it and jump the goddamn thing."

Sam and Harry glanced at each other and shrugged. They veered left to outrun the leading tip of the fissure. At the same time, they were running away from the airplane hangar.

"We're not going to outrun the damn thing," Sam said.

Harry watched Daniela and Hope shrink in the distance. But the fissure still appeared too wide.

O'Connor spat out the remains of her cigar. "Just go for it." She alternated her gaze between Sam and Harry. "I trust you. And if we die, then at least I die with two of the best."

Sam spun his head in a double-take but couldn't afford to take the time to process O'Connor's words.

"I'm going to go wide so we can approach the crack head on. With me, Sam?"

"Yeah."

"Okay. Synchronize our steps and... GO!"

Harry headed left for several feet before turning a hundred-eighty degrees in a short arc. The two of them, with O'Connor suspended between, headed straight for the fissure. Sam and Harry's legs ran in time, each of their strides matching the other.

"Kick it, Sam. Three, two, and..."

They sailed over the fissure which looked black and bottomless from their brief vantage point. But they didn't have the speed to cover the entire distance.

Their hips hit the edge of the fissure, knocking them forward. Sam sank his fingers into the turf and began clawing them forward.

Harry had the wind knocked out of him and it took a moment for him to regain his focus.

"Be thankful you don't have tits because... *fuck* that hurt." O'Connor unhooked her arms from Sam and Harry's necks and clawed her way forward using her knees and one hand.

The grass under Harry gave way. "Shit!" He reached out for the only thing within reach: O'Connor's right leg.

O'Connor managed a quick look back. "Sam!" She threw her body flat on the ground to maximize the friction and clawed the grass.

Sam was back on O'Connor in a second. He grasped her forearms and heaved with all his strength. "Climb with your feet, Harry."

Unbeknown to Sam, Harry had already been working his legs at a furious pace, but it appeared the resort had been built on a foundation of sand. He couldn't get any traction.

A pair of arms wrapped themselves around Sam's waist and pulled. It was the boost that they needed. O'Connor and Harry slid over the edge and out of the fissure. But instead of stopping, Sam and his unseen assistant continued to pull O'Connor and Harry across the lawn until they met the asphalt of the airstrip.

Sam let go of O'Connor's arms and turned to find Hope panting, hands on her knees. He smiled, breathing hard. "Your black fingernail polish gave you away."

Hope shrugged. "The odds were pretty good it'd be me."

Harry scrambled to his feet and lifted O'Connor up. Daniela took Sam's place and secured O'Connor's arm over her shoulder.

Exhausted and caked with dirt, the team ran for the hangar as fast as their bodies would allow.

The airstrip's windsock hung halfheartedly atop its pole, held aloft by an easterly breeze. The airstrip was the last intact structure on the island, but the eastern corner of the asphalt had already started to disintegrate. The remaining island had become a collapsing time bomb.

HARRY RAN PAST the Gulfstream and caressed the fuselage like he was calming a horse after an earthquake. He looked back at the eastern section of the runway. Chunks of asphalt fell away at a steady pace.

There was still time. He continued toward the Cessna six-seater parked on the opposite side of the hangar.

"Wait. We're not taking the jet?" O'Connor deflated, one arm still draped around Daniela's shoulder. "After all we've been through, we got to take *that* bucket of bolts?"

"You don't start a Gulfstream up with a turn of a key like your beloved Buick. It'll take more time than we have to get it off the ground." Harry looked back at the approaching destruction as he beckoned to the rest of the group. "The runway's disintegrating and it's going to hit the jet first. If you want a sixty-five million dollar coffin, be my guest. Otherwise..." He arrived at the side door of the Cessna to discover it locked. He ran his hands over his pockets even though he knew they were empty. "Fuck."

"Locked? I can pick it," Hope said with a grin. "Anyone got a paperclip?"

Harry pointed at the eroding runway, now halfway to the hangar. "No time." He ran to a small toolbox set against the wall of the hangar and flung the lid open. He extracted a wrench from the contents and ran back to the Cessna's side door, pulling the blocks from the wheels as he passed by. "If we're not on that runway before it collapses, we're dead."

Harry raised the wrench and smashed a hole in the door's Plexiglass window. He reached into the jagged opening, unlocked the door, and stepped into the plane. "Pile in folks. And buckle up." He watched the collapsing line of asphalt catching up with them through the Cessna's windshield. "Hurry. Time's ticking."

Sam hopped in first and helped O'Connor up.

"I call shotgun." O'Connor hopped into the co-pilot's seat and pulled on the headset.

Sam assisted Hope and Daniela into the plane. Daniela took the left seat of the front row, just behind Harry and O'Connor, and Sam and Hope took the back row of seats. All three buckled themselves in.

Harry cast O'Connor an uneasy look. "Buckle up and for fuck's sake don't touch anything." He flipped the pilot-side visor down and a set of keys fell into his lap.

"Seriously?" O'Connor raised a brow at him.

Harry shrugged. "No one at the resort knows how to fly a plane except me so security isn't that much of an issue." He inserted the key into the ignition switch and began the Cessna's start-up procedure, pressing buttons, flipping switches, and setting the engine controls correctly for engine start.

Daniela peered out the shattered window. "Don't mean to backseat-fly but—"

"I know…" Harry was fully aware of where the line of no return was on the runway, a crumbling line that continued to consume the asphalt as it advanced. He bypassed the written start-up checklist and chose to go by memory instead.

A substantial chunk of asphalt fell away from the eroding edge. The far corner of the hangar dropped and the corrugated walls began to buckle.

"Oh fuck." O'Connor looked out the windshield, past Harry carrying out his rapid pre-flight sequence. "You were right about the jet."

Harry peered left for a moment before returning to the Cessna ignition sequence. A chunk of concrete under the Gulfstream's left landing gear had cracked and sunk, causing the jet to lean to one side.

"I know a few things." Harry offered O'Connor a stress-filled grin.

The Cessna's engine whined and the single prop in front began to spin up. Vibrations shook the little aircraft as the prop morphed into a spinning blurred disc.

"Here goes nothing." Harry adjusted the choke to the engine and guided the plane out of the hangar.

Sitting in the back row, Hope reached for Sam's hand. They interlaced fingers tightly and shared a look of panic.

Daniela spotted their reliance on each other and smiled to herself. She felt a tap on her shoulder and looked over the backrest. Hope had extended her free hand between the seats. It was a perfectly timed gesture. She took Hope's hand and mouthed the words "thank you."

The Cessna cleared the hangar and progressed down the runway but not fast enough for O'Connor. "Let's go, Harry. Make this bucket of bolts *move*."

"Doing my best, but there's this little thing called physics getting in the way." Harry adjusted controls on the dashboard and engaged the flaps on the wings.

The advancing asphalt edge continued its relentless pursuit. The back wheels dipped, tilting the plane upward as the edge threatened to consume the back end of the plane. Sam placed his free hand on the roof of the cabin and squeezed his eyes shut.

Harry throttled up the engine and pulled ahead of the expanding crack. But his success was short-lived. "Goddamn it..."

"What is it now?" O'Connor's attitude disappeared when she saw the color drain from Harry's face.

He pointed straight ahead. Not only was the runway eroding from behind, but ahead as well. The available asphalt was disappearing twice as fast as he had anticipated.

O'Connor stared at him with a face as serious as she could

muster. "You're going to have to gun it and hope for the best. Either we die or we don't."

Harry returned a look of concern mixed with determination. "I think you're right. Pretty smart for someone who's never piloted a plane before." The Gods were smiling down on him. The windsock near the runway indicated that the winds had picked up and favored a westward departure. The headwind would shorten his takeoff distance. Reassured, he advanced the Cessna's throttle all the way to full power and started his takeoff roll.

The engine screamed as the plane accelerated down the runway, pressing everyone back in their seats.

Harry watched his airspeed increase and available runway decrease. "Come on, come on... you bucket of bolts." He raised a brow at O'Connor but she either ignored him or didn't hear him. Instead she focused on the end of the runway.

There was nothing else Harry could do except let the plane accelerate. "It's going to be close! Hold on!"

The Cessna met the end of the runway and dipped. Harry pulled back on the yoke to compensate and nosed the plane toward the sky just enough to clear the crumbling ground. He eased the yoke back to avoid a stall, reset the flaps, and let the plane accelerate and climb.

"Not today not today not today..." Sam repeated this mantra supposedly to himself but had spoken loud enough for Hope to hear. She squeezed his hand and he opened his eyes, distracted.

The vibration of take-off fell away and left the buzz-whine of the engine.

Hope shook her head and smiled. "Not today," she returned softly.

"Harry, my man. You fucking *did* it!" O'Connor roared with laughter, as much a compliment as a release of anxiety. She reached out and tapped his shoulder. "I'd celebrate with a cigar but as luck would have it..." She patted her pockets and came up empty. "Got any Jack Daniels?"

Harry glanced at O'Connor, his relief easy to spot. "Sorry to be a buzz-kill. No smoking, no drinking on this flight." He twisted in his seat to face Daniela, Sam, and Hope. He pointed at the headsets hanging from the sides of the cabin and tapped his own. He grinned and winked at Daniela before returning to face front.

The three got the message loud and clear. They pulled on the headsets connected to the plane's electronics by coiled umbilicals and positioned their mouthpieces.

"Sorry for the bumpy ride," Harry said, his crackling voice transmitted to everyone else in the plane.

"We're alive because of you, Harry." Hope beamed from the back row of seats. "You're the god among us."

"Let's not get carried away." Harry banked the plane in a wide arc. Near the center of what used to be Mar-A-Verde, sharks fed on the remaining acidbacks. The water had adopted a temporary purple bullseye. Boats filled with staff and guests peppered the submerged shores. Some waved at the plane as it flew past.

"Holy shit." O'Connor plastered her face against the side window. "It's gone. All of it. Even the runway." She looked back at Harry. "Sorry. We did that."

"Nah, you didn't." Harry smiled and adjusted the engine's throttle. "The ball was rolling before you got here. You just helped speed things along. You probably saved some lives too."

The graphical interface on the dashboard showed Marjerio Cay, existing only digitally on the map now, with Freeport and Grand Bahama to the north and the Bimini Islands to the south.

"We're three-quarters of an hour away from civilization." Harry set a course for Palm Beach, Florida, as Marjerio Cay continued to decompose into the ocean behind them.

CROSSROADS

TRUE TO HIS word, Harry touched down at Palm Beach International Airport forty minutes later. Despite the buzz of the Cessna's engine and the wind noise from the broken side window, Sam had managed to sleep through the entire crossing. He had used Hope's shoulder as a pillow which she hadn't minded.

The small bump as the plane's three wheels hit the runway was enough to pull Sam from sleep. He lifted his head and took a moment to get his bearings.

Hope smiled and handed him his headset. "Welcome back to reality, sleepyhead."

"Did I miss anything?" Sam wiped sleep from his eyes.

O'Connor twisted in her seat to look back at him. "Sam, if I catch you sleeping on the job again, your ass is as good as gone." She waited a beat before breaking into hysterics.

Hope rolled her eyes in annoyance. "Just a lot of *that*." She thumbed back at O'Connor.

Daniela reached forward and gave Harry's shoulder a squeeze. "Thanks for getting us off that island safely. We all owe you our lives."

"All in a day's work." Harry communicated with the tower and navigated the Cessna back toward the Mar-A-Verde hangar.

Just as in days previous, the hangar door opened on its own when the Cessna was within range of the automatic lock. Bruce with the Detest-A-Pest trailer sat parked to one side of the covered space. Without the Gulfstream the hangar felt massive.

"Bruce!" O'Connor's eyes lit up like she was seeing her beloved Buick Century for the first time. "Can't wait to spread my body across his vinyl seats."

Harry raised a brow. "Whatever floats your boat." He entered the hangar, turned the Cessna around to face the large doors, and began his power-down sequence. As the propeller stopped, Harry turned to the rest of the group. "Thank you for flying with Mar-A-Verde for the last fucking time."

Everyone laughed as Harry popped open the side door of the plane. He stepped out first and helped the others down, O'Connor last.

"Sam? Hope?" O'Connor raised her eyebrows in an expectant look. "Help your boss to the company car?"

Sam pursed his lips as he exchanged a sly glance with Hope. "Do we have a spare set of crutches in the equipment trailer by any chance?"

"No. You're going to have to carry me." O'Connor grinned and batted her eyelashes at him.

Sam and Hope lifted O'Connor by the shoulders, one on each side, and transported her to the Buick.

O'Connor leaned over the car, spread her arms, and kissed the pristine white hood. "Brucy-baby, I didn't think I was going to see you again."

Harry and Daniela swapped a look that had "she's crazy" written all over it.

"Just keep your clothes on." Sam patted O'Connor on the shoulder.

O'Connor straightened up and pointed at Harry. "Two things. First, let's take care of business. Then we find mass quantities of Jack Daniels."

Harry jiggled his phone in his hand. "Already done. Check your email. Same password."

O'Connor pulled out her phone. After a few taps, she looked up and smiled. "Pleasure doing business with you. Sorry for destroying the resort."

Harry shrugged indifference. "In a way you set me free." He glanced down at Daniela's hand and slipped his fingers around hers. "Who knows what adventure awaits?"

"About that Jack Daniels..."

"I know just the place." Harry grinned. "And *I'm* driving."

O'Connor's gaze jumped between Harry and the others in the group. "What do mean you're—"

"You're in no condition to drive."

"Harry's right," Sam said. "After everything that's happened, this isn't the hill to die on."

O'Connor nodded.

Harry ran to the side office, retrieved the keys to Bruce, and unlocked the doors. He opened the passenger side door with a flourish. "Your chariot awaits."

Everyone piled into Bruce, O'Connor calling shotgun of course. After clearing the hangar, Harry closed the doors manually, marking the last time he would fly under the banner of a Strunk enterprise.

Twenty minutes later Harry pulled into the parking lot of Gusto Grande. He found two connected stalls and parked Bruce and the Detest-A-Pest trailer.

"Mexican? Are you shitting me?" O'Connor looked at Sam in the back seat sandwiched between Hope and Daniela. "Did you tell him?"

Sam shook his head. "Said nothing, I swear."

Harry killed the engine and propped his right elbow over the seat-back. "Tell me what?"

"In L.A. last summer O'Connor got a taste of authentic Mexican food," Sam said. "Since then she's become quite the fan."

Harry hooked a thumb at the modestly sized restaurant. "This place is great. I'm sure you won't be disappointed. Let's go."

The group piled out of Bruce and into the restaurant, Sam and Hope reprising their roles as O'Connor's support staff.

Harry singled out a corner booth in the back, as far away from other customers as possible, and slid across the upholstered bench seating.

"Hey, why so far back?" O'Connor craned her head to survey the restaurant's diners.

Daniela parked herself next to Harry. "In case you haven't noticed, we look and smell like death warmed over."

O'Connor sniffed. "You got a point." She took a seat, followed by Sam and Hope. "Dinner's on me. If you got a problem with that... too bad."

A server approached the table with menus under her arm. She didn't appear to care about their grubby appearance. "Welcome to Gusto Grande. My name's Veronica and I'll be your server tonight. Our specials—" She had begun to distribute the menus when O'Connor stopped her.

"We're not going to need those, honey," O'Connor said. "Give us one of everything, plus a bottle of Jack Daniels."

Sam raised his finger. "And a club soda."

"Yeah. And a club soda. Can you do that?" O'Connor sported a playful grin.

Veronica raised a brow. "You're joking, right?"

O'Connor looked around the table, at Sam, Hope, Daniela, and Harry. They smiled and nodded back.

"No joke." She relaxed into the backrest and crossed her arms. "We'll start with the Jack Daniels and the appies."

"And a club soda," Sam said.

"Yeah, a club soda. Sorry Sam."

Sam shrugged it off. Veronica collected the menus and returned shortly after with a tray of shot glasses, Sam's club soda, and an unopened bottle of Jack Daniels Tennessee whiskey.

O'Connor cracked the cap and filled the four shot glasses. "Here's to the future and good friends."

Everyone clinked glasses and downed their drinks.

"Another round?" O'Connor's eyes gleamed in the low light of the booth.

"Let's pace ourselves," Hope said.

Daniela nodded. "I'm with Hope."

"Bunch of lightweights." O'Connor glanced at Harry and flashed her eyebrows. "Harry Harcourt?"

Harry pushed his shot glass across the table. "Why not."

O'Connor filled their glasses. "Bottoms up." She tossed back another one and a half ounces of Tennessee's finest. "Now that hits the goddamn spot."

Veronica carried a stack of plates to the table. "Quesadillas and nachos will be out in a few minutes."

Daniela took the plates and handed them out. "So O'Connor, what now?"

Sam nodded. "Especially since you hired me less than a week ago."

O'Connor poured herself another shot of whiskey and shrugged. "I don't know. After losing all my equipment, retirement does sound mighty good right about now. That Kill-O-Matic was one of a kind." She downed the shot in one gulp.

"What happened to 'no rest for the wicked?' " Sam grinned.

"I think my wicked has up and left."

Harry clasped his fingers. "Maybe the world is trying to tell you something."

O'Connor turned to him. "Like what?"

"Like becoming a landlord." Hope smiled. The whiskey had

brought a warm glow to her cheeks. "Sam and I need a place to live."

"You two shacking up?"

"No, I meant separate places." Hope glanced at Sam, her cheeks now more red than pink.

Sam hung his head but smiled at the same time. "I'm crushed." Hope gave him a playful smack.

"Maybe you should start making and selling your own extermination equipment," Harry said. "Not many outfits can claim to have destroyed an elite golfing resort."

O'Connor pushed Harry's shoulder. "Not sure that's something I want to call attention to." She spotted Veronica approaching with two large platters of food. "But *there's* something that demands my attention."

Veronica set platters of mixed nachos and quesadillas on the table, plus smaller dishes of sour cream, guacamole, and pico de gallo.

O'Connor filled her plate and began to shovel food into her mouth. "What are your plans, Harry?"

"I'll probably go help with the rebuild after hurricane Dorian. There's still lots to do. After that..." Harry placed a quesadilla on his plate and shrugged. "Strunk was kind enough to give Daniela and I generous bonuses, so who knows?"

Daniela narrowed her eyes and gave Harry a sideways look. "What did you do?"

Harry smiled and winked at her. "I just cashed in our meal credits. Made sure my crew got theirs as well."

Daniela tapped his chest. "You didn't..."

Harry shrugged. "Couldn't use them any more so..."

Sam sipped his club soda. "How about you, Daniela?"

"My life is in the Bahamas and doctors are always in need." Daniela glanced at Harry. "Want some company, Harry Harcourt?"

"Abso-*fucking*-lutely." Harry clinked Daniela's glass and slid it across the table toward O'Connor. "If you're pouring, I'll take another whiskey."

"Coming right up." O'Connor filled Harry's glass, then her own. "Anyone else?"

Daniela and Hope presented their glasses and O'Connor filled them to the brim.

"To Gusto Grande!" O'Connor and the others raised their glasses again and drank.

Hope lit up. "Hey, remember that sink hole at the White House? Maybe we could work our magic and get it to collapse into the ground too."

O'Connor nodded, slow at first. "You know, with everything that's going on, that's not a bad idea."

Sam munched on his nachos. "No, it *is* a bad idea. That sink hole was a geological blip."

"The White House could use some shaking up," Daniela said.

"Right. And just think of the publicity we'd get." O'Connor's eyes began to glass over as the gears in her brain turned. "We already know they got a rat infestation."

Sam shook his head. "After what happened at Mar-A-Verde, we'd never get clearance."

"I've got a few favors I can call in." O'Connor stroked her face in thought.

"No."

O'Connor glanced at Hope, then back at Sam. "As an employee of Detest-A-Pest, you're obligated—"

Sam grit his teeth and slammed his glass of club soda on the table. "Then I QUIT!" Silence descended among the group as he cast a steely gaze at O'Connor.

Harry, Daniela, and Hope exchanged uneasy looks.

Sam's visage of seriousness melted into a huge grin. "Just fucking with you."

Everyone roared with laughter, not a thought spared for their uncertain futures as Veronica brought the next round of food.

October 14, 2019 - June 27, 2020
Victoria, BC

***Note from the author:** If you like this book, may I ask three things? First, please leave a review. I must manage my time and since I write in multiple genres, I will pay more attention to the books/genres with the most reviews. What I focus on next depends on you, the reader. Help me to make the most of my time. Second, please join my reader group at LeeGabel.com/signup. There, I can keep you informed of future books and giveaways. And third, please recommend this book to your friends. You can also ask your local library to order it for you if they don't have it yet. My sincere thanks.*

Titles by Lee Gabel

Detest-A-Pest Series
Molerat 2.0
Arachnid 2.0
Vermin 2.0

Standalone
Snipped
David's Summer
Tied

Afterward

Like it? Rate it. Share it.

If you enjoyed *Molerat 2.0*, please rate it and spread the word. With your rating, you take part in this book's success. If you're interested in joining my Reader Group for updates and advance notice of upcoming releases, please sign up by going to LeeGabel.com.

Note from the author

Thank you for reading my sixth novel. I hadn't planned on writing a series of Detest-A-Pest novels, but the characters **and most importantly you, the reader** have asked for more. How could I refuse? I'm not sure where I want the Detest-A-Pest crew to go next, but I'm open to ideas.

As you know by now, I enjoy writing about real places. I use real street names where appropriate but change addresses and make up most locations and businesses. In *Molerat 2.0*, the resort Mar-A-Verde as well as the island, Marjerio Cay in the Bahamas, are fictional. However, you may notice similarities to another resort located nearby. In my defense, it was safer to make up a location so I could destroy it, than use a real location. In this respect, *Molerat 2.0* was both fun and cathartic to write.

Many thanks go to my wife and editor Sheila. She's the shining star behind my success. To my readers, thank you for going on this ride with me. I'm not a fast writer and I appreciate your patience. And to my family and friends who supported my decision to quit my job to write full time four years ago (still the most difficult decision I've ever had to make in my life), you were right. I am your number one fan now.

About the author

Since 1992, Lee has worked within the visual and dramatic arts landscape as a graphic designer, illustrator, visual effects artist, animator, screenwriter, and author. He's contributed to an Emmy award and once walked 63.5 kilometers in 13 hours. Traditionally trained as a screenwriter, Lee has moved to writing books in order to share his stories.

Lee has spent most of his life living on an island in the Pacific Northwest and he writes in multiple genres that interest him. Why? In his own words: "Writing is magic. I'll never understand how it works the way it does, but I do know if I put energy into writing, it rewards me in strange and wonderful ways. Even if I know where I'm going in a story, often I'll end up pulled in directions by my characters that I least expect. What ends up on the page never ceases to surprise me, and that's super cool. Writing continues to be one of the most difficult and most rewarding aspects of my life."

Find Lee on the Internet:

Want to join Lee's Reader Group or find out more about Lee and the books he writes? Please go to:

LeeGabel.com

LeeGabel.com/facebook

LeeGabel.com/twitter

Or follow Lee on BookBub at LeeGabel.com/bookbub

Two sisters. One wants in. One has a plan. But gang loyalty cuts family ties and even the best plan can derail.

Jess works, spends time with friends, and earns good grades in school. But she's also sole provider for her drug-addicted mother... And she hates it.

Her sister Nova holds a high-profile position in the Dynamite Queens. Within her turf Nova enjoys fame, fortune, freedom, and respect – at a cost of family life.

But Jess wants what Nova has and is willing to do anything to get it. After one explosive argument, Jess joins a rival gang, a decision that leads her down a path of brutal consequences.

South Central L. A. erupts with violence as two gangs – two sisters – wage war on each other. For the winner, victory could be unforgiving...

Note: This novel contains strong language and gang violence.

Tied: A Street Gang Novel (**316** pages)

A family in crisis. An impossible choice. A race against time.

An unplanned pregnancy turns the lives of Deanna, her husband Max, and her teenage son upside down. But there's something else wrong...

After baby David receives a cancer diagnosis, Deanna drops everything to focus on finding a cure. Max has other ideas.

Based on his own troubled past, Max challenges Deanna to consider quality of life versus quantity. Their opposing opinions throw their marriage into chaos and Deanna seeks treatment options alone.

Caught in the middle, Alex must navigate this family crisis on his own. An unexpected friendship with a cancer survivor may offer the perspective he needs.

With the clock ticking, Deanna stops at nothing to save baby David's life... but will her relationship with her family survive the process?

David's Summer (310 pages)

"Get snipped," they said. "It will solve all your problems," they said. Unfortunately, Ted listened...

Five years ago, it was love at first sight. Now, it's life on autopilot as tumbleweeds roll through Ted and Iris's bedroom. Their lackluster love life is driving Ted nuts. Iris's solution to their bedroom blues: get snipped.

Kunal and Ray, Ted's best friends and sworn enemies of Iris, agree with her for once. All roads seem to lead to a surgical solution, but Ted's not going there... until an explosive argument changes everything. A vasectomy seems like Ted's only play to win Iris back.

The antics of his precocious next-door neighbor complicates matters. Ted's ill-conceived decisions jeopardize everything important in his life, including his nuts.

But life was about to throw Ted a romantic curveball aimed straight at his heart...

Snipped: A Cutting Comedy (300 pages)

www.ingramcontent.com/pod-product-compliance
Lightning Source LLC
Chambersburg PA
CBHW031628200726
48288CB00019B/398